I0581582

BOOK ONE OF
THE CROWNED CHRONICLES

OF LEGENDS AND ROSES

ASHLEY W. SLAUGHTER

OF LEGENDS AND ROSES
Book One of THE CROWNED CHRONICLES

Library of Congress Cataloging-in-Publication Data
Name: Slaughter, Ashley W., author
Title: Of Legends and Roses / Ashley W. Slaughter.
Description: First edition. | Santa Rita, GU: AWS Writing, 2021.
Identifiers: LCCN 2021908838 | ISBN (hardcover) 978-1-7369638-0-7 | ISBN (paperback) 978-1-7369638-1-4 | ISBN (ebook) 978-1-7369638-2-1

First edition, August 2021
Revised first edition, September 2022

Edited by Gina Kammer
Cover Design by Lena Yang
Published by AWS Writing

For more information, visit ashleywslaughter.com

BOOK ONE OF
THE CROWNED CHRONICLES

OF
LEGENDS
AND
ROSES

ASHLEY W. SLAUGHTER

A MAGIAN PENINSULA NOVEL

ADRIAN ICE SHELF
Pax Pass
Borea
TARASYN
Viridi
Flecte
Pruin
Ripa
BERYL FOOTHILLS
THE WEST LANDS
SILVER MOUNTAINS
Ferox Pass
Vespost
HIDDON
Vena
THE HAREN DESERT

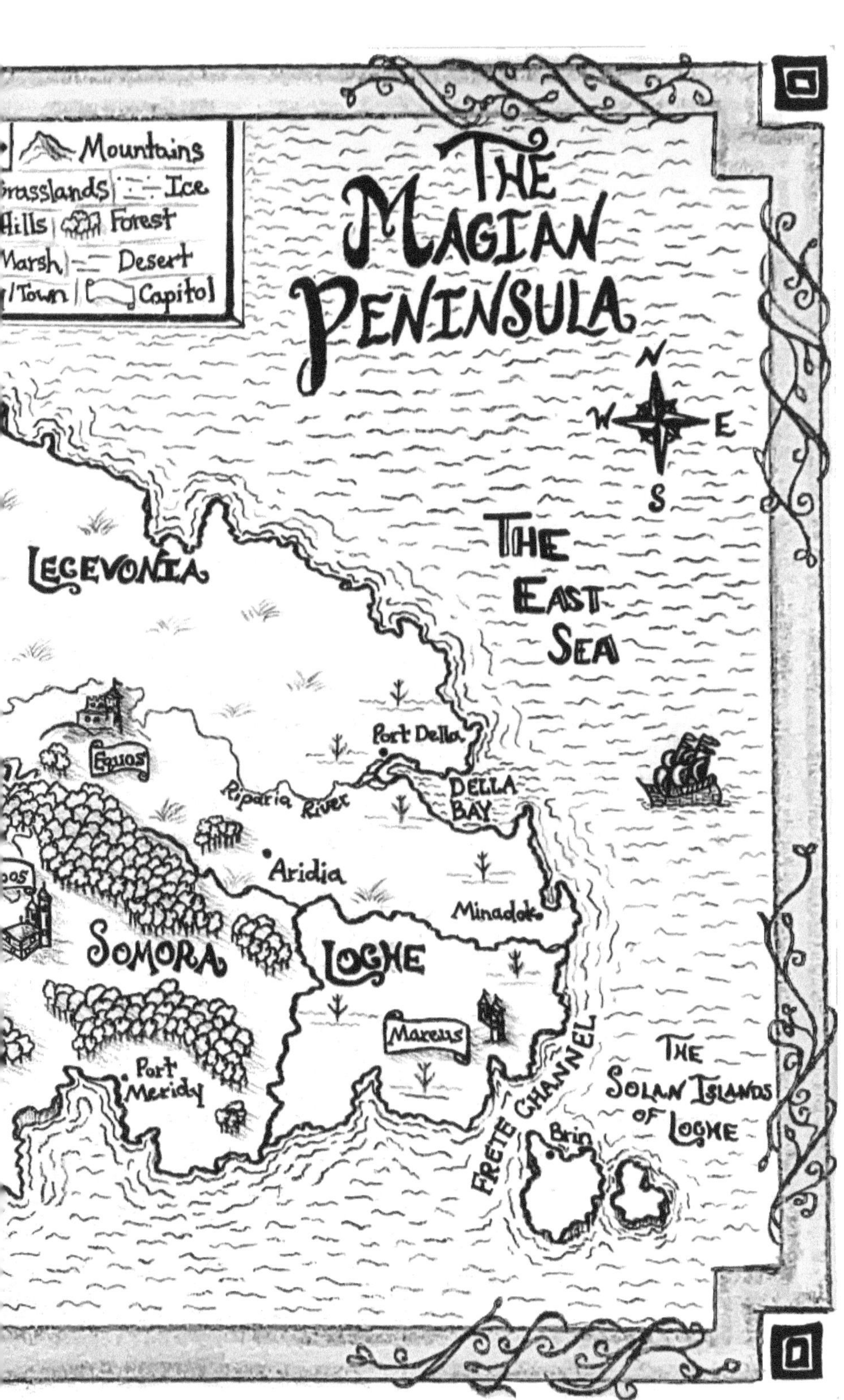

Mountains
Grasslands
Ice
Hills
Forest
Marsh
Desert
Town
Capitol
THE MAGIAN PENINSULA
N
W
E
S
THE EAST SEA
LEGEVONIA
Equos
Port Della
Riparia River
DELLA BAY
Aridia
Minadote
SOMORA
LOGHE
Mareus
Port Meridy
FRETE CHANNEL
THE SOLAN ISLANDS OF LOGHE
Brin

TABLE OF CONTENTS

*For Nick.
I would not have accomplished
this without you.*

OF LEGENDS AND ROSES

BOOK ONE OF
THE CROWNED CHRONICLES

A MAGIAN PENINSULA NOVEL

1

CHAPTER ONE

I WAS ALIVE.

This thought kept my focus off the fate that awaited me as Midas and I careened through the forest, flying against the leaf-woven tapestry of trees and brush. The adrenaline pumping through my veins seemed to channel into Midas, his dark eyes wild with excitement, his pitch-black mane fanned out with our speed. In this moment, we were of one body and one spirit. He snorted as the sound of competing hoofbeats reached our ears through the wind's sharp whistle.

But I wasn't going to get caught yet. With a quick click of my heels, I urged Midas faster, and he blasted forward with a renewed energy. We bent around the curve of the wooded trail before the gray dust had settled behind us.

I was surprised, really, by the skill of the soldier that was after me. He seemed to be keeping up with me better than others could, even as we crashed through the slow stream and sailed over the silent boulders.

With every hoofbeat, I felt my life soaring. Trusting Midas to keep us from barreling into a tree, I chanced a glimpse behind me and caught a flash of chestnut through the brush, accompanied by the cobalt and carmine of the kingdom's army uniform. And it was closer than I'd expected.

"Boars," I cursed aloud. Dread began to inch into my mind as my saddlebag bounced heavily with the weight of the queen's crown nestled inside it.

In a split decision, I cut sharply from the path. Suddenly, branches were stinging my face, leaving scratches that Hazel would surely fuss over later. But Midas hardly protested as we forged through the dense brush, grunting happily with the challenge of new terrain. The shrill whinny of the guard's horse behind me became lost in the rustle of leaves, and my lips stretched into a small, playful smile. I was free once more, if only for a few stolen moments.

The slow babble of Equos's stream drifted to us from close by, so, no longer in immediate danger of capture, I slowed Midas until the steady rhythm of his hooves came to a stop near the mossy banks of the creek. Midas shook out his mane and pranced his feet across the forest floor, throwing his head back with a joyful snort.

"Midas, you fearless boy," I cooed from atop his back as I picked leaves and twigs from the base of his cascading tail. "You are the only horse in the Five Kingdoms that can fly like that." His bloodline was truly unmatched, descended directly from the original horses of Equos. His proud eyes gleamed at me now, along with his powerful stance lording over the forest, made me wonder if the old legends that surrounded Lecevonia's horses had some truth to them.

Still, those old legends were hard to believe, with their magi and abilities and nonsensical tales.

I leaned back against Midas's flank, skirts gathered at my knees, and peered up through the trees to the pinpoints of blue sky, reveling in this last moment of peace. I welcomed the warm sun rays and spring breeze pushing away the last lingering weeks of a frigid winter. The snapping of nearby branches made me want to bolt, but I knew the time had come for me to face my demise.

With a heavy sigh, I let the soldier and his horse approach loudly through the woven leaves and branches. The life I'd felt earlier faded as he finally tumbled to the banks of the stream, his chestnut mare holding a stubbornly disdainful glare.

"I see why they sent for an ex-cavalryman to find you, Your Majesty." The man panted. He slid down from his horse's back and bowed. "Sir Thomas, at your service." Then, he collapsed to the ground and leaned against a tree trunk. "I'm too old for this."

I chuckled as I opened my saddlebag and dug around for my crown. "Not at all, Sir Thomas. I was impressed that you were able to keep up."

"I haven't ridden a horse like that since my thirties," he said with a groan, stretching his legs out one at a time. "Your meeting starts in a few hours. I'm meant to escort you back to the castle."

The familiar weight of the golden crown rested upon my head, the kingdom upon my shoulders. "I know." Even here, swathed in the secluded sunlight passing through the trees, I could not hide from my duties. The plethora of news from this morning spun through my head once more.

Another home was set ablaze by the Rebels of the Red Sun, Your Majesty, and the owners plead for money to rebuild . . .

One of our trading vessels sank on its path toward Somora, Your Majesty; we will need to discuss our product losses . . .

We have arranged a meeting with another suitor, Your Majesty . . .

The last was most horrid. It was the reason I went for a ride in the first place.

In my first year as Queen of Lecevonia, I had learned to solve the minor problems of the kingdom and had even handled a major problem or two. The Corvid Incident that occurred earlier that year crossed my mind, then, causing me to shudder. I had never seen the streets littered with so many disease-ridden crows, nor had I heard so many rumors of a horrible omen.

That last piece of news, though, I could not resolve.

I had never been one to shirk my duties, and, of course, I knew where they lay in that moment. My advisors had made it very clear since my first day of lessons with them after Papa and Mama had died that Lecevonia needed to strengthen its foreign relations once again. And their solution was offering my hand in *matrimony*.

I'd been open to it at first—excited, even. Marriage meant strength, security, that I was doing my job correctly. However, despite my efforts and cooperation with my advisors, I could not bear to willingly marry any of the princes I'd had the "pleasure" to meet. Some of the more memorable men returned to my mind, then: Prince Marcus DeGrey of Hiddon hadn't given me even a glance and had instead gazed upon himself lovingly in any nearby reflective surface; Prince Pertos Terrowin of Loche had made scathing remarks about anything his eyes rested upon—our courtyard, Lecevonia's coat of arms, my gown—and was *still* shocked when I dismissed him from my court; and his brother, Prince Rowon, had been simply dull, with his indifferent sigh and glazed stare. I'd have thought that someone out for the position of king-consort would at least make an attempt at flattery . . .

Lecevonia is only as strong as its leader. Papa's words hung heavily in my mind as I patted Midas's shoulder. My parents had been strong. Papa had been a revered king, with statues erected to him in Equos's city square and legions of men dedicated to him. And Mama's femininity and grace were remembered through the streets of every city and village in the kingdom to this day. Together, they were a couple bound in fortitude. I'd loved them, and I'd wanted to *be* them.

But they hadn't been strong enough to beat Atroxis. Papa and Mama were only two of countless lives throughout the Peninsula claimed by the disease, with its terrible fever and lungs as heavy as lead. I'd only been thirteen.

Now, I *needed* to be my parents. Both of them—my father's regality and my mother's poise—until I found a king-consort to rule by my side.

I sighed at that thought and turned back to Sir Thomas. "What do you do when there is something you've sworn to do, but every fiber of your being is screaming at you to run in the opposite direction?"

"That depends," the old guard started thoughtfully. He groaned as he stood back up to his feet. "Is it your smarts telling you to run? Or fear?"

I smiled ruefully, knowing full well which one it was—not that I would ever admit it.

"Well, then, I suppose we should get moving." I reached behind my head and cringed to feel the intricate bun Hazel had so artfully put together this morning hanging loosely at the nape of my neck. Ah, well. She was going to be upset at my filthy appearance, anyhow.

Might as well face the dragon.

"Please, not the red dress, Hazel!" I exclaimed. I sat on the edge of my bed, cuddled in my chemise and drowning in my dread as Hazel rummaged through my wardrobe.

"Why not, my queen? It accentuates your figure so perfectly!"

I struggled to stifle my groan. "That is exactly why, Hazel. The neckline is too low, and it hugs *everything* too tightly." I looked at her pointedly. "It just isn't appropriate for this occasion."

"I think it's perfect," Hazel murmured, running her hand lovingly over the velvet.

"I wish you would listen to me when I tell you what kind of clothes I will *actually* wear."

"Oh, nonsense, my queen. If I did that, your closet would be full of browns and grays."

"That is not true," I muttered.

Hazel just huffed in defeat and turned back to the armoire, beginning her search once again. This time, she returned to me with a jeweled violet gown draped over her arm.

"Does it have to be purple, Hazel?" Where were my browns and grays?

"My queen, this is one of your best. You will look stunning *and* modest."

My defeated huff mirrored Hazel's, finally assenting. She hadn't been too angry about my mud-splattered dress from riding, and she'd easily concealed the scratches across my cheeks from the branches, so I decided I shouldn't test my luck. I stepped into the dress as Hazel held it open for me, slipping my arms through the long satin sleeves. Another one of my handmaidens, Thea, laced up the back of the gown, pulling the high neckline taught and trapping me in for the day.

As Hazel started brushing the knots and twigs out of my hair, there was a knock on my chamber door.

Through the mirror, I saw Thea answer the door, and one of my guards entered with a bow.

"Your Majesty," he said gruffly, "Sir Ezekiel wishes to see you."

Hazel groaned and rolled her eyes, tutting her tongue in

disapproval. "Oh, we don't have time for this."

But I completely ignored her. I fought to keep a cool expression as excitement fluttered through me. "Thank you. Please let him in."

The guard disappeared behind the door, and a few moments later, Zeke took his place. As usual, he gave no pretense of formality as he strode into the room and leaned against the bedpost like these were *his* chambers, and *I* were the intruder.

Relief flooded my mind as soon as I saw him standing there, his perfect teeth flashing. Then, I couldn't help myself anymore. I stood from my vanity stool with Hazel mid-brushstroke and rushed across the room to him, launching myself into him. "I was told you weren't expected to return for another week!"

Zeke laughed and ensnared me in his arms, his eagerness radiating all around me. "I finished my assignment early."

"I've been worried," I admitted. This time, his scouting assignment had taken him away for nearly two months. I had heard no word from him since he last left the castle, so I'd had no idea if he had been sick, hurt, or worse—captured.

He looked down at me in mock disapproval. "I always come home in one piece, Rose."

But I just shook my head and turned my face upward to look at him. I had to crane my neck, as he was so much taller than me. No matter what he said, I'd always worry about my oldest friend. "You need to cut your hair." I reached one of my hands to the top of his head and ruffled his wavy blond hair.

He waved my hand and my comment away. "I'll get to it."

I finally stepped back and took a better look at him, his dirty uniform, and the thick stubble on his face. "You must've just gotten back."

The corner of his lip turned up into a tiny half-smile. "Haven't even checked in with Colonel Burnstead yet."

My eyes zeroed in on his left forearm, where a crimson stain on his tunic had blossomed through the cotton. Tendrils of concern began to crawl their way into my mind. "One piece, right? Have you been to a healer yet, Zeke?"

He looked at the blood on his arm as if just remembering it was there. "Ah, I'll get to that too. It's nothing."

I glared at him as a hint of anger rose in my chest. "Nothing? Like the broken foot after your last assignment?"

He met my glare with an indignant gaze and yanked up the sleeve to his elbow, exposing a long but shallow cut already scabbed over.

The non-severity of the injury silenced me, though I still internally fumed.

"You see? It's nothing." He roughly pushed his sleeve down and crossed his arms over his chest. "I grazed the edge of my own dagger." He motioned to the small knife tucked into his belt with his hand, then turned his glare on me.

I looked down to the crimson rug tucked beneath my bed and took a deep breath. "I'm sorry. I'm just . . . stressed."

He put his fingers under my chin and lifted my head to meet his gaze. There was an inexplicable little jolt in my chest at the sudden touch, and he smiled my favorite half-smile. "It's all right, my Rose. If I'm to be honest"—his smile turned into a teasing smirk—"it's a relief to know that someone worries so much about me."

"Leave it to you to turn around my apology." If a tone could kill, mine would have slaughtered him.

Hazel then cut in and took hold of my arm. "Okay now, enough. Come, my queen—we still need to finish your hair. We only have another half hour!" She belligerently dragged me back to the mirror and practically pushed me onto the stool.

"As if it takes thirty minutes to fix my hair, Hazel!"

Zeke's brow pulled together. "Another half hour until what?"

"She has another meeting with a suitor," Hazel answered him, her eyes widening suggestively. Then she huffed and turned back to me. "And I can fix your bedhead in five minutes, but we will take all the time in the world for you to look your best." She began parting my hair into strands for an intricate braid.

Zeke leaned against the bedpost once more. "That seems to come quite naturally to Rose."

I made no attempt to hide my eye roll. "Your flattery does not work on me, Zeke. Just because every woman in the Five Kingdoms falls for you does not mean I'm going to do the same."

"Oh no?" There was something strange in his voice, a new playfulness. Then, out of nowhere, his arms were around me and lifting me from my stool. My indignant shriek was interrupted by a laugh that bubbled through my lips as he spun me in a circle. His lips brushed my ear as he murmured, "Surely, I could change your mind in a heartbeat if you allow me."

His husky breath coaxed spontaneous little goosebumps to rise along my neck, but I shook my head at his teasing. As if he hadn't already had nineteen years to do so.

Hazel suddenly shouldered her way between us and slapped Zeke's arm. "You, away. I'm almost finished."

After a few finishing pins here and a hair tuck there, she stepped back from her masterpiece with a look of accomplishment. "You're ready, my queen."

I stood and studied myself in the mirror. My emerald green eyes were dancing in the filtered sunlight, their color popping against my olive skin—which was glowing, no doubt due to Hazel's new bath soap. My brown hair shined, wrapped in a series of beautiful, neat braids and collected into a chignon at the nape of my neck.

I felt regal.

Suddenly, Hazel, upon noticing the length of the shadows on the floor, inhaled sharply. "It's time!" She rushed to my desk in my chambers' office and opened a dark wooden box forever situated on the desk's corner. She returned with my crown, its golden twists glinting in the sun's light through the window after having been cleaned after the morning's ride, and gingerly placed the crown on my head, careful not to disturb the intricate braids. As its weight settled, I had to admit that its presence gave me a sense of authority—something that, even after almost a year, I still struggled to feel.

Zeke cleared his throat and walked over to me. With a theatrically deep bow and playful smile, he offered me his arm. "Would you allow me, a poor and lowly man, to escort you to your meeting?"

I laughed and curtsied just as dramatically. "Why, I am honored just to be in your poor and lowly presence!" Though he was *far* from poor and lowly, living here in the castle when he wasn't away.

We exited my rooms and began walking down the wide corridor, which surprisingly lacked the bustle of a typical morning. I felt the weight of Zeke's stare on me, and after a few long seconds of silence, I turned my face upward to look at him. "May I help you?"

His brown eyes shifted only slightly to meet my gaze, and he shook his head softly. "I just haven't seen you in a long time, Rose. I miss you." His voice had dipped down an octave, taking on a more serious tone.

Against my wishes, my cheeks began to warm under his stare. I narrowed my eyes and pulled them away from his and toward the stone stairway.

Zeke had been in my life as far back as I could remember. His family had resided in the castle, as did all Lecevonian scouts and their families. And as children, we had been inseparable. We had spent countless days exploring every inch of the castle and its grounds.

Then, when his father never returned from an assignment one night, Zeke had been able to lean on me. In turn, I had depended on him for strength when Atroxis had taken Mama and Papa away from me. He was my confidante, my most trusted friend.

But Zeke's clear feelings for me struck my heart with guilt like a dagger each day. I had known my entire life that I would one day marry royalty; otherwise, I may have entertained the idea of a future with Zeke. But that had never been feasible. I'd been careful to build a barrier for my feelings, strictly keeping Zeke only as a friend in my mind.

And Zeke must have also known his wishes were impossible because he left his feelings for me unspoken between us—for which I was grateful.

Still, just like this stubborn blush of mine, some feelings were determined to stick around.

After another quiet moment, when my cheeks had finally cooled, Zeke's voice returned to its normal light manner. "So, how has it been here at Hillstone? Have I missed anything exciting?"

I groaned. "Oh, you've missed absolutely nothing. Besides"—I jabbed him lightly in his ribs—"you haven't been here to cause trouble."

He laughed. "I do make things interesting, don't I?"

"Oh!" I suddenly exclaimed, as the earlier morning came to my memory. "I do have news! I ran into Isabele early this morning—just before dawn on my way to the stables. She was acting strange. She was in quite a hurry, but she claimed to simply be going to the kitchens. And she seemed. . . *very* cheery."

Zeke looked at me dubiously. "You mean cheerier than normal?"

I gave a fervent nod. "And she blushed as red as raspberries when

I asked her where she was headed."

"It's a boy, I guarantee it."

I reeled backward with a snort. "What? I don't think so."

"Why not? She's seventeen, now."

"I suppose so . . . Even so, Isabele would surely tell me if she had any feelings for someone." Or had I been so absorbed in my own responsibilities that I had failed to see my sister's inclinations? A wave of guilt made me drop my gaze to the floor.

Zeke chortled. "It isn't as if you would recognize the hints, anyway. You've never given any man the time of day."

I shot him with a glare, feeling defensive. "Not all of us can afford to spend time on crushes when one must learn how to rule a kingdom." My annoyance was short-lived though, and uncertainty took its place. "And, as you can see, my job is to focus on exactly that right now."

Zeke must have picked up on that telltale involuntary tremor in my voice, for he stopped walking and turned to face me. We were near the bottom of the stairway, our shadows bouncing on the wall in the light of the nearest torch. Setting his hands softly on my shoulders, he ducked to look me in the eye, guilt creasing his forehead. "My Rose." His teasing tone had shifted to one of sincerity, and he offered a rueful grin. "I sometimes forget that your responsibilities have changed since we were young."

I let out a quick, humorless laugh. "Quite different," I allowed, mental defeat threatening to take hold. "Zeke, each meeting with a new suitor is exponentially draining. And you know my troubles go further than finding a husband." As we began walking once more, the morning's lengthy news report circulated in my mind again.

In all honesty, the transition had been . . . admittedly difficult for me. Though I'd been crowned the previous year at the traditional age of eighteen, I never did have much in the way of a mentor. I, of course, was forever thankful for my advising council, but none of them could compare to my father. They had never ruled a kingdom. The decisions still ultimately fell on me, and I simply did not feel prepared for the role. The role of my parents.

Instead of speaking my true thoughts, however, I only added, "It has not been the easiest time since my coronation."

"You will continue to adjust, Rose." Then, his eyes widened in amusement. "Remember the stories of magic we were told as children?" he asked wistfully. "Imagine how much easier your position would be if you had a Talent to help you along. Mind reading, or perhaps perfect judgement." His joy at the idea lightened his entire expression, and he laughed giddily.

Though I rolled my eyes, my mood lifted with his as I appreciated his attempt at a distraction. "Please, Zeke. That type of magic faded long ago from the kingdoms—you know that. It is as if it never existed." I waved away the thought with my free hand.

But Zeke didn't relent quite yet. "Rose, entertain the thought, just for a second. What do you think your Talent would be?"

"Well . . ." I tried to recall any Talents I'd heard about, but I only remembered ones from the old nursery tales. Ridiculous ones, like the ability to make plants grow. I glanced at him through my periphery, and his eyebrows were raised playfully. "Mental strength, I suppose." Yes, more of that would be nice.

Zeke considered that for a second before eventually nodding. "All right. I can agree. Though, maybe *hardheadedness* would be the more appropriate term." He eyed me tauntingly.

An indignant gasp escaped my lips. I looked around us quickly, and seeing that there were no witnesses, I flicked the side of his head. Hard.

That garnered a startled grunt of displeasure from him, so I was satisfied.

Zeke then sighed, taking on a more subdued disposition, and turned his gaze toward the bright hall windows. "Suppose this prince turns out to be the one you choose. Would you feel a little less burdened?"

I was silent for a moment as I thought, then snickered. "Yes, I suppose it would be one less burden to bear." My heaviest burden. However, my hope on the matter had been long ago spent.

The responding silence dragged until we reached the dark, imposing doors of the council room. Zeke seemed to regain his playful mood as he turned to me with a deep bow. "Your prince awaits, *Your Majesty.*"

I couldn't help but laugh. "Thank you, *Sir Ezekiel.*"

He kissed my hand and opened the door for me.

CHAPTER TWO

THE COUNCIL ROOM, though magnificent with its high windows, heavy redwood doors, and polished mahogany table, never failed to somehow make me feel imprisoned. Maybe it was because this room was where my history lessons were as a child, or perhaps the heavy velvet carmine and cobalt banners raining down the wall triggered claustrophobia. I never could quite place it.

The mysterious new prince was sitting at one end of the large table with one of my advisors, Lord Brock, close to his side. They seemed to be chattering pleasantly, making small talk about the market, the weather—no doubt something trivial. As I walked in, they both stood and bowed to me. I lowered my head respectfully and took my seat at the other end of the table, awaiting my punishment.

Lord Brock stepped forward. "Queen Rosemary Avelia," he said formally, "it is my pleasure to introduce you to Prince Hirum Redona."

The name rang a slight bell in my head.

"You may remember him from family functions," Lord Brock

continued. "He is of Somora."

Somora? I groaned internally. Mama was a Somoran princess before marrying Papa, which meant that this man was my cousin. Was this truly the level to which my advisors had resorted?

Now, Prince Hirum Redona was not Prince Charming. From the thinning of his red hair that I glimpsed as he bowed and the hard-set lines of his face, I guessed his age to be no younger than forty. Still, it was not as unnerving as the eleven-year-old Prince Maddox I'd met with last month.

My intuition immediately told me that this was not a match. However, I shook the feeling for now. Perhaps he was a gentleman.

So, I painted on a polite smile. "It is lovely to meet you, Prince Hirum."

"The same to you, beautiful Queen Rosemary," he said with a reedy grin. "You *are* ravishing."

Oh, no. Not a gentleman. I narrowed my eyes and silently cursed my advisors.

They wanted to play games? All right, then. I began playing a game of my own.

"One of your brothers came to see me last week, did he not?" I asked, my voice portraying innocence.

The question undoubtedly rattled Prince Hirum, and he swallowed loudly. "I—well . . .," he stammered before continuing, "If he was, Your Majesty, I was not aware of it."

"Hmm. Well, I do remember every prince I meet." Of course I remembered; he had been another cousin, though he'd been in his thirties rather than forties. I feigned a confused expression, pinching my eyebrows together and frowning. "Yes, I am certain that last Tuesday, I met with Prince Berinon Redona of Somora. Did I not, Lord Brock?" I turned my gaze to my advisor, my faked ambiguity transforming into a tumultuous glare.

Though Lord Brock's eyes had settled on the floor, his answering glower was intended for me.

I finally let my irritation show. "Do you see the dilemma here, gentlemen?" I asked, glancing between the two. "Is it truly appropriate to seek the same hand as your brother?"

My questions had the desired response. Lord Brock could not meet the eyes of Prince Hirum, and the visiting prince shifted on his feet uncomfortably.

Though I wanted to snicker, I set my mouth in a hard line. My tone shifted to artificial remorse. "I seem to have caused some slight tension here. I am terribly sorry."

Prince Hirum just stared at me, dumbfounded.

"I apologize, Prince Hirum, but as you can see, this will not work." I stood from my chair and bowed my head in a way I hoped seemed apologetic. "I do hope that you have safe travels returning to Somora."

Without waiting for a response, I slowly turned on my heel and strode out of the council hall, dismissing our gathering. I heard Lord Brock expressing apologies behind me.

As I stepped into the corridor, my flustered advisor hurried after me before the heavy redwood door closed.

"That was inexcusable," he chided. "There was no need to bring his brother into the conversation. You thoroughly embarrassed him."

"Did you see the way he was staring at me? He was practically *salivating*!" I crossed my arms over my chest, shaking my head in disgust. "Lord Brock, he is forty. That is twice my age! My parents would never have approved."

"If King Doran and Queen Ryia knew the fragile situation you were in right now, they would consider these same measures."

My voice turned to ice. "I would beg to disagree, but queens do not beg."

Lord Brock closed his eyes and inhaled deeply, most likely in a dire attempt to cool his temper, before starting again. "my queen, I am sorry to put you in such a fuss. I truly am. But whether you approve of it or not, if you do not have a future king of Lecevonia—"

"King-consort," I corrected him vehemently.

He bowed his head in apology and continued. "If we do not have someone standing by your side soon, we will have no choice but to plant one there for you." He heaved a deep sigh and turned to leave. "This does not have to be so difficult, my queen."

With that, he walked briskly away from me, leaving me standing in the middle of the corridor.

I was still seething after I had watched him disappear around the stone corner. I let out a loud groan of frustration, which unwittingly attracted the attention of several eyes in the hall. Now under their sudden scrutiny, I straightened my shoulders to at least appear a bit more in control and made my way outside to the courtyard.

As I walked, I tried to speak myself into seeing reason. I knew Lord Brock was trying to help me, and though I didn't want to admit it, he was right. Lecevonia needed strong alliances. It would only be a matter of time before other kingdoms of the Peninsula would begin to challenge my kingdom's strength.

Though my parents had maintained reliable alliances with Somora and Loche and had begun to kindle a relationship with Hiddon, I could not be sure of their stance now that my parents had long passed. They had each been very supportive in the immediate period following their funeral; King Merek of Somora and both King Jarin and Queen Seraphine of Loche had personally attended the ceremony, and Hiddon had sent a year's supply of their fine honey and a generous stock of furs. And of course, King Merek, as my mother's brother, had too generously offered any assistance I might have needed. Though his idea of assistance had undoubtedly included one of his own sons on the Lecevonian throne.

However, the kingdoms had since been quiet. None had come to my coronation. Even my Uncle Merek had kept distant. I supposed we had maintained good trading relationships with each of them, but I truly had no idea where Lecevonia currently stood in the minds of the other rulers.

Lecevonia was only as strong as its leader. And I needed a king-consort in order to be stronger.

Still, I could not fathom marrying any of the men I'd met.

Once outside in the spring air, though, I didn't feel so confined to choosing one of them that minute. No, Lecevonia needed a man that exuded confidence and kindness. I nor the people of my kingdom would settle for less. I collapsed onto a nearby bench and closed my eyes, thankful for the distractingly warm caress of the sunshine.

I was so absorbed in my own head that the loud whistle directed straight into my ear completely took me by surprise.

I sprang from my seat, my heart speeding to an uncontrollable rhythm. Then, once I saw my youngest sister and one of the older gardeners guffawing near the bench, I rolled my eyes. "Oh, I should have known it was you, Clara. And Sterling!" I crossed my arms over my chest and shifted to one foot, wearing an expression of mock offense. "You just assisted in fooling the queen!"

"I apologize for my minor act of treason, Your Majesty," he said, bowing deeply at the waist. "We could never have done it if you weren't in such deep thought. So, we had to take our chance. It's very hard to catch you off-guard."

"You two are the best tricksters I know," I said, catching Clara around the waist and tickling her neck.

Clara laughed, wriggling and twisting until she finally escaped from my arms. Then she plopped down next to me on the bench. "What's the matter, Rose?"

Hm. I apparently needed to practice a bit more poise. "Nothing you need to worry your curly little head about, sweet girl. What were you doing out here?"

Thoroughly distracted, her little eyes suddenly lightened as a huge smile spread across her face. "I was picking flowers for the dining table for my birthday!"

I looked down and noticed for the first time the small bouquet of orange blossoms in my sister's clutches.

"You do remember it's tomorrow, don't you?" Clara's eyes narrowed.

"Of course I remember your birthday! You've been talking about turning eight for six weeks now." Truthfully, however, I had completely and horribly forgotten, as my own troubles had unfolded and refolded daily. Another sister's life events I'd been overlooking, it seemed.

"Well," Clara announced, her voice alive with excitement, "I'm going to go put these flowers in water. Aren't they so pretty, Rose?" She didn't wait for my opinion before bouncing away, heading for the castle doors.

I sighed and settled on the bench to delve into my thoughts once again.

Sterling remained, his kind old eyes regarding me. "You do look rather distressed, my queen," he said, leaning on his rake.

I took a deep breath and let my thoughts flow into words. "Each new prince I meet makes me feel as if this entire endeavor is pointless. My advisors are upset with me, I'm a horrible older sister—I haven't even *talked* to Lisette this week—and I don't know what to do. I'm not pleasing anyone." I closed my eyes and rubbed my forehead.

I felt the bench shake ever so slightly as he settled next to me. "Have you tried flipping a coin? That usually works. Heads, you worry about the problem. Tails, you don't."

"Sterling." My lids lifted just enough to look at the old man.

"I know, my queen. I am only joking," he chuckled, pleased with himself. "You made Clara happy just now because you were excited about her birthday," he pointed out. "You make me happy by listening to my rambling about peonies. That's two people you've pleased right there." He glanced above us to the forsythia blossoms just budding on the lush green trees. "Please remember, as your mother did always say"—he turned his gaze back to me with a slight smile on his face—"trust your judgement. There is no rush to choose a man."

"There *is* a rush, though, Sterling," I said. "My advisors are growing impatient—an arranged marriage surely isn't far off."

Sterling huffed. "Well, who said that you had to show up for the wedding? Who said that you had to proclaim, 'I do'?" He patted my hand with such love and compassion that, in my emotional turmoil, a knot rose into my throat. "Are you aware that you do not *have* to do anything? You are, after all, the queen."

He did have a point there, I supposed.

Sterling was silent for a second, giving his words a chance to sink in before standing up from the bench with a loud stretch. "And now I must go back to raking leaves. Because I am not the queen." He turned to me one last time and winked. "Have confidence, Your Majesty." He began whistling as he strolled away, a familiar tune that I couldn't quite place.

Alone in the courtyard, I replayed Sterling's words in my head. I really did love that old gardener. He had already been here at Hillstone in my earliest memories, and Mama had been so fond of

Sterling. Now, he was less of a castle worker and more like family.

And he was right, after all. I was the queen, reigning power of Lecevonia! I didn't have to do anything I wished not to.

But where was the line drawn between my own desires and my duties to the kingdom?

I lifted my head and peered up at the forsythia trees, the first plants to blossom in the courtyard in the middle of March. The butter-yellow flowers gave off a pleasant, smooth fragrance, which seemed out of place to me given how my day had been so far. No doubt Sterling had pruned these trees, keeping them as beautiful as they were now.

I was just starting to enjoy the quiet solitude of the courtyard when another of my advisors, Lord Clark, at long last found me.

Lovely.

He bowed quickly as he halted in front me. "Queen Rosemary— I've gone through half of the castle until I came across Sir Ezekiel and asked him where you might be."

Boars. Zeke knew where I was after every meeting. "And what do you need me to know so urgently, Lord Clark?"

"You'll be meeting with another prince this afternoon."

At first, I thought I'd heard him wrong. Surely, they wouldn't plan this.

But as he stood there, anticipating my response, I realized that he'd said exactly what I'd feared.

I sat there and stared at him. "Is not one enough for the day?"

"I'm sorry, my queen," Lord Clark said, and he did sound genuinely apologetic. "We did not anticipate his arrival so quickly—we were expecting him next week, actually." He looked a bit chagrined, as if this prince's early arrival displeased him too.

I decided to try Sterling's advice. "Then tell him that I will meet with him tomorrow," I said firmly. "If he's coming so unannounced, then he should understand that some *planned* things take precedence, shouldn't he?"

But Lord Clark shook his head, stubbornly refusing to give in. "He's come a long way to meet with you today, Your Majesty."

I wanted to groan, to shout out loud, to storm off to my chambers. But none of those were acceptable for a queen. So, I simply glared straight ahead, refusing to meet Lord Clark's eyes.

"I assure you that this meeting will not be as dreadful as this morning," my advisor said softly. "You haven't had any suitors from this particular kingdom yet. I know how these meetings . . . disgruntle you."

Disgruntle was an understatement. "If I could choose with whom I meet, perhaps I would be a tad more enthusiastic," I said under my breath.

Lord Clark did not miss a word, however, and he frowned. "Then you would never arrange a meeting." He turned back toward the walkway leading to the castle steps. "The meeting is in four hours, a bit after lunch."

"I shall see you then," I said, my words underlined with sarcasm. Lord Clark did not turn, so my tone must have been subtle enough.

And I was left alone once more.

My advisors must have been delirious, allowing this to happen. And how had I not met with anyone from this kingdom before? I began recalling each of my suitors, shuddering as certain ones came to mind. Somora, Loche, Hiddon . . . And that was all. Huh. Sure enough— there was one more. A northern kingdom that even Papa hadn't discussed very much.

I would not give it another thought for now. Instead, I looked at the clear sky, where only a slight smattering of clouds was visible over the distant mountains, slowly extending to the nearer foothills. It was one of those rare days where the weather was perfect for just about anything. The warm sunlight felt too nice, and I decided then that I should not waste it. I still had four spare hours, right? I stood quickly from my bench, my eyes fixed on the stone path to the stable.

With space for more than three hundred horses under its roof, our Royal Stable was the largest horse stable in the Five Kingdoms, and Lecevonia's proudest feature. The brick walls were lined with spacious stalls, twenty-five on each side of an aisle, with many aisles leading off the main entryway. The cobblestone floors were always somehow kept clean. And behind the stable was a series of vast, green pastures that seemed to go on without end. Though several of the horses here belonged to capitol citizens, most formed the Cavalry Division of the Royal Army—another formidable aspect of my kingdom.

The stable was always a busy place, with people rushing around and tending to the needs of every horse housed here. But the moment I walked through the sliding stable doors, every one of the stable workers stopped his or her tasks, turned to me, and bowed or curtsied before returning to their work. I sighed, reminiscing the not-so-long-ago days when I could visit my horse without so much as a glance in my direction.

Trying to ignore the unwelcome attention, I bent down to pet the tawny tabby cat that always greeted me when I came to the stable. "I don't mind *your* attention, missy," I murmured, scratching her behind one of her ears.

When I straightened, I caught sight of Celeste leaning against the far wall, her head resting against a nearby wooden beam, eyes closed.

I immediately felt my mood lift once again; next to Zeke, Celeste was my closest friend. Her father had been a stable worker, so we had effortlessly bonded over horses when we were both young girls.

I walked up to her silently, trying my best to go undetected, and when I finally sidled up next to her, I said, "Better get back to work before the queen catches you slacking."

"Better start trying to be a little less noticeable, Your Majesty," she responded, eyes still closed.

A tiny, surprised bubble of laughter found its way through my lips. "Oh, I *do* apologize for disturbing you then," I said, feigning sincerity with a pouted lip and scrunched forehead.

Her characteristic bold smile spread across her face, and she opened her eyes just a tad. "I knew it was you when everything and everyone around me went silent for a second."

"Hmm" was my only answer. I might never be able to be stealthy again.

I walked to Midas's stall and unlatched the door with a metallic clank. "Hello again," I greeted him quietly with a gentle pat of his sleek black neck. In response, Midas nudged my shoulder and nickered softly. His dark accusing eyes seemed to say, *Twice in one day? You are too much.*

"How has he been since this morning?" I asked Celeste as I clipped his lead rope to his bridle.

"He's been a bit cranky, but that's really nothing new," she shrugged. "Otherwise, he's fine." She took the lead rope from me with a knowing smirk. "I'll get him ready for you. You can't be getting dirty, with your next meeting in a few hours."

"How did you know about my meeting?" I asked, my eyes squinting in surprise.

Celeste's smirk turned smug. "Word travels. I also heard about your little performance with the prince from Somora."

I crossed my arms over my chest. "I don't regret what I said to him."

"Good!" She placed a saddle blanket on Midas's back. "I'm proud of you, Rosie—he sounded disgusting."

I heard a familiar giggle then, and my gaze flitted toward the sound. To my surprise, I found my sister Lisette talking to one of the stablehands. No, more than talking . . . Flirting?

I'd missed this too?

But Lisette was only fifteen! Oh . . . Fifteen? Truly?

When I looked back at Celeste, I saw that she'd followed my gaze.

"That has been going on for a few months now," she said, nodding in my sister's direction.

I sighed heavily. This only reaffirmed my thoughts during my conversation with Sterling. "Becoming queen also meant I've turned into a terrible older sister."

But Celeste quickly shook her head. "No—you just have larger things to worry about now." She held Midas's reins out to me. "Go clear your head."

I gratefully took Midas's reins and, with my skirts hiked up to my thighs, stuck my foot into the stirrup. As I swung my other leg over and steered him toward the door, I heard Celeste call out, "And relax for me!"

I took my favorite path, one that anyone rarely rode because of its undesirably rough terrain. Midas and I, however, knew this path so well that neither of us had to worry about the obstacles anymore. I closed my eyes for a long moment, enjoying nature's quiet liveliness as I swayed from side to side. The low-pitched songs of starlings rolled through the air while a gentle breeze rustled Midas's black mane and tail and danced through the trees' leaves. Once again shrouded in the cover of the woods, I felt peace fully overtake me.

I guided Midas through the shallow stream and meandered around a tight curve. But Midas disapprovingly lifted his head and pawed the ground with his front hoof. *What about this morning? Where is that Rosemary?* I chuckled, reading his mood, and accelerated first to a trot, then to a canter. After a while, I finally let him loose to a gallop. At full speed, Midas shook his mane and snorted in satisfaction.

We rode swiftly down the rocky, overgrown trail, the trees on either side of us a blur past my purple skirts. My ears no longer picked up the sounds of the forest, only the whistle of the speeding wind. My frustrations, my anxiety, my self-doubt all wheeled out of my head with the passing gusts. How could anything trouble me when I was flying?

But as the wind rushed through my woven braids, Hazel's disappointed face emerged in my mind. She would be so upset if her morning's masterpiece were ruined. With a disgruntled sigh—for neither I nor Midas was ready to slow—I pulled back on Midas's reins.

His resistance told me that he wasn't pleased as we slowed to a walk, but he got distracted almost immediately, suddenly pricking his ears forward.

Then I heard it too.

A rustling, too big for an animal.

The crack of a branch.

I locked eyes with the archer in the low branches of a nearby oak in the same instant that he let his arrow fly.

There was no time for me to think. On some instinct, I ducked as the arrow whistled past my right ear and lodged itself into the trunk of the tree directly behind me. I swept my eyes wildly through the branches, knowing my looming death could come from any angle. The next time my eyes found the archer, his arrow was aimed for Midas's flank.

No!

I twisted Midas out of the arrow's wickedly accurate path just as another set of hooves pounded against the dirt path behind me. *Great, he is not alone,* I thought, my fear bubbling to the surface.

But the horse streaked past me in a flash of white, so closely that Midas reared onto his hind legs and squealed, eyes wild. I thought I'd made out a man and a horse, but the rest was a blur of action.

What in Haggard's name was happening?

I saw the archer hurriedly jump down from his branch and into the brush below. The flash came to a sudden stop at the edge of the path, and the new arrival jumped from his horse's back and bolted into the trees toward the archer.

Bushes thrashed angrily for an unending second, and I immediately considered fleeing down the path. I'd felt vulnerable before, but never like this. This new vulnerability in the face of death weighed more heavily on my mind than anything. I hated it, this weakness. I needed to leave this place.

Lecevonia is only as strong as its leader.

Fleeing did not feel strong.

I held my ground atop Midas.

The newcomer again emerged with his sword withdrawn from its sheath and held against the archer's throat. As the man brought him forward out of the brush, the archer's bow fell to the forested ground with a soft thud.

"Do you regret attempting to harm this woman, now?" the man raged, his deep voice booming.

"I—I'm sorry," the archer stammered fearfully, his gray eyes peering up at the man through his stranglehold. "I was assigned. I'm only doing what I was told!" He closed his eyes. "Please, I beg for forgiveness . . ." He trailed off, incoherent murmurs and pleas rolling into each other.

"Don't ask me—ask the woman you were to kill," the man growled.

His gaze shot toward me, his teeth gritted together.

I instinctively stood straighter and hardened my expression. In an instant, I had changed from frightened woman to the reigning Queen of Lecevonia. I glared at the archer, ready to announce a death sentence.

But I hesitated. I had never condemned anyone in such a way. Besides, he must have some information.

When I spoke, my voice rang clear, not a tremble to be detected. "Tell me, who sent you?"

For a moment, there was only silence in the forest. Then the archer's eyes shot open, suddenly glaring, cutting through me. I watched his feigned fear morph into a shrewd defiance, and, moving with the speed of a snake, he unsheathed a hidden dagger. Before I could acknowledge it, he wildly swiped it in an upward arc toward the man holding him captive.

The man exclaimed a profanity and flinched out of the dagger's path. But his hold had loosened just enough for the archer to slither out of the man's grasp. Before either of us could react, the archer had disappeared into the brush.

The forest was quiet then, aside from Midas's hooves trampling the ground nervously.

Still cursing under his breath, the man sprinted toward the surrounding bushes, but I somehow knew the archer had already made a silent escape. The man emerged again with only an angry sigh. He moved to sheath his sword—a masterful weapon with an ornate silver hilt and embellishments of swirling dark metal—but he seemed to notice something and paused, examining the black blade.

Then I saw it too—a small trace of crimson at the sword's edge. The archer must have injured himself while making his escape.

The man wiped off the blood with moss from the forest floor

before sliding the sword into its leather scabbard. At his feet, the archer's bow lay forgotten among the weeds.

"Ah," he said, mostly to himself, as he picked it up and examined it. "At least he is weaponless, then." He turned to me for the first time, with a small grin.

He was not much older than me, three or possibly four years, with curls so dark they were almost black, and piercing sapphire eyes that were striking against his fair complexion. They gleamed in the sunlight now, softening as he looked at me. His ornate red vest was threaded with gold and exhibited an unfamiliar crest on the shoulder, but nonetheless fit for a prince. Well, he certainly had the air of a pampered prince. And, as much as I hated to admit it, his little grin was . . . charming.

"Are you all right, Your Majesty?" The young man interrupted my evaluation, his tone gentle. Genuine concern touched the edges of his words, and his arms outstretched cautiously toward me. "Are you hurt in any way?"

I had a feeling that my wide eyes and hard-pressed lips were not helping my "calm" charade. Nevertheless, my hand slowly drifted to my golden crown, assuring its place atop my head.

I was suddenly aware that this man was performing his own assessment.

So, I straightened my shoulders and attempted to smooth my expression, but I stayed upon Midas's back and held his reins firmly. "Yes, I am fine. Thank you. If you would not have come when you did, I may very well be dead right now . . ." My eyes fell to the ground, and I nearly trembled as this reality began to sink into my mind. I refused to dwell on it in this moment though. "May I ask what you are doing here on this trail?"

He walked to his horse and secured the archer's bow to his saddle.

"The terrain of this path attracted me to it," he admitted with a small smile, patting the horse's alabaster neck. "She prefers the mountains, so this trail best suited her."

"Who are you? Why are you here?" My questions had come out more demanding than I'd intended, so I felt the need to elaborate. "I apologize—I don't recognize the crest on your garment."

The man smiled a little wider, unbothered, and bowed deeply at the waist. "I am Prince Gryffin Danicio, of Tarasyn. And I believe I am here to meet with you this afternoon." He eyed me as he straightened.

. . . Oh.

Prince Gryffin looked to the trees edging the path once more, seeming to be fighting indecision. After another long moment, he faced me again, decision made. "May I escort you back to the stable? To ensure that our friend doesn't try to return." He had probably attempted to sound light and teasing, but apprehension hardened his tone.

Though I hardly ever felt the need for an escort, I could not fool myself—I didn't want to be alone right now. What was more, as our eyes met, the strongest sensation of trust I'd ever felt overcame me. "I'd appreciate that. Thank you, Prince Gryffin."

As we rode, his eyes kept sweeping the surrounding forest, the high branches, and brush bordering the path. His vigilance gave me a surge of comfort, for that new brand of vulnerability still clung to the edges of my mind.

The resolve I was desperately holding together began to splinter, like a ceramic pot on the verge of breaking.

I made an attempt to distract myself. "So, *you* are the suitor with whom I'm to meet this afternoon," I said, playfully scrutinizing him out of the corner of my eye.

The prince chuckled. "Indeed, Your Majesty. I hope I meet your expectations."

"Well, though my *standards* remain high," I said carefully, "after this morning's meeting, my *expectations* are fairly low."

Prince Gryffin looked at me inquisitively. "Just this morning? Huh . . ." He paused for a moment, his mouth set into a contrite grimace. "I apologize if my early arrival is inconvenient."

Well, he was considerate at least. One point for him. I could not stanch my sudden flicker of hope. "Well, if you're different from the others, Prince Gryffin," I said, taking on a teasing tone, "perhaps I will forgive you." We led our horses through the small stream, water splashing loudly around us. "Though, I suppose I do already owe you my gratitude."

"I assure you. I'm just as grateful to have arrived when I did as you are." He turned his eyes toward me. "I must admit, you're rather calm right now. Are you sure that you're all right?"

I could not break yet. I couldn't allow myself.

But I also didn't have the spare energy to lie.

"If you knew the effort I am putting into staying together right now, your mind would be more at ease," I admitted. To stay grounded, I focused only on Midas's swaying beneath me. Left, right. Left, right.

When I glanced toward the prince again, I saw that concern had deepened his expression. "Once I inform someone of what's happened here, soldiers will be scouring the woods, and they will find your assassin." His eyes turned fierce. "You *will* be safe."

Suddenly, the idea of guards pacing the castle and scouts—Zeke, I thought painfully—searching the forest flooded my mind, and panic slithered its way in with the image.

"No!" I very nearly shouted.

Prince Gryffin's horse jolted its head upward in surprise and grunted, jostling its reins.

I began again more softly. "Prince Gryffin, I must ask that you don't tell anyone of this. I will, in my own time. I just . . . need to make sense of it first." I didn't want Zeke out there, nor did I want guards posted around my every waking moment.

He studied me out of his periphery, seeming to scrutinize my sanity for a moment—which was completely reasonable—before bowing his head. "As you wish, Your Majesty."

I heaved a soft sigh of relief. "Thank you."

We were approaching the trailhead near the stable now, and I could just make out the figures of a few stable workers through the open barn doors. I looked at Prince Gryffin once more. "I do have another favor. My advisors would not be thrilled to know that I met you before our official meeting with them. And, well, word travels," I hinted, echoing Celeste's words from earlier. "Would you mind . . .?"

Prince Gryffin's small grin reappeared. "Our secret. I'll continue riding for a bit, then search the woods. But I'll be watching until you are inside the stable."

I wheeled Midas around then, toward the stable. "It truly was a pleasure meeting you, even if I am to meet you again in just a short while. And thank you, again, for coming to my aid." I let a mischievous smile play on my lips and exhaled a dramatic sigh. "A mere damsel in distress."

"After seeing how you handle yourself, I don't think that you truly ever *can* be a damsel in distress, my beautiful queen," the prince said with a wink.

At his words, I expected the anger I so often felt when a stranger called me beautiful. I anticipated it.

However, no anger rose. If anything, a bit of an unfamiliar feeling, something like giddiness, fluttered through me.

Hm. Strange.

I shook away this feeling, amounting it to my totally disheveled mind, and rode the last stretch to the stable unaccompanied.

When I reached Midas's stall, Celeste rushed to me and took the reins out of my hands. "You are cutting it very close, Rosie."

"I know. I'm on my way up to the council room." I gave her a quick kiss on the cheek. "Thank you, Celeste." If she saw my unraveling resolve in my eyes, she did not say so.

When I exited the stable, I patted my hair to make sure that the elaborate braid that Hazel had worked on so hard this morning was still in place. Everything felt right. I quickly smoothed out my violet gown; there was no dirt, which surprised me, and even after all that had occurred, the dress was only slightly wrinkled from riding. Passing my private inspection, I lifted my skirts and hurried up the stone path to the castle.

CHAPTER THREE

I LET MYSELF in through the old gates that had once marked the edge of the castle grounds and let them swing closed behind me, the creaking of the rusted iron hinges quickly fading as I rushed into the castle courtyard. Birds whistled loudly in the trees, and a squirrel ran past my drumming feet to avoid getting trampled. Clara was back to picking flowers for her birthday, and she waved to me as I ran by.

I sprinted up the stone stairs, pausing only for the guards to heave open the thick wooden doors for me. I saw Zeke leaning against the castle wall, and when I didn't slow for him, I heard him grumble. Soon, he was in stride next to me in the main corridor. "Why are you in such a hurry, Rose?"

Now inside the castle, I came to a stop with Zeke beside me. "Well," I said, my breath coming in little huffs, "I'm meeting with another prince today, and I can't be late." And, I knew that if I stopped moving, the fractures in my mind caused by this feeling of unforgiving vulnerability might finally break open. "Now, I have to—"

But he held his arm out in front of me. "Not yet." He looked at me accusingly with his deep brown eyes, crossing his arms over his chest. "Since when are you in a *hurry* to meet with a prince?"

Leave it to Zeke to notice. I knew it was not exactly *queenly* to rush like this, but I would never hear the end of Hazel nor my advisors if I were late. And, if I was being honest with myself, I did feel a strange excitement to see Prince Gryffin again. "All right!" I finally exclaimed. I raised my hand, gesturing to him to follow me. There were too many eyes in the hall.

I led him to a secluded corner near the end of the corridor, which looked out through a massive window facing west. I moved behind the last grand stone column in the corridor and finally turned to Zeke.

"I'll tell you. But you cannot tell anyone else. It would become too much of a fuss."

Zeke scoffed. "Rose, as long as we have known each other, have I ever told one of your secrets?"

It was my turn to give an accusing look. "You let it slip to Lisette that I let her pet bird out its cage, and it flew out of the window, never to return."

He shrugged, not fazed. "We were both, what, ten?"

"She was angry with me for three *months*, Zeke."

Zeke sighed. "You have my word that I will not tell anyone." He uncrossed his arms and set one above his head, resting on the pillar, and the other to his hip. He looked at me expectantly.

I sighed and looked down to the floor, folding my hands together in front of me. With a deep breath, taking comfort in the fact that I could trust Zeke with anything, I conveyed everything that had happened in the woods. As I talked, Zeke's brow furrowed, and he frowned, the corners of his lips sliding farther down as he listened.

I had just barely gotten through my experience with the archer and

Prince Gryffin's timely appearance when his face buckled with rage. "You—" he began shouting, but my pleading eyes made him lower his voice to a hiss. "You were almost *killed*? And you don't want me to tell anyone about that?"

I could feel my resolve finally breaking, that ceramic pot near to bursting. Tears threatened to flow. "The last thing I want is to be guarded as I walk within my own home. Everyone would just have unnecessary concern for me."

"Unnecessary?" He looked at me incredulously. "What part of protecting you is unnecessary? What if he tries to return?"

"What if this is an isolated attempt?" I countered. I knew he could also be right, but I just couldn't make sense of anything right now. Not until I could think. "Zeke, please, just . . . let me figure this out first." I used the same line I had with Prince Gryffin, but the uncertain lilt in my voice unveiled any charade of confidence this time.

"Well, while you're 'figuring it out,' I will have to take care of this matter myself," he said harshly, turning away from me.

The image of Zeke in the woods, put at risk hunting the ruthless archer, returned to my mind, and panic slipped through the growing cracks. "No!" I grabbed his hand and stopped him, pulling him back to me. I rested my hands on either side of his face. "You just came home, Zeke. You need your rest. There's no need to go after anyone."

Zeke looked at me, all anger gradually leaving his features. In its place, a mixture of amusement and faux disbelief claimed his expression. "Why, is that concern for me that I hear from you, Rose?"

I dropped my hands immediately and looked to the floor. But I spoke in earnest. "It is no secret that I worry about you, Zeke. If you need me to admit it again, fine. You always cross my mind when you are away. I get worried sick at night, wondering if you are all right, if you are coming home. The days on which you return are some of my happiest. There," I concluded, stubbornly raising my eyes to meet his gaze. "Are you satisfied now?"

The amusement on his face had materialized into a smirk. "Just barely, my Rosemary."

I rolled my eyes not so discreetly. Still, his teasing acted as mortar, slowly working to seal the cracks of my overwhelmed mind. I could feel my resolve solidifying again. "Again, your flattery does not work on me, Ezekiel." Then I sighed, and my expression turned serious. "You will not tell anyone?"

He just slowly shook his head, his blonde hair cascading into his eyes.

That was enough of an answer for me. "And you still need to cut your hair."

"I'll get it done, Rose." Zeke raised his hand and brushed my cheek with his index finger, and I turned away quickly. We were beginning to cross our carefully placed barrier.

"I have to go, Zeke."

"All right. Go meet with your lovely prince." He wore a reluctant grimace. "I do suppose I owe this one my gratitude. Where did you say that he was from?"

"I don't remember," I admitted, a bit ashamed. "There was so much happening. I didn't recognize the kingdom immediately."

"Hm," was Zeke's simple, thoughtful answer. "Well, as always, I would say good luck—but I do hope it goes terribly," he laughed. Back to his normal self it seemed.

I shook my head and smiled. I could forever count on him to lighten any situation. "Goodbye, Zeke."

"Goodbye, my Rose."

I turned away then and left Zeke standing there behind the column.

As I walked toward the council room, I could feel his eyes lingering on me before I finally heard his footsteps begin to fade in the opposite direction, toward the stairs to the kitchens.

Just as I rounded the corner of the main corridor, I found Lord Clark shutting the council room doors behind him. When he caught sight of me, he clapped his hands. "Ah! Impeccable punctuality!" As he took my arm and escorted me toward the council room, the corner of his mouth turned up into a smirk. "If you truly don't like him, you can still send him home straight away."

I offered him a small smile; Lord Clark didn't rattle my nerves nearly as much as Lord Brock did.

He pulled open the heavy redwood door for me, and I stepped into the council room for the second time today. This time, however, I was not shrinking away.

Lord Brock appeared through the door in the far-right corner—the door to the advisors' office. "Queen Rosemary Avelia," he called out formally, "I have the pleasure to introduce to you Prince Gryffin Danicio, of Tarasyn."

Ah, Tarasyn! That was it! The Peninsula's northernmost kingdom—though my knowledge ended there.

Lord Brock waved his hand in a large arc behind him, and I almost giggled—the whole affair was much more grandiose than this morning. My advisors must have had a good feeling about this one.

Prince Gryffin strode into the council room from the office and bowed. I could study him a bit more closely now, and my first assessment had been correct—Prince Gryffin was, without a doubt, charming. His presence already felt familiar.

"It is a pleasure to meet you, Prince Gryffin."

"And you, Your Majesty." His blue eyes were edged with concern, asking me an unspoken question. *Are you all right?*

As I sat in my usual place at the head of the table, something about his gaze made it possible to muster up a smile, a genuine one that reached my eyes. Yes. I was fine for now.

Lord Clark interrupted our silent conversation. "Prince Gryffin is the second eldest of his family in Tarasyn. We have yet to form any sort of trade agreement with his kingdom, which is rather surprising, given the kingdom's proximity to our own." A tinge of confusion spiked his voice. "We don't have *any* ties to Tarasyn, in fact."

"Tarasyn has only recently opened its borders, sir," Gryffin answered as he sat at the table, already looking quite at home, and folded his hands in front of him. He shifted his gaze to me. "We've actually been in quite a tumultuous time for the past few decades. My grandfather and father were both harsh rulers, and, well . . . I'll simply say they were not viewed positively by the people of the kingdom."

A pummeled landscape engrossed my mind, with scarred mountainsides and mistreated, disgruntled people. Sympathy filled my chest.

"However, my older brother now rules Tarasyn," Prince Gryffin continued, "and the state of the kingdom is very much improving."

"Well, that's good!" I said, perhaps a bit too excitedly. Though, really, I was relieved for the Tarasynian people. A war-torn life was no way to live. "How long has your brother been king?"

"Five years. Almost six, now. I take pride in being under his reign."

I heard the clear admiration in his voice, saw it in his smile, and, for the first time during a meeting with a suitor, I was intrigued. "You care deeply for your brother then, Prince Gryffin?"

"Very much. He is my most trusted, Your Majesty."

He was caring and unafraid to say so—another two points, as I continued my tally. "What of the rest of your family?"

"I have two younger brothers—twins, in fact—and one sister." Gryffin chuckled as he seemed to recall a memory. "My poor sister had to grow up in the midst of four older brothers, which I can only imagine was not easy for her."

"Surely not!" I still sometimes imagined what it would be like to have a brother instead of three sisters. Less melodrama, I was sure. "You all watch over her though, I assume."

"She can take care of herself, but with four older brothers, I assure you that she is well protected." His eyebrows lifted in amusement. "Though she has seen her fair share of skirmishes and tricks among us."

I pictured a little girl, about Clara's age, dancing around two curly-haired boys who were caught up in a brotherly brawl, probably over some trivial thing like who would have to muck the horse's stall that night, and I snickered at the image.

Then, before I could take hold of the direction of my thoughts, the boys morphed into Gryffin and the archer in the woods, wrestling in the dirt of the forest floor. The little girl turned into a younger version of myself, helplessly staring at them with wide-eyed fear.

My laugh was cut short by a guttural gasp as this new image filled every corner of my mind, and I felt the fissures of my resolve further split.

My breakdown was imminent, and I needed to be alone.

I tried to cover my sudden unsteadiness by plastering on another bright smile. "You will have to tell me of these skirmishes and tricks in the near future, Prince Gryffin."

Lord Brock cleared his throat loudly. "Does this mean, then, my queen, that you'll permit Prince Gryffin to stay for a time?" Though

Lord Brock maintained his professional demeanor as always, I heard a hint of excitement in his tone—now that I had finally shown interest in a suitor. His happiness held me together for a moment longer.

I studied Gryffin, taking in again his deep blue eyes and strong, kind complexion.

Well, he wasn't forty.

"Yes, Lord Brock. If you would accept my invitation, Prince Gryffin, I ask that you stay here at Hillstone for a while. My kingdom has much to offer, and I'd like to get to know you."

A wide, brilliant smile spread across Gryffin's lips as he bowed his head. "Of course, Your Majesty."

I felt an unfamiliar little thrill run down my spine at his reply, and my etched delight became a little bit more authentic. "Lord Clark, please prepare a chamber in our guest wing for Prince Gryffin. Strive to make his time here as comfortable as possible."

As Lord Clark hurried off, I stood and walked around the table to Prince Gryffin. "It really has been a pleasure to meet you. I'd like to see you again soon." I bowed my head, a new, sly grin pulling at the corners of my mouth. "Now, Lord Brock will lead you to your rooms."

"Thank you, Your Majesty," he said, his answering grin matching mine. As soon as Lord Brock was out of earshot, Gryffin stood and leaned toward my ear. "No more archers for today, yes?"

I couldn't stop the sudden blush that rose to my cheeks.

Then he leaned back, nodded to me one last time, and followed Lord Brock out of the council room.

Finally. Alone.

With no witnesses and no eavesdroppers, I collapsed down into my cushioned chair and caved in on myself. My little mental ceramic pot shattered, shards flying everywhere as I finally let the gravity of today's events consume me.

I could have been killed today.

That lone thought sent me into a fit of hyperventilation.

This morning could have been the last time I had seen my sisters, spoken to Celeste, walked through the hall with Zeke. My last of the wind whistling past me as I rode Midas. This morning could have been my last *everything*.

I'd never felt so vulnerable as I'd been, held within the sights of that archer. So easily able to be disposed of. In a matter of seconds, Lecevonia could have lost its ruler. Would Papa have shaken his head in disappointment that I'd gone out for a ride when so many other responsibilities rested upon my shoulders? I'd never felt unsafe flying through the forest, but now even that seemed like a stupid decision.

Strangely, however, the tears that had so nearly spilled earlier did not return now. Instead, a flow of relief began to affix to my every fiber, for this morning had *not* been my last. And this relief helped me to slow my breath, my chest rising and falling a bit more calmly as I sat there, eyes closed.

But a string of questions tormented me.

Who had sent the archer to assassinate me?

Who in my kingdom would want me off the throne? And for whom to rule? My sister Isabele? Isabele was too gentle; she would be crushed under the weight of the Crown.

No, it must have been someone who wishes to do away with the Crown altogether.

The Rebels of the Red Sun crossed my mind, but I quickly dismissed the thought. They were no real danger, only hardheaded zealots who tried to make statements by terrorizing the little villages of the countryside every so often. They weren't capable of something such as this.

Then who?

I wondered if I was wrong for not immediately informing my advisors.

But for some reason, I felt that I had time to consider my next course of action. Not many people could afford to hire an assassin more than once, and the attempt had failed. Or, if the assassin did show his face again, the next attack would not be soon. Whoever had sent the archer would now know that I escaped and that I had the capability to raise an alarm. They would wait, if only to gauge the castle's response.

I almost scoffed. The castle's response would no doubt result in increased guard shifts. And decreased freedom. A nonstop entourage of soldiers posted around me. To the council room, to the Great Hall, to my chambers. No, it would not be a decrease in freedom—it would be *no* freedom.

Yes, I had time. And I knew that this time was thanks to Prince Gryffin, for appearing in the woods when he did.

This thought led to another matter.

Could I have possibly met the man I was to marry?

The idea dumbfounded me. I had never truly thought I would meet someone in whom I felt so . . . confident. So promising, as if he really could be everything I had been seeking. A prince, and a rather remarkable one at that, seemingly worthy of the position as husband and king, had walked through my door as if he'd been hand delivered at just the right time.

I pictured him now with his gentle expression, a smile on his lips, and his eyes—his most striking feature—exuding perpetual warmth. My imagination then started to take over the picture, and I saw his steady hand pulling through his dark hair, his eyes crinkling at the corners as he laughed. My heart gave the smallest yet surprising flutter, just as it had in the woods.

Marriage? Indeed, marriage meant security, and security meant strength. But I felt a tugging in my chest, pulling me away from the image. I could certainly appreciate his charm, his bravery, his calming demeanor. But I felt that I was not ready to share my life so intimately with someone else quite yet.

As I sat in my chambers that night, so very mentally ready to retire from the day, Hazel bombarded me with questions concerning Prince Gryffin as she combed through my hair. The adrenaline from the morning had faded, leaving me utterly exhausted. I was, however, grateful that my intricate braid had been undone, leaving my hair to flow freely down my back in gentle waves with no headache. So, I entertained Hazel's curiosity tonight.

"Was he tall? He must have been tall."

"Fairly tall, yes—"

"Is he practiced with a sword? A bow and arrow? I wonder if he has seen battle."

"Well—"

"What color are his eyes?"

"This *striking* blue—"

"What does Tarasyn have available for trade? Silks maybe?" Hazel paused only to gasp excitedly. "Oh, I hope silks! I could make a gorgeous dress for you using new silks!"

Finally, I just laughed and held up my hand to stop Hazel's inquiries. "I've only just met him today, Hazel. I will most certainly tell you *everything* once I've learned more about the man."

Hazel's eyes became starry. "Oh, my Queen Rosemary, to think you may marry this one. It *is* rather hard to fathom in all honesty. I was beginning to think you would never choose a man." Tears began to sparkle in her eyes. "Soon, you will be a bride. A most beautiful bride, I assure you."

"Hazel," I sighed, "enough about a wedding. It's my *duty* to marry."

"If you have a more positive outlook, marriage may not seem so detrimental to you," she huffed. "Would it really be horrible to have this Prince Gryffin as your king?"

"King-consort," I corrected the older woman quietly. Still, the quick image of Prince Gryffin standing beside me made me smile, instantly answering Hazel's question. "I know you're right, Hazel," I said. "Marriage doesn't scare me, I suppose, but rather the man ruling beside me. How can I be certain that the man standing there is the one that will make me happy for the rest of my life?" More importantly, how could I be certain that the man standing there was the right man for my kingdom?

Hazel slowly set the comb down on my vanity. "I suppose no one *truly* knows that when they marry, my queen. It's more of a . . . daily choice."

My answering stare must have displayed my utter lack of understanding because Hazel finally sighed and shrugged her shoulders. "As in your mother's words, follow your own judgement, my sweet queen."

I didn't know if I could trust my judgement.

Just then, there was a brisk and heavy knock against my door. I could hear some sort of commotion just outside my door, like raised voices and swearing.

Then, Zeke swung open my door. He rushed into my chamber, followed by one of my night guards, Amos.

"You cannot enter, Sir Ezekiel! Her Majesty is retiring to bed!"

But Zeke completely ignored Amos's protests and walked quickly to my vanity, taking long strides, his expression intense. "You met with a Tarasynian prince today?" His question shot out with an accusing edge to it.

I looked up at Zeke, my eyes wide with shock. Where had *this* come from?

I slowly nodded to Amos. "He may have his say. Leave us."

My guard hesitated very briefly, before gruffly mumbling, "Yes, Your Majesty," and sauntering back to his post, closing the door behind him.

I then turned to Hazel. "As should you. I'll call for you when Zeke leaves." I gave what I hoped was a reassuring smile.

Hazel had a grave look on her face, an expression of warning for me, but she simply nodded and silently exited through the maids' door in the far corner of my chambers.

Once we were alone, I turned my eyes back to Zeke. "How did you know that he was from Tarasyn?"

"I am a scout, Rose," Zeke answered snidely. "I know what happens around here. And I'm sure everyone on the castle grounds has heard about 'your prospective husband, the charming Prince Gryffin' by now." Zeke spit the words out as if they were poison.

I crossed my arms in front of me defensively. "Why does it matter where he is from?"

He knelt in front of me and took my hands in his—normally a common gesture between us, but tonight, his grip felt urgent. "Rose, please, you cannot entertain the idea of marrying a Tarasynian prince. It could be your downfall."

At this, I froze. "What do you mean? What's wrong?"

Zeke groaned in frustration then and sat on the edge of my bed, pulling me down beside him. When he finally answered, his voice was quieter, but it still burned with the same intensity. "I can't answer that. But you must trust me—please, Rose, Tarasyn is *not* a kingdom with which we want to have ties."

I felt my eyebrows pinch together. "Why not? Prince Gryffin said that his kingdom is getting back onto its feet, after decades of distress. It is such a near kingdom, Zeke, and so *in need* of good relations! As are we. Why would we not want to create ties?"

"Rose, please." Zeke's chocolate brown eyes scorched insistently.

I heard Zeke's urgency, but I didn't understand where it was coming from. "Zeke, I can't make a decision like that if you aren't making any sense."

He groaned again, irritability quickening his breaths. "Rose, you know I can't tell you everything I discover from my assignments. You have to trust me."

"Assignments?" My eyes squinted critically. "You've been to Tarasyn?"

Zeke seemed to realize he had let information slip through the cracks. His expression hardened, eyes narrowed, as he released my hands. He stood and slowly walked to my window, peering out into the darkness of the courtyard below.

The silence drew on, the only sound was the crackling wood ablaze in the hearth.

Finally, once he gathered himself, he turned back to face me, a very small smile on his lips. "Ah, my Rose. Always clever. Nothing slips past you." He walked back to the edge of the bed, taking my hands again. He sighed and murmured carefully, "I can't say." Though his answer confirmed it for me.

Despite the serious tone of his words, I snorted. "Zeke, please, it is only me. You've told me about so many of your assignments in the past. Besides, I am the queen. You know Colonel Burnstead reports all of the scouts' assignments to me once complete."

"We haven't yet gathered enough information to make a firm report." He knelt in front of me again and leaned over our hands, folded together in my lap. I felt his lips just barely brush against them as he spoke, "Rose, please trust me. I care about you too much to see you as a puppet in Tarasyn's hand."

A puppet?

Some emotion began to rise to the surface inside me then. A puppet could be manipulated, controlled. I was certainly stronger than a *puppet!* "Excuse me?" I shook away his hands and stood from the bed, my voice rising with me. After a moment, I identified my emotion as . . . anger. True anger. "Do you doubt my judgement? Do you doubt my strength as Queen?"

Zeke looked up at me, at first shocked by my outburst. Then, his expression grew indignant as he too jumped to his feet. "Of course not, Rose! You know better than to think I would ever have that opinion about you."

I vehemently shook my head and turned away from him. "How do I know that . . ." Then I hesitated.

"How do you know what?"

I shouldn't say this. But I could not stop myself. I was too angry.

I turned to face him again, seething, my hair viciously whipping around me. "How do I know that you are not simply jealous of Prince Gryffin?"

Zeke's face blanked. He was speechless for a moment. Then, as if the sun's rays had been overcome by a thundercloud, his face darkened. I watched as his expression shifted through shock, confusion, and finally landed on ferocity. His fists clenched at his sides. "That crossed a line, Rose."

I knew it, but I could not rein in my words now. "What else am I supposed to think? You barrel into my chambers like a bull and claim that marrying Prince Gryffin would be detrimental to my kingdom, yet you cannot give a reason as to why! Do you remember that Prince Gryffin actually *saved* my life just hours ago?" I threw my hands into the air in exasperation. "For all I know, you could be using your job as a scout as an excuse! It is convenient, no? You have solid reasons as to why I should listen to you, but you can't tell any of them to me? Despite having done so in the past!" I folded my arms across my chest, unmovable in my resolve.

Zeke took one long step toward me and grabbed my shoulders. His face was just inches from mine, his brown eyes boring down into mine so intensely that I could see my angry reflection in his pupils. His face calmed as he looked at me, but a sense of desperation remained in his gaze. "Rose." He gave one short, breathy, incredulous laugh. "Rose, you cannot actually believe that."

I stared back into his eyes, and I felt my heart skip a beat. *Stop, Rose,* I chided myself. The Zeke-corner of my mind must stay nice and dark, unexplored. I hated that I was forever hurting my closest friend. But my judiciously established barrier must hold.

I articulated my next words carefully. "Zeke, I think you should leave."

He released my shoulders suddenly as if I had burned him.

Hard anger set his features into livid stone. "Indeed, Your Majesty. Who am I to worry about you?" Bitter sarcasm clipped his words. "Just a common scout amongst your ranks—nothing more."

He turned away from me and yanked open my chamber door, spitting upon the floor as he did so. "Enjoy your prince." Then, he walked through the oak door and slammed it shut behind him, his boots clicking sharply against the stone down the hall.

CHAPTER FOUR

I AWOKE THE next morning still completely exhausted.

Even with my near-death experience, my argument with Zeke had drained me more than anything else yesterday.

Yesterday. I laughed to myself incredulously. Yesterday had been one of the most eventful days of my life.

Before I'd even emerged from beneath my bedsheets, I decided to work within my chambers today. So many emotions conflicted with each other as I stumbled sleepily through the previous day in my mind, from overwhelming anxiety to bright fear to simple happiness, all through to ending my day with immense emotional pain.

But, to my surprise, I also felt a hint of excitement as I remembered that I could again see Prince Gryffin today.

I sat up, rubbing my eyes relentlessly, finally feeling an urge to get my day started. But then I caught a glimpse of myself in the ornate mirror across from my bed and cringed.

Meeting with Prince Gryffin perhaps had to wait until later in the day.

A wonderful, warm floral smell reached my nose, and I caught sight of Hazel standing near the window, draining rose and linden buds from steaming water.

The lines etched into my face immediately relaxed. Mmm . . . Tiliarose. My favorite.

Upon hearing me stir, Hazel looked up from the tiliarose.

"My queen," Hazel said with sympathy as she took in my tired eyes. "I see you did not sleep well. *And* you didn't send for me last night." She clucked her tongue disapprovingly as she walked slowly to my bedside, careful not to spill the brimming cup.

As she handed it to me, warmth from the ceramic cup swathed caressing wisps around my nose. "I'm sorry, Hazel. Zeke's visit ended poorly." An understatement. "And I was too worked up. I needed to be alone to calm down." I sighed as I took a sip of the comforting floral brew.

Hazel gasped, taken aback. "Ezekiel? Are we speaking of the same man? His visits have never caused a sleepless night for you!"

"I suppose there is a first for everything, Hazel." I glanced out my window at the spring sunshine. A new beginning. "Would you mind fetching him for me? I would like to . . . to apologize. For what I said to him."

"I'm sorry, my queen, but Ezekiel is no longer in the castle. He left on his horse early this morning on an assignment."

I looked down at my sheets bundled in my lap. "Ah" was all I quietly said. Zeke always told me when he was leaving. A first for everything. My apology would have to wait, then. I already missed him, and I was painfully aware that I had driven an enormous wedge between us.

I sighed and swung my feet over the side of the bed, resting them on the rug. I ran a hand through my long wavy hair, and my fingers caught knot after knot. "Hazel, would you mind finding Lord Brock? I'd like my meals and work brought to my rooms today, please." I looked at my reflection in the mirror again. "If I am to meet with Prince Gryffin, I need to look and feel rejuvenated."

Hazel grinned. "You care about your appearance for this one, my queen."

"And?" I tried to sound nonchalant, as if I weren't acting completely out of character.

"Nothing at all, Your Majesty," Hazel answered. Her voice carried a hint of smugness. "Shall we dress you in your red dress today?"

My first reaction was an obstinate *no*. But, as much as I hated the ostentatious red dress, Prince Gryffin may think otherwise. And I could not bring myself to run this prince off as readily as I had the others. "All right, Hazel, I'll suffer through the day wearing your beloved red dress."

"It is *your* beloved red dress, my queen!" Hazel sang over her shoulder, already rushing to my armoire.

Once I was trapped in the gown, I turned to look at my reflection in the large mirror. The fiery red velvet hugged my body before broadening gracefully around my hips, steadily spreading into a wide train on the floor, pooling around my feet. The dress's sleeves fit snugly to my arms and flowed open at my hands, allowing the long cuffs to drape elegantly down my sides.

Then I turned my attention to the neckline and winced. Yes—any man would most likely fall to his knees if he were to see me in this dress. However, I couldn't deny Hazel's talent. This dress fit exactly as it should, from the snug shoulders to the gem-studded bodice to the long train that followed me like a rippling scarlet river.

Hazel arranged my hair into an elaborate twist as I sat eating my breakfast near the window. Beneath me, in the courtyard, I spotted Isabele and Lisette walking alongside each other, embracing the morning sunshine streaming into the garden. For a moment, I felt a longing to be there in the courtyard with them, as we used to do before my coronation. But the weight of yesterday's events and my sleepless night quickly returned, and I sluggishly turned my gaze away from the window.

"Has my paperwork for the morning arrived yet, Hazel?"

"Yes, Your Majesty, the stack is anxiously awaiting your attention on your desk in your office."

I suppressed a heavy sigh. Though I longed to crawl right back underneath my warm blankets, the thought of my work as a distraction carried me to my desk.

After a morning of shuffling endless pages of parchment and advisors scurrying in and out of my office, it finally felt as if yesterday had been a distant nightmare. The dark circles under my eyes had finally lifted, and the angle of the sun streaming through my window told me that the time for lunch was drawing near.

As I just finished signing my name for what felt to be the hundredth time this morning, there was another knock on my chamber door, and one of my day guards walked into my office.

"Prince Gryffin of Tarasyn requests to see you, Your Majesty."

I felt my eyes brighten with my smile. "Yes, of course. Let him in, please."

The guard bowed and walked away, and a moment later, Prince Gryffin appeared in my office doorway. I stood to greet him.

His eyes widened at the sight of my dress, but he impressively kept his composure. He simply said, "Queen Rosemary, you look stunning," as he took my extended hand in his and lightly kissed it. Then, eyeing the stack of papers on my desk, he chuckled. "Your morning appears to have been rather eventful."

I widened my eyes theatrically and shrugged my shoulders as I returned to my chair. "Well, if by 'eventful' you mean reading through agreements and requests until I am cross-eyed, then yes. *Very* eventful." With two meetings yesterday, the paperwork had piled up. But before I could get overwhelmed by the work I had yet to tend to, I grinned at him. "And how has your morning been, Prince Gryffin? Are our arrangements for you to your liking?"

"Please, simply call me Gryffin, Your Majesty. And I can definitely say that Hillstone's guest chambers exceed expectations. The hot lavender bath was certainly more than I'd anticipated." His laugh bounced off the walls, and his charming little grin returned. "We still have some work to do at Snowmont," he admitted. "However, I was beginning to wonder if I'd see you today." He narrowed his eyes, his lips pursed.

Though I felt a smidge of guilt, I refused to shrink into my chair. Instead, I playfully challenged his words. "I'm sorry, Gryffin." It felt a little too nice to use his first name. "I meant to ask for you, but then I became completely ensnared in running a kingdom." I gestured to the stack. "So ensnared that there was just no escape."

"Perhaps I can provide an escape now?" Gryffin suggested. His grin was still respectful, but very confident.

His suggestion brought an unexpected heat to my cheeks, so I turned away quickly and looked out my window. "What do you have in mind?"

"Well, I know *I'm* rather hungry. And you?"

"Famished," I answered with a small smile. When I was certain my cheeks had returned to their normal color, I returned my attention to Gryffin's sapphire eyes. "How do you feel about a picnic? The weather is beautiful again today, and I'd like to stare at something other than these stone walls. And," my smile widened, "I know of the perfect picnic spot."

A frisky skepticism danced across Gryffin's face. "The *perfect* picnic spot? Well, now you have to share."

I stood from my chair, suddenly excited. I absolutely loved picnics, and, thankfully, it'd be another distraction. "Excellent! Come with me, down to the kitchens."

"We'll be packing our own lunch, then?" Gryffin asked, sounding a little surprised.

"If I let everyone do everything for me, I will surely become helpless." I walked to my armoire and threw it open. I gathered a knitted blanket that had been stored on the top shelf into my arms and examined it. "Yes, this will do," I muttered, mostly to myself. Then, I turned toward my chamber door and, without waiting for him, walked through it and into the hallway.

I could hear Gryffin chuckle from behind me as he hurried to catch up.

I led him through the corridors and down several sets of stairs until we reached the ground level. The warmth of the kitchens had already reached us, and when we came upon a set of thin wooden doors, I halted and turned to face Gryffin. I shot him a quick, coy grin before opening the doors.

As it was so close to lunch time, the kitchens were bustling with staff. At every turn of the head, workers were delivering and preparing ingredients, chopping vegetables, kneading bread. Still others were piling cooked food onto waiting plates, ready for deliverance throughout the castle. As each person slowly caught sight of us, they would bow or curtsy quickly before returning to their work.

One girl, about the age of nine and one of my favorite faces to see around Hillstone, hurried over to us with a beaming smile. "What may we do for you, Your Majesty? Have you changed your mind about having your meals brought to your room?"

I stooped down and smiled at the young girl. "I have, Lucinda. I will prepare a picnic for Prince Gryffin and myself. I think I can handle that." I winked at her. "However, could you please fetch me a basket?"

"Of course, Your Majesty!" Lucinda curtsied and bounced off, intent on her new mission.

Gryffin looked at me with an impressed expression. "Do you know the names of all of the people who work here?"

I smiled a bit proudly and placed the blanket on a nearby table. "I try my best to recognize my staff," I responded, turning to the stacks of fruits. Fresh produce was not Lecevonia's strong suit, but we managed to keep a nice supply for ourselves and for trade. I picked up four apples and examined them before laying them on the table next to the blanket. "But really, I know Lucinda because she and my sister Clara are close." I held a bunch of green grapes up by the stem and, deciding that they looked nice, placed it next to the apples. "How is the staff in Tarasyn?"

"My father was very particular about how things were run," Gryffin began slowly, picking up one of the apples and twirling it in his hand. "So there weren't many people to remember. Less staff meant less room for error to my father. That being said, my siblings and I were all close to each one of the staff members. They all watched us grow. With such few people and with no trade partners, there were a few shortcomings—no large dinners or fine linens like you have here, for example—but my father was never bothered as long as every task in the castle was done correctly and efficiently."

I had walked over to the rack of cheeses and had chosen a white block of gouda, cut in half by the staff for easy serving. I hadn't thought about that, what it must be like to have no trade partners. How had they sustained themselves all these years? "Were you close to a particular staff member when you were younger?" I had my Hazel; surely, he'd had someone too.

Gryffin's eyes lit up at the question, as if drawn to a memory. "I often found myself in the company of an older man named Stephen. He was like a father to me, when my own was not." The light slowly left his eyes as he trailed off, and his features darkened.

As I was pouring wine into a small bottle, I sensed by his silence that Gryffin's thoughts had taken a dark turn.

What had happened to Stephen?

I placed the bottle onto the table and rested my hand delicately on top of Gryffin's. I looked up at him and offered a gentle smile.

"Stephen reminds me of our Sterling," I said quietly. "He's been like a father—or grandfather, I suppose," I shrugged, "especially since our father passed."

Gryffin managed a smile, and my heart suddenly hurt for him. To have no father figure? How had he become the man he was today?

Just then, Lucinda came rushing over to us carrying a wicker basket, her small arm looped under the handle. I gave Gryffin's hand a very light squeeze before turning to face the young girl as she skidded to a halt in front of me, holding out the basket. "Your Majesty, will this do well enough?"

I laughed lightly and accepted the basket from her. "Yes, it is perfect! Thank you for finding such a lovely basket for us." I tapped her on the nose with one finger.

Lucinda, positively glowing with pride, curtsied and scampered off to continue her duties. I packed the basket silently, feeling the weight of Gryffin's eyes following me. After folding the blanket over the food, I turned to him. I felt as if my face was glowing with excitement. "Now, to the stable."

"To the stable?" Gryffin asked with an incredulous laugh. "How far away is this perfect picnic spot? And . . . will you be able to ride your horse in your dress?" He eyed the red velvet hugging my body.

"Trust me, it is well worth the ride. And never doubt a woman's ability to do anything she wants while still looking magnificent."

I led the way riding Midas, Gryffin and his horse following close behind. The spot I had in mind was down at the far end of the pastures, almost to the edge of the capitol city's boundary. The towering stone wall surrounding the city could be seen in the distance, but it soon disappeared as we descended into a valley between the hills.

The sun was now high in the sky with hardly any clouds to block its rays, but a gentle spring breeze kept the air feeling cool. We rode until my ears picked up on the babbling of running water, and I finally halted my horse and dismounted. I led Midas by the reins over a small crest in the landscape, which then gently sloped down toward the stream that ran through the outskirts of the city.

I untied the picnic basket from my saddle and released Midas's reins, of which he showed his great appreciation by a ferocious shake of his mane before trotting a short distance away and beginning to graze. Gryffin's horse shot past me to join Midas, and I heard Gryffin's footsteps crunching over to me through the greening grass.

I felt the pressure of his arm circling lightly around my waist, and the unexpected touch might have made me jump had I not been more surprised by the sudden delight that surged through me.

"You were right," he said, incredulousness painting his voice. "This is indeed a beautiful place."

I smiled. "As I said, it's well worth the ride." I gently twisted out of his arm and waltzed into the shade of a large willow situated right on the bank of the stream. "And here," I said, placing the picnic basket on the ground, "is the perfect picnic spot."

Gryffin nodded with a dazzling laugh. "It does seem quite perfect, Queen Rosemary."

I meticulously placed the food and wine on the cool grass and spread the blanket out over the ground. After I settled onto it, my legs to one side beneath me, I patted the spot beside me, inviting Gryffin to sit.

"You must tell me," Gryffin started as he picked up an apple, "did you picnic often when you were younger? You seem to know exactly what you're doing."

His correct deduction triggered a delicious warmth inside my chest, and I nodded enthusiastically. "My sisters and I have always loved to picnic. Our mother would often take us here for the day. It would give us all a chance to escape the walls of the castle for a while." I grew quiet as a memory of Mama, sitting in this same spot, flashed into my mind. She'd been pregnant with Clara at the time. Oh, Clara would have absolutely loved this. She'd be like Isabele had been, dancing in the grass and splashing through the stream to the opposite bank.

Coming back to the present, I turned my eyes to Gryffin. "Did your mother or father take you and your siblings out very much?"

"My mother actually did," he answered cheerfully. "She would take us horseback riding, and she would take my sister down to the gardens for her reading lessons almost every day if the weather allowed. Then,

Atroxis took her from us." His eyes darkened. "And my father did not care so much for outings as my mother did." Gryffin was silent for such a long time that I wondered where his thoughts were, so far away from this shaded blanket by the stream. I placed my hand atop his, and his eyes snapped back to me, regaining his light composure with a new light dancing across his face. "My mother taught me to ride, and she and my father gave Lucy to me for my ninth birthday." He gestured toward his white horse grazing near Midas.

"Lucy! Such a nice name—it suits her. So, I suppose it is *her* that I should be thanking for getting to me so quickly yesterday!" I nudged his arm teasingly.

His entire frame shook with a belly laugh. "Yes, she is undoubtedly the true hero! You know, her original name was Lucifer, until I found out that she was a filly," he rolled his eyes as he took a bite of the apple in his hand. Then, he focused his blue gaze on me. "How are you, after yesterday?" Concern coated his question.

"Shaken," I admitted, looking down with a grimace I could not control. "I just can't make sense of it. The kingdom adored my parents, and I've only reigned for one year thus far. I haven't had time to *drastically* change anything." Even in the years between my parents' death and my coronation had been relatively calm, as my council had kept things steady until I was old enough to rule. They hadn't had the authority to make major changes. Who was unhappy, now?

I shook my head in an attempt to clear it and placed my hand on top of Gryffin's again. "But I'm all right. Truly, I can't thank you enough."

Gryffin turned his hand upward to take gentle hold of my fingers. His hand was rough, surely from years of riding, but warm. "Have you told anyone?" he asked quietly.

His question made me hesitate, wondering how much I should

really tell him. "Just one person. One of my closest friends. He won't tell anyone."

Gryffin's eyes narrowed in worry. "Are you sure you don't want anyone else to know of the incident? You could very well be in danger, Queen Rosemary." His tone had become very serious. "Assassination is no game."

"No." I shut his suggestion down quickly. "The very last thing I want is to be surrounded by guards throughout the entire day. It would drive me mad." However, I did have to admit that his words raised my own concern. Indeed, assassination was no game. "If I have any suspicion of another attempt, I will consider increasing my personal security."

This conversation had begun to cloud my mind with anxiety, so I eyed Gryffin with a wide, mischievous smile. "But the archer seemed rather afraid of you! You had him babbling like a fool!"

My teasing seemed to work, for Gryffin's expression lightened as he laughed and gave my hand a gentle squeeze. "Then I may just have to become your personal guard," he suggested playfully, leaning back onto his elbow.

He was almost touching my leg, and my heartbeat picked up to a subtly faster rhythm at the proximity. "I wouldn't be too opposed to the idea," I said a little breathlessly.

My gaze locked onto his eyes, becoming mesmerized for a second. The blue was deeper than a sapphire, as I'd originally thought, more how I remembered the ocean at Lecevonia's western border. Flecks of silver reminded me of the shimmering waves, emphasized by the natural light emanating in his eyes.

What on Haggard's green earth was I feeling? Clear attraction, without a doubt, but possibly something a bit . . . more. More comfortable, more trusting. Simply *more*. I didn't understand it.

"Your eyes are a beautiful shade of green, Queen Rosemary."

For once, I did not mind the compliment. "My eyes are like my father's. Though I do hope my appearance is not what draws you to me." I squinted my eyes in lighthearted accusation.

But Gryffin looked genuinely offended. "Of course not, Your Majesty." He looked away for a quick, thoughtful second before meeting my eyes again. "Your *passion* is what keeps my attention," he clarified. "You are very passionate about your kingdom—about being a proper ruler yet staying true to your own wants and needs. You are passionate about your freedom."

With his words, I recognized the truth behind them. So caught in the current of reign, I'd sometimes been quick to overlook *why* I gave every moment of my days to Lecevonia. And at the center of my passion was the inherent fact that I'd been born designed to rule.

I hoped to live up to my design.

Gryffin then lifted my hand slowly and kissed it. "Though I cannot lie, either," he continued with wide eyes, "I *am* still a man, and I easily get distracted when I see you."

Though the corners of my lips wanted to pull upward into a smile, I rolled my eyes as I gathered hold of my wits once again. "Perhaps that distraction will play in my favor, one day." I reached for the block of gouda and tore off a corner. "Would you pour the wine, please?"

Gryffin, with another mouthful of his apple, nodded and filled each chalice before passing one to me. He took a sip from his own and was about to say something, then froze. He took another sip, paying attention to the taste this time, and finally nodded approvingly with widened eyes.

"This wine is delicious." He looked at me incredulously. "What is it?"

"Blackberry spice wine," I answered with a laugh. "Why are you so surprised?"

He smiled a bit ruefully. "I'm not used to visiting other kingdoms and tasting better wine than our own. I was convinced Tarasyn's wine was the best on the Peninsula."

"Well, Tarasyn cannot provide charming princes as well as the best wine in the five kingdoms, Prince Gryffin," I teased as I sipped from my own chalice.

Charming princes? Was I . . . flirting?

"Charming, you say?" Gryffin's smile widened. "Do you think I'm charming, Queen Rosemary?"

I shrugged lightheartedly. "I may." Then, as I reached across Gryffin for the bunch of grapes, I added, "and you may call me Rosemary." *Queen* was getting to be a bit too much.

Gryffin, his face now only inches from mine, took my chin in his free hand and gently turned my face to his. He looked at me with a small, mindful smirk. "Why do you tease me, Rosemary?"

Warmth immediately blossomed across my cheeks and I smoothly turned my face away, hoping he hadn't seen. Why did he have this unfathomable *effect* on me? I was not accustomed to feeling so nervous. I chose to focus instead on the grapes nestled in my hand.

Gryffin leaned back on his elbows once again. "You don't let many people into your personal life."

Well, that was quite an assumption. Yet, he was right again. How could I truly have a personal life when my kingdom was meant to *be* my life? "No, I don't. That isn't really a luxury I have."

He nodded quietly, but he didn't seem bothered by my answer. "Caution is good, especially as someone in your position. It's smart." He was silent for a moment, his gaze drifting across the stream and into the trees of the sloping hill. When he next reached for his chalice, he looked back at me with gentle eyes. "I hope that you can let me in one day."

At his words, under his gaze, my heart drummed a little harder. "You're certainly on the right path." I turned my attention away from him, to the less confusing sky through the weeping willow's branches, the sun now beginning its descent into the west.

I was not quite sure what to do with myself. I felt so comfortable with Gryffin, but a reluctance still tugged on me. With Zeke, I'd always had to actively push his emotions away from me, to spare both him and myself. I had never wanted a man's affection before, and now that I clearly had it from Gryffin, I didn't know what to make of it.

To distract myself, I whistled for Midas, who lifted his head from grazing and gazed lazily in my direction. I tossed an apple toward him, and Midas gladly accepted.

Gryffin stood with an apple in his hand and walked to his horse. But when he offered it to Lucy, she didn't even care enough to lift her head.

I shook my head in disbelief. "I've never seen a horse that does not like apples."

He sighed and offered the apple to Midas instead, who did not hesitate to receive a second treat. Sometimes I was certain my horse was actually a pig. Then Gryffin turned back to me. "May I have a few grapes?"

I looked at him quizzically. "Grapes?"

He laughed at my doubtfulness and walked back to me. "Lucy loves grapes."

I slowly plucked a few grapes off the main stem and handed them to Gryffin. "Truly? Grapes?" I asked again.

He held his hand once again out to Lucy, and this time, she willingly ate his offering. "Yes, grapes. Lucy is old and has seemed to grow tired of apples, the spoiled mare." He looked at his horse in mock chagrin.

"And, well, Tarasyn has many vineyards. I tried grapes one day, and she found a new love. I would be willing to wager that she would drink wine if I let her." Gryffin patted Lucy's neck before returning to my side.

"So, you must tell me, Rosemary," he suddenly said, tearing a small piece off the cheese block, "who *do* you let into your personal life? I may need to ask them to bestow their wisdom upon me." He winked at me and popped the bit of cheese into his mouth.

I threw the plucked-clean grape stem into the stream. "Well, all of my friends are people I've grown up with here in the castle. There is Celeste in the stable—her parents were stablehands when we were both young. Her father still works here, actually. There is my chief lady-in-waiting, Hazel, though she is more like my grandmother than an attendant," I chuckled. "Then there are my sisters, naturally. And there is Zeke."

Gryffin's attention piqued. "Zeke?"

"Yes. We grew up in the castle together. He's my closest friend." But I felt a pang in my chest as his too-long hair and angry, hurt eyes came to the forefront of my mind. "Don't mind him for now. And I've already mentioned Sterling," I said with a smile. "He's one of our gardeners, and he's the one I typically trust to give me the most reasonable advice." Though he did not have many words of wisdom regarding my marriage . . . "Sterling is especially close to my youngest sister, Clara. She is turning eight, actually!" I suddenly remembered.

Then I froze.

"Rosemary?" Gryffin pressed.

But I couldn't answer. The oncoming rush of guilt was too great.

Clara was turning eight *today*.

After no response, Gryffin touched my shoulder, his brow pinched in concern. "Rosemary, are you all right?"

I finally turned to him, in a sudden shame-ridden panic. "Clara's birthday party is *tonight.*" I gasped and looked to the sky again, at the sun hanging low just above the tree canopy across the stream. "Her party starts in just a couple of hours!"

But there was still time.

I burst into action, hurriedly placing what was left over from our picnic into the basket. "I can't believe I forgot. She had mentioned it to me just yesterday!"

I bent down to pick up the blanket, but Gryffin had already folded it and was holding it out to me.

"A lot happened yesterday," he calmly reminded me.

I took the blanket from him, hardly hearing his words, and stuffed it into the basket. "She had been so excited! Lucinda did not mention anything about it earlier, did she?" I was mumbling mostly to myself now as I stood with the haphazardly packed basket. "I need to change my dress—Gryffin, I can't be late!" More importantly, I couldn't let myself forego my sisterly duties again.

Before I could rush off to Midas, Gryffin took a small step forward and placed his hands gently on my shoulders. "Rosemary, calm down." He bent down to look at me, eye-level, and his blue eyes were already working some odd calming magic. "You will make it to Princess Clara's party." His voice was soft and reassuring, and a tiny smile played at his lips. "Our horses ride fast. You will be there in time."

I stared into his eyes for a moment longer, reveling in their steadiness. My mind, though still racing, slowed enough for me to think straighter than before. "You're right," I finally muttered. My voice strangely sounded gruffer than usual, and I had to clear my throat. "Yes, we will make it."

Still, I hurried to fasten the basket to Midas's saddle.

CHAPTER FIVE

I RODE STRAIGHT into the Royal Stable without slowing. My mind had once again begun to frenzy as we rode, and when I reached Midas's stall, I quickly jumped off his back, the skirts of my red dress flying behind me. I noticed briefly that the hem of the dress had gotten filthy during this swift ride back to the stable. Hazel would be furious.

"Celeste!" I called out. She'd whispered to me as we'd left that she would want each and every detail of our picnic, so I was sure that she would be close by.

True to form, Celeste slinked out from around the corner of the aisle, a full water bucket in her hand. But, even from her distance, she must have seen my not-so-subtle panic, for she hurriedly placed the bucket on the ground with a *thunk* and jogged to Midas's stall.

"You forgot about Clara's party, didn't you?" she immediately accused.

I groaned. "Not now, Celeste."

"Must have been a nice outing." She waggled her eyebrows

suggestively, a tiny smirk crossing her features.

I pursed my lips and refused to answer. "Celeste, I am so sorry to do this again, but could you tend to Midas? I need to get to my chambers before Hazel resorts to nervous shock."

"Of course, Rosie," Celeste answered, taking Midas's reins from me. "But that's two days in a row. Midas is going to start thinking that you don't love him anymore."

"I promise I won't make a habit of it." I untied the basket from my saddle. "Can you also be sure that this basket gets back to Lucinda in the kitchen?"

"I can manage that," Gryffin's deep voice murmured from behind me. He still held his horse's reins in his hand, but he took the basket from me with a roguish smile.

"I truly am sorry for such an abrupt ending to our picnic," I apologized breathlessly. "Had I remembered Clara's party, I would have planned our day a bit better."

"No need to apologize, Rosemary. I thoroughly enjoyed my time with you."

As he bent down to kiss my outstretched hand, Celeste eyed me with high eyebrows and a risqué smile. I had to look away from her—and from Gryffin—before my entire face could be painted scarlet.

When I was able to catch my breath again, I peered at him. "I will see you at the party, yes?"

"Am I invited?" His blue eyes looked a little surprised.

"Of course! The queen herself has just officially extended the invitation to you," I said. "And I know my sisters will want to meet you."

Gryffin smiled. "Then I will be there."

Not needing any more prompting, I turned and hurried out through the stable doors, ignoring Celeste's gloating stare.

I followed the stone path up to the castle and passed quickly through the old iron gate. I made my way through the courtyard, trying to avoid anyone setting up for the party, and entered the castle through a small wooden side door, a shortcut to my chambers that Zeke and I had found long ago.

After climbing the spiraling steps, I burst into my rooms to find an agitated Hazel pacing near my armoire, and my other handmaids standing quietly in the corner and out of her way.

"Oh, my queen, look at you!" Hazel's dismayed *tut-tut* sent a flood of guilt through me. She rushed across the room to me and held out the cuff of one of my sleeves. "Your dress is practically ruined! And your hair—!" At a newfound loss for words, her frown only deepened as she unfastened the laces of my dress.

"I know, Hazel, I'm sorry." I began unpinning my hair from the twist, releasing my brown curls one by one. "Work your magic!"

Hazel went to the armoire and started digging through my dresses. She brought a brown dress to me and sighed. "I have no time to convince you to wear any other color tonight, my queen. You'll have your way just this time."

With the dress on and hair brushed through, I looked at myself in the long mirror and smiled. On this rare occasion, I looked and *felt* like myself. I did not look like Queen Rosemary Avelia, Sovereign of Lecevonia—simply Rose, attending my little sister's eighth birthday party.

Hazel's finishing touch was a jeweled pin on each side of my hair, each holding back just a few strands from my face. Still, she seemed unsatisfied.

She disappeared into my office and reemerged with a small golden tiara, which had been a gift from Uncle Merek after my coronation. She worked it into my hair and secured it with the pins on either side of my head.

"There," she nodded, finally pleased. "Now, go!"

I gave her a quick hug around the shoulders. "Thank you, Hazel. I will see you at the party!" With that, I opened the doors of my chambers and swept out into the hallway.

At the main entrance leading out into the courtyard, I found Isabele and Lisette waiting near the massive oak doors. They both turned at the sound of my quick footsteps.

"Rose!" Though Isabele tried to keep her voice hushed, there was no mistaking the alarm in her tone. "Where have you *been*? Clara will be here any moment!"

But Lisette looked at me with a knowing smile. "I heard that you rode into the stable just an hour ago accompanied by Prince Gryffin."

Isabele's perpetually kind eyes widened in shock at the news. "Prince Gryffin?" She looked at me accusingly. "Rose! Why haven't you told me anything about this?"

"Lisette, would your source of information happen to be the stablehand with whom you were flirting yesterday?" I snickered as Lisette's cheeks turned a bright red.

I then braced myself and reluctantly turned to face Isabele's hurt expression. I took hold of her hand and squeezed it. "I'm sorry, Isa. So much has happened so quickly. I will tell you everything after Clara's party."

As if on cue, Lord Brock and Lord Clark rounded the corner of the hall, leading Clara and her chief lady-in-waiting toward the entrance. When she saw us standing near the doors, she pushed past my advisors and catapulted herself to us, giving out happy, eager hugs.

"Is everything ready?" she asked, her tiny voice chiming with excitement.

Lisette chuckled. "Of course, Clara—Sterling ensured that all is *perfect.* Everyone is awaiting your arrival."

Isabele took Clara's small hand and twirled her in a circle. "Your birthday dress is gorgeous! Katerina has done a *lovely* job." She smiled at Clara's lady-in-waiting, who nodded in thanks with a tiny grin.

Clara beamed and gathered her skirts in her hands, swinging from side to side. The light blue fabric swayed lightly as she moved, and embroidered little golden flowers shimmered in the light of the setting sun streaming through the high castle window. "Thank you, Isa! It is my new favorite dress."

Smiling widely at my youngest sister, I stooped down and held her small hands. "Happy birthday, Clara. Are you ready to greet your guests?"

She nodded excitedly, and, after inhaling the largest breath her little body could take, faced the oaken double doors.

Lord Clark stepped through one of the doors into the courtyard, and a moment later, I heard his voice just outside. "Good evening, everyone. On behalf of the royal family, I would like to thank you all for joining us for our Princess Clara's celebration of her eighth birthday. I now welcome, as she is so aptly called the Darling of Lecevonia, Princess Clara Avelia."

Clara straightened her shoulders as both doors were pulled open, exposing the four of us standing side by side. A crowd larger than I expected welcomed us with reverent bows and curtsies. Then, as they all straightened once more, the mass of people erupted into thunderous applause and loud shouts.

The entire kingdom loved Clara.

Sterling was the first to step forward. He bowed and held out his tanned arm to Clara with a smile, and Clara accepted it with a grin just as wide as his. The old gardener quietly wished her a happy birthday and led her through the crowd to mingle, Clara's light brown curls bouncing as they went. I smiled as they walked away, assured that Clara would be well looked after under Sterling's watch.

The large crowd had begun to disperse throughout the gardens, and light string music was now weaving through the forsythia trees. The castle doors closed behind us, and I turned to see Prince Gryffin securing one of the door handles.

I flashed him a flirtatious grin. "How were you recruited to become doorman?"

Gryffin scratched the back of his neck in mock confusion. "Well, I'd been making my way down to the party when a guard intercepted me and asked if I would open the door for you and your sisters. The right door, specifically," he said with a smirk, theatrically gesturing to the door he had just fastened shut. "Apparently, one of the guards had not shown up for duty, and they appeared to be in a pinch. Anyhow, I couldn't let the opportunity slip by." With a deep bow, he lifted my hand and kissed it softly. "Good evening, my Queen Rosemary."

A new alluring desire in his tone sent a wave of heat crawling up the back of my neck, and I impulsively turned away from him to hide my sudden nervousness. "Come, meet my sisters," I said, trying to distract him from my reaction. I was going to have to get a better grip on these new emotions.

I sidestepped over to Isabele and Lisette, who were both wearing mischievous grins and pretending not to have heard our brief exchange. I sighed and attempted to push away my nerves as I gestured to Gryffin.

"My dear sisters," I said, hearing an odd lilt in my voice, "I'd like you to meet Prince Gryffin Danicio of Tarasyn. Prince Gryffin, these are my sisters, Princess Isabele and Princess Lisette."

Gryffin bowed to my sisters and smiled. "It is a pleasure to meet you both, Your Graces."

Isabele and Lisette both curtsied in return.

"The same to you, Prince Gryffin," Isabele responded in her soft voice. Her brown eyes flitted between me and Gryffin. "My sister has not yet gotten a chance to tell us very much, but we look forward to learning more about you."

Gryffin grinned effortlessly. "I pray that she will tell you only positive things about me. I hope to make a nice impression."

Lisette snorted, breaking all formalities. "It will be a feat for Rose to say anything nice about a man seeking her hand in marriage."

I gasped indignantly, already feeling a rising blush. "All right, you three have visited enough. Go on, mingle with our people!"

I quickly hugged Lisette, who was laughing under her breath. As I moved in to embrace Isabele, her quiet voice whispered into my ear. "Take care of yourself, Rose. This one seems to be quite the charmer." She smiled at me one last time, but her eyes were full of wariness. After a moment, she turned away and followed Lisette through the crowd.

What had that meant?

But Gryffin's chuckle interrupted my confusion. "I think that went very well." He extended his arm out to me. "May I be your escort tonight?"

I threaded my arm through his with only a smile and began making my way toward the crowd. The gardeners had no doubt been working unceasingly for hours today, turning Hillstone's formal courtyard into a beautiful party setting. Countless candles flickered throughout the gardens, lighting the entire area with a nice ambient glow. Trails of intertwined flowers had been wrapped around the trellises and benches, and long, thin blue ribbons that matched Clara's dress came together in arching canopies above the crowd.

I recognized many castle workers in the crowd attending as guests, which did not surprise me in the slightest. Clara made friends with everyone so easily. Even Celeste had been able to come up from the stables for the party. I saw her hunting around the pastry table.

No sign of Zeke though, and I tried not to be too disappointed. He really had left, then.

Men and women bowed or curtsied as I walked through the crowd, and I always responded with a bowed head and polite smile. I also noticed that the crowd's eyes were not only focused on me, but on Gryffin as well.

"I'm sure everyone must be wondering, 'who is this handsome man that escorts the queen tonight?'" I murmured quietly, eyeing Gryffin through my periphery.

"A man, a prince, a doorman." Gryffin shrugged his shoulders.

I let out an exaggerated gasp. "Oh! A jack of all trades!"

He smiled and placed his free hand atop mine. "Truthfully, he is simply a man that is honored to be by your side tonight."

A charmer . . . Isabele's words echoed in my thoughts, but I still could not stop the swelling pleasure that made my heartbeat bound to a new rhythm.

As we walked, I noticed that the initial stares of passersby were only that; the crowd was not focused on me nor Gryffin but on Clara tonight. And for that, I was thankful. I walked farther away from the visitors and led Gryffin to a quieter section of the gardens. Only a few visitors and staff meandered in and out of the scene.

I had only just spotted Clara's curly head in the distance when Gryffin spoke again.

"You seem different from this afternoon, if you don't mind me saying so. Tonight, you seem . . . at ease."

I smiled softly. "You speak as if you already know who I really am, Gryffin."

"I'm speaking in true seriousness, and out of curiosity. What makes tonight different?"

I met his eyes with an analytical gaze of my own. Could I let this man in? Let him see a different side of me, a side that always seems to be at odds with the Queen of Lecevonia?

If I wanted a husband, I needed to. And this man struck me as worth the chance.

I looked out to my people again. "Did you see how the crowd was looking in directions other than mine? Do you see the plainness of my appearance?" I plucked a flower off a nearby bench and sat down, inviting Gryffin to join me. "This is closer to my true character than you have yet to see. I truly enjoyed this afternoon," I said, turning back to face him, "but tonight, as Clara is reveling in attention, I am reveling in peace."

Gryffin nodded, reflecting on my words. Through his eyes, I could see his mind working, making sense of a queen that would rather be overlooked. After a moment, he picked up a flower that had fallen onto the stone ground and took my flower out of my hands.

"As beautiful as you were this afternoon—please, never get rid of that red dress"—he interrupted himself with a husky chuckle—"I see an even more intriguing woman sitting here now." He handed our flowers to me, now tied together by the stems. He let his hand linger on mine, and I lifted my head to find his ocean-blue eyes boring into me.

This time, I could not convince myself to look away. Nor did I want to. Not as he brought his hand gently to my cheek, not as he began to lean in toward me.

Only when our lips met was I able to close my eyes. And I melted into him.

Melting. That is exactly what I felt. My barrier, my caution—softened by Gryffin's warm lips against mine, liquefied into a new kind of resolve. A resolve that allowed me to feel heat, excitement, sanctuary. I had never allowed myself to feel these new emotions with a man, having barred them away for Zeke's sake, until now.

Ah, Zeke . . . I refused to visit that corner of my mind right now. Instead, I reveled in Gryffin's soft touch, his hand against my cheek. I parted my lips as I breathed in Gryffin's sweet tenderness, and his warm caress enveloped me as his hand traveled to the base of my neck—

But the moment was ended by Clara's bloodcurdling scream.

CHAPTER SIX

I REELED BACKWARD and met Gryffin's wide eyes for only a fraction of a second.

Then, I leapt from the bench and sprinted back down the cobblestone pathway. The daze lingering from the kiss collided harshly with the surge of adrenaline that was working to clear my mind as I pushed through the panicked crowd, Clara's continued scream ringing in my ears.

It was a sound of unrelenting agony and complete terror.

As I finally made it to the center of the thickening mob, I found Clara on the ground, kneeling next to Sterling.

He'd collapsed onto the hard, unforgiving courtyard stone, and an arrow protruded from his back. Blood had begun to seep from the wound and pool into the spaces between the cobblestones, crimson rivulets traveling across the ground.

For one horrible second, my feet were rooted in their steps, my eyes glued to Sterling's outstretched hands, clutching at the air.

Then I rushed to my baby sister's side. I wrapped my arms tightly around her, but her screaming did not cease.

Sterling's eyes dashed around wildly, and as he gasped for a breath, unable to draw in vital air, more blood trickled from his mouth. His eyes stopped spinning for a moment and settled on my horror-stricken face, but as he tried to speak to me, his speech only came as a gurgle.

Clara's scream cut off with a pained, broken wail.

The events after were a daze.

I recalled Sterling's face, his unmoving stare as castle guards dragged Clara and me away from him, Clara fighting with all her little strength against the grip of the guards.

I recalled being lifted from the ground and ushered quickly through the heavy doors of the castle, the words of the guards at my side reaching through the sudden ring of my ears. "The arrow was too deep."

And I recalled Gryffin securing the doors behind us anxiously as I was rushed down the long halls of the castle to my chambers, where my windows and doors were immediately locked.

Only then, in the sanctuary of my rooms, did I begin to process what had happened.

Sterling had been killed. Murdered.

I sat at my parchment-strewn desk and covered my face with my hands, suddenly gasping through dry sobs.

Yet my brain still tried to make sense of it all.

Unlike yesterday, this arrow hadn't been meant for me; that much was certain. The attack had happened nowhere near where Gryffin and I had been.

But had it been meant for Sterling? Why would someone attack an old gardener?

An old gardener, true, but also so much more . . . Someone must have learned of Sterling's role in our lives, how close he'd been to Clara—and had killed him. At Clara's *birthday party*, no less!

Who could be so cold?

Perhaps since the attack against me yesterday had failed, they'd chosen to take a different route. A more sinister, hurtful route.

But *why?* To send a message? To prove that we were vulnerable?

I felt my mind beginning to spiral, and these threads of thought became so tangled that it seemed hopeless to unravel them on my own.

I sat at my desk for what felt like hours, and with my windows shuttered, it was impossible to tell how late it'd gotten. My gasping had finally stopped, for my lungs had grown too tired. But no tears came; my mind was still too distracted to process my grief any further.

A quick knock on my door interrupted my thoughts. One of my guards—I was too flustered to recognize him—appeared in the doorway just as I straightened my shoulders, taking on my role as Queen of Lecovonia once again. "Your Majesty, Prince Gryffin would like to speak with you."

Gryffin. "Of course, let him in."

Gryffin entered my chambers, remaining composed until the guard was out of sight. Then, he rushed into my office and knelt in front of me, taking both of my hands in his. He met my gaze with eyes full of such genuine concern that my tears almost made their way to the surface. He started to speak, but I stopped him with a shake of my head.

"Please, do not ask if I am all right. We both know the answer to that."

He nodded once, slowly. "Of course, Rosemary."

"My poor little Clara . . ." I released one of my hands from his, only to collapse the weight of my head into it. Here, in front of Gryffin, I felt that I could let my grief show. "Sterling was like her father. She did not know our own—she was too young when the sickness took them. And she did not have a chance to tell Sterling goodbye.”

“Death often comes too quickly, my queen. Goodbyes are not always possible.” Gryffin gently placed one hand beneath my chin and lifted my head, his eyes meeting mine again. Even now, how did his ocean-blue eyes have such a calming effect?

There was a curt knock on my door, causing me to break our eye contact. Without waiting for an answer, the same guard marched briskly into the room. Amos, I remembered. “Your Majesty.” There was an air of urgency as he approached, and he completely ignored the proximity between me and Prince Gryffin. He had a piece of folded paper in his hand. “This was tied to the arrow,” he said, offering the paper to me. But the paper was sprayed with dark red stains, and, knowing whose blood had splattered the paper, I could not bear to touch it.

“What is written on it?”

Amos unfolded the paper and held it out for me to read. The words written in a heavy, scrawling cursive sent chills racing through my body:

Soon, I will stop your heart.

Under the weight of this threat, the same vulnerability I’d felt with the archer in the woods promised to crumble my will. *Lecevonia is weak,* it assured me, *because you are weak.*

But the stubborn daggers surrounding my heart rose against the threat.

I pushed myself up abruptly from my chair and strode to the doors of my chambers, throwing them open with any strength I could muster. “Hear me now,” I addressed each of my guards outside. My voice sounded as merciless as I felt. “I command that security be doubled across the castle grounds, tripled around each member of the royal family. I do not want anyone arriving or leaving the castle grounds without strict clearance. One of you, report this to your colonel. I want this effective immediately."

As one of the guards sprinted off down the hall, I turned back to my office. Gryffin still stood there, and Zeke's warning from the night before— was it just the night before?— replayed in my mind. My resolve began to harden once again, barriers reinstated. "It is best if you return to your chambers."

He looked at me in confusion, his expression unsure. "Rosemary, you are in a fragile state—"

Fragile? No. "I am Queen, and you will do as I say while in my kingdom," I said firmly.

But still, my heart softened as I gazed at him. I hadn't forgotten how Gryffin had made me feel, the confidence he'd given me. I instead decided to take a different approach. Maybe not all barriers needed to return. "My family is under attack, Gryffin. This is a threat to my kingdom. A foreign guest such as yourself should not be involved in these matters. I'm sorry." I took a step closer to him. "Thank you for your concern, and thank you for understanding. Please, return to your chambers."

Gryffin sighed, his face now a hard mask. "As you wish, Your Majesty." He took a few strides toward my door, but he paused as he passed in front of me. Carefully, he took my hand in his and pressed it to his lips gently. Our kiss this evening returned to my mind, and I felt my cheeks warming as our eyes met now.

Then Gryffin quickly left my chambers, his boots echoing in the quiet hallway.

I closed my eyes and sighed deeply, and for a moment, I allowed myself to wonder what a normal nineteen-year-old in the countryside of my kingdom would have done after a kiss, on a normal evening. Perhaps I would have been able to go home to my family at the end of the night and dream of whichever boy had been brave enough to do it. Or perhaps the kiss would have gone a step further.

But I shook my head. *Thinking of kisses when the security of your kingdom has been breached. Keep your thoughts in line, Rose.*

I walked to my doors and addressed the guards one more time. "I would like the security increased around Prince Gryffin's chambers as well. I will speak with General Gambeson first thing tomorrow morning regarding our next course of action. Thank you all for your service."

As I closed my doors, Hazel rushed into my rooms through the maids' door. But before she could speak or fret, I held up my hand. "I must see Clara." I finally felt the sting of tears in my eyes, and my voice faltered as I spoke. "Will you please accompany me?"

As we approached Clara's rooms, I saw with satisfaction that my order had already been put into effect. Six guards stood outside Clara's doors.

They bowed in unison. "Your Majesty."

"I am here to see my sister."

"Of course," the lead guard answered solemnly as he unlocked the heavy wooden doors. I picked up on some emotion as the guard's voice faltered in its firmness, which I eventually placed as worry. With Clara's sweet demeanor, I had no doubt that everyone in Hillstone worried about her.

As we walked through, I addressed the guards in earnest. "Thank you all for the quick response. Your service to the kingdom and my family is of utmost importance and deeply appreciated."

My eyes darted across the room until they found Clara. She sat in her nightshift at her vanity at the far end of the room with Katerina slowly combing her light brown curls, still damp from her bath.

If Clara heard us enter, she did not show it.

Her three other handmaidens, Mary, Ruth, and Diane, seemed paralyzed as well, standing in a tremulous pack in the corner closest to the door, unsure of exactly how to handle themselves. Her once beautiful birthday party gown lay in a shimmering blue and bloody heap on the floor near the bathroom, and the sickly scent of rusted iron blanketed the room.

Without warning, a fierce anger began to boil through me. *Why hadn't they cleaned this up yet?*

I addressed Diane. "Take Clara's gown down to the laundry wing. And please, try to clean up this mess. It is no wonder that Clara is in this state with this smell still present."

The edge in my tone seemed to provide the force needed to set the chambermaids in motion. The trembling girls became a flurry of movement as Diane swept up the dress and disappeared through the maid's door, leaving Mary and Ruth to hastily scrub away the drying blood from Clara's floor.

I made my way to my sister, taking care to soften my eyes, my hands, my every movement. I knelt in front of her and gingerly took Clara's unfathomably cold little hands into my own. Her green eyes stared endlessly into the space above my head, unseeing, and her small body seemed frozen. Her face almost expressionless save for a soft frown, her shoulders sunken into the chair behind her. I heard Hazel whimper behind me as she also took in Clara's state.

With almost a whisper, I rubbed my thumb against my sister's frigid cheek. "Clara?"

No response. Not even a twitch in her hands.

"She's been like this since she's been brought back here, my queen," Katerina said, her old voice quiet but alarmed. "Through her bath, her dressing down . . . No movement, and no word."

My poor sister. Joyful, sweet, young Clara.

Before tonight, she had not known the cruelty of the world. Even when Mama and Papa passed, Clara had only been a few months old. Katerina has since been her mother, and Sterling had been her father. She spent her days in the gardens, the stable, the kitchens, parading around the grounds, doing whatever pleased her little heart. Her life had been blissfully spent inside the sanctity of the castle grounds.

And that sanctity had now been breached. Her father figure had been stolen from her in a matter of short moments in front of her eyes.

As I studied my sister's vacant face, the overwhelming urge to cry returned.

I wanted to cry for Sterling, for Clara, for my kingdom now at risk. But as I felt my tears threatening to cascade, I blinked them into nonexistence. I had to be strong for Clara, and if Clara saw her oldest sister's resolve splinter, she would surely crumble into unfixable pieces.

Instead, I leaned forward and pressed my forehead against Clara's clammy brow. With my hands resting on her cheeks, I closed my eyes as I tried to find soothing words. "My sweet sister, I know this is unbelievable, that it feels so impossible . . . And you will feel so many different emotions for a while. In your own time, you will allow yourself to feel them, to understand them. But please, come back to us," I begged. "We are all here for you."

I opened my eyes to find Clara's blank gaze on me.

"I killed him."

Clara's first words, so full of guilt, hung in the air heavily.

Then she began to wail.

I gathered Clara off her chair and into my arms, trying with every ounce of my strength to hold Clara's pieces together. Despite my own confused emotions, I made such an effort to keep my voice comforting. "No, Clara, you did not kill him. Of course you did not kill him."

Through the gasps of grief, Clara continued wailing, "I killed him! I killed Sterling!" She wriggled in my arms and peered up at me, her big eyes brimming with anguish. "We were dancing—and then we turned, and he saw—he pushed me, and the arrow—" This was as much as Clara could manage before collapsing against my chest.

The arrow had been meant for Clara.

Icy horror pooled in my mind, followed by shame and rationality. *Of course it was,* I chided myself. How could I have been so stupid? Why would someone want to kill one of our gardeners?

Knowing now that my sister was the intended target, I knew that even Sterling would not have wanted this to happen any other way. I still clung to Clara's trembling frame, feeling the tremors start in the lower back of my own body. "Shh. My sweet Clara, shh. It's okay. This is not your fault . . ."

I continued my cooing as Clara's wailing slowly decreased to whimpers, and eventually to silence. Clara had exhausted herself to sleep.

I gave my little sister one last kiss on the forehead before passing her to Katerina. Now that Clara could find a few moments of peace in sleep, my own exhaustion began creeping into my bones. The sky through the high windows must have been dark for a few hours. What time was it? "Please, Katerina, keep her comfortable as long as you can."

"Of course, my queen," the old woman responded as she took Clara to bed. I stood, joints creaking, and Hazel and I quietly took our leave.

I fervently wished that I could still be bundled up in Hazel's arms as Katerina did with Clara. I wished I could even lay my head on Hazel's shoulder. But with my guards surrounding us in the hall, I could not bear to show weakness. Instead, I simply took hold of Hazel's hand and let an unspoken, thankful love pass between us.

Without informing my guards, I took the turn down the hall leading to Isabele's chambers. My other sisters must have been roiling in the aftermath of the night's events too.

I found both Isabele and Lisette in Isabele's chambers, sitting on her bed. Isabele's grief was clear from her puffy eyes and reddened nose, and even Lisette, as stern-faced as she always tried to be, had glistening eyes.

They jumped up from the bed and rushed into my open arms. We embraced each other fiercely, holding on to one another as if any one of us could be taken away the next moment.

"Poor Sterling," Isabele managed to say through her tears. "He was so good to all of us, and he's just . . . gone."

"I wish Mama were here," Lisette said, her voice cracking.

"I know, as do I," I murmured, smoothing the back of Lisette's brown hair. I wanted Mama, more than anything, to embrace us all and assure us that we will be all right. And Papa, to tell me what to do next. For now, though, the only thing I felt I needed to do was hold my sisters closely to me. My own tears threatened to spill over, but still I refrained, letting Isabele's waterworks suffice for all three of us.

With a heavy sigh, I pulled back slightly and looked my sisters in the eyes. "I know things are frightening and confusing right now. But you two are old enough to understand what is happening." I hoped the gravity of our situation was evident as I emphasized each of my next words. "Our kingdom is under attack."

I relayed my experience in Clara's chambers, explaining how, not Sterling, but Clara was the arrow's intended destination. However, I did leave out the note tied to the arrow, which still made me shudder. They did not need to know that an additional threat had already been sent.

As I spoke, Isabele shrunk back from me, her eyes growing wide with terror and disbelief. Lisette, always striving for maturity, kept her gaze locked on the stone floor.

I closed my eyes as I finished speaking, no longer able to meet my sisters' stares. "That arrow could have been for any of us."

This realization struck them both into silence.

My eyes flashed open once more. "We all need to be extremely vigilant. I've ordered for an increase of guards posted around each of you at all times—I can't take any chances with your safety."

Then, an apologetic smile stretched across my lips. "And now I have to act as Queen. I order you two to stay within the castle walls until further notice." I held up my hand to silence Lisette's shriek of indignation. "I know. I'm not thrilled about it, either. But I need to do what Mama and Papa would have wanted us to do." I gave them both one last embrace before turning toward the door. "Try to get some sleep. And please, above anything, try to stay strong for Clara. Sterling would have wanted that, and she needs us now more than ever."

Both of my sisters nodded quietly. "And what about you?" Isabele asked.

"What?"

"Are you all right?" Her gentle voice cracked as she took my hand in hers.

No. The denial came quick, shot like an arrow through my

determination to stay together. But I *would* stay together. Lecevonia is only as strong as its leader. I felt so much gratitude for my sister, always so empathetic, as I squeezed her hand. "Don't spend any worry on me. I'll be fine."

When I exited into the hallway, I glanced through my periphery to Hazel. "I am *immensely* looking forward to returning to my rooms," I sighed as we fell into step.

"Of course, my queen," Hazel responded softly. The corners of her mouth turned up into a gentle, warming smile. "We will get a nice bath drawn up for you, and a pot of warm tiliarose—"

But she was interrupted by a young soldier, who'd hurriedly turned the corner and whipped his head around quickly. When he spotted us, he ran down the corridor and skidded to a halt before me.

"Your Majesty." His eyes flashed as they met mine. "We have the archer."

CHAPTER SEVEN

I FELT MY eyes immediately steel over. "Take me to him."

The hot bath and tiliarose would have to wait.

We flew through the halls of the castle, drifting around corners and running down the spiraling stone staircase. We descended further and further down, until we could go no lower.

The prison.

Hillstone's prison had been hewn out of the hillside, making it the foundation of our keep. Since it was technically underground, a perpetual humidity permeated through each of the cells, leaving droplets of dew on the walls and iron bars. I made it a point to not come down here too often; we rarely had prisoners, anyhow, aside from the occasional drunken troublemaker.

I lifted my skirts as I followed the soldier through the dank, stale air and across wet stone until we halted in front of a dark holding cell. Through the narrow spaces between the metal bars, I first glimpsed a ring of angry guards and Zeke's yellow hair.

Zeke?

What was he doing here?

Then, I realized Zeke was holding a man in a chokehold. The man was dressed in a Lecevonian soldier's uniform, the cobalt and carmine ridiculing me, and a dark hood lay on the ground at his feet. His hands and feet were bound behind him with rope, and his gray eyes dashed around madly at the sound of our approach. His hair was matted to his forehead with sweat, and a long, jagged wound that seemed to have only recently scabbed over stretched across the side of his neck. A heinous smile was plastered onto his face, but he stayed silent.

My gut wrenched as I immediately recognized him.

The archer from the woods.

My mind started reeling, but foremost I felt complete and utter disgust.

First for the archer, as his daring grin burned everlasting scars into my memory. Then for myself, as the unforgiving realization quickly dawned on me: had I told someone about the assassination attempt yesterday, as soon as it'd happened, perhaps they would have captured this man before he released his killing arrow tonight. Before he took Sterling's life.

Before he put my kingdom in jeopardy.

"Rose," Zeke growled, all formalities escaping him, "we found something for you. Wrapped it up and all."

My unforgiving glare bored into the man, for my decision had been made from the moment I met his hideously excited gray eyes. "Execute him. At once."

As I turned away, I heard the man's last burst of maniacal laughter pierce through the stone corridor before the sharp snap of his neck cut it off forevermore.

My face the following morning hid no ounce of my fatigue. The sun had not yet risen, and the three hours of deep, exhausted sleep had done nothing but refuel last night's emotions. Grief for Sterling's death. Relief that Clara had survived. Fear for myself and for my sisters. Lingering shock from sentencing a man to death.

And, above all, guilt for failing to report the archer's first attempt—no, not failing, I reminded myself remorsefully, but *choosing*— and thus setting this mess into motion.

As Hazel readied me for the day in a sensible dark green gown, I knew I must come forward about the archer this morning during my meeting with General Gambeson and my advisors. Shame flared in my chest, but I could only lay my head in my hands and groan while Hazel fixed my hair into a practical bun.

"My queen, I know how draining yesterday was for you," Hazel said softly. "If I could take even a portion of the weight off your shoulders, I would do so in a heartbeat." She stuck a final pin into my hair before gently squeezing my shoulders, a small sympathetic smile shining through the mirror.

But the last thing I felt that I deserved was sympathy.

Hazel went into my office and quickly returned with my golden crown in her hand. She gently placed it atop my head with a delicate sigh. "There. You are ready."

"I am not close to ready," I muttered, mostly to myself. My mind was frayed by fatigue and anxiety, and I was trying to rule my kingdom with a guilty heart.

I suddenly became angry with myself. *Stop it, Rose.*

I could not wallow in this shame. Lecevonia needed a strong-willed ruler now more than ever. I'd made my decisions, and there'd been consequences. What I needed to do now was protect my family and the people of my kingdom from the threats that lay ahead.

Though it took an exorbitant amount of effort, I held my chin high as I rose from my seat. The assassin's note lay unfolded on my desk, the crimson bloodstains now dried to burnt burgundy reminders of the night. Not allowing myself to dwell on it, I grabbed the haunting paper and strode through my doors.

To find both Zeke and Gryffin standing outside my rooms.

Well.

This was something I did not have the energy to unravel.

Zeke leaned against the opposing wall with his arms folded across his chest, though not as comfortably as he normally would when visiting me. Gryffin stood a bit more refined, his hands folded behind his back. Both men had dark circles under their eyes.

"Good morning," I said to them, a slightly surprised lilt in my voice.

They both bowed.

They greeted me simultaneously "Rose." "Rosemary." Each turned to look at the other for an incredulous second at the familiarity in the greeting—then with hardened eyes.

Oh, I *really* did not have the energy for this.

Zeke stepped forward. "I was coming by to see how you are doing," he said, his eyes finally leaving Gryffin to look at me. The lines of his expression, though stiffened by Gryffin's presence, were filled with worry.

"As was I," Gryffin said with a small smile that did not quite touch his eyes as he looked at me. The shadow of concern on his face was just as present now as it had been last night. Gryffin was accompanied by two guards, as I had ordered. I couldn't tell in his features what he thought about that.

My heart fluttered, but I was too tired to discern which man was the culprit. Other, deeper emotions stirred, but I would have to think about them later. I had a kingdom to save.

I gave each of them a tired smile. "Thank you both for your concern—I truly appreciate your thoughtfulness. However, I have a meeting to attend. I will have to speak with both of you later."

Almost with relief, I turned from them and continued down the hall, my guards in tow.

I was really touched by Gryffin's return, even after the manner in which I'd sent him away last night. However, given his gentlemanly reputation, I was not very surprised.

Our kiss returned to my mind—how warm his lips were on mine, how strong yet gentle his touch was as his hand rested on my cheek, an unfamiliar heat rising inside me. I had felt my barriers wavering earlier yesterday, during our picnic. I hadn't felt anything like it before. I'd wanted to let him into my innermost self, and the kiss had only begun to finish the job.

Until Clara's scream.

I wondered what he thought of all of this. How weak he must think Lecevonia was, with two nearly successful assassination attempts on the royal family in two days. Was he now regretting his choice to court me? Or was a weak kingdom better than no kingdom?

But I internally shook away my thoughts. Lecevonia was not weak.

Zeke's presence was more surprising. Hazel had just told me that Zeke had left on an assignment. What was he doing back so soon? How had *he* been the one to bring in the assassin?

If I were to be honest with myself, Zeke was the one I really wanted to talk to. How was he after last night? What a fool he must think I was now, for not mentioning the assassination attempt in the woods.

I worried at the inside of my lower lip with my teeth as I recalled the assassin's hasty execution. Carrying out such deeds was not Zeke's normal role. Did Zeke know of the archer's true intentions to kill Clara?

These circulating thoughts still tormented me as I approached the doors of the council room with my entourage of guards. My sergeant at arms opened the heavy doors, and I strode into the usually stale room, which was now alive with energy.

Each one of my advisors sat in his usual place: Lord Brock to my left, Lord Clark to my right, Lords Castor and Quince on either side of them. Sterling had been a castle employee almost as long as any of them had been serving the monarchy, and his death had visibly taken its toll on them. Lord Quince was never one to bury his emotions, and he unrelentingly exhibited sorrow in the slump of his shoulders, the swollen circles under his dark eyes. Even Lord Castor, usually hotheaded and stoic to no end, could not conceal the grief-stricken vacancy in his eyes.

My chair remained unoccupied at the head of the large table, and across from me at the other end sat General Gambeson, flanked by Colonel Holland, commander of Lecevonia's cavalry, and Colonel Burnstead, leader of the Royal Army's foot soldiers and scouts. Zeke's commanding officer.

The strong sensation of urgency hung in the air between the quiet chatter of conversation, and the company stood abruptly as I entered the room.

"Good morning, gentlemen," I greeted them. "Before we get to our pressing business, let us first pause for a moment to recognize the absence of one of our own, Sterling Carfale. He served the royal family for many years, and his sacrifice does not go unnoticed."

A respectful length of silence fell over the large room, weighing heavily in the air as grief still stained the faces of my advisors.

I settled into my seat, and as soon as the grating of the wood chairs against the stone floors ceased, I slapped the folded paper in my hand onto the table. "This message was attached to the arrow that killed Sterling, delivered to me last night by one of my guards. He must have noticed it as they removed Sterling's body."

I passed the horror-stained paper to Lord Brock, and the threat on my life continued its journey from hand to hand until it reached General Gambeson. Despite the distance, the elegant cursive letters still mocked me.

General Gambeson's gruff voice was the first to burst into speech. "Your Majesty," he began, "increased security has successfully been implemented as you ordered, doubled surrounding the castle and tripled around each member of the royal family. I assigned lieutenants to begin organizing the guard rotations as we speak." He placed the message down on the table, and I foolishly wished he would have hidden the writing from view, tucked it away out of existence.

"Thank you very much for your quick work, General. As you all can see," I continued, addressing the table, "last night was only the beginning of this threat against our kingdom. I visited Princess Clara last night. She described the events as best as she could remember them"—Clara's small, grieving face resurfaced in my memory—"and informed me that Mister Carfale shielded her from the arrow." I met the eyes of those around the table. "This was an assassination attempt on Princess Clara. This could have happened to any one of the princesses, and I am intended to be the next target."

I then looked down to the mahogany table, gathering my courage, before raising my eyes to those around me once again. My heart loudly thudded deep in my chest. "I have a confession to make. This was not the first incident." I had to pause, then, and take a deep, quaking inhale. "Two days ago, I was attacked while riding my horse down the southeastern riding trail. The same archer was the culprit of last night's crime. Prince Gryffin of Tarasyn caught the archer, but the man then escaped."

General Gambeson made quick eye contact with the two colonels then turned his gaze back to me. "We are aware, Your Majesty."

Surprise touched my eyes.

Colonel Burnstead gave a stiff nod. "Sir Ezekiel informed us. He and a few other scouts were assigned to track and capture the assassin the following morning. Unfortunately, our scouts did not find any sign of the assassin until late yesterday afternoon."

Well, naturally Zeke told his commanding officers.

Once again, naivety reigned. Why would he keep an assassination attempt against the queen quiet? Of course, he wouldn't. And *couldn't*, really. I hadn't given him a direct order, and his sole job was, at its core, to protect the kingdom.

"I assure you, Your Majesty, the Royal Army is prepared to protect the Crown." General Gambeson bowed his head. "Colonel Holland and Colonel Burnstead have their men standing ready for further instruction. Our cavalry men and horses are trained and ready, and our foot soldiers stand at nine thousand strong. And of course, once word spreads that the Darling of Lecevonia was the target of an assassination, we expect enlistment to increase."

I thought of these numbers for a moment. From my frequent visits to the stable, I knew that the Royal Cavalry stood at two hundred and fifty soldiers, all very well trained. The cavalry horses received the best treatment in the Royal Stable, and it seemed the soldiers trained constantly in the surrounding pastures.

Nine thousand footmen may have been on the lower side. Atroxis had claimed the lives of many in the kingdom, and young men were no exception, causing a drastic decrease in numbers of the Royal

Army. Still, I was encouraged. A portion of them could be sent to the kingdom's borders for patrol while a good many could remain at the castle to be trained for combat. If these assassination attempts called for an invasion . . .

I then turned to Colonel Burnstead. "Have you and your men gathered any information regarding from where the assassin may have been sent?"

The colonel hesitated for a brief moment, flipping through papers that lay in front of him but not truly referring to them. Assignment reports, no doubt, already memorized. He answered with dissatisfaction weighing his voice. "We do not have solid evidence of such information, Your Majesty. Only leads."

"Where are you suspecting?" I pressed.

Colonel Burnstead's steeled eyes rose to meet mine. "We have reason to believe that King Roderich Danicio of Tarasyn has ill will against Lecevonia."

What?

"Tarasyn?" My voice betrayed my disbelief. "What made you come to this conclusion?"

"Through previous assignments to the kingdom, we have collected word of the king's desire to expand the borders of his kingdom. And with Lecevonia as his neighbor, well, we have reason to believe that we may be his target." Now Colonel Burnstead actually referred to his papers. "King Roderich has been building his armies over the past five years since his coronation, eleven thousand men strong. Little to no cavalry, however."

Lord Clark broke in. "As you are aware, Your Majesty, he is a young ruler such as yourself. However, while your mother and father passed on a strong kingdom to you, King Roderich's father and grandfather left a crumbling civilization in their wake. After a civil war of seventy-odd years, I'm sure you can only imagine the pressure King Roderich feels to strengthen his kingdom."

"And pressure, Queen Rosemary, can be a dangerous thing when forced upon the wrong person," General Gambeson added gravely as he folded his hands in front of him.

I tried to absorb this new information. "Why wouldn't King Roderich first try to reach an agreement with me? Why would he send an assassin?"

"We were hoping to gather a bit of information from the assassin himself," Colonel Burnstead's accusing smirk, though quick, did not go unnoticed. "However, after his quick execution last night, that is no longer possible."

I wanted to throw my hands up into the air. Well, I wasn't doing anything right, it seemed!

"However," the colonel continued cautiously, "you are not the only one with a note, Your Majesty." He looked at General Gambeson, who nodded his head once.

"Go on, tell her."

Colonel Burnstead rifled through the papers in front of him and, so slowly, slid out a smashed scroll of parchment. "This was found in the assassin's cloak."

The scroll was passed along the table to me, carrying with it the smell of horsehair, dirt, and leather. With a deep breath, I unwound the parchment and peered down at the writing. It eerily resembled the swooping script scrawled onto my note, but these letters made no sense, seeming to have been thoughtlessly strewn together into unrecognizable words.

A cipher.

"My men have not figured it out, yet," admitted Colonel Burnstead, his voice hardened by disappointment. "But we will continue to work on it, day and night."

"Is this perhaps the Rebels of the Red Sun?" I asked. "This coding seems to be something they would do."

General Gambeson shook his head. "This is more advanced than anything the Rebels of the Red Sun have shown to be capable of."

"I agree," said Colonel Burnstead. "If decoding this message reveals anything to do with Tarasyn, I would not be shocked. What's more, perhaps King Roderich *was* trying to make an agreement." He looked around the table pointedly. "What of Prince Gryffin Danicio?"

This took not only me, but my entire advising council by surprise.

This was a thought that had obviously not entered any of their minds. Clearly, my advisors had not known of Tarasyn's possible ill wishes when they arranged for Prince Gryffin to meet with me.

Colonel Burnstead looked at them incredulously. "Has it truly never occurred to you that His Grace could be here on his brother's behalf?"

His words tried to plant a seed of doubt, but that little seedling didn't take root. Rather, it was quickly overtaken by a strong wall of rejection as Gryffin's kind, concerned eyes from this morning flooded my memory as the ocean floods the shore. No—Colonel Burnstead's thought wasn't possible. Gryffin was not capable of faking that much compassion. I shook my head, unable to think clearly anymore, and looked away from my council, down to the table once again. "I will speak with Prince Gryffin myself." Once I discovered what his true intentions were, I would make my decision from there.

Steeling myself, I forced my gaze upward to Lord Brock. "In the meantime, what do you suggest that we do?"

Lord Brock glanced around the table at my other advisors before answering. "We suggest stationing men along the Lecevonian-Tarasynian border. We also suggest closing the castle walls to outsiders. Which will, of course, put an end to meeting with potential suitors for now.”

The last comment almost made me laugh. They could not actually be concerned about this now. Instead, I let only one chuckle escape my tight lips. “Surely. There are clearly more pressing issues than finding a husband right now.”

My intense gaze passed between General Gambeson, Colonel Holland, and Colonel Burnstead. “I will abide by my advisors. Send five thousand men to our northern border immediately, along with several scouts. Have our scouts gather as much information of Tarasyn’s intentions as quickly and as safely as possible,” I rolled up the beaten parchment and passed it back to the colonel, “including anything about this message. The remaining four thousand men will guard the castle grounds and continue to train new recruits. Perhaps one hundred or so of the most skilled can be promoted to our cavalry.”

My stare trailed out the window, where the rising sun was now sending strong rays across the room. “The capitol’s gates shall be locked to any foreigner. Lecevonian citizens may still come and go, but reduce entry only to essential business.” I returned my eyes to my council. “The increase in guards will remain in effect until we have a clear understanding of King Roderich’s plans.”

“Yes, Your Majesty.” All three bowed their heads.

Lord Clark spoke hesitantly. “What of Prince Gryffin, Queen?”

Lord Castor scoffed. “Surely we must send him back to his kingdom. We cannot have a Tarasynian inside the castle walls.”

“I disagree,” interjected Lord Quince. “If we send him home, he may have information he can relay to his brother. We cannot risk—”

“He most likely already has a way of communicating to those in his home kingdom,” Lord Castor pointed out gruffly. “We cannot risk him gathering even more information than he already has—”

"He cannot leave. There may be no telling what he's found out—"

"Enough," my sharp voice interrupted the two men. "Thank you both for your opinions." I'd meant my thanks to be genuine, but I felt that the edge still present in my tone had come off wrong. Though my mind was once again reeling, I attempted to stay level. "Prince Gryffin will remain here in the castle, and he will continue to be heavily guarded." He could be innocent in all of this. I would keep holding onto that hope. "As I said, I will speak with him. No action will be taken against him until I say otherwise."

I looked to Lord Brock and Lord Clark, and both gave me the subtlest nods of approval.

"And a last order of business," I continued, addressing my advisors. I softened my tone. "I'd like to arrange a memorial service for Mister Carfale. I believe my family as well as his will benefit from it. In three days' time as is custom, and it may be held in our courtyard. Lord Quince, may I put you in charge of such arrangements?"

"Of course, Your Majesty," my advisor answered solemnly. I knew Lord Quince would be the best for the job; when emotion was wanted, Lord Quince never failed to deliver.

Drawing the meeting to a close, I pushed back my chair and stood, and the others around the table followed suit.

"Thank you all for your insights and your service to the kingdom. I will surely see all of you again very soon." I gave them a small smile. "Please, stay safe."

I exited the council room and let the heavy wooden door close with a definitive thud behind me.

CHAPTER EIGHT

AS MY GUARDS flanked me, I ran through once more the next courses of action laid out for my kingdom. Soldiers at the borders, good. Soldiers at the castle, even better. Scouts sent into Tarasyn, a necessity. I would need to speak to Zeke soon as I assumed he would be one of the scouts assigned to further investigate our shady neighbor.

The image of Zeke and Gryffin both standing outside my door this morning returned to my mind, and my heart fluttered.

My mind drifted into comparisons.

In the presence of Prince Gryffin, I melted. No other man had made me feel so empowered, so appreciated, as he had in the few days he has been here. The way he gazed at me, his blue eyes so relaxed and genuine . . . I felt as if I could let myself unfold with Prince Gryffin, and if we explored this clear attraction stemming between us, perhaps I truly could be comfortable with him.

But then again, with Zeke, I was always comfortable. I felt the "Zeke corner" of my mind slowly nudging against its careful barrier, despite my better judgement. I knew that I truly wanted to speak to Zeke, and I ached to catch him before he left again.

However, my conversation with Prince Gryffin could not wait. His intent while in the capitol and at Hillstone was really of utmost importance. Besides, I figured Zeke would find me before he was supposed to leave again.

I turned to my guards. "Please, escort me to Prince Gryffin's chambers." Then I paused and gave each of the men a warm smile. "Also, I'd like to start learning your names. It seems we all will be spending a lot of time together."

I knew Amos, one of my regular night guards, and I recalled Thomas from the woods on that day that seemed so long ago now— the ex-cavalryman that had been able to more or less keep up with Midas. As we walked down the long corridor to the guest wing, I gathered that the other four soldiers on this shift were Hugh, Robert, Roger, and Geoffrey.

Robert, Roger . . . Robert, Roger . . . I repeated these two while studying their features, knowing if any names were to give me trouble, it'd be these two. Despite their similar names, however, they looked about as similar as a horse was to an oak tree. Robert was more of the horse, lean but muscular and possessing rather small ears. Roger was, well, an oak tree. Towering and broad-chested, with thick limbs and large feet. His dark armor only added to the effect. He dwarfed the nearby men, and I decided I felt very safe under his watch.

I learned that Hugh had five children—one son and four daughters—and another arriving soon, and that he hoped the child would be a boy.

"A boy would keep my oldest company, see?" he'd stated very pragmatically. The thought of five children alone made my head whirl. I knew that I wanted to be a mother one day, but certainly not before a few years from now. Still, his family life intrigued me. What must it be like to have *six* children, and a loving spouse awaiting your return home?

Geoffrey, on the other hand, was proudly single and seemed to be thriving. He reminded me of Zeke in that aspect. He has been with the Royal Army for almost three years, making him the newest soldier in this rotation.

Amos has been serving in the Royal Army for seventeen years, alongside Thomas, who had fourteen years in. At the time they'd met, Amos had just been promoted to Second Class and had been set to oversee the training of a batch of new recruits, Thomas being among them. During archery trials, Thomas had let loose an arrow that was so off-target that Amos had required him to wear *blocks of cheese* on his temples during training, held steadfast with rope, to block Thomas's peripheral vision. After several days of relenting to the embarrassment, Thomas had had enough. As revenge, Thomas had melted the cheese blocks over a fire after his training and poured the molten goop into Amos's boots while Amos was bathing.

"I had thought certain death would be waiting for me the next day," Thomas admitted with a chuckle. "Instead, though, Amos had only given me a nod of grudging approval from across the archery field. We have been good friends ever since."

"Though the stench of pungent cheese had followed me for weeks afterwards," Amos interjected indignantly.

Their story had us all cackling as we approached the third set of guest chambers. Gryffin's two guards stood on either side of the oaken door, and they bowed their heads before returning to their attentive stance.

I inhaled deeply, and all humor suddenly evaporated, replaced with a new apprehension as Hugh's knock reverberated through the hall.

The heavy door opened quickly, and Gryffin's comforting smile greeted me. "Queen Rosemary," he breathed, his low voice exuding relief as he bowed deeply.

I couldn't help but smile in return. My mission was to see if Gryffin could be trusted, and I already felt as if I were getting my answer. "How does breakfast sound to you?"

"Quite remarkable, actually." He stepped out into the hall and, after closing the door behind him, offered his arm to me. "Shall we?"

My hand found his outstretched arm so naturally, as if he'd been escorting me all my life. Gryffin's guards fell into step behind mine as we strode down the corridor toward the Great Hall.

"I apologize for having to leave so abruptly this morning," I began, though I wasn't really feeling very remorseful. I had *not* been ready for his and Zeke's bombardment this morning. "As you can imagine, my advisors and I had a good bit to discuss after . . . after last night." Again, a sudden wave of grief assailed me, and tears pricked the back of my eyes. But I would not let them spill over—not in the middle of a bustling corridor.

"It's quite all right, my queen." Gryffin reached with his free hand and gave mine a reassuring squeeze. He peered down at me out of the corner of his eye. "Would you like to talk about any of it?"

I quickly conjured up a nonchalant smile. "Oh, no, this is not something you should be worried about. You are our guest, after all." It was not as if I could share details anyhow.

It appeared that we had arrived at the Great Hall toward the end of the morning rush. Nearly all the small wooden everyday dining tables had been cleared, and hardly anyone aside from kitchen workers were milling through the grand room. However, I did briefly catch the eye of Isabele, who was seated at a small rectangular table set in the far-right corner. Seated across from her was a boy whom I did not recognize, but from the way their heads leaned in close together over the table, I had a feeling that this was far from their first meeting.

So Zeke had been right! I could see Isabele's blush from where I stood.

A soft sigh escaped my lips as we settled at a table near the front of the Hall, near the ornate mahogany table perpetually set for the royal family. Our guards loosely arranged themselves at surrounding tables, not overcrowding but still ensuring a close watch.

I wasn't yet sure how I would determine Gryffin's innocence. I supposed I'd just see where our conversation led. But for some inexplicable reason, sitting here now across from Gryffin, even after learning of Tarasyn's possible involvement, I felt an almost overwhelming sense of trust. Perhaps it was simply because he'd been there in the woods? That he'd saved my life? That was a fact that couldn't be overlooked.

I glanced across the table, and Gryffin was looking at me expectantly. I realized he had asked me a question which I had completely missed.

"Hmm? I'm sorry. My mind wandered." I gave a small apologetic smile.

Gryffin only chuckled. "It's all right, Rosemary. I can only imagine in how many different places your mind must be this morning." His ocean eyes grew soft, and he reached across the table to lightly grasp my hand resting on the table's edge. "How are you?"

I turned my gaze down to our hands. "Tired," I admitted. "And still absorbing. I cannot wrap my mind around the fact that I will no longer walk through the gardens and run into Sterling pruning the cedars or watering the peony bushes . . . Peonies take a while to bloom after planting, you know," I pointed out, smiling through my resurfacing grief. "I learned that small fact from Sterling. He'd say,

'Many gardeners often give up on peonies, but given time and a little coaxing, peonies will bloom into the largest flowers you will ever lay eyes on.' One of his favorite teachings." This time, when the prick of tears came again, I felt two mutineers escape and roll down the slope of my cheek. I tried to discreetly use my napkin to dab the droplets away, pretending to wipe the corners of my mouth.

Gryffin gingerly lifted my chin, and the expression I encountered on his face was so sweet, so caring, that my breathing hitched a little. His eyes emitted sympathy, and a little furrow creased between his eyebrows as his lips pressed together.

"Loss is fickle like that. You suddenly remember the small details." He gently ran the back of his finger along my jaw. "I'm so sorry that you and your family must go through this grief, now of all times."

Though battling my own sorrow, I gathered the strength to give a real smile. "Thank you, Gryffin."

The mood surrounding our quiet table shifted as castle workers began setting plates of food down in front of us. When I caught sight of the jam-slathered bread and roasted pork, I felt an emptiness in my stomach for the first time this morning, and my mood immediately lightened as the plates hit the table.

"So," I began as I casually sliced my knife through the warm ham, "while I've been narrowly avoiding assassination, what have you been doing in your spare time?"

"Well, aside from saving your skin?" Gryffin retorted with a playful grin. "I've been spending a lot of time in Hillstone's library." He gave a high-pitched, impressed whistle. "That's what I call a nice collection. How on earth have you gathered so many books?" he asked, placing a pork slice on his plate.

My answering smile was a bit smug. "One of two printing presses in our kingdom is here at Hillstone. Our press operator lives here with her family. Naturally, the castle gets the first edition of any work she gets her hands on.”

“And the map of the Magian Peninsula hung in your library’s archway is utterly remarkable!” Gryffin’s eyes widened in awe. “It is massive and so detailed! How often is it updated?”

“With any major change on the Peninsula, I suppose . . .” I trailed off as I slowly chewed the ham. In my nineteen years, I had not noticed any changes to the hand-drawn map. Granted, I really only paid attention to the smaller version of the map in my office. “Have you found any books sparking your interest?”

“Well, I’ve mostly been focusing on Lecevonia’s history.”

My hand, which had been in despicably plain sight reaching for a hard-boiled egg, flinched against my control. I knew that a suitor interested in my kingdom’s history should be pleasing to me. It would show that he actually had some regard for the welfare of Lecevonia, not just a title. However, with Tarasyn as a possible imposing force, I was not quite sure how much I wanted Gryffin to delve into *any* information regarding Lecevonia.

I tried to recover, again reaching for the boiled egg and returning it to my plate with a smooth expression. “Oh?” I responded, feigning indifference. “Anything to your interest?”

Gryffin, though, was too sharp, and my reaction hadn’t gone unnoticed. He again reached for my hand, slowly weaving through the plates and drinkware. “Is there a problem?”

“Of course not.” My attempt at a recovering laugh was a tad too loud.

His brow knitted together, and the sting of suspicion began to prick his eyes.

Rosemary, get a hold of yourself. I decided to try a different tactic, and, without breaking eye contact, I gave him a sheepish smile. “I’m sorry, Gryffin. I know that I am not necessarily myself right now." I turned my hand over, palm facing upward, and squeezed his fingers. "I admit that I am a bit . . . jittery, after last night. And I . . . I feel that I can let my true emotions show a bit more than normal when I am with you."

I lifted my eyes to gaze into the oceans of his, and I saw his brow beginning to soften, his eyes becoming clearer once more. So, as an extra touch, I lowered my voice to an inviting tone. "Really, I'd like to know what you've found interesting about my kingdom."

Finally, his gentle fingers wrapped around my hand in return as he smiled. Then, the sunlight through the window glinted off his blue eyes as they narrowed lightheartedly. "Have you read much about the magic of the Magian Peninsula?"

Magic. I rolled my eyes. *That* was what he'd been studying? "You sound like Zeke, and I will tell you just as I told him—magic has not existed in the Five Kingdoms in a very long time."

"Ah, but it did exist, correct?"

I felt the corners of my eyes taper. "Maybe. What are you getting at, Gryffin?"

Gryffin hesitated. He withdrew his hand and picked up an apple from the tray of fruits. "Well, simply that its existence should not be ignored. As I'm sure you know, the magic had had a very strong influence on the formation of the Five Kingdoms." He took a bite into his apple and looked at me with an odd expression. "You really don't give any credence to the Peninsula's magic?"

I shrugged my shoulders. Why would I care about something so irrelevant now?

Gryffin shook his head with wide, incredulous eyes. "All right," he said, holding up his hands in surrender. "My little discovery wouldn't mean much to you, then."

"Well, that's not fair! Go on, what do you think you found?"

Gryffin pursed his lips, and I tried to look as serious as I could. Finally, he relaxed his mouth into a smile. "Do you recall the legend of Haggard and the Five Talented?"

"Of course." I scoffed. "It's an old bedtime story." I adopted a deep, mystical voice, imitating my father. "'Haggard was the last of the magi in this land, grown old and unwell . . .'" With a little snicker, I reverted to my normal voice before reciting the old story. "On his deathbed, he gifted his magical abilities to his five mortal children, 'Talented' as they were later called. Each of the Talented would become the first rulers of the Five Kingdoms."

I'd recalled the tale with a surprising lack of effort, the memory of Papa sitting in the candlelight by my and my sisters' bedsides easily resurfacing. I reached for my chalice of honey mead. "What of it?"

"Do you remember the abilities he gave to each of his children?" Gryffin pressed.

One corner of my mouth lifted as I squinted at him, for I was unable to admit that the finer details of the story evaded my memory.

"I believe I've made a connection." His smile grew. "I believe that still, even to this day, each of the five kingdoms' strongest attribute and trade stem from the Talent of each of the first Talented. Think about it—Lecevonia is prized for its quality horses, yes?" His eyes were bright with excitement. "Every kingdom on the Peninsula buys horses from your kingdom's stables! And Lecevonia's first ruler was able to—"

"To design horses of any natural material," I finished for him, feeling awe for the first time since this conversation began. Of course, Papa had told me the stories—Equos, our first ever king and our capitol city's namesake, making horses of clay, water, stone. He could not breathe life into them himself, however; some higher being breathed life into his creations in the night. With his Talent, he was able to build half an army overnight.

Curiosity got the best of me. "What of Tarasyn?"

Gryffin shrugged. "Our produce and wine. Our first ruler, Viridi, could coax plants into substantial growth. Which is quite helpful, given our location—snow and rugged mountains don't necessarily make for fertile soil." Then his eyes narrowed in chagrin. "Still, not nearly as impressive as Equos in my opinion."

I could feel my amusement gleaming through my widened eyes. The bedtime stories had a lot of truth behind them, it turned out. I wondered briefly what the other kingdoms' legends told. Neither my parents nor my advisors felt that the stories of the Talented were pertinent to ruling a kingdom now. The Talented were quite literally ancient history.

With that last thought, I was brought back to practicality, and my eyes tightened in scrutiny. "While that is a very interesting connection—and I applaud you for it—" I said sincerely, "I still fail to see what prevalence this holds now. That line of magic died out long ago." I seized a slice of bread smothered in grape jam and brought it to my lips. "Besides, Talents were so rare to begin with. The first Talented may have shaped our kingdoms, but even their descendants so rarely possessed Talents. No one has been born Talented in . . . what? Four centuries?"

Gryffin seemed to want to say more. He inhaled animatedly, but an internal battle raged as his eyes flashed between excitement and some other emotion that I could not quite place. Wariness, maybe? Caution?

Instead, he heaved a sigh deep from his chest. "I suppose you're right. I am simply delving into history. Tarasyn is very in tune with our Talented roots, though our resources are few." A smile returned to his lips. "That's why I spend so much of my time in your library. Resource upon resource, available to whomever may be so inclined!”

“Does Tarasyn believe in Talents, then?”

“Of course, we do. Why shouldn’t we?”

“Do you believe that Talented people still exist?”

Gryffin held up his hands. “I never said that, exactly. Just that Tarasyn is . . . different, I suppose. You and I were raised very differently.”

Raised differently. Hmm. “Will you tell me more about Tarasyn?”

Gryffin laughed in surprise. “Truly?”

I nodded.

He squinted his eyes in disbelief. “Why?”

I could not exactly tell him that I was hunting for information, but I didn’t have to lie, either. “Well, all I know about Tarasyn is that the kingdom keeps to itself. Besides, it’s only fair,” I reminded him as I smugly crossed my arms over my chest. “You’ve been reading everything there is to know about Lecevonia.”

He leaned back in his chair with a chuckle. “I suppose you’re right.” He lifted his eyes to the large sunlit window, then back down to me. “What would you like to know?”

“Well, you’ve bragged twice now about your kingdom’s wine. Are there vineyards as far as the eye can see?”

“In some places, yes. Throughout the countryside, if you aren’t standing in a vineyard, you’re standing in a vegetable farm or fruit orchard. Of course, this is relevant to land that wasn’t burned down to the dirt during the civil war.” His eyes darkened as he grimaced. “Some farmers have been able to rebuild, but others weren’t so lucky. Many of them moved into the cities looking for work.”

“What are the cities in Tarasyn like?” In fact, as I thought about it, I shamefully couldn’t name a single city in his kingdom aside from their capitol, Viridi. I tried to recall the map of the Peninsula, but my mind drew a hazy blank as it reached Tarasyn's border.

"Improving, thanks to my family, after seventy years of neglect." Gryffin offered a half smile. "Our capital, Viridi, is nestled in a deep valley, with the Silver Mountains towering around it. And Borea, settled in the north, sits near the upper ridge of the range. Though there is no longer travel through the nearby Pax Pass, the city remains as prominent as ever."

"No travel? What happened?" There were only two mountain passes connecting the Peninsula to the West Lands, so I thought it odd that one would be completely out of commission.

Gryffin shrugged, but I caught the slightest tension flash through his eyes. "My only guess is that travelers no longer wanted to face the dangers of a war-riddled civilization—which is understandable." He leaned forward, resting his elbows on the table, and helped himself to a final slice of bread. "Travelers from the mainland now use the Ferox Pass in Hiddon, though it is much rougher. Narrow roads on high ridges, dense forests . . . And that is *after* crossing the Haren Desert!"

My sarcastic chuckle scrunched up my nose. "That sounds like a lovely journey."

Castle workers quietly began roving the table, clearing our spent breakfast, and I smiled as little Lucinda approached us to collect our goblets.

"Ah! Hello, little one!" Gryffin exclaimed, recognizing the little girl. He squinted as if in thought and put his hand under his chin. "Lucinda, yes?"

Lucinda, utterly charmed, beamed up at him and curtsied.

"Did Gryffin return your basket to you, Lucinda?" I asked, eyeing Gryffin in mock suspicion. Teasing him took no effort, much like how it felt with Zeke.

"Yes, Your Majesty." She glanced back and forth between us. "Did you have a nice picnic?”

Our picnic seemed like an eternity ago, in another world. A happier world, a world full of Sterlings and unbreached walls. My lips turned upward in a small smile as I met Gryffin's steady gaze. “Why yes we did, thank you.”

“Did you kiss?” Lucinda blurted, her eyes wide with excitement.

“Oh!” My cheeks felt as if a flame were held to them, and I heard Gryffin's bright laugh boom through the Hall. “Oh, no, we are not talking about this! Silly girl,” I mildly chided. Then, as my thoughts returned to another usually silly girl, I quietly added, “Why don't you go up to Clara's rooms sometime today? I believe she might need a friend.”

Lucinda's eyes turned downcast as she understood my meaning. “Yes, Your Majesty,” she agreed. “I wouldn't want to be alone right now, either.” Then, with a smile that showed all of her little teeth, she shouted, “Don't worry, I'll cheer her up!” With that, she sprinted away with our chalices.

“She's not a shy one, is she?” Gryffin said, still shaking with quiet laughter. He stretched his hand across the now empty table, palm facing upward.

“She never has been,” I answered with a rueful shake of my head. I laid my hand softly in his and smiled, leaning across the table attentively. “Tell me about your family.”

“Well,” Gryffin began thoughtfully, “you know I am the second eldest, with my older brother three years my senior. Roderich.” The respect in Gryffin's voice embraced his brother's name like a warm blanket. “And my two younger brothers, Michael and Laris, both eighteen—twins, you see—and my youngest sister, Kathryn. Her seventeenth birthday passed not too long ago.” He chuckled quietly, then. “Kathryn would like you and your sisters. She's a little crass,” he admitted, "but that's what happens when you grow up with only brothers, I suppose. She has always wanted sisters."

I smiled softly. "Perhaps one day we may meet her. From what you say, I like her already."

I tore my eyes away from his face and for a moment gazed at the carmine and cobalt banners hanging throughout the Hall, embossed with silver strands to create the familiar horse's head, Lecevonia's crest, encircled in the dove's wings of the Avelia family's coat of arms.

The banners grounded me as they brought back to my mind why I was here, sitting across from Gryffin and asking about his family.

"What of your oldest brother?" I inquired, my eyes meeting his again. I attempted a vaguely interested expression and dearly hoped it was convincing.

At the mention of his brother, Gryffin smiled. "He and I have been through much together. It was only us two for five years, until the twins were born. He is there in my earliest memories. As the two oldest, and with our mother often sickly, our father held us responsible for our siblings. And—seeing as the twins never had a true chance to ascend to the throne—well, Roderich and I received the brunt of Father's attention." His smile turned down into a scowl, and his forehead knitted together as he seemed to descend into a memory. "As dreadful as that may have been."

The dark tonal shift was almost frightening. His ocean eyes flickered to mine, serious as he seemed to deliberate how much to tell me.

"There is more you should know," he finally said, "if you are to understand how far Tarasyn has come and how proud I am of my brother." Gryffin inhaled a deep breath and held it at the top of his lungs, steeling himself. "Remember how I mentioned that Tarasyn is quite in tune with our Talented past?"

I nodded softly, unable to speak in the shadowed dusk emanating from him.

"That wasn't always the case. It started with my grandfather. He was so *sure* that the magic still ran through the veins of some older families. He passed his beliefs down to my father, and they wasted each and every one of their days scouring the kingdom for someone with a Talent." He glowered down at the table. "They were both obsessed. They would corral Tarasynian citizens and . . . *force* them to expose their Talent. Unfortunately, if they could not show any type of ability, there were consequences. Horrible consequences. Betrayal to the Crown, you see. Treason for 'hiding' special abilities against the King's orders." Gryffin grunted under his breath, dark thoughts clearly raging. "My grandfather's actions were the spark of our kingdom's years of unrest, and my father had only been worse. We call it a civil war, but really, the Tarasynian people had no power against the Crown. They rebelled, but it did not stop my father from murdering his own people." These last words were forced through Gryffin's disgusted sneer.

I could only stare open-mouthed as the harsh reality of Tarasyn's past sank in before sudden indignation flooded my mind. How could someone do that to his own people? I tried to imagine Lecevonia in the same state, my people so afraid of me, hating me to the point of rebellion. The mere idea repulsed me. "That's barbaric."

Gryffin looked pained. "I know—better than most. My siblings and I were no exception to their designs, though we were spared from the harsh executions. Father couldn't off his own children, nor do I think he really wanted to." His gaze remained fixed on the wooden grains of the table. "He was very hard on Roderich, especially. Even I was not allowed to accompany them on a number of their private lessons. It is truly amazing that Roderich turned out as well as he has. Perhaps our father's unfaltering control backfired in the best way."

"It's amazing that *you* are doing as well as you are, as well," I said, my voice steeped in sympathy. "Or any of your siblings, for that matter."

Gryffin looked up at me then with a half-smile. "No need to pity us, Rosemary. Tarasyn can only rebuild from where we are now."

I saw an opportunity to dig a little deeper into Roderich's motivations. "How do you feel Roderich's rule is going?"

"He is slowly but assuredly piecing the kingdom back together. The citizens approve of him; they actually *rejoiced* when he was crowned. Roderich's been on the throne for almost six years now, and we have seen vast improvement in our kingdom's morale in just those few years. We may not be where we were one hundred years ago, before my grandfather's rule, but we're working in the right direction." His smile widened. "My coming here is actually our first attempt to improve relations on the Peninsula." Gryffin's eyes stayed locked on mine, and I could only see his utter certainty as he spoke. "I hardly see him, really. He spends his days either in his office organizing some project or visiting the towns of our countryside. He is doing good work."

And at that moment, as the truth he so fervently believed burned in his ocean eyes, I felt I had all evidence I needed to make my decision.

He had no idea of any malicious intent his brother may have had against Lecevonia. For all he knew, Roderich was parading through the streets of Viridi right now, throwing gold coins in the air and kissing babies.

But did that mean Gryffin's lack of knowledge was trustworthy?

"How is Princess Clara?" Gryffin's gaze was now searching my own, brimming with concern.

The sudden subject change triggered a bit of turmoil as last night's anguish crept into my thoughts. "Very shaken, but she will be okay." A weighted sigh rose into my chest. "She's so young. She hasn't seen anything like this before—even during Atroxis, she was barely old enough to crawl." I rubbed my temples, attempting to massage away my anxiety. "Things have been nonstop since last night . . . Though it feels as if I am in more of a waiting game now, as we gather more information." I let my hand drop to the table with a thud.

Gryffin leaned back in his chair, his jaw hardening. "Any leads?"

There was my barrier. The conversation had entered territory into which I should not venture.

But I considered, for the first time, telling Gryffin about Colonel Burnstead's allegations. And why not? Didn't he have a right to know of his kingdom's own doings?

Besides, as a suitor to my hand, he must hold *some* loyalty to me and to Lecevonia. Perhaps I should invite him to the next council meeting—he may have some insight about his brother—

Rose. Think.

Perhaps I shouldn't. He was a Tarasynian prince, after all, very much so before a potential Lecevonian king consort. Could I possibly ask him to betray his family, his home?

And how could I expect him to react upon the news? I could already imagine how the conversation would go.

"Gryffin, we believe your brother is behind the assassination attempts."

"What? No. Roderich has never shown any inkling!"

"Please, Gryffin, tell us everything you possibly can about your brother."

A pause. "Perhaps I should return home, try to sort this out with Roderich myself."

And that was why I could not tell Gryffin. I must avoid anything that might cause him to feel the need to leave the castle. If he tried, my men would have to stop him . . . ultimately making him an enemy. And since I wanted to marry him, that simply wouldn't do.

This mental deliberation passed all within the time it took me to take a loaded inhale, and as I let out my breath slowly, I began to draw swirling designs on the back of Gryffin's hand. "As I said before, no need to worry about that. You are our guest." But my lips turned down. "Some time to visit. You've been here for three days now, and it must seem as though assassination attempts are a regular occurrence."

"Let's avoid one today, shall we?" He gave a humorless laugh.

I rolled my eyes at his levity but answered in the same tone. "I couldn't agree more."

Through the high windows, the sunlight shone brightly to the stone floor, signaling that mid-morning had approached. So, I sighed heavily and looked toward the entrance of the Great Hall. "I suppose it's time for me to face the rest of my day." A queen's duties never ceased. "Thank you for joining me for breakfast, Gryffin," I said with a genuine smile. "It was much needed."

"Of course, my Rosemary," he responded sincerely, and with such tenderness, he leaned over the table and gently pressed his lips to my hand. This small, sweet kiss sent a thrill through my abdomen. "I'm glad we had the opportunity to talk in the midst of the chaos." He raised his head, and his face was suddenly inches from mine, his nose just barely grazing my own. His blue eyes bored into me, and I felt frozen in place, though warmth from his gaze coursed through me. "I really am worried about you."

It was all the strength I had to turn my face away from his as my blush returned to my cheeks.

I stood from my chair then, wood sliding against the stone floor.

Gryffin and our entourage of guards followed suit, disrupting the quiet Hall.

As we walked back toward the entrance of the Hall, I looked up again at Gryffin, ablaze with curiosity once more. One final answer had not yet been given. "I do have one more question, and I cannot help but ask now."

Gryffin met my gaze, his expression curious and amused. "Anything, Rosemary."

I decided to ask blatantly. "Why are you here?"

His expression lost a bit of its amusement. "I beg your pardon?"

"In Lecevonia."

He looked at me with pursed lips, confused. "Well, as I mentioned before, Tarasyn is working on outside relations—"

But I shook my head. "That's not what I mean. Why are you *still* here?" Why, even after my kingdom, my very *keep*, has been proven breachable, hadn't he gone home? Why was he still seeking my hand in marriage even after this weakness had been exposed?

Not weak, I reminded myself sternly. Caught off-guard, yes, but not weak.

"Ah," he murmured, finally seeming to catch my meaning.

Out in the corridor, he turned to face me. "I am here," he began slowly, "because a brilliant woman stands in front of me." He lifted his left hand to catch a piece of my hair, dangling loosely near my ear. "*She* seems to still want me here," he continued, tucking the piece of hair back into place, "and after just a few short days, I find myself so taken that I'm willing to do anything she asks of me."

His hand remained on my cheek as a gentle smile pulled at the corners of his lips. "And," he added, "I see a woman and a kingdom very much worth protecting."

I could not deny it any longer. I was completely and utterly charmed.

I felt my barriers melting once again. I leaned my cheek into his warm hand, and despite feeling the blood rush to my cheeks once more, I didn't want to look away. My chest began to ache, and I realized I had been holding my breath. I let out a long, shaky exhale, my widened eyes smiling.

Though I felt as if I could stand there, completely blissful, for the rest of the day, I was aware of the guards around us, the bustling of the castle corridor. I was the first to break eye contact and look down the hall. "I must go . . ."

Gryffin blinked, seeming to suddenly return to the present as well, his face soft. "Of course." His hand left my cheek and brushed down the length of my arm, leaving a new trail of goosebumps, to take my hand dangling at my side. He slowly raised it to his lips and kissed it just as tenderly as before, his eyes never leaving mine.

Finally, he released my hand with a gentle squeeze. "I will see you again soon," he promised with a confident smile. Then he turned on his heel and strode down the hall, presumably toward the library, his two guards following closely behind him.

CHAPTER NINE

I WAS NOT quite ready to return to my rooms, so instead, I turned to my guards with a new plan. I only had one place in mind, a place where I was certain to have a little peace. "Would you all please accompany me to the chapel? I . . . I have a lot to think about."

To my surprise, Amos smirked. "I bet so, Your Majesty."

His retort caused the rest of my guards to whistle and snicker.

Eyes wide, I looked at Amos and pursed my lips as I tried not to smile. "Oh hush, all of you! Can't a woman work through her thoughts without judgement?" I countered, but I made sure to keep my tone lighthearted.

Our parade continued up to the third floor of the castle, and up the spiral staircase of the castle's only turret. Small, narrow windows welcomed sunlight into the otherwise dark stairwell.

The castle's chapel was small, meant for only intimate family ceremonies, but the grand stained-glass window facing eastward compensated, making the room feel twice the size. The window depicted a colorful image of a nerys lily, Lecevonia's representative flower. It thrived in the briny air embracing the limestone cliffsides of the coast and, as told through generations, could supposedly make one feel well-fed for days with just one petal. Though, more realistically and according to Hazel, its crushed stems made a lovely moisturizer for the skin. The sunlight passing through the slender blue petals cast azure beams across the short rows of cushioned chairs, and the red of the flower's pistil and stamens shimmered on the large wooden tabernacle situated in the front of the chapel. An endless gradient of other hues, from jade to magenta to sienna, danced across the walls.

I made my way up the small aisle and seated myself in one of the cushioned chairs near the edge. Roger and Robert turned to face the door while the rest of my guards situated themselves loosely around me. Thomas looked about ready to lean his head back and take a nap.

The chapel's quiet atmosphere, like the courtyard, made it one of my favorite places to escape to, even if just for a moment.

And it was inside the castle walls. Safe.

The gentle pressure of Gryffin's warm hand on my cheek still lingered, and I couldn't shake the image of his face, his earnest ocean eyes, his kind smile out of my head. His concern for me as well as my sisters, his silly tales of magic, his proud expression as he talked about his own family—these all stirred a warmth in my chest and sent a confusing surge through my stomach. Something about this morning with him stayed with me, something that had been a sort of enlightenment, but I could not place it quite yet.

I recalled my assurance of Gryffin's innocence—stopping by my advisors' office should be my next course of action. At the thought, strong relief flowed through me once more. Gryffin felt *trustworthy.*

But why?

Why did I care so much whether or not Gryffin knew nothing of his brother's possible actions against my kingdom?

I knew that I had *wanted* him to be innocent; I had known that even during the council meeting this morning. After all, that had been the driving force behind my desire to talk to Gryffin personally. And I knew that I did not want to send him away from the kingdom, despite the danger Lecevonia faced. Yes, it had been Lord Quince's suggestion that convinced me that my train of thought made sense, but I was also aware that the thought of sending him away . . . upset me. I wanted him to stay simply because I liked his company. I *wanted* his company.

And that was the moment that one of my thoughts from breakfast returned to me, ringing through my mind, chiming clearly through the muddled mess.

And since I wanted to marry him.

I froze, staring straight ahead at the dark wooden tabernacle, this new realization tethering me down into my seat.

I wanted to marry Gryffin.

When had *that* evolved?

I knew that I didn't love him. It had only been three days, so of course not. Still, I couldn't deny the strong pull I felt toward him, and he seemed to feel it too. He had said as much just earlier, hadn't he? As he'd rested his hand upon my cheek. . .

No, I didn't love him—yet. But I so easily could.

Suddenly, I was able to see our future as if I were witnessing it happen right before me. I saw myself in a dazzling cream gown, its train brushing the floor as I walked down the short aisle of this small chapel, with ivory flowers and green ferns and ivies raining down on either side of the bunch in my hands. A glorious veil cascading behind me, my jeweled golden crown nestled atop my head. And waiting for me at the end of the aisle, stunning in a cream and golden-threaded vest bearing both the coats of arms of Tarasyn and Lecevonia, was Gryffin, with his ocean-blue eyes standing out against his wavy brown hair.

Then, a new image, the two of us sitting in the thrones that my own mother and father had claimed in the Great Hall. Our hands interlocked, smiling out toward a gathered crowd in the Hall. Perhaps even a brown-haired, green-eyed little girl playing at our feet.

I closed my eyes and found myself smiling. This could indeed be my future. My future with Gryffin, my family, my kingdom. I wanted it. It may even solve this new, sudden tension between Tarasyn and Lecevonia.

But my eyes shot open once more at that thought, my smile slowly dropping. No, assassination attempts were not excusable.

However, with Gryffin as king consort, he could assist me in Tarasynian relations. He could help me decide what to do about his brother—if Roderich truly was behind these heinous actions. The idea of having someone by my side during this confusing and frightening time really enticed me.

But, then again, someone was already always by my side.

Zeke.

I sighed and shifted in my seat. Zeke would always be beside me. In my image of my wedding, there Zeke would stand, in the first row of cushioned seats, looking handsome in a cobalt and carmine vest with the Lecevonian coat of arms embroidered in silver thread on the left side of his chest. He'd gaze back at me and offer a genuine smile— but with a subtle hint of sadness behind it—as I walked down the short aisle. And he would be there in the Great Hall, his golden hair shining in the bright sunlight entering through the high windows, laughing as my child ran across the cobblestoned floor.

He would always be there, and I liked the idea of that too.

Thomas's sudden snore grated against the walls of the stone chapel, snapping me out of that future. The rest of the soldiers jolted upright, and Thomas looked just as shocked.

Amos immediately berated his friend, swearing in whispers too low for me to decipher. After a moment, a deep and quiet chuckle rumbled through the small room. Roger.

I could not help but smile as well. "It's all right, Thomas," I said softly, assuring him. Then, with a groan, I stood to my feet. "It's time for me to return to my duties, anyway."

Upon exiting the spiraling stairwell, I yearned so strongly to take a right and return to my rooms. However, I stayed true to my own word and made my way down the main staircase to my advisors' office.

Though Lord Castor was not pleased with my conclusion, I held my stance, and after a fiery bickering match, he and my other advisors bowed their heads in compliance. Gryffin was not to be arrested or sent away.

I then paused as I turned to leave, worrying at my bottom lip. "Lord Brock . . ." I began slowly.

"Yes, Your Majesty?"

I considered telling them that I made the decision to marry Prince Gryffin. Lord Brock would surely be ecstatic. But I stalled now, thinking that now was not really the time. Maybe after Sterling's funeral service. My heart panged again as Sterling's gentle voice filled my mind.

Peonies take a while to bloom after planting.

I instead asked a decidedly more pressing question. "Has there been any new information relayed to you this morning regarding Tarasyn?"

Lord Brock glanced down to the floor, looking defeated. "No, my queen. General Gambeson will give us all a briefing the morning after next, unless some lead is discovered beforehand." He then turned his gaze to me, eyes intense. "We *will* know who has done this to you and your family, Queen Rosemary. And they will pay for their crimes before they can attempt to hurt you once more."

A wave of gratitude suddenly rushed through me as I met Lord Brock's eyes, fierce and ever loyal. I did not doubt his devotion to the Crown and to my kingdom. Even my meetings with potential suitors had been, as he thought, in best interest of the kingdom, although I had relentlessly disagreed with him.

I opted once again to complete my work in my rooms, ready to face the parchment that had no doubt piled up on my office desk after last night. But first, I had one more task I *needed* to do today.

I turned to Thomas. "Would you mind finding Sir Ezekiel? I'd like to speak with him."

Thomas bowed and was about to turn away as we rounded the corner of the third floor's corridor. However, down the hall, leaning against the wall across from the doors to my rooms, was Zeke.

A smile immediately burst across my face. I began walking a little faster, my guards following. "Hello, Sir Ezekiel." The formalities grated against my elation.

He bowed his head. "Queen Rosemary." When he lifted his head and looked at me, his eyes held such an intensity. "I had hoped that I could see you this afternoon."

"Of course. I was hoping the same," I admitted. "I'll have Hazel bring up lunch for us."

I nodded to each of my guards. "Thank you all for your time. I know following me around may not be the most glamorous way to spend your day."

This time, it was Hugh to laugh. "Think nothing of it, Your Majesty. We happily do it."

These men really were so good.

Hazel awaited inside, her back turned to us. She was smoothing out fresh sheets on my bed, and without looking up she greeted me. "Your paperwork is on your desk, my queen."

Then she lifted her head and saw the two of us in the doorway. "Ah." She offered an almost relieved smile. Funny—normally her reactions toward Zeke were no less than annoyed. "I will leave you two. Would you like lunch brought up to you?"

I smiled gratefully at the old woman. "Please. Thank you very much, Hazel."

Hazel came around the bed and laid her hand on my cheek for a moment.

Then she turned and pointed her finger accusingly at Zeke. "You be good." She wagged her finger at him, a threat embroidering her tone. Back to normal, it seemed. After glancing back and forth once between the two of us, she walked to the corner of the room and disappeared through the maid's door.

I turned to Zeke, all formalities aside now. There was so much that I wanted to say, to ask him. A flurry of emotions battled within me, from grief for Sterling, to fear for my kingdom, to regret over our argument, to concern regarding the assassin's execution, to relief that he stood here now. But I could manage only one word as I looked up to him. "Hi."

He smiled one of my favorite half-smiles. A smile that said, *we're okay.* "Hi, Rose."

Then I closed the distance between us, wrapping my arms around him in a vise. I tucked my head into his chest, and finally, the tears I had been holding in for so long spilled over.

As I let my grief finally take hold, it felt as if rough stones were being raked across my chest as my sobs shook my entire frame. My throat burned as I gasped between jagged breaths. The weight of Sterling's death, my kingdom's safety, my sisters' lives all fused into an impossible heaviness that finally crushed me.

And Zeke simply held me, his arms tight around my shoulders, holding me together as much as he could. Had I been with anyone else, I may have been embarrassed, ashamed for showing this weakness.

But not with Zeke. I never truly felt shamed with Zeke.

Even still, neither the strength of his arms nor the comfort they brought could compete with the weight of my crumpled resolve. My sadness, stresses, and fears all manifested into a rearing monster, biting away at my strength, striking again and again until every ounce of my energy lay in shreds, weak and defenseless, on the floor of my mind.

But Zeke still stood there, holding me, his head bent to rest on top of mine. His lips brushed words of reassurance against my hair that I sometimes caught, things like *you are doing amazingly* and *if anyone had just half the strength that you have. . .* But mostly, he hummed soothingly. After listening closely, I placed the tune as one my mother used to sing to me and my sisters. A short, simple bedtime lullaby, sung in every Lecevonian household, and I whispered along in my head.

On the Beryl Hills,
The verdant grassy sea a lull,
See the world now so still
Settling in, save for a lone gull.

Hush now, my sweet darling,
Oh, the pink hues of the sun creep.
Hush now, and just maybe
On Equos's horses you will sleep.

He hummed the sweet melody over and over, letting me weep.

I didn't know how long my tears spilled. Long enough for Hazel to slip in and set our lunch on the table near the window, though I had completely missed her entrance. I finally reached a point where I could comprehend that my tears had reduced to just one or two sliding down my cheeks, and my sobbing breaths had dissolved into small sighing hiccups. I was suddenly aware that I was ruining Zeke's vest, my tears probably seeping to his tunic underneath. So I turned my head to the side, my ear against his chest now, and kept my eyes closed, waiting for a bit more control to return to me.

When I could focus my breathing into even, albeit shaky, breaths, I found my voice. It sounded as if I had swallowed water. "I'm sorry. Thank you, Zeke."

He only hugged me more tightly, still humming.

"My Rose," he finally said, "you have been holding an entire kingdom together. It's only fair that I may help to hold *you* in one piece." He smiled down at me, a sad smile laced with sympathy.

I unfurled my arms and brought my hands to my face, covering my eyes. I could feel the red heat, the swollen skin of my eyelids and cheeks from crying. I rubbed my fingertips against my closed eyelids, wiping the last bits of moisture away. But I kept my hands pressed to my cheeks as I continued to even out my breathing, and I felt Zeke's hands gently squeezing my forearms.

When I finally slid my hands down to my chin, I opened my

stinging eyes to find Zeke stooping down, his face directly in front of mine, brow furrowed. "Rose, you do not *realize* how strong you are. But I do. So much stress, so much responsibility . . . and you are only just now letting yourself place it all down?" He grinned halfheartedly. "Most people would consider that unhealthy, you know."

"Most people have the choice." I sighed heavily and closed my eyes once more. Fatigue had wrapped itself around me as if it were a heavy blanket, weighing down my shoulders.

I felt Zeke's hand slide down my arm and take hold of my hand. "Come," he said with a gentle squeeze. "Try to eat, before your lunch gets any colder."

I let him lead me to the little round table at the window, but I couldn't pay much attention to the meal. I only registered the slice of mulberry bread that I was tearing into crumbled bits.

"Zeke, after last night . . ." The sound of the assassin's neck snapping rang in my ears, making me flinch. "How . . . how are you?"

Zeke smirked without humor, peeling a boiled egg absentmindedly. "I did not sleep much better than you, I'd wager."

I could only focus on my hands, on the shreds of bread, unable to meet his eyes. "I'm so sorry that you had to—that I put you into that situation." My voice trembled, and I wanted to cry for my friend. But my tears were now spent.

"I'm not, Rose." He reached one of his hands across the table and took hold of mine, and his other he placed underneath my chin, gently lifting my head. My eyes met his, and I suddenly found myself unable to look away.

"If he were to live," Zeke continued, "he would've found some way to attack again. He would've tried *endlessly*, until he'd succeeded . . ." He trailed off for a long moment, in thought, before returning to me. "He was a danger to you and your sisters. He could not be allowed to live." His brown eyes were intense, but something dark lay behind them. I knew then that the execution had affected him more than he was letting on.

"The snap haunts me," I whispered.

"I know, Rose," he said, his eyes hazy. "I hear it too, ringing, echoing, bouncing off the stone walls."

We stared at each other, sharing the horror. The responsibility of robbing one of his life.

Zeke snapped out of it first with a quick shake of his head. "It had to be done, Rose."

I sighed as I absorbed his words. "Yes, you are right. He was a danger." Which led to another matter. "And that's why you informed Colonel Burnstead."

"Ah." Zeke looked away now, glancing toward the window. "I should have figured that that would be a topic of discussion in the council meeting this morning."

"I'm not upset, Zeke. I understand why you informed them. And it was wrong of me to ask you to do otherwise."

"I wish I would have gone to them directly after you told me, instead of mulling over it for the entire afternoon." He cursed under his breath, and he spoke through gritted teeth. "If I would have just *gone* to them! Then maybe we would have found him earlier, and no one would have been lost." His face settled into a defeated scowl.

I squeezed his hand. How could he blame himself? "*None* of this is your fault, Zeke. This is solely on me."

He looked at me with an accusing grin. "You're right, it is." Of course, leave it to Zeke to affirm hard truths. "If you had gone straight away to your advisors—"

I interrupted him, holding up my free hand. "I know, Zeke." This was one thing of which I didn't need reminding. I looked toward the window, welcoming the warmth of the sun as my body had run cold with grief. "I'm learning."

And I was only still learning, after all, even if my teachers were ruthless facilitators of the most painful lessons. My parents' deaths had taught me grief. Sterling's death had taught me regret. In this moment, I felt so small. So much smaller than my parents had been.

I could feel Zeke studying me, and though I knew my lip was quivering, I determinedly held onto an otherwise inscrutable mask.

Thankfully, he pressed onto another subject. "How did the council meeting go?"

With this distraction from my guilt, I was able to effortlessly shift into the Queen of Lecevonia. "With the information that we have, we are taking cautious but passive action against Tarasyn, until we know more. Sending troops to the border, sending scouts ahead, training new soldiers and assuring our cavalry is ready . . . precautionarily." I looked at him through my periphery. "Were you the one to find the message in the assassin's cloak?"

He nodded and made a disgruntled sound. "I wish I could understand it."

"Me too." I sent my gaze downward to the floor. "But I understand your warning now, I suppose."

Zeke sighed, with a relieved set to his mouth. His hand tightened around mine. "I'm glad that you see, now." He watched me, treading carefully as he spoke. "Prince Gryffin cannot be trusted, Rose."

I turned in my seat to look at him head-on. "That isn't what I meant. I see your reasoning to be cautious of Tarasyn. But—" I had to pause, to be sure that each of my next words left my lips with purpose. "But I do trust Prince Gryffin, Zeke."

That stopped him short. He drew his hands away ever so slightly, resting them on the table now. "What?" His eyes widened for just a second, before settling into a scowl.

But I did not break eye contact with him. He *must* understand. "Zeke, I really trust that he is unaware of his brother's malintent."

"How so?" he fired back, crossing his arms tightly across his chest.

"The way he so wholeheartedly believes in his brother, believes that Tarasyn is improving, the sincerity with which he speaks of his brother's rule. He cannot possibly be aware of these plans! And . . ." I ventured on, I knew, at the risk of angering my friend. "And he said as much, after he and I visited this morning over breakfast."

He sneered at me. "You had a chat with him this morning, did you?"

"For Haggard's sake, Zeke, please don't do this." I reached my hands across the table, palms facing upward. Zeke uncrossed his arms and placed one of his hands in mine, though he still did not look at me. So, bravely, I tried to explain. "I had to determine Gryffin's true intentions—"

"Ah, on a first-name basis now?"

I ignored his snide remarks. My eyes, wide in sincerity, bored into his furrowed forehead as I continued. "And do you know what he said? He said 'Lecevonia is worth protecting.' Zeke, if you could have *seen* his eyes!" Now I was pleading with him, urging him to trust me, just as I trusted in Gryffin.

Zeke continued to stare down at our hands, his eyebrows pinched. For a long moment, we sat in silence.

Hazel returned and, after meeting my warning gaze very briefly, silently stacked our plates to take down to the kitchens. I, of course, always appreciated Hazel putting Zeke in his place, but right now, the last thing I needed was a snarky remark from her. The thick tension surrounding the little table must have been enough explanation because she quickly disappeared through the maids' door again, avoiding further eye contact.

Once Hazel was gone, Zeke looked up at me and finally spoke. "So, you truly believe that the man is innocent in all of this."

However inexplicably, I was certain of Gryffin. "I trust him," I repeated. "And, Zeke. . ." Was now really the time? Would any time truly be appropriate? It did not matter when I told him; I would still hurt him. "I am choosing to marry him."

Zeke's eyes flashed, shifting from incredulous to . . . livid. "What?" he said again.

But I held my ground and tried to speak reason. "He may be able to help with Tarasynian relations. Even you must agree with that, don't you?"

Zeke rose from his chair. "You're going to marry him?"

So much for reason.

His anger painfully pierced through me, but I refused to let him see that. "Zeke, he is a good man—the best of any of the suitors I have met! Please, Zeke—you knew this was coming."

"But to *him*?" He raised his hand, gesturing ambiguously toward my doors. "To an enemy?"

Now my own anger was rising, and my voice rose with it. "*Gryffin* is not the enemy!"

Zeke threw his extended hand in the air in exasperation. "Oh, no, he is just the enemy's brother," he shouted. "Don't let *that* be a deterrent, surely!"

I refused to answer him—his hurtful words didn't deserve a rebuttal. We glared at each other for a long moment, neither one backing down.

I knew that this was painful for Zeke, but truly, how else would I tell him? I wanted to be the one through whom he heard it, rather than through unrelenting gossip that would surely ensue once I told my advisors. And I knew, ultimately, I wanted Zeke's support. No—I *needed* it. I needed him by my side, just as I had envisioned in the chapel. I could admit that much.

Finally, Zeke broke our silence with a loud, drawn out sigh. "I did not come here to argue with you, my Rose." He stepped toward me and took my hands in both of his once more. "I do not agree with you in the slightest, and as your friend, I won't let you forget that." He lifted my hands to his lips, and he kissed each one softly.

Then, he gently released my hands and adopted a more formal air with a deep bow. "However, as my queen," he said pointedly, "I respect your judgement." He turned away toward the door, and when he looked at me again, he wore a sad smile. "I have to go, Rose."

I took a step after him. "Why? Surely you don't leave again so soon?"

He let out one short laugh. "We are in a time of malicious uncertainty, Rose. I have my job to do. Scouts are needed more now than they ever have been." He looked away from me then, back toward the door. "I'm going to offer to go to the front lines, to be positioned at the Tarasynian-Lecevonian border."

The front lines?

No.

"Zeke—"

I stopped myself. I knew this was selfish. I should let him leave, and I should no longer hurt him. But I could not bear to see him go off once more, only to possibly be captured. Or worse.

No. I couldn't let him go.

"Zeke, please stay."

He looked at me, puzzled. "Rose, I cannot do my job from the castle."

"Become part of my personal guard, then. Or my sisters'. Or Gryffin's! Keeping an eye on Gryffin all day would surely make you feel better, right?" It would suit his paranoia, at least.

I saw a flash of shock whisk across his features. It was just for a split second, but I caught the small inhale, the slight raise of his eyebrows. He leaned back slightly on his heels, as if my request had been a sudden, surprising whoosh of air.

Then he scoffed. "Rose, that's not what I've trained my entire life to do. That's not my job."

"Please, Zeke."

He glared down to the stone floor.

"Even if just until Sterling's funeral," I amended. "You want to be here for it, don't you?" I wanted him here, and I knew Sterling would as well. It was only a couple of days from now, but perhaps I could convince him to stay in that time.

He kept his gaze on the floor and was silent for a long moment. "I will see what I can do." He rocked back on his heels one more time, then sighed and launched into a big step toward me, closing the distance by gathering me into his arms.

"Goodbye, Rose." His soft breath sifted through my hair.

He released me with the smile I loved, kissed the top of my head, and strode out of my chambers hurriedly before I could talk him into anything else.

The rest of my day was consumed by my work, and I found myself thankful for the distraction. I had been able to allocate funds to the family whose house had been burned down—this Rebels of the Red Sun would need to be controlled, somehow—and I was glad that I would be able to make a difference among my people, even if that difference was only a small one.

The sunken trading vessel to Somora, well, that was another matter. Looking at the supply list aboard the ship and the kingdom's general ledger, I knew that the loss would be sizable. No merchandise, which was mostly wheat and fresh produce, had been able to be salvaged before the ship filled with water and dropped into the depths of the East Sea.

Fortunately, the crew had been able to abandon the vessel, and they would all be able to return to their families. The same could not be said, however, for Lecevonia's largest loss: the handful of horses that had been aboard, also on their way to Somora. The crew had released them all from their ties before boarding the small skiff, and I could only hope that they would make it to some distant shore; perhaps the Solan Islands of Loche were their best bet. And the cause of the wreckage was yet to be determined.

Though King Merek, of course, understood that mishaps out at sea did happen, he had openly expressed his wishes for a new shipment in two weeks' time, before he would send his own vessel stocked with linens and timber for Lecevonia. So, my afternoon consisted of arranging wheat, corn, and grapes to be subtracted out of Lecevonia's own stock and having quality horses set aside for the shipment, as well as timber for a new ship.

Lord Clark did appear at one point and reported that ten teams of scouts, two men per team, would ride toward Tarasyn that night, and two thousand soldiers would begin their trek to the Tarasynian-Lecevonian border the next morning, splitting into groups of five hundred and taking alternate paths in an attempt to avoid raising suspicion in Tarasyn. The remaining three thousand would move out the day after next. They would not cross into Tarasynian territory, but they would be prepared for any attack.

Neither he nor any of my other advisors reported any new information regarding Tarasyn, and so my waiting game continued.

Even still, as I lay under my sheets that night, I remembered the small family I was able to help—a mother and father, with two young boys—and the warmth of accomplishment spread through my chest.

CHAPTER TEN

I WOKE WITH a panicked scream. I jerked upright, and I whipped my head to either side, trying to find the archer in the woods. Hadn't I just been fighting with him?

I looked down at my ivory night shift and cobalt sheets. No, they were not covered in dust and dirt from the forest floor. I lifted my hand to my hair and found no leaves and twigs. But when I slid my hand across my forehead, a sheen of sweat dampened my fingers. And I was so *tired*. Every one of my muscles ached.

I collapsed down onto my pillow, and I willed my eyes to glance to the corner of my darkened bedchamber.

No, Gryffin was not there, simply standing to the side, looking on with an expression of helpless sympathy on his face.

I turned my gaze straight up to the bed's canopy above me, trying to even my breath, when a quick knock on my door echoed urgently through the room. The intruder waited for no response. A second later, I gasped and sat straight once more as my room was flooded with flickering light from the candlelit corridor. The faces of two of my guards cast in black shadows peered into my room through the cracked door. I did not recognize them, so they must have changed shifts.

I gathered my sheets in my hands at my chest, trying to mask the rapid rising and falling as I fruitlessly struggled to slow my breathing. Upon seeing me still tucked in my bed, both shadows relaxed.

"Your Majesty," one of the shaded faces spoke, "are you all right? We heard you shout."

"Would you like us to do a sweep of the room?" the other shadow suggested.

"No, no, I'm fine." I sounded breathless even to my own ears, so I took a deep lungful before continuing. "I apologize. I've just awoken from a dream." Yes, only a dream. Another deep breath. "Thank you both for your concern. I am all right."

Both heads bowed, allowing another sliver of light into the dark room.

"We are here if you need anything at all," the first face spoke again. Then they both backed out of the doorway, sliding the door shut behind them. The room was cloaked in darkness once again.

I slowly rolled back down onto my pillow. I nestled there, though my muscles refused to release their tension, and stared upward at my canopy once again as my eyes adjusted to the darkness.

Only a dream. I had not actually been fighting with the assassin in a battle that seemed to go on endlessly—one that I never really had the upper hand in; I could only defend myself as well as I knew how, with no weapons of my own, no combat skills. While he had his bow and his arrows, his dagger, his strength. I would slip my arm free only to have my leg seized. When I would wriggle my foot loose, the string of the bow would be shoved into the hollow of my neck, and I would fall to the ground. A constant fight or flight decision had raged in my frightened mind as I tried fruitlessly to escape his grasp . . . while his maniacal laugh infested the trees and the brush . . .

I clutched my heaving chest. I hadn't realized that my breathing had morphed into hyperventilation.

The incident in the woods would have never happened to Papa. And he wouldn't be plagued with these nightmares of weakness.

As my eyes, now adjusted to the darkness, registered the sleepy gray tinge of the dawning sky framed in my window, I decided that I would never feel that helpless, unrelenting terror again.

Once the morning had reached an acceptable hour, I set my plan into action.

"Hazel," I said as soon as she appeared in my rooms, "I'd like to wear trousers today, and a tunic. And a vest."

My gracious lady-in-waiting looked appalled. "Pardon, my queen?"

Now I felt a bit sheepish, but I held my ground. "Yes, Hazel. Please."

"And what will you be doing today that requires men's clothing, Your Majesty?" Hazel crossed her arms and glared.

"Not men's clothing, Hazel," I corrected, "but practical clothing." I lifted my chin, hoping I seemed confident.

We remained like this for a moment, in a standoff, neither one of us budging.

But in the end, my resolve proved stronger than Hazel's, and when Hazel threw her arms into the air, I couldn't help but smile at my little victory. After last night, *any* little victory was welcome.

"Why do I even bother with you, some days?" the old woman said in exasperation, shaking her head. "I will see what they have down in the laundry wing." With a disgruntled sigh and a glare, she marched through the maid's door.

After dressing in what Hazel was able to scrounge up for me, I strode down the hall with my new set of guards and assessed my new attire. Admittedly, this was my first time ever wearing trousers; a princess's days endlessly consisted of dresses and gowns, and as a queen, even more so. I initially thought that the trousers were rather uncomfortable. I felt that my legs had more freedom in the billowing skirt of a dress. The feeling of the cloth coating each of my legs would be something to get used to. The tunic was my favorite piece, as it hung loosely on my bodice, though the buttoned burgundy vest subtracted from that slightly. Still, I appreciated no neckline to worry over. And the cobalt and carmine floor-length coat, which Hazel had relentlessly insisted on even as I had protested, was a nice touch after all. Though the sleeves were open, revealing the cotton arms of the tunic, the coat was fastened closed in front with a leather belt, giving the entire outfit a slightly more feminine feel. Hazel had opted for a smaller tiara, which I had inherited from my mother, and had worked it snugly into my braided hair.

Though different, I embraced the new outfit. At least my leather riding boots were familiar as they clicked down the hall with my steps.

My guards—whose names I learned were Hector, Rowan, Arthur, Brom, Ulric, and another Geoffrey—and I descended the main stairwell while I replayed my conversation with Gryffin yesterday. I recalled his words. *I see a woman and a kingdom very much worth protecting.* As I entered the castle's library, I hoped he would see this as an opportunity to do just that.

It was not difficult to find him, sitting in a cushioned seat amongst the history section of the library. He was leaning forward, immersed in some book, with two other volumes lying at his feet. His two guards looked utterly bored, though one did peer over Gryffin's shoulder, seeming to absentmindedly read along. The other stood farther back, leaning against a nearby bookcase, his chin tucked into his chest. Probably dozing.

Only when both of his guards suddenly stood at attention did he turn his gaze upward to us.

An incredulous grin broke across his face. He stood and bowed at the waist, but his eyes never left mine. "Good morning, Queen Rosemary."

He approached me in two strides and gathered my hands in his. Still smiling, he lifted my arms up, his eyes in disbelief, and in a surprising flourish that made me squeal, he twirled me around by the hand as if in a dance. My coat billowed in a wide circle around me.

My startled exclamation was quickly cut short by my laughter. His playful twirl left me energetic, cheeks warm. When I wound to a stop, I curtsied spiritedly. "Good morning, Prince Gryffin."

"You look magnificent." Gryffin beamed. "What activity do you have planned today that requires such a change in attire?"

"An activity that you will assist me with, I hope." I looked at him seriously. "I want you to teach me how to use a sword."

Gryffin paused, stiffening just a bit, his incredulous expression turning confused. "And what gives you that need?"

Hm. Not quite as willing as I had hoped.

I lowered my voice. "Well, given the danger my family and I currently face, I . . . I want to be prepared."

"Rosemary, that's what these men are here for." He lifted his hand, gesturing to the soldiers loosely arranged around us. He took one of my hands and pressed it to his chest. "That's what *I* am here for. You don't need to be afraid. We are all here, ready to protect you." He brought my hand toward his lips, but before he could kiss it, I loosened my hand from his grip and sighed.

"Gryffin." I stepped closer to him, my voice hardly above a whisper. I lowered my eyes to the floor. I didn't want to admit my fear; I'd already shown so much weakness in front of this man. But he needed to understand. "I had a dream last night—a nightmare, really. About the archer in the woods. I awoke, terrified, and I realized I have never been as *helpless* as I was in the woods that day."

"Anyone would have been taken off their guard, Rosemary."

"If you hadn't been there, I would have been killed." I lifted my eyes to meet his. "What if you are not there next time? Or if these men are not there?" I gestured toward my guards. "I'd be killed in a second, and I want to change that. I want to be able to defend myself."

Gryffin studied me for a long moment before a yielding smile lightened his eyes. "Well, how can I say no to that?" He leaned forward and softly kissed my forehead. "First, though, we need to find you a sword that will fit you."

What did *that* mean? To mask my confusion, I turned from him and marched toward the library doors. "All right, then. We can visit the spare armory."

However, finding a sword that "fit" me proved to be more difficult than I thought. They were all so much heavier than they looked. Gryffin had suggested starting with a wood-crafted sword for my lesson, but I scoffed at the idea, feeling that the quickest way of learning was to throw myself into it wholly. Eventually, after several respectable weapons had ended up in my discard pile on the stone floor of the armory, I had found a sword that was light enough for me to handle but still held some weight of its own.

Since no visitors were currently allowed inside the castle walls, the

Great Hall's silence hung eerily in the air. However, our presence did attract a few castle workers. Several people lingered around and lounged around the Hall, and a hint of excitement buzzed through the grand room.

"All right," I said, sword in hand and scabbard tied around my waist, "what should I know first?"

Gryffin chuckled. "First," he said, approaching me in our impromptu training arena, "is how to properly unsheathe and hold your weapon." He loosened my sword from my hands and slid it casually into its scabbard.

Then he stood across from me with his own sword sheathed, the silver hilt with twisting dark metal shining. "First, with your dominant hand, establish a strong grasp"—slowly and deliberately, he gripped the hilt—"just below the cross-guard, no lower"—he indicated with his left hand the long bit of metal at the base of the blade, which had always reminded me of wings—"and unsheathe your sword fully from the scabbard before holding in front of you, at the ready," he concluded, extending his sword out in front of him with both hands.

I snickered quietly to myself. Easy enough. I reached across my body, gripped my sword just underneath the cross-guard as he'd said, and swiftly pulled the sword from its sheath. Too easy.

But as I straightened my weapon in front of me, the tip of the sword caught the very end of the scabbard, and my grip faltered just enough for the weight of the sword to fall from my hand. The sword clanged to the ground at my feet with an earsplitting metal-on-stone clatter. The Great Hall turned silent.

My face burned, and the sword lying at my feet mocked me.

"*Fully* remove it from the scabbard," Gryffin reminded me. He picked up my sword from the stone floor and carefully slid it again into its scabbard at my waist, letting his fingers brush my side. "Sheathing and unsheathing are how many men lose fingers or toes." He backed away. "Try again."

So, with a bit more concentration, I repeated the movement, this time assuring that the tip of the blade cleared the end of the scabbard before straightening it out in front of me. I brought my left hand just below my right, feeling a hint of pride over something so simple.

Gryffin nodded in approval. "Better, overall. Take mind where you place your other hand," he said, laying his hand over my left. He slid my hand farther down the hilt, to the pommel. "You will have better leverage this way." We stood like this perhaps just a bit longer than necessary, certainly long enough to distract me, before he finally took a step back to assess me. "How does your stance feel?"

I turned my attention to my feet and shifted a bit. Yes, I felt more grounded now. I looked up at Gryffin again, and he nodded. "There you are, a tad more comfortable."

He pursed his lips then, evaluating as he circled me. He took a step toward me again and gently placed his hands on my shoulders. With a smirk, he squeezed my shoulders and leaned in closely. "Relax. Your shoulders are not saying anything that your ears need to hear."

I rolled my eyes and drew my shoulders down my spine in response. Though I would never tell Gryffin, my arms did feel sturdier.

Gryffin stepped back again, and officially granted his approval with a smile of encouragement. "Now, take a swing."

I paused, confused. Gryffin's sword lay untouched on the stone floor. "Well, aren't you going to be my opponent?"

Gryffin laughed. "I will, but I want you to practice a bit first. Get a feel for the weapon in your hand."

I frowned. "So, I am supposed to simply swing into empty air?"

A snarky but familiar voice interrupted us. "Are you too nervous to face Her Majesty, Prince Gryffin?"

My eyes shot toward the voice, refusing to build my hopes, and there was Zeke striding toward us from the entryway of the Hall.

I relaxed my arms, my sword tilting toward the floor, and a wide smile spread across my face. "I assumed that you had left last night."

"No," he answered, his words light through a smirk. "I'm reporting for duty, Your Majesty."

I saw now that he was in his uniform vest, emblazoned with the Lecevonian coat of arms on its chest, and his own sword was secured to his waist. My smile grew. "Duty?"

"Indeed." Zeke turned to one of my guards on post, Hector. "Sir Hector Mead, I am your relief." He reached into his vest then and retrieved a small yet hefty piece of paper. An official order.

Hector glanced over the paper, which seemed satisfactory enough for him, and turned to me with a bow. "Always an honor, Your Majesty."

"Thank you, Hector," I responded with a slight bow of my head. I turned to Zeke in disbelief. Of course, I had wanted it so badly, but I hadn't truly expected him to choose to miss out on the excitement at the border. "You were able to convince them, then?"

Zeke smiled. "I'm on Colonel Burnstead's good side right now, and General Gambeson's, for that matter. You know, after I informed them . . ." he trailed off. "They both actually thought it would be smart for a scout to stay behind at the castle, anyway. I may catch something that others would not." He shrugged nonchalantly, but I caught the slight narrowing suspicion of his brown eyes.

He scanned my outfit then and spoke low enough for only my ears. "Busy today, aren't we?" He raised his eyebrows and grinned.

I wanted to punch him in the shoulder, but the public eye reeled in my desire. However, I did little to hide my eye roll.

And then my anxiety began to set in. Having weapons so close to each of these men might not be a good idea . . . Had they even officially been introduced, yet? I cleared my throat exceedingly loudly. "Sir Ezekiel, have you met—"

"We have," Zeke interrupted me, eyes tight. "Yesterday morning actually, outside your rooms." Though it seemed to pain him to do so, he stiffly bowed his head. "Prince Gryffin Danicio," he said formally, "I hope you are well." Though his tone suggested just the opposite.

Gryffin, cordial as always, lowered his head respectfully. "Likewise, Sir Ezekiel." Though his smile was radiantly kind, his answering tone had the same bite to it. "I am well, in fact. First thing this morning, Queen Rosemary sought me out in the library and requested my assistance in learning a little bit of defense." He gestured to me, my small sword still in hand.

The tone in his voice could only be pride, but I felt no flattery. Both he and Zeke were too important to me, and I wouldn't stand for hostility from either of them. Not over me.

I took a step forward and placed myself diplomatically between the two men. "Isn't it a wonderful idea, Zeke?" I eyed my friend pointedly, no longer addressing him formally in an attempt to lighten the atmosphere. *Be nice.*

Zeke met my eyes briefly, before sighing and forcing a smile. "A fine idea, Rose. Now, what is this about 'swinging into empty air'?"

Gryffin laughed, all tension dissolved as his confidence returned. "To answer your earlier question with honesty, I *am* a bit hesitant to face Rosemary with a sword just yet." He narrowed his eyes at me with a teasing smile. "She may do more damage than she means to."

Zeke looked at me analytically now, as a soldier would look at a new recruit. He returned his gaze to Gryffin out of his periphery. "Perhaps you should show her a few defensive stances?"

Gryffin nodded in terse agreement. "That was our next step." *Before you interrupted,* his tight smile insinuated.

Then, Gryffin looked back to me, unsheathing his sword. "Now, the beauty of using a sword as a weapon is that it is designed to be used both defensively"—he firmly held his sword in front of him, the flat face of the blade guarding his throat—"and offensively." He swung his sword sharply in a downward thrust. "And sometimes, both at the same time." He brought his sword in front of him again, angled downward so that the wide, strong portion of the blade protected his face while the narrow, weak portion closer to the point skewered an imaginary opponent. "You've actually already learned one defensive move," he said with a keen smile. "The most basic and instinctual. Hold your sword upward again, hands at your hips."

I did as I was told, holding my sword with the tip pointing upward toward the far corner of the Hall's ceiling.

"That stance," Gryffin continued, stepping a bit closer, "is called plough guard. You can move to block many attacks from this position. If you aim your sword directly at your opponent's throat"—he stepped even closer, lightly touching the tip of the sword and moving it down just slightly, until it pointed directly under his chin—"you have an excellent defense already in place, which could quickly turn to offense if needed." He met my eyes and smiled. "If you took one step forward right now, I would be done for."

So I dared not move.

Zeke stepped in. "I've got a useful one."

Gryffin narrowed his eyes in irritation, but he consented, taking a step back and sheathing his sword. "Go ahead."

Zeke planted himself in front of me with a smug smile. "All right, Rose. Point your blade downward toward the ground again." He lowered his voice, his smile turning into a teasing grin. "Just as you were when you relaxed as I entered the Hall."

I scrunched my nose at his comment, but I did as he instructed, letting my sword tip fall toward the ground.

"But this time, *don't relax*."

Ah . . . I stiffened again, trying to keep my arms rigid, my grip on the sword's hilt tight. When I was in position, Zeke circled around me. A chill ran down my back as I felt his eyes on me, taking in my stance, my feet, my shoulders.

Then to my surprise, he shoved me, hard, with one finger from behind. With a gasp, I stumbled forward, my feet no longer planted onto the stone. My sword's tip bounced off the floor loudly. Out of the corner of my eye, I saw Gryffin take a quick step forward.

Infuriated, I wheeled around to face Zeke. "Why did you do that?"

His little chortle tolled in my ear. "You were too relaxed."

". . .Oh."

"That could have been dangerous, Sir Ezekiel," Gryffin called. His voice slipped into anger.

Zeke glared in Gryffin's direction. "Well, how else is she supposed to learn?"

"I'm fine!" I interjected loudly, waving both of them off. I set my gaze on Zeke. "Again." Determined, I took my stance again, this time forcing my whole body into a tense rock, as tense as the air of the room.

Zeke circled me again, and this time, when he pushed me, I was as firm as a statue.

"Good," Zeke affirmed with a smiling nod. "This is called fool's guard, because you don't seem at all ready for a fight. Your opponent will be more inclined to attack. When in reality"—he unsheathed his own sword then, and moved swiftly from fool's guard to plough guard with one small hand adjustment before continuing—"you can shift into a more offensive position very easily, and you may even be able to take your opponent by surprise." I thought I saw his eyes land on Gryffin as he spoke.

Intrigued, I gripped my sword firmly and snapped up into plough guard. The whoosh of the air as the blade of my sword cut through the air exhilarated me, and I smiled wickedly as the power of a weapon settled into my hands for the first time.

Without a second thought, I lifted my hands high and tilted the blade over my shoulder. I cut the blade down swiftly, slicing through the emptiness in front of me that I'd mentally occupied with the archer in the woods. First his left arm, then his right arm. A giggle bubbled through my lips.

What power! I *dared* the next assassin to challenge me.

Gryffin laughed and shouted, "Very good! That was the quick guard, or vom tag. It is much more of an offensive move, and you executed it beautifully."

I felt so energized. Invigorated. "What else should I know?"

Gryffin chuckled. "All right, I'll demonstrate one more defensive stance, one that I find very useful."

With his right hand under the cross-guard and left hand at the pommel, he brought the hilt of his weapon to the left side of his face, the sword's tip facing outward toward his imaginary opponent. "This is the left ochs. A purely defensive stance. It can protect practically every angle of your body."

As I watched him move his sword, I noticed that his left hand controlled the weapon by the pommel, creating a seesawing effect in front of him. He was right—his entire front could easily be defended. He could even reach his hands overhead and block an attack from above.

"And," he continued, "you can easily move into a right ochs, which is an offensive stance." He twisted his sword across the front of his body, left arm traveling under his right, until his hands were on the right side of his face. His left arm was twisted underneath his right, which looked complicated to me, but Gryffin still moved with ease as he thrust his blade into the empty space in front of him.

Doubtfully, I tried to copy his movements with my own sword. The left ochs was easy enough, but its right counterpart proved to be a bit more challenging. I couldn't comfortably lunge with my arms twisted like that, which Gryffin blamed on the sword not fitting me quite properly.

"A balanced sword makes every difference," he reminded me, after my umpteenth attempt at an offensive attack. "Your muscles are compensating for the imbalance rather than putting all of their energy into the strike."

I sighed. The muscles in my arms were beginning to shake with fatigue. I'd have to put an order in with the blacksmith soon.

I continued to take my different stances, making moves from each position. I felt that I was improving, and the sword was indeed becoming more comfortable in my grip as Gryffin had said. I was practicing certain cuts and thrusts, a few defensive moves here and there, and was even making a fair amount of parries against my own imaginary opponent. It was easy to envision slashing through the archer in the woods. Gryffin's words ran into Zeke's as they both encouraged and coached me, and I felt the space between them shift from tension to a sort of unwilling comradery.

Still, my strength was fading, and I felt droplets of sweat rolling from my temples. After a while, Gryffin placed a hand on my arm. "Why don't you sit for a minute? Give your arms a rest."

Then Zeke chimed in from the sideline. "What if Rose watches how a fight might ensue?"

Gryffin's eyes widened in amusement. "Are you suggesting that you and I demonstrate?"

Zeke shrugged. "I don't see why not. Rose?" His voice housed a little too much excitement.

But I immediately stiffened. "Absolutely not." The thought of Zeke and Gryffin lunging back and forth at each other was not something I wanted to picture. I trusted Gryffin, but Zeke . . . Well, I didn't know if Zeke could hold back a damaging blow.

Zeke groaned. "Please, Rose. Just a little fun. I'm not going to hurt your precious prince. Besides, I'm dying for a bit of action after watching you slice the air into shreds." His teasing grin did little to calm my nerves.

Finally, I rolled my eyes and sighed. "If either one of you is harmed, I'll hold you both personally responsible." I eyed both men directly with my threat before ebbing to the sidelines.

As soon as I collapsed into the chair, I realized how tired my body really was. My arms felt gelatinous, and my legs just about screamed in gratitude to have all weight taken off them. I rotated my ankles and wrists in circles, back and forth, trying to loosen them. And I watched nervously as Zeke and Gryffin took their stances, face-to-face, swords drawn.

First, they stood unmoving, each seeming to measure his opponent. The crowd standing by to watch had formed a wide rectangle around the two men, but neither seemed to notice the onlookers. Or, if they did, they were not bothered in the least. In fact, both were smiling as if they'd just received the best gifts for Solstice Day.

Then, Zeke made the first move. He lunged with a quick and powerful slash downward toward Gryffin's right shoulder. But Gryffin deflected it with his own weapon held firmly above him, and the blades clashed together. A sharp metallic screech sliced through the Hall as

Gryffin parried and trapped Zeke's sword under his own.

Zeke slid his sword backward to free it just before making a daring cut toward Gryffin's torso. Again, Gryffin's sword was already there, fluidly blocking the jab. Then, with surprising speed, Zeke twirled his entire body around, his sword traveling in a wide sweep around him, and finally rested his blade against Gryffin's shoulder, close to his throat.

The Hall was silent, aside from the small gasp that had escaped my lips, until Gryffin chuckled and lowered his sword. "Very nice, Sir Ezekiel."

Zeke answered with only his usual cocky smirk.

Without hesitation, they returned to their beginning stances and began again. This time, Gryffin was the first to make an offensive move, thrusting his blade toward Zeke's left forearm. Zeke had barely enough time to jump backward and counter with a cut toward Gryffin's waist, which Gryffin deflected.

The shriek of metal clashing upon metal had attracted more bystanders, and the growing crowd had begun to murmur. I heard several groups wagering amongst themselves as to who would win. Zeke's victory in the first round made him a favorite, it seemed, but as this fight continued, Gryffin playing more on the offense, he also began to grow a group of supporters.

Gryffin moved forward again, and with a complicated twist of his arms, he managed to confuse Zeke, who had moved to protect his lower body, while Gryffin arched overhead and brought the hilt of his weapon to float above Zeke's head. No doubt a damaging blow at full force.

Zeke sighed and lowered his sword. "You are no stranger to a sword, yourself." But under his begrudging words, I heard an excited lift to his tone. He was certainly enjoying himself.

Their practices went on for the next hour, each man repeatedly gaining the upper hand. I noticed that Gryffin's style was a bit more grandiose, with more finesse and accuracy in his twirls and twists, which often gave him an advantage. But Zeke's fighting techniques were quick and straightforward, with strong lunges and slashes that frequently outpowered Gryffin's fancy moves. I tried to memorize their different methods and tricks, but my main takeaway was that I would quickly lose a fight against either of them.

Finally, a few of the kitchen workers began moving among the crowd, placing tables around the Great Hall and setting them for supper. Grumbles traveled through the crowd as the gathering slowly dispersed, leaving Zeke and Gryffin standing alone. Both men were panting, sweat gleaming on their faces from exertion.

Gryffin straightened and sighed breathlessly. Sword pointing down behind him, he walked over to Zeke with a smile and outstretched his hand out in front of him. "A fair draw, wouldn't you agree?"

Zeke chuckled and, without hesitation, reached forward and shook Gryffin's hand. "A fair draw."

At that moment, watching the two most important men in my life now, I felt a surge of hope course through me. This moment of true comradery between Zeke and Gryffin, however brief, brought with it an optimism that I couldn't extinguish. Perhaps Zeke *could* be happy after I was married off, if he approved of the man.

But I frowned. It would take more than a fun sword match for Zeke to approve of Gryffin.

The three of us stayed in the Great Hall for supper, seated at the front table always reserved for the royal family. I sat at the head, with Gryffin directly to my right and Zeke seated beside him. I vaguely heard their conversation, discussing Gryffin's sword and its strange black metal and comparing techniques that I should learn, as roasted lamb and salted potatoes were placed in front of us.

Isabele joined us before long, followed by Lisette just moments after. They sat to my left with muted greetings to Zeke and Gryffin. Clara's chair to Lisette's left remained empty.

I looked to Isabele solemnly. "Clara won't be joining us, then?"

Isabele slowly shook her head. "She asked that her meals be taken to her rooms today." She sighed softly. "Poor little sister."

But Lisette had a hard set to her mouth. "I understand that she is grieving, but she should really try to continue on with her day as normal."

I clicked my tongue in disapproval. "Oh, Lisette, come now."

Isabele nodded fervently at my words and turned in her seat to face Lisette. "She's only eight years old," she added. "Sterling was so important to her, and you know that. Please, give her a bit of sympathy!"

"I was only eight when Mama and Papa passed," Lisette immediately shot back. "And I did not spend my days wallowing in my rooms." Her voice broke at the very end, though, and she looked down at the table abruptly.

The table was quiet for a moment, and the only sound was Lisette's fork and knife sliding across her plate, roughly cutting into her slice of lamb.

Isabele and I glanced at each other across the table. We had glimpsed, for the first time, a weakness in Lisette, and it had surfaced because of us.

Surprisingly, Gryffin was the one to break the silence. He hesitantly reached his hand forward and patted Lisette's hand holding the knife. Her knife stopped vigorously tearing the meat apart, and the quiet snuffles she had been so desperately trying to hide could now be heard.

"Everyone grieves in their own manner, Princess," he said quietly.

"Not everyone might be able to pick themselves up and continue on as you did." He smiled reassuringly and retracted his hand.

Zeke followed with his own words of encouragement. "You were always the mature one among this group," he teased. "How about you give Clara at least through Sterling's service? Perhaps that will give her the closure she needs."

I nodded sadly. "Isabele and I are very sorry, Lisette." I looked to Isabele for assistance, but I saw that my sister had her own tears in her eyes. Ah, always the empathetic one.

Isabele began to blubber. "Oh, Lisette, I'm so sorry for being so insensitive! I—I should have—" she broke off in a quiet sob.

I had flashbacks to when our parents had passed, to this exact table, to two sisters crying. Except back then, it was myself and Isabele. Lisette had always been the stoic one. Would this become a replay of the sad memory?

However, from what I could see now, Isabele's outburst seemed to be exactly what Lisette needed. She had always thrived off having to take care of Isabele; that's why the two of them were so in tune with one another. Lisette hugged Isabele tightly, taking on her usual role of holding Isabele together.

I glanced at the two men with a silent thanks. Zeke flashed his smile that I loved, and Gryffin's kind ocean eyes gazed back at me warmly.

The meal returned to its former lighthearted air after that, with Zeke's banter with Lisette over which books in the library were most interesting. Gryffin chimed in a bit, having spent so much time there recently, claiming that the history books were most interesting.

Lisette vehemently disagreed, claiming that the volumes on trading techniques were far superior. Still, Zeke cast a wary glance toward Gryffin at his answer. Oh, for Haggard's sake, was he truly unable to trust Gryffin even with history books? Hoping to distract him, I laughed loudly, claiming that Lisette would make for an excellent queen.

Isabele cast her own vote for the endless supply of stable care books.

"Lecevonia is, after all, the kingdom of horses," she pointed out.

"The kingdom of horses!" Gryffin exclaimed. "Just as Equos intended."

Zeke's ears perked. "Equos? So you pay attention to the legends, as well, then?"

"Unlike Rosemary." Gryffin ran his thumb across the back of my hand with a smirk. "Yes, I believe there are truths to many of them."

"Are these the old nursery tales Mama and Papa used to tell us?" Isabele asked with an interested cock of her head.

"Indeed, they are, Isa," I answered, taking a sip from my wine. "And that is all they are—nursery tales."

"I wouldn't call stories of the Talented bleeding out of their eyes nursey tales," Zeke countered.

"Bleeding out of their eyes?" Lisette chimed in with her own eyes widened.

Zeke took advantage of Lisette's sudden interest. "There is a legend about a Talented man named Morthius. He was Talented with the ability to turn *anything* into gold coins just with his touch, but he used his Talent so often that he bled from his eyes and died of his affliction. It became a word of caution to all those Talented; 'the greedy will bleed while the righteous will heed.'"

Lisette gasped. "*That* is where the old adage comes from?"

"Though I do think that particular legend might be an exaggeration," Gryffin shrugged.

"Thank Haggard that Clara isn't here, after all. You two would be giving her nightmares." I wagged my finger accusingly at Gryffin and

Zeke, though I was feeling too happy to mean it seriously.

At my accusation, Zeke snickered while Gryffin held up his hands amicably.

After a little while longer, with the final bread roll in Zeke's hand, I stood from my chair. My tired legs immediately protested, and the glass of wine I had drunk with my food made my world spin.

"I believe it's time that I go on to bed," I said, a bit ruefully. My good mood from Zeke and Gryffin's comradery still lingered, and my mind was drifting effortlessly like the thick spring clouds that lay over the northern hills. Perhaps the wine was playing a larger role in my mood than I thought.

I walked behind my two sisters and hugged them both around the shoulders. A massive wave of gratitude for my sisters suddenly overcame me, and as I looked at them, I saw the backbone of my support team. I looked back and forth between both of them, and my words were earnest. "I love you. So much. You do know that, yes?"

Isabele squeezed my arm. "Oh, of course, dear sister."

Then, I turned to Gryffin, and immediately I felt a smile spread across my face. "Thank you for your lesson today. Again tomorrow?" The thought of tomorrow, practicing sword in hand, sent a rush of excitement through me. Then, I groaned quietly to myself as I remembered certain queenly duties. "After tomorrow morning's council meeting."

Though that thought threatened to dampen my good spirits, I pushed it away, willing it into tomorrow's worries.

Gryffin chuckled. "That sounds like a wonderful plan, my queen." He reached for my hand and gingerly brought it to his lips.

At that moment, Gryffin's mere presence brought upon me such an immaculate happiness. So strong, that I didn't stop myself from placing my hand on Gryffin's chest, reaching up onto my toes, and kissing his cheek, just above his jaw.

I heard Isabele's quiet gasp, but I didn't care. I only focused on my heart racing in my chest, even just from that quick kiss.

I backed away with a smile. "I will see you tomorrow, then," I reiterated.

Gryffin's returning grin was dazzling. "Tomorrow."

As I turned away from the table, my guards took their positions around me, and we exited the Great Hall in a flourish. I remembered then that Zeke was still here, as a member of my guard, and I turned to him with a smile. But he avoided eye contact with me, looking only straight ahead and more on edge than I'd seen him all day.

I felt my smile turn slightly downward. Perhaps my brief kiss for Gryffin was not a good idea.

Then I shook my head to myself. No, Zeke was being ridiculous. That kiss was hardly anything. He would need to get used to it.

Upon reaching my rooms, I truly began to feel the fatigue of my muscles. With the fuzzy aura still shrouding the corners of my mind, I thanked each of my guards, squeezed Zeke's hand in mine reassuringly for a moment as I passed him, and bid them good night.

CHAPTER ELEVEN

THE SUBDUED SUNLIGHT streaming through my windows surprised me when I woke the next morning. I looked toward my window overlooking the courtyard, past Hazel preparing my tiliarose, and saw only clouds. A thick layer covered the sky, threatening to empty its rain to the ground. I sighed. The stretch of beautiful spring days had ended, making way for the next round of vernal rains that had been looming over the foothills.

I stretched upright in my bed, and my muscles protested as never before. With a pop here and a crack there, I felt as if I had just been out riding Midas for hours on end.

"You are my knight in polished armor, Hazel," I moaned gratefully as she handed me my cup of tiliarose.

I dressed similarly to yesterday's attire, and Hazel had been kind enough to have a new pair of trousers fitted to my size. Though she didn't question my new wardrobe choices, a strained look of worry never left her eyes. Hazel arranged the top half of my hair into a long braid, while the lower half tumbled freely down my back in waves. But while Hazel was turned away to collect my crown, I stealthily slipped a leather band around my wrist. I was sure that I wouldn't want my hair flying around my face while swords swung through the air.

When I exited my rooms, I found that my old round of guards had returned, excluding Geoffrey. Zeke stood in his place, instead.

Zeke was *still* here? I just barely grazed my friend's hand as we began our trek down to the council room, and I narrowed my eyes accusingly. "You need sleep."

But I noticed that, despite being awake all night, he didn't seem tired. His brown eyes were alert, his tone chipper when he responded, "I'm all right, Rose. My shift ends this evening." He winked at me with a waggle of his eyebrows. "We *are* trained to function off little sleep, you know."

I rolled my eyes at his little joke. "I'm sure."

With a heavy sigh, I paused before the dark doors of the council room, and an all-too-familiar terror began to set in. My waiting game might be over now.

I felt Zeke gently squeeze my shoulder, and he leaned in close to my ear. "Remember, you don't realize how strong you are," he whispered.

I offered him a thankful smile. "I will try to keep that in mind." Then, I drew my shoulders down, straightened my back, and strode into the council room.

The men were arranged around the large table in the same seats as before, and when I entered the room, all the men stood in greeting.

"Good morning," I bowed my head. As I settled into the cushioned chair, I noticed that, like my chambers, the room was darker as the sunlight struggled through the shroud of clouds. I didn't normally put much faith in bad omens, but sometimes that ominous feeling was hard to ignore.

With a deep inhale, I addressed the general, ready to hack through the weeds. "General Gambeson, your report, please."

The General cleared his throat. "As has been conveyed, two thousand troops moved out yesterday morning to our northern borders. Two hundred and fifty men were ordered to keep post in Flecte, to establish a connection between nearest supplies and our base encampment. The rest of the two thousand are currently camped in the forests at the base of the Silver Mountains, in the Beryl Foothills.

"The remaining three thousand have begun their trek at dawn, and they should arrive at the encampment by dawn tomorrow morning. Two hundred and fifty more will stay stationed in Flecte as well."

I nodded. "Excellent. So, four thousand five hundred men are at the ready at the border, then." Four thousand five hundred at the border, four thousand remaining here at the castle, and five hundred stationed in Flecte between the two locations. The good numbers erased a bit of my gloom.

I turned to Colonel Holland. "How is our cavalry?"

"Training nonstop, Your Majesty," he assured. "The horses are in excellent shape, and our men are well skilled."

I nodded again, and then hesitated. "Should we send a number of our cavalry to the border? Just in case?"

"I don't believe that is necessary, Your Majesty," General Gambeson answered. "Once we see Tarasyn's army moving, we can send our cavalry where they are needed. Riding hard, they would be able to make it to the encampment in just six hours. But for now, I believe they should stay near the castle. You and your family are what the assassin's employer is truly after."

I felt my face fall. Once Tarasyn moves? "I take it that our scouts keeping an eye on King Roderich have not had any action to report, then."

Colonel Burnstead was the one to answer my question this time, his face grave. "Two of our scouts returned this morning. You are correct—no movement on Tarasyn's end. They've reported that the areas surrounding the castle and the border were unnervingly quiet."

My hands involuntarily thudded down on the tabletop in frustration. "Quiet? Where would you hide an army of eleven thousand men?" My intense gaze flickered between each of the men around the table.

"He may have divided them among Tarasyn's cities," suggested Colonel Burnstead. "Our scouts reported roughly two thousand men near the capitol. Perhaps the other nine thousand are spread between Borea and surrounding villages." He grunted disdainfully. "In the mountains, it is—unfortunately for us—quite easy to hide an army."

I sighed in annoyance. If a battle did arise, my troops would most definitely be at a disadvantage; foothills were one thing, but snowy, forested mountains? That was something that no one in Lecevonia was used to. "Can we send our scouts to the cities?"

Colonel Burnstead nodded. "One step ahead, Your Majesty. Six of the nine remaining scout teams on Tarasynian land are headed to Borea as we speak. The other three are to stay near the capitol."

"And anything of the assassin's message?"

"We've only found one phrase in the assassin's scroll, 'at first light,' but there is nothing incriminating as of yet. The cipher is proving . . . complex."

I felt my frustration rising even still. "If there haven't been any movements, are we still almost certain that King Roderich is behind the assassination attempts?" I questioned heatedly. "What if our focus is in the wrong place?"

Colonel Burnstead grimaced. "I assure you, Your Majesty, you are not the only one frustrated. King Roderich has been hiding his tracks well—even I can admit that. But as I said, Tarasynian action has been *unnervingly* quiet. Even movement inside the castle itself is still." He looked down to the table, a look of concentration on his face. "Our scouts report that hardly any firelight comes from inside the castle walls, even in the evening. What are they *doing* in there?" His voice grew quiet as he asked himself this painstakingly unanswered question. With an exasperated grunt, he shot his gaze to me once more. "Something just is not right, Your Majesty."

"Perhaps they are preparing for a massive move?" Colonel Holland offered. "Their troops may be stationed in the surrounding cities to protect the citizens from backlash. Or—" Suddenly, his eyes were calculating. "To perhaps launch from those cities into action against us." He snapped his head to the left, meeting General Gambeson's stare. "Imagine it. Attack with their small two-thousand-man section of the army, retreat, and entice our troops to advance onto their turf. They would have the upper hand in the mountains, and our cavalry would be almost useless."

General Gambeson folded his hands in front of him, his thick gray eyebrows furrowed. "That would be an effective battle plan on Tarasyn's end."

I could paint the picture so easily in my mind: eleven thousand men hidden throughout the dense forests of the Silver Mountains, picking off my troops one by one. Frostbite would take care of the men they missed. I shuddered, as if the snowy gusts of wind were whipping around my own body. "Our men would not survive a battle in the mountains. We must command them to fall back into the foothills— entice Tarasyn's army onto *our* land."

"Onto our land!" Lord Quince gasped. "Surely, not!"

But General Gambeson nodded slowly. "I would normally oppose inviting a war inside Lecevonian borders, but the alternative is too grave." He maintained firm eye contact with me. "But I must warn you—our countryside may suffer if we bring the fighting here."

"Then we won't let them get to the countryside," I insisted. "Our men will hold at the border, until the remainder of our army and cavalry can arrive."

Even as I said this, I knew it was no guarantee; if our army could not hold back eleven thousand men at the border, the northern hills would be the next obvious hit. And they *would* be hit, hard. Stables and produce farms pillaged, wheat fields burned to stubble, my people—the backbone of this kingdom—hunkered down in their small stone houses with their families. And that was only the best possible scenario.

But I couldn't let my entire army be decimated in the mountains of Tarasyn.

I leaned back in my seat before continuing, not as adamant as before. "And this is all, of course, if Tarasyn strikes against our men first. Correct?" I looked back and forth between the officers.

"Indeed, Your Majesty," answered General Gambeson. "We will not spark an attack without provocation, nor without your approval."

I let out a long exhale. Sitting here in a reaction state did not sit well with me.

Lord Brock cleared his throat. "Perhaps, Your Majesty, we should send some word of warning to Hiddon? They share a border with Tarasyn as well."

Hiddon! Of course!

"Lord Brock, you are a mastermind!" It's been a few months since we've had any contact with them; perhaps they may have even noticed some unusual activity at their northern border. What an opportunity to build relations, and I had nearly missed it! I grumbled internally, chagrined with myself.

I turned to Colonel Burnstead. "Would it be possible to send out the two scouts that have returned to Hiddon?"

Colonel Burnstead seemed to take a mental stock of his men before nodding slowly. "That shouldn't be a problem, Your Majesty. I believe the eighteen scouts left in Tarasyn can handle sending any news that may arise on their end."

I smiled widely. "I will have a note for King Theon and Queen Alys ready by noon today. How long is the ride to Hiddon's capitol?"

"About a day and a half. Around twenty riding hours."

"Excellent. We may hear news within the next three days, then."

Another thought returned to me then, but I sank back into my chair, doubting if I should even voice it. Surely, no one would agree with me.

But I couldn't stop myself.

"Perhaps Prince Gryffin would have some insight on Tarasyn's strategies?"

For a split second, a heavy silence hung around the table. Then a chorus of voices spoke over one another.

"I don't think we should involve the prince, Your Majesty—"

"Can you be sure that he is loyal to Lecevonia? His home kingdom—"

"He would never betray his own brother—"

I held up my hand, palm out, to silence the men. "I trust him. Why not?"

Lord Clark spoke quietly. "You are right in thinking that he may very well have some idea of how his brother would lead their army. But, Your Majesty, even though you are sure that Prince Gryffin is unaware of his brother's actions, can you be sure that he would side with Lecevonia?"

I replayed Gryffin's words in my head, that Lecevonia was a kingdom worth protecting. Lord Clark did have a point, though. Would Gryffin still stand by his words if he knew that the danger to Lecevonia was very likely his own kingdom?

I sighed. "We cannot keep this information from him much longer."

"And if he decides to leave?" Lord Quince inquired.

Lord Castor cut in before I could answer. "You know that we cannot allow that, Your Majesty. He would become a prisoner."

"He could immediately be a liability," agreed Lord Brock. His voice held a tinge of disappointment. "The risk is too great."

I dropped my head into my hands. There seemed no way around it, then. Gryffin would eventually discover Lecevonia's allegations against Tarasyn, and he would either side with Lecevonia, or remain in the castle as a prisoner. Those were the only two possible outcomes.

I sighed heavily and lifted my head. "Of course," I relented. "We will continue to keep him out of the conflict as long as possible."

Finally, I turned to Lord Quince. "Are all the details in place for Mister Carfale's memorial service tomorrow morning?" I struggled to keep my voice strong, unwavering.

My advisor nodded somberly. "Yes, Your Majesty. Though, seeing the clouds that are moving in, the service may have to be held in the Great Hall rather than the courtyard." He pursed his lips, clearly displeased with the notion.

But I shook my head. "We can have canopies set up if needed. Mister Carfale would have liked his service to be among the rose bushes and peonies."

As Lord Quince jotted this note down with his quill, I stood from my seat. "Thank you all once again, gentlemen. I expect we will meet again once our scouts return to us?"

"We expect all eighteen of our scouts in Tarasyn to return to us in one week, give or take a day or two," answered Colonel Burnstead. "The length of their assignment depends on the information they find."

"Our men traveling to Hiddon may be back before then, Your Majesty," General Gambeson stated.

"All right. We will all reconvene then." I bowed my head to them once more. "I truly appreciate the work each of you do. Please, reiterate my thanks to our men in the field as well. Keep well." I smiled at them all before exiting the council room.

I leaned my head against the heavy doors and looked up toward the ceiling. In my line of vision, a candelabrum mounted on the stone wall lit the corridor with its flickering candles.

I truly hated keeping this much from Gryffin. He *would* discover our thoughts, our accusations, somehow. And then what? Would he despise me for keeping such pertinent information from him? Would he wish, ultimately, to return to Tarasyn? I tried to imagine how I would feel, if Lecevonia were the one attacking an unsuspecting kingdom. Would I side with my family and want to return home? And, deep in my mind, I knew the answer would probably be yes.

As I watched the small tongues of fire dancing in the drafty hall, I let out a sigh. Just as the little flames withstood the gusts of wind, I would handle my own gusts as they came.

I pushed myself off the door and found my guards already in their positions, with Zeke looking at me with a worried gaze. As we began walking back to my rooms, he sidled his way beside me.

"How did it go?"

I glanced at him through my periphery. "Well, I believe. And then not so much. We were productive in discussing strategy at the border, but it is still all precautionary. Our *neighbor*," I whispered cryptically, to avoid giving too much away to any wandering ears, "has not given us much information."

"Hmph," Zeke mumbled. "Why precautionary? Why not act first? We may have surprise on our end as an advantage."

"I don't *want* a war, Zeke. Especially with Gryffin's brother. But," I said, against Zeke's protests, "at least we are prepared. We're sending a couple of scouts to Hiddon to ask if they have seen any strange activity on their end."

"Hiddon! I haven't been to Hiddon in ages!"

I narrowed my eyes as we rounded the last corner to my chambers. "Your guard shift does not end until tonight. Don't get any ideas."

He relented, holding his hands in front of him peaceably. "I promised I'd stay until Sterling's service."

Still, I hinted a longing in his voice, and I was reminded that it was in fact *very* selfish to ask him to stay in the castle.

Upon entering my rooms, I walked immediately to my office desk and slid a piece of parchment in front of me, dipped my quill into my inkwell, and began scratching onto the paper.

King Theon DeGrey of Hiddon, and Queen Alys,

I do hope that you both are well.

As Lecevonia is learning more of the kingdom of Tarasyn, we have growing concerns regarding their intent toward their neighboring kingdoms. As we each share a border with Tarasyn, I desired to inquire about any activity you may have noted. If there is any news at all that you may be able to share, I would be grateful.

I hope that we may be able to continue correspondence once again as in the past, and I wish that we may gather again soon.

I paused for a second, quill hovering over the parchment. Was this too serious? I knew it was of course a serious matter, but I hadn't spoken to King Theon or Queen Alys in such a long time. So, I decided to send along a bit more comradery. I'd arrange it with my advisors.

Please, accept this wine as a token of thanks and well wishes.

Warmest regards, Queen Rosemary Avelia of Lecevonia

There. Concise and direct.

I folded the parchment and sealed it with a dab of molten wax, pressing Lecevonia's coat of arms into the yielding blue drop.

After handing off my letter to my advisors, I turned to Zeke and smiled. "Ready to continue my lessons?"

From my entourage of guards, Amos exclaimed, "Ah! So, it's true! We heard that the queen was learning self-defense." He side-eyed me with an approving wink.

I laughed. Amos was definitely my favorite. "I'm sure you and Thomas can show me how it's done, as well," I promised, returning his wink.

We made our way to the Great Hall, the rest of my guards arguing over which moves were most important for a beginning swordsman. When we entered the open room, the clamor of a hundred voices took me by surprise. I then guessed that, as Celeste always said, word had very effectively traveled.

Gryffin was already there, lunging at the empty air with his sword. He smiled widely and bowed as we approached. "Perfect! I was hoping that my opponent would show soon." But he was eyeing Zeke, and I was suddenly sure that Gryffin had not been talking about me.

Gryffin took my hand in his and brought it to his lips. "Mmm," he murmured, and his eyes shifted upward to glance at me. "Good morning, Rosemary."

I felt a flirtatious smile spread across my face. "Good morning, Gryffin."

But he didn't stop after his initial kiss. The tip of his nose brushed my skin as he planted his lips lightly and quickly several more times, up to my wrist, before releasing my hand. Goosebumps had involuntarily risen on my arms, and I was grateful for the convenient sleeves of the tunic.

Despite my internal fluster, I managed a bright laugh and clapped my hands together in front of me. "What's your lesson plan for today?"

"Well," he began, wrapping his arm lightly around my waist and leading me forward, "I suppose we should review the stances we practiced yesterday. Then perhaps, very slowly, we could begin practicing a bit of one-on-one combat?" He ended his sentence as if it were a question. He was leaving it up to me.

Though the thought initially terrified me, I steeled myself. My father, and every ruler before him, knew how to defend himself with a sword. Why should I be an exception?

But before I could answer, Zeke interjected with a brazen snort.

"Of course she should practice one-on-one combat. She can't be left to defend herself with only theory."

Gryffin turned his head to face Zeke, a mischievous smile on his lips. "Maybe a few more examples before then?"

Zeke narrowed his eyes combatively. "I am always ready for a competition," he responded, already reaching for the hilt of his sword at his waist.

"Excuse me," I interrupted them, "are we here so that I may learn or so that you two can have playtime?"

The two men, both leaning toward each other eagerly, straightened and looked at me. Zeke grumbled something imprudently while Gryffin cleared his throat.

"Indeed, my Rosemary." Then he pointed his index finger at Zeke. "Later, you and I will see definitively who the better fighter is." His promise was threatening, but I wasn't sure if his smile could grow any larger.

Then he held out his hand and motioned me forward. "All right, let's review our stances."

For the next hour, I maneuvered my way through each of the guards I had been taught, even making new lunges and blocks every so often. I found that the sword felt more comfortable in my hands today, but my muscles screamed relentlessly for the first fifteen minutes of the practice. Eventually, their piercing throb settled into the background as a stubborn but manageable ache.

Being more comfortable with my weapon meant a bit more bravery surged through me today, and I dared to try a few of the twisting moves that I observed Gryffin perform yesterday. I found that I could more easily predict where my imaginary opponent's sword may be, and I would parry with an offensive move of my own. With every successful thrust of my blade, my sense of vulnerability lessened. All the while, Gryffin's words coached me, with suggestions and approval taking turns.

At one point, he had come forward and placed his hands on my hips, claiming that my stance wasn't aligned properly, and Zeke had yelled from his seat accusing Gryffin of distracting his opponent.

Gryffin chuckled quietly in my ear. "I will have him to contend with for the rest of my life, won't I?"

"He means well," I responded softly. I lowered my voice an octave.

"Maybe he's right, though. Perhaps you *are* trying to distract me." My eyes met his, and my gaze held him there.

Just long enough for me to twist out of his hands and, from my right ochs, thrust my blade near his left ear.

A gasp ran through the Hall as the small, gathered crowd watched from the sidelines.

Gryffin stared at me, his ocean eyes completely shocked. Then, as he registered what I'd done, a smile spread across his face.

An energetic murmur now traveled through the room, a joyful buzz, as if the crowd were on the verge of applause.

Gryffin pressed his lips together in approval and nodded. "Excellent, my Rosemary." I thought I might have heard a bit of pride in his voice. "So, I take it that you feel ready to get into some actual practice now?"

I answered only with a devilish grin, standing at the ready in my best plough guard.

But the air of the room had changed.

My guards were all on their feet, standing tense. Zeke had his arms tight across his chest, his face hard-set. The crowd that had been so joyous and excited just a moment ago now emitted waves of wariness, urgent whispers flowing through the people.

I didn't understand what had caused such a shift in the atmosphere, but Gryffin cleared his throat and slowly sheathed his sword.

"Perhaps, one of your guards would like to practice with you? I believe that I may be more helpful as an observer—you know, so that I may coach you to victory." He smiled teasingly at me, but his eyes were tight.

Then I understood. To my people, facing off with Gryffin would not have been acceptable. He, a foreign guest, could not be allowed to pick up a sword against the queen. My guards surely would have had to intervene to stop him, even if this was merely practice. I huffed out a displeased exhale. I trusted Gryffin entirely. And I trusted my judgement.

But no one seemed to do the same.

Fine. Once I told my advisors that I'd chosen Gryffin as my king consort, the kingdom's attitude toward him would change. So, I would comply today, to keep peace. I looked to my guards, expecting Zeke to be the first to answer.

But he stayed silent, arms crossed over his chest. He wouldn't meet my eyes.

How strange.

Instead, Amos stepped forward. His voice strived for ease as he said enthusiastically, "I'll take the challenge!"

He stopped to stand in front of me, and I smiled at him gratefully.

He returned my smile with a mischievous grin of his own. "Let's test your skills, then, my queen."

We both stood at the ready, and I began to analyze.

Amos, of course, looked much more comfortable than I felt, with his practiced sword hovering lightly in front of his body. I decided that I would wait for him to make the first offensive move. He was quite a lot taller than me, so I figured I should most likely focus on lower targets—his legs, his abdomen. And, of course, his stature was much broader than mine. Not as starkly drastic as Roger's frame but still enough of a difference. I doubted I would be able to get around him in any way. So, I focused on his front.

Why hadn't he made a move yet?

I decided to feign a thrust to the right. He moved only slightly, but he quickly saw through my trick.

I had to be more convincing, then.

I slashed my sword to the left, with more fervor than last time, pulling back just before I would have had to commit to the full swing.

This time, Amos went for it. He moved his sword to block, leaving his left side undefended. I lifted my sword above my head, ready to slash downward toward his arm, but I hadn't done this move before. I didn't realize the amount of time it would take to heave the weapon above my head, and I lost my advantage. Amos recovered quickly and moved to cover. A loud clang echoed off the stone walls as our swords clashed. Then he moved from his defensive stance and thrust toward my right shoulder.

As I saw the blade plunging fast toward me, a flurry of adrenaline sharpened my mind. I felt as if I could feel the pressure of air changing around me as death—or, so it would have been if it weren't Amos's sword—fell closer. Without truly thinking about it, I twisted to the left, swiveling out of my opponent's sword's reach, and my weapon whipped around with me. I heard Gryffin's shouts of praise, and I smiled wildly. Excitement fluttered through my stomach as I faced Amos head-on again, my weapon at the ready.

This time, the adrenaline had raised my confidence enough for me to make the offensive move. I stepped toward Amos in a right ochs, intending to lunge toward his abdomen.

But my move must have been too obvious, for Amos adopted a left ochs stance and deflected my blade with an easy adjustment. And, before I could think of my next tactic, he slid his weapon free, blades running together in a deafening shriek, and jabbed toward the side of my neck.

There his blade hovered, and I knew I had lost.

I exhaled and lowered my sword to the ground.

Amos smiled and removed his sword from my neck. Experience had won this time.

But that didn't stop Gryffin's praise. He approached us with bright eyes. "Excellent job, Rosemary!" In his excitement, he grabbed my free hand, planted an enthusiastic kiss on my thumb, and held my hand tightly to his chest. "Your feint in the beginning was fantastic. And the twist away from his attack? Phenomenal!"

I laughed, his eagerness leaching into my own mood and leaving me giddy even after he'd released my hand.

Even Zeke had seemed to recover; he walked over and hugged me around the shoulders with one arm. "You really did well, especially as your first time facing someone else." He smiled at me and rubbed my upper arm with his hand. "But remember, never forget to have your own back. Protecting yourself should *always* be your first priority." He squeezed my arm softly.

I nodded admittedly. "You're right. I did get a little too caught up in my offensive move."

"Still, well done," he said, his smile proud.

Then I turned back to Amos. He was standing casually, his weight shifted on his right leg, his sword nonchalantly tucked underneath his arm. "Again?" I requested.

But Gryffin stepped in. "Why don't you take a rest, Rosemary?"

"I'm fine," I countered. Really, I felt as if I could fight ten more rounds. I'd never had so much energy!

Still, Gryffin shook his head. "I'd like you to see a multiple attack." He looked to Zeke and Amos. "Would you two like to demonstrate with me?"

The hours passed, and I watched as Gryffin demonstrated different strategies in fending off multiple attackers. Keep eyes on both at all times, but remember that only one can be a target at a time. Judge which attacker is most prevalent in that instant, and act. And always, self-defense is first.

Gryffin and Zeke even got in a few more solo rounds, and I found

I enjoyed watching them. Their movements were mesmerizing in a way, with Gryffin's finesse and Zeke's swiftness. Gryffin seemed to twist his weapon and his body effortlessly out of Zeke's strike, but then Zeke's sword would quickly find a new target. Or Zeke's direct movements would seem impossibly fast, but they would be a bit too predictable; Gryffin could twist his way into making his mark.

Their fighting styles reminded me of their personalities. Zeke lived by the seat of his pants, and Gryffin, from his gestures to his phrasing to his mere voice, was always smooth. As I studied both of them, I let myself forget the turmoil with Tarasyn, the dangers my life now faced. I dared to find a moment's peace.

Our practice took us to supper before I had a chance to go one-to-one with Amos again, which I had a feeling was on purpose. And after dinner, I kissed Gryffin on the cheek again as a good night. This time, he leaned into it with a smile.

Then his smile turned sad, and his voice lowered to something more subdued. "Perhaps tomorrow we take a break from our practice, yes?"

My good mood quickly began to dissipate as several emotions flooded into my mind—returning grief, guilt, sadness.

Tomorrow morning would be Sterling's funeral service.

I looked down to the floor. The wine from dinner battled against these emotions, trying to give each of them fuzzy edges. "Yes, perhaps we should put off any lessons for a few days."

Gryffin placed his finger under my chin and lifted my face to his again. His ocean eyes delved into my emerald ones, emanating sorrow and sympathy.

I could have kissed him then. Even in the middle of the Great Hall, in front of my sisters, I could have easily leaned into him and closed the inches that stood between us now. And I found that, truly, I wanted to. I wanted to feel his warm lips on mine, his arms holding me to his chest. I wanted to feel as I had during Clara's party, before everything had started to shatter around me. I wanted to feel something other than sadness.

But instead, I only let out a small sigh. I would not do that here. My advisors would about have a heart attack. And Hazel! Goodness, Hazel would surely have a fit.

Instead, I grasped Gryffin's hand once more, just for a moment, holding on to the feeling as long as I dared, until, finally, I had to turn away from him. "Good night, Gryffin."

"Good night, my Rosemary," he murmured after me. His deep voice sounded as if he were trying to hold on to that moment too.

CHAPTER TWELVE

THE KNOCK UPON my chamber door startled me, tearing me away from my book and back to the present of my study. The wine tonight was still lingering, feathering the edges of my mind, so I had been trying to will it away before lying down for the night.

I placed the ribbon to mark my page and laid the book down beside me on the bench before straightening into a seat and tightening my blanket over my night shift. I heard Hazel open my door and mutter something quietly to whoever was on the other side.

Then I heard Hazel's resigned sigh, and that gave me an idea of who my visitor might be.

I smiled widely and rose from the bench, though my head spun a little, as I heard Hazel close the door, the click of the latch catching. The sound of boots across the stone floor thumped closer, and Zeke appeared through the doors of my study.

At my smile, Zeke chuckled. "Why are you always so pleased to see me, Rose?"

"Because," I began, extending my hand to him, "as irritating as you can be, you are . . . a light." A light? Yes, that seemed right. At least, I thought it did.

Zeke froze for a second, narrowing his eyes with a skeptical grin. "A light, huh?"

"Mhmm," I murmured. "You are a light, and you are always casting your beams through the haze." But, with Zeke's scrunched eyes still looking at me in cynicism, I sighed and sat back down on the bench. "Never mind, I don't know what I'm saying. Just babbling, I suppose. It's the wine." I shook my head, trying to clear my own haze, and looked up at my friend again. "Done with your shift?"

Zeke picked up my book and sat beside me in its place. "Feel free to babble—I believe you were giving me a compliment." He smiled smugly, his brown eyes glinting from the candlelight. "And yes, I'm relieved for the night."

"Good. You need sleep."

"Rose, don't you remember? We can perform off hardly any sleep." He winked.

Now that it was only him and me, with Hazel rummaging around in my bedroom, I punched him in the shoulder as I had wanted to in the Great Hall.

Zeke, unable to control his laughter, held up his hands in surrender. "All right, no teasing." He held out the book I had been reading. "*Haggard and the Five Talented, and Other Tales.* Some light bedtime stories before you sleep?" he joked.

"Just passing the time as I wait for my head to clear a little," I said. "I don't know if my brain would be able to handle any heavier information at the moment."

He leaned his back against the wall. "I thought you scoffed at the thought of magic."

"I couldn't stop thinking about that story you told during supper yesterday. And then, there was something Gryffin said the other day, about Tarasyn being in tune with their magical past—it's made me curious, I suppose."

"'In tune' with magic is an understatement," he muttered.

I jolted upright. "What do you mean? Have you seen someone Talented?"

"No, no." He shook his head and widened his eyes incredulously. "To see the first Talented in three hundred years—I wouldn't keep that to myself! No, I haven't had contact with any Tarasynian during my assignments. But Tarasyn has . . . a different feel to it." His voice lowered. "The whole place seems to *ring* with something. Some sort of pressure, some . . . vibration through the air." His eyes glazed as he seemed to struggle to describe his memory. "Their forests almost feel alive with it."

I tried to comprehend his words, to imagine that feeling of a different gravity—a different force than what I felt here. But I was trying to make my muddled mind do too much. "Well, that last bit makes sense, after all, since Viridi's Talent was to control plant growth," I mumbled, lost in thought.

Zeke shook his head. "I suppose you're right," he said, his voice lightening again. "You're doing amazingly, by the way. With the sword lessons. And the wardrobe change?" He winked. "Breathtaking."

I rolled my eyes. "Thank you *so* very much, Zeke," I said, sarcastically batting my eyelashes at him.

"I mean it. You're doing very well. What made you want to learn?"

I shifted uncomfortably. I still felt embarrassed by my nightmare. But this was Zeke. I could tell him anything. "I had a dream about the archer in the woods. The assassin. I couldn't defend myself. It was a never-ending struggle . . . I never want to feel that way again. So, I asked

Gryffin for help.”

He pouted. “Why didn’t you ask me?”

“Well, I didn’t know that you were still here,” I said, poking him in the shoulder. “I thought that you had gone with the other scouts, the night before, to Tarasyn.”

“Ah.” He sat thoughtfully for a moment. “You know, I would have told you if I were leaving.”

“Well. You didn’t last time, to hunt the archer.”

He pursed his lips, then bowed his head once. “Fair enough.”

I turned to him, suddenly remembering. “Why didn’t you want to practice with me?”

He looked at me, puzzled.

“Sword fighting. Since you enjoy it so much with Gryffin, I assumed that you would’ve been the first one to volunteer.”

“Ah.” He frowned, his eyebrows knitting together, seeming to think of his answer. “I couldn’t envision you as an opponent. Scrutinizing different maneuvers to defeat you—I just couldn’t do it. Whereas Gryffin”—his tone lightened again with a chuckle—“well, he’s easy to see as an opponent.”

I slowly nodded my head. Of course he would be.

Then he shifted, clearing his throat. “Speaking of Gryffin, that is actually why I’ve come tonight.” His gaze dropped to the floor.

My back stiffened. Frankly, I was not in the mood for one of Zeke’s sermons, nor did I have the energy to fight with him tonight. “Zeke, I don’t want to hear your opinion—”

“It isn’t what you expect.”

So, with a sigh, I rigidly folded my hands in my lap. “Go on, then.”

After a moment, he turned his brown eyes on me again. “He is a good man,” he admitted.

That was enough to make my eyes widen. But as I was about to ask him what on earth had changed his mind, he laughed and placed a finger on my lips to stop me. "Don't say anything quite yet." He held his finger there until I relaxed from a bit of my rigidity. Then he lowered his hand, absentmindedly opting to take my hands into his.

"He is a good man," he repeated, "and I can see now that he cares for you. That he wants to protect you. I must admit that . . . my jealousy was partially why I was so stubborn to see that."

I looked away from him then, unable to meet his eyes. I wasn't ready for a conversation about Zeke's feelings toward me. Especially not right now, when I already could not think straight.

Still, he continued, though I could hear that his voice was pitted with pain. Perhaps he had looked away too. "After the last two days, now that I've removed my prejudice and learned who he is as a man, I've accepted that you deserve a man such as Prince Gryffin to be by your side as you rule Lecevonia."

In my silence, my mind roiled in chaos. I wanted to be happy, so utterly happy, that Zeke finally approved of Gryffin. Yet, hearing his acceptance also made me feel unexpectedly hollow. Almost as if I were lost. No, more as if I had lost *something*. Something that I didn't know how to function without.

It didn't make any sense, and my muddled mind sure wasn't helping me figure any of it out.

"This does not mean that I trust Tarasyn," he clarified, unaware of my internal battle. "Not at all. I still have deep reservations regarding the entire kingdom, and I don't believe that Tarasyn is up to anything good. However, if anyone can help you maneuver Tarasynian relations, it would be Prince Gryffin."

I chanced a glance at him, and I found his eyes fixed on my face. I heaved a deep exhale and tightened my hold on one of his hands as I urged myself to speak. But I didn't quite know what to say. So, I spoke of one thing that I knew without a doubt: the deep gratitude I felt. "Zeke, thank you." I turned my face to directly look at him. "I know how hard it must be to try to see Gryffin as I do. And your support is what I truly need. I'm so grateful that you're able to give it to me."

He leaned in and sighed a quiet, pained laugh. "Please, don't thank me, Rose." He brought my hands to his lips and kissed them softly.

Then his eyes flashed. "You are going to tell your advisors tomorrow, yes? After the service?"

I nodded. Had I told him about that? I couldn't remember; my mind was useless right then. I looked down at our hands. "It seemed most appropriate to wait."

Zeke slid one of his hands beneath my chin and lifted my face again. "I'm glad that you thought as much," he said earnestly, his hand drifting to my cheek. A very involuntary jolt coursed through my chest. He leaned a little closer, close enough that I could see the small apricot flecks in his brown eyes. "There is something that I have to do—*want* isn't a strong enough word—before you're a betrothed woman." He chuckled, still leaning closer into me.

Oh, no. "Zeke—"

To my surprise, he froze in his place and closed his eyes. "Please, Rose . . ."

He wouldn't kiss me unless I allowed it.

I shouldn't. I had been so careful, my barriers around the Zeke-corner of my mind so artfully built to withstand any surge of emotion. But the edges of my mind were softened by the wine now, and my barriers felt wooden instead of stone. A small draft flowed through the cracks in the wood, but this wind came from *inside* the Zeke-corner. And this trapped wisp of wind threatened to blow down years of construction.

But here was my best friend, raw and defeated in front of me, giving me exactly what I had wanted—his blessing to marry the man I wanted by my side. Was it fair to keep what *he* wanted away from him? Or would it cause him even further pain? Still, the draft escaping through the wood continued to blow, calling me to drift forward. The wind caressed my hands as I approached the poor, weathered barrier.

Without deciding, I found myself gravitating toward him, leaning forward until I had closed the gap that separated us.

The moment my lips touched Zeke's, a sweet sense of *belonging* blanketed me. A soft moan of relief escaped both of us, and we laughed breathlessly. Zeke's hand remained soft on my cheek, and he brought his other hand to rest on my other cheek, framing my face, holding my lips to his.

The wind whistled louder through the splintered wood.

This kiss was so different than the one I had shared with Gryffin. With Gryffin, the exciting newness of a man's affection had caused heat to rise quickly to my skin and had caused a melting of my resolve, of my barrier to keep any man shut out.

I now realized that I had constructed that barrier, that resolve that Gryffin had melted, out of fear for what I felt for *Zeke*. Subconsciously, I must have been so sure that if any man raised in me even a hint of romantic feelings, my feelings for Zeke would slowly sneak out of their corner. And now, they were. Or rather billowing. Indeed, Gryffin had melted my barrier like butter, but that had only cleared a path for these emotions I'd refused to acknowledge for years.

So, no, this kiss wasn't a melting. Instead, it was a familiar warmth, welcoming me home as if I had always belonged here, in this moment.

The final gust blew the lazy wooden boards of my weakened barrier down to the floor of my mind, and my Zeke-corner gusted through my entire mind, even blowing away the last bit of fog left by the wine.

I curled one hand around Zeke's wrist, and my other gently wound into Zeke's golden hair. I pulled myself closer to him, scooting toward him on the bench until my hip touched his, our legs pressed against each other. I felt his hand softly trail down my shoulder, around my waist, to the small of my back. He pressed his palm lightly against me, and my body bowed against his.

Every emotion, every moment I had tried to tuck away for years now displayed themselves like a peacock, its feathers so ostentatious that it did not seem possible that I had not understood them before. My joy when Zeke walked into any room, my relief when he returned from his assignments, the twist of my stomach every time he took hold of my hand, and even when I was a young girl, when he smiled—these were so much more than friendship.

And my own stubborn dutifulness had made this peace, this liberation so elusive.

Our lips slowed then, and Zeke moved his mouth to my cheek, my jaw, my nose—which caused me to smile as I worked to catch my breath. I caught his lips with my own a couple more times when his traveled too closely on their venture, and I breathed in the sweet scent of Zeke's hair as his lips traced my neck.

Finally, he rested his forehead against mine and breathed a ragged exhale. His hands, so warm against my cheek and my back, held me to him.

We sat like that for a while, and I felt an unimaginable release. I had been denying Zeke for so long, tethering any feelings I may have felt to that very back corner, never to be revisited. Now, with those feelings drifting freely through my mind, I said the words that I had planned to never utter. "I love you, Zeke."

I felt his breathy laugh brush across my face. "I know, perhaps better than you do." He moved his arms down, snaking them around me in a hug, and sighed. "My Rose. I've always loved you too."

Now it was my turn to laugh, and I opened my eyes, boring into his. "I know."

I noticed then that Hazel was silent in the other room. Perhaps she had made an escape. So, I allowed my mind to dream. I allowed myself to picture yet another future.

A future with Zeke.

A wedding ceremony, where I was wearing the same cream gown and carrying the same waterfall of flowers. But now, Zeke stood in a cream-colored vest at the end of the aisle. He looked as handsome as he did every day, and a glorious, triumphant smile claimed his features. And in the Great Hall, there we were sitting in the king and queen's thrones, grasping each other's hands, while a little golden-haired, green eyed boy ran around at our feet. The image brought me a bliss I didn't know was possible.

But the last image was only hazy, not sharp.

Because Zeke could not belong there.

Zeke could never sit upon the king's throne.

Tears stung behind my eyes. "But, Zeke, I cannot marry you."

He closed his eyes. "I know."

And the pain in his voice riddled me to my very core. So much that I felt it too. The injustice of it shook me. Had I been born anyone else, as a kitchen maid, or a stable hand like Celeste, I could marry Zeke. Instead, as Queen, though I knew that so many other luxuries were afforded to me, the luxury of marrying for love was never mine. It had been a silly notion on my part.

"But I cannot marry Gryffin, either." The realization hit me as a mallet meets an anvil, sending fiery sparks flying in every direction.

Zeke opened his eyes, perplexed. "What?"

"I can't marry Gryffin. Not when I feel for you this way." I refused to lose this part of myself, Zeke's part, to my duty.

Zeke leaned back from me. "Rose, is that wine still sloshing around in there?" he asked with a chuckle, rubbing his thumb across my forehead. His hand rested on my cheek.

"I took an oath to dedicate my life to Lecevonia," I said firmly, "and I cannot serve Lecevonia if I feel any hatred toward my kingdom for forcing me into something such as marriage." I felt in my heart that Mama and Papa would have thought the same too. Lecevonia was only as strong as its leader, and if its leader did not feel in control at her strongest, what was the point?

Zeke rolled his eyes. "Oh, yes, your advisors will go for *that* with no trouble."

"They'll have to," I said quietly, leaning into his hand. "I am their queen."

Still, I couldn't ignore a small but relentless tug in my mind, a tug that led me back to the safety and assurance that was Gryffin.

CHAPTER THIRTEEN

THE THICK CLOUDS held their rain just long enough for all of those attending Sterling's funeral service to enter through the castle doors. Thunder had rumbled menacingly throughout the service, and as soon as the thick oak doors thudded shut, the clouds relented to the weight of the rain they held, dropping watery sheets to the ground.

I watched as the Great Hall filled with people, my arms draped over Clara's shoulders in a gentle hug. Silent tears still traveled down Clara's little cheeks, as they had through the entire ceremony. Isabele stood to my right, crying quiet tears of her own, with Lisette next to her. And Gryffin stood to my left, his arm wrapped loosely around my waist. His gentle smile was what held me together now, though in its own way it also made me want to shatter.

Before Zeke had left my rooms the night before, I had stressed that he and I could not be realistically be together, that we should nip this in the bud before neither of us could bare to lose it.

"Even if I wish otherwise," I had amended despondently.

"I know, Rose," he had answered, yet he still grasped my hand to his chest, his eyes closed. "But please, let me just enjoy this while I can."

So we had sat there quietly, Zeke brushing his lips across my palm, my fingertips, my wrist. I had allowed myself to feel at peace in that moment, and I attempted to memorize every feeling there with Zeke that I was able.

And that sealed our kiss as our last.

The wine must have finally drifted me to sleep, because I had then found myself under my sheets in the darkness of early morning, utterly disoriented. Finding Zeke no longer with me had opened a new wound in my chest, and I had turned my head and cried silently into my pillows until the gray light of dawn inched its way through my window.

Then, upon remembering what was happening today, my tears had gushed even more heavily. When Hazel had appeared to start brewing morning tiliarose, my face had been puffy almost beyond recognition.

The beautiful old woman had simply sat on the edge of my bed, her arms wrapped tightly around me. She hadn't even fretted about my face until the time came for me to dress.

So there I stood, in a flowing black gown embroidered with silver peonies, with the light pressure of Gryffin's arm against my waist.

The ceremony really had been nice—everything Sterling would have liked. Even the weather. He loved rain. He had always said that Mother Nature was helping him do his job by watering the flowers.

And Lord Quince had really done well putting the entire thing together, from the flowers to the canopies. Sterling's presence had been so evident in the draping forsythia, the fresh-cut peonies and roses gathered masterfully with greenery in iron vases. Even the rich sky blue of the canopies—I could not fathom how difficult it must have been to dye the leather to that shade of blue—matched the old man's eyes.

I turned my tired gaze to Gryffin. "It's as if Sterling is commanding the weather today."

He offered me a sad smile. "He must know that this day is hard for everyone here. The weather should be the last thing anyone has to worry about." He hugged me a little more closely to him. "You're doing marvelously, Rosemary."

I sighed. "Unfortunately, this family is no stranger to death."

I had said as much in my tribute, my 'Queen's Address,' for Sterling. I had held my tears, kept my voice steady until my final words: *Thank you, Mister Carfale.* Only then had a tear slid quietly down my cheek.

"But, thank you," I added quickly, hoping to sound a bit less morbid.

Gryffin's kind, concerned ocean eyes reminded me that he would have been a good choice. Though I panged for someone else now, I hadn't forgotten how Gryffin made me feel as well. My mind raged in angry torrents of emotion, but what roared most dreadfully was the task of telling Gryffin I could not commit myself to marriage.

Castle workers normally held private ceremonies for their passed loved ones at the home of family members, and the king and queen would have granted any family members a few days' absence to grieve.

But Sterling was different—he *was* family, no matter how unofficially. And he had no family of his own in Lecevonia. I had granted the gardening staff the day off if they chose to take it, and to any worker who wished to attend Sterling's service I had granted pardon. It seemed as if the entirety of the castle were milling around in the Great Hall now.

However, despite the enormous amount of people, the atmosphere was still hushed, subdued. Grieving.

Through the crowd, I saw Lucinda's black hair bouncing as she made her way to the throne. She so dutifully had her little eyes set on Clara.

As Lucinda curtsied to us and held out her hand toward Clara, I felt a surge of gratitude for the little girl. If anyone should be with Clara on this day, it should be Lucinda.

I squeezed Clara's shoulders once more and squatted down to meet my youngest sister's eyes. "You'll be all right?"

Clara nodded—she still hadn't said a word yet today—and hugged me around the neck. Then she tightly took hold of Lucinda's hand, as if it were the only thing tethering her here in this moment, and meandered away with her slowly, toward a table set to our right.

Once Clara was gone, Isabele and Lisette both sighed and let their shoulders fall. I hadn't realized how much grief they also had been hiding. I cast a sad look toward my sisters and wrapped my arms around both of them. "Thank you both, so much," I whispered solemnly. Taking a step back, I kept my hands on my sisters' shoulders. "I think we need today just as Clara does."

Isabele nodded, her eyes glassy. "Mama adored Sterling so much."

"He was the first one to visit all of us after Mama and Papa passed," Lisette murmured, reminiscing. Though she had no tears in her eyes, sadness thickened her voice. She met my eyes with utter sincerity. "We'll be sure to keep an eye on Clara. We know you have so much going on." Then she glanced around the Hall subtly. "Any news on the assassin?"

Isabele reached across me and sharply tapped Lisette's hand. "Now is *not* the time to be asking about this!"

"Why not? The assassin is the reason why we are doing this today!" Lisette's hushed voice had risen, just enough for a few nearby people to glance our way.

I gave them both a warning look, but truthfully, Lisette made a valid point. "No new news, but we are hoping that will change soon." I began calculating in my head, thinking back to when the scouts had left. "Perhaps the day after tomorrow, we may have more defined information."

Lisette sighed. "All right. Just—*please*— keep us updated." Her eyes narrowed, suddenly accusatory. "I feel as if we never know what is happening in the kingdom. We are *not* just castle ornaments. We'd like to be informed too. It's our life and our people in danger too."

I was silent for a moment, eyes widened. I didn't realize that Lisette felt this way. Just a *castle ornament?* Surely not. However, I suddenly realized that a silent little eight-year-old girl no longer stood in front of me, but a woman of fifteen years—and so vastly more mature than that. Lisette had grown before my eyes, and in this moment, I felt as if I had completely missed it. I felt my face soften as I answered, "Yes, of course. I'm sorry, Lisette."

Lisette nodded once and wrapped her arms around me. As she stepped away, she looked to Isabele. "Ready?" she asked, extending her hand.

Isabele squeezed Lisette's hand but let it drop to her side after a moment. "I'll follow you in a minute." She turned back to me. "Can I talk to you later?" Her eyes flickered toward Gryffin, seemingly subconsciously. He was still standing with me, just a few paces back, but he wouldn't have been able to hear my sister's hushed voice. Her tone sounded urgent, and I tried to understand what was running through my sister's mind; but in this rare instant, Isabele's face was unreadable.

Though confused, I took Isabele's hand in my own. "Of course. After the guests leave?"

Isabele dipped her head once in agreement, and after giving me one last tight hug, she trailed after Lisette into the crowd.

I sighed and turned toward Gryffin again. He had been quietly observing the Great Hall, now filled with everyone from the courtyard. The table of food was quickly being scoured, and I eyed a few blueberry pastries in passing hands.

Gryffin turned toward me then with a small smile and took hold of my hand. "How are you?"

"I am holding myself together," I answered honestly. "I can feel Sterling's influence in almost everything. It's as if he put this entire morning together himself. It makes it harder to forget that . . . that he isn't here anymore." With a deep sigh, I added, "And I must be honest, I'm dying to try one of those blueberry pastries."

He chuckled and kissed my hand. "I bet we can work our way down there."

As always, people bowed or curtsied as we passed through the subdued crowd, and I lowered my head to them in acknowledgement.

As we walked, I squeezed Gryffin's arm. "Thank you for being here," I said sincerely. And I knew that Zeke was here too, somewhere, supporting me from afar. Even as I scanned the faces around me now, I did not find his familiar brown eyes.

However, I did find Celeste. She was walking toward us, carrying a few beloved blueberry pastries in her hands. When she reached us, she curtsied and met my eyes with a consoling smile. She handed one of the pastries to Gryffin with a quiet, "For you," and then turned and hugged me tightly around the shoulders.

"Oh, my Rosie," she murmured. "I'd ask how you are doing, but I imagine you're getting tired of that question. And besides," she released me and handed me one of the pastries, "I wouldn't like having to lie and say, 'I'm all right,' repeatedly, either."

I chuckled quietly. "Thank you, Celeste." I felt my mood lifting; it had been days since I'd been able to go down to the stables and visit. Not since the archer in the woods. The warm blueberry pastry in my hand also helped my spirit, and I treasured the soft bread and sweet, gooey berries in my first bite.

"How is Midas?" I asked. My voice cracked under a little surge of guilt. Poor Midas probably felt neglected by now.

"He's all right, cranky as ever when he gets lonely. I try to take him out at least once a day." Celeste shrugged. There was no accusation in her voice, but the way she had said it as if it were just another fact made me feel guiltier. Perhaps I could chance a walk out to the stable soon.

But a ride was still out of the question.

Just then, the familiar brown eyes I had been searching for made their way toward us through the mass of people.

Our eyes met for just a short second before I had to drop my gaze. The new wound in my chest throbbed from the harsh thudding of my heart.

Zeke's boots clicked to a stop in front of us. "Rosemary, Gryffin," I heard him greet us. "And beautiful Celeste!"

Steeling myself, I glanced up, in time to see Celeste roll her eyes.

"Hello, Ezekiel. Still the flirt, I gather," Celeste answered as Zeke lightly kissed her hand.

Zeke was much better at this than I was. Granted, he had years of practice hiding his emotions. So, I forced myself to smile. "I'm fairly confident that he won't ever change," I teased.

Nothing had changed for Zeke last night. He had always known his feelings. His days would go on just as they always had—suppressing his love behind an arrogant smile.

But everything had changed for me.

At least I had the excuse of Sterling's service to be scatterbrained, which in itself was not a complete lie.

Zeke exhaled heavily. "What a morning."

Celeste nodded in somber agreement. "Sterling had been around here so much longer than any of us," she said with a sigh. "It's odd glancing toward the courtyard and not spotting him clipping the rose bushes or sweeping leaves off the pathway."

"Or dancing with little Clara," Zeke said with a chuckle.

"Even in the short time I had known him, I could instantly tell that he had a kind mind," Gryffin commented gently, adding in his own fond memory.

"My mother adored Sterling, you know," I said quietly, my gaze drifting toward the far wall, out the window to the rain. "When my mother moved to Hillstone after marrying my father, Sterling had come with her from Somora."

"Truly?" Gryffin asked, his tone incredulous. "A gardener accompanied the princess? Not a guard?"

I shrugged. "Mama had apparently been close to Sterling since she was a little girl. Like my grandmother, my mother loved plants, especially flowers and herbs. So, she had always been in their castle's courtyard, often in Sterling's shadow while he worked. So much so that my grandparents had offered for Sterling to accompany her here, to Lecevonia, should Sterling wish. And he did, 'without a doubt,' as Sterling had always said." I turned my eyes back to our little group with a small smile.

"I wonder what of his family," Gryffin continued to inquire. "Did he have a wife and kids?"

I answered with a nonchalant shake of my head. "None that he ever mentioned."

"How odd," Gryffin muttered, gaze drifting off, now in thought.

I pursed my lips. I had never thought so—it was simply a story that my parents had always told me. I had always found it endearing but nothing more.

Gryffin's eyes returned to mine. "King Merek is your uncle, yes? He's rather old."

I nodded, confused by his question. "My mother was born seventeen years after him."

"Seventeen years!" Gryffin's eyes widened. "And the princes of Somora are your cousins, albeit much older than you."

"Indeed," I said, my nose wrinkling as I once again remembered my recent visit with Prince Hirum. But now I was getting suspicious. "How is this relevant?"

Gryffin grinned. "I'm just speculating. It's probably nothing."

"Well, now you have to tell us," Celeste interjected. "What are you thinking?"

Gryffin pursed his lips. "Sterling had no family of his own, correct? And your grandparents sent him away with your mother, who is so much younger than her *only* brother. And you've been told that your grandmother loved the gardens . . ."

Zeke seemed to catch on first to whatever Gryffin was insinuating, and he snorted. "Not a chance."

"What?" Celeste and I questioned at the same time.

"Though, now that you put it in such a way . . ." Zeke allowed.

That was when I realized what Gryffin had been implying. "No! You think that my grandmother might have had an *affair* with Sterling? I . . ." But, as I thought further, even *I* couldn't deny the possibility. My mother was so much younger than Uncle Merek, and sending off Sterling with my mother . . . well, it could have been an easy way to rid my grandparents of the daily reminder of my grandmother's actions. "But—then that would make Sterling our *grandfather*!"

Celeste burst into laughter. "This is the best part about funerals."

"What? Lifelong secrets coming to the surface?" Zeke chortled.

"No! Why are you laughing? This is madness!" I exclaimed. Sterling, my grandfather? And Isabele's and Lisette's, and Clara's . . .

Ah, little Clara. My heart softened as my little sister's bouncing ringlets danced across my thoughts. Clara had not had just a father figure, but an actual grandfather. Maybe we all had.

And as I thought about it more, the less incredulous I felt. It did possibly explain how Uncle Merek was the *only* heir, and how Sterling had been more than happy to accompany my mother anywhere.

Now there was no wonder why Sterling had loved us all so much.

I had believed that I had never met my grandparents—the king and queen of Somora had both passed when I was just a child. Now, to think that my own grandfather might have been here, at the castle . . .

"But wouldn't this change *something*? Possibly even my right to the throne?" My mind began on a downward spiral. My royal heritage could be in question all due to, however amazing of a man Sterling may have been, a commoner.

"Does it, really, though?" Zeke asked. "I mean, Queen Ryia was still a royal princess, though maybe half-so. Her mother, your grandmother, was still queen."

Gryffin nodded in agreement. "Of course, Rosemary. You and your sisters *are* still royal by blood."

"But, if my grandfather was not actually my grandfather, then I have *no* Somoran royalty in my heritage. I have only Loche's, where my grandmother was from . . ." I shook my head and groaned, shielding my eyes with my hands. "This is too confusing."

"You have Lecevonian royalty, Rosie," Celeste reminded me. "That's what truly matters."

"Your *Majesty*," Gryffin emphasized, lifting my hand and kissing it softly, "this changes nothing."

To my right, Zeke shook his head. "Nothing at all." And when I glanced at him, though he was smiling, his eyes were sad.

If only it *had* changed things, if it had made me a commoner too. I couldn't help but share in his sadness.

But I had to remind myself that being queen was more than a bloodline. I cared endlessly for my people, and I had the power to make my kingdom stronger. So, I belonged here, on the throne of Lecevonia. A small blip in my heritage didn't change that. And, truly, if I had been able to handcraft a grandfather, I would never have been able to design a better man than Sterling.

Finally, accepting this insane possibility, I sighed and smiled wryly. "All right then, who else has a secret lineage they'd like to share?"

Our group's laughter, rising above the somber crowd, had caused several heads to turn in our direction.

"I wonder if Mama knew," I mused aloud.

"I sincerely doubt so," Gryffin responded. "That is something that your grandparents would have kept *very* secret, I'm sure."

"Unless Sterling told her himself," Celeste pointed out.

"It's no matter, I suppose. Word of this cannot spread," I said quickly, eyeing Celeste. After all, she was the one who had enlightened me on how fast rumors flew here. "You all might be forgiving, but I doubt everyone will think the same. Right now, the last thing this kingdom needs is doubt about who belongs on the throne."

"I don't know, Rose, maybe transparency would be better," Zeke suggested.

He might have had a point; secrets hardly ever boded well. However, if this were to get out, I didn't think I could handle the repercussions right now. "Really, we don't even know if this is true. Besides, there's time for transparency once things settle again," I said quietly.

"I suppose I can find other things to cause talk in the stable,"

Celeste replied, a playful smile tugging the corner of her mouth. "Which, I suppose, I should get back to."

I looked around us, not having realized that the guests were starting to trickle out of the Great Hall, returning to their duties.

By the door, Celeste gave me a parting hug and made me promise that I'd come down to the stable soon.

"We have a lot to talk about," Celeste said pointedly, eyeing Gryffin. Then her eyes shifted to Zeke. "And you have to tell me what's going on *there* between you two," she added, lowering her voice to whisper.

I grimaced. "I'm just as confused as you are, Celeste."

"Oh, I'm not confused. I see it. But come talk it out with me. Down in the stable. *With Midas,* who misses you dearly."

"Yes, Your Majesty," I teased.

After Celeste had gone, I looked around the Hall for Zeke and Gryffin, who had snuck off during goodbyes. I finally spotted them near the pastry table, picking the scraps left by the crowd. As I approached them, it looked as if they were bartering over an apple tart and a lone raspberry turnover. None of the blueberry pastries were left, of course, the last one having been devoured by the hungry crowd over an hour ago.

One of the kitchen workers, who had been sweeping crumbs around the table, must have heard them, because she stopped sweeping for a moment and said very quietly, "There is a plate of pastries set aside for Queen Rosemary in the kitchen."

"Oh!" Zeke exclaimed. "Well, I'll take care of that," he said, shooting a mischievous smile in my direction. As he started walking away, he called over his shoulder, "Don't worry, I'll deliver the rest of them to your rooms on my shift this afternoon!"

Then he strode off across the Hall, toward the stairs to the kitchens.

That left me with Gryffin.

And my entourage of guards, whom I had honestly forgotten about during the service. They had blended in so seamlessly, made themselves invisible. I wondered then if they had heard our conversation regarding my possibly newfound lineage.

I may have to discuss that with them.

But now, I turned to Gryffin. There was an enormous weight on my heart that I had to tend to. "Would you like to go for a walk?"

He smiled, his perfect teeth gleaming. "I'd love to. As long as we don't go out in *that.*" He nodded toward the windows, where sheets of rain could be seen still plummeting down from the dark sky.

"Of course, not," I said, looping my arm through his. My voice thickened with chagrin. "I'm confined to the castle walls, anyway."

As we exited the Great Hall, I let out a sigh that felt as if I'd been stifling it for a while. "Thank you, again, for being there with me. Even though you didn't know Sterling very well, I'm very glad that I had you here."

Gryffin laid his other hand on top of mine. "Funerals are not held for the ones who have passed. They are held for the ones still here, remembering them." He glanced down at me with a small, sincere smile. "I am more than content to be here for you."

When I met his gaze, an excited spark quickened the rhythm of my heartbeat. He certainly was not making this any easier.

"Oh," he continued, as we walked down the cavernous hall, "I never asked you—how did your council meeting go yesterday?"

"Well, and not so well," I hedged, the same description I had given Zeke. "No new leads on the assassin, but we are ready for an attack."

"An attack?" His voice deepened. "Do you expect an attack?"

Hm. I remembered my advisors' words, and my promise to keep Gryffin out of the conflict as long as possible. So, I dodged around the question while still answering honestly. "Well, we aren't entirely sure."

Still, he pressed on. "An attack from where?"

I had to hold my ground. "We aren't entirely sure of that, either."

From a glance at Gryffin's face, he already knew I wasn't telling him everything. But his eyes, though skeptical, were soft as they looked back at me. No accusation, no questions.

He stopped walking then, rather abruptly, and he held my hand to his chest. "Rosemary," he murmured, shaking his head incredulously, "you have me." Then he laughed, mostly to himself, and kissed my hand briefly before meeting my eyes. "You have me," he repeated, a bit more loudly this time.

Though I didn't completely understand what he meant by that, I couldn't stop a blush rising to my cheeks under his stare. I then sensed that, if I was going to tell him what I needed to, I needed to stop him now. "Gryffin, I—"

But the admiring gaze in his ocean blue eyes intensified, and I was trapped.

He had *me.*

"You are here," he began softly, "a queen reigning for only one year, already battling an assassination attempt. Some kings don't even *see* an assassination attempt in their entire rule. And yet, you are still poised, regal, steadfast. How are you doing it?" He stared at me with astounded eyes. "And learning to fight with a sword, on top of everything!"

He slowly brought his hand to my cheek, and the other to my waist. "You are a remarkable woman," he murmured. Gryffin's intense eyes never left mine, and his large, warm hands held me so perfectly.

What I would have done for a moment of privacy.

My thoughts were chaos, tangled together and shrouded with a thick, confusing mist. The strong, sure thud inside my chest was beating for this man in front of me, but I couldn't help but wish I were looking into another man's eyes, with another man's hand on my waist. The beautiful wedding image returned, but the man standing at the aisle's end kept flashing to Zeke, no matter how hard I tried to place Gryffin there. The only constant, as the man phased back and forth between my two most important men, was Gryffin's eyes. Secure. Trustworthy.

And, just like the ocean, I could see no end to their depth.

Why had I dared let myself think that I wouldn't marry either one of these men? I'd been a fool to even entertain the idea. I had been right. There had only ever been one choice.

"Would you like to stay here?"

Gryffin froze, his hand a stone on my cheek "Excuse me?" he asked.

That choice was my kingdom. And my kingdom did not need a rogue queen. It needed security.

So, I steeled myself with a deep breath. "I would like you to stay here. As the King-consort of Lecevonia. As my husband."

Husband. What a word.

Gryffin stood, still frozen, long enough that I began to doubt his response. Was this not what he wanted?

Then, his look of bewilderment shifted into the greatest expression of happiness I had ever seen on his face. His smile stretched across his perfect teeth, and his sudden outburst of incredulous laughter boomed through the corridor.

I felt both of his hands on my waist, and my feet left the floor. He spun me around, my laugh joining his, before setting me on my feet again.

Then, his hand caressed my cheek, and he kissed me. Right in the corridor. Before our parade of guards, before the castle workers meandering in the hallways after the service.

And, rather than embarrassment, I felt that familiar melting.

It was a quick kiss, but it lacked nothing in fervor. His lips crushed mine, and he held me to him so tightly that I melded against him. I felt that same heat rising to my skin. It was not as welcoming as the caressing warmth of Zeke's touch, but it was a very close second.

Then, as quickly as he had bent down to kiss me, he lifted his head and gazed at me. His eyes glowed of happiness, of sureness, of . . . triumph? Whatever it was, I decided that I loved to see that expression on his face.

"My Rosemary," he whispered, his face scanning my face, my smile.

I couldn't deny that I liked hearing that from his lips. "Will you accompany me to tell my advisors?" I smirked. "They will be *utterly* overjoyed." My advisors, then my sisters . . .

My sisters! I felt my face immediately fall.

"Oh, boars," I cursed, closing my eyes. I wanted to cover my face with my hands. "I told Isabele that I'd visit with her. She's probably been waiting this entire time . . ." I turned on Gryffin teasingly and wagged my finger at him. "Why do I always forget things with you?"

Gryffin chuckled and hugged me a little closer. "Maybe I am simply too—what's the word you've used? 'Charming'?" He lifted his eyebrows.

I rolled my eyes, laughing. "Yes, that must be it." 'Charming' was an understatement. I took a step back, out of Gryffin's arms. "Meet me at my rooms in two hours. *Then* we will make Lord Brock's day."

As I turned and walked away, I tried so fervently to ignore the aching wound in my chest. I knew that only one man could heal that wound, and I could not have him. The ache would have to be a simple price to pay.

I rushed up the stairwell and through the corridors, my guards walking briskly alongside me.

"Are congratulations in order, then?" Amos asked, smiling hugely.

An involuntary grimace set across my features. "I apologize that you all had to witness that. I don't mean for your orders to subject you to my endless romantic endeavors."

Roger, with his impossibly deep voice, surprised me with his boom of laughter.

And Thomas, also chuckling, shook his head. "No need, Your Majesty," he assured me. "It's actually refreshing from our days of training and drills."

I slowed as we turned down the hall to Isabele's chambers. My sister's serious expression floated in front of me once more, and a new gravity entered my mind, conflicting with my sheer relief from just a few moments ago. For indeed just minutes ago, my life had changed courses. I had secured a good man for myself and for my kingdom, and one best suited to help with this strife with Tarasyn, at that. My people would be safe, I would be wed, and I would rule with a king-consort by my side.

Worrying at my bottom lip, I began to take deep breaths in an attempt to calm my mind. Isabele deserved my full attention.

My sister's guards posted outside must have already informed her of my arrival, for her door had been thrown wide open. Isabele stood in the door frame, and as I came into view, she held her arms out toward me.

"I'm sorry, Isa," I said quietly, walking into my sister's arms.

Isabele simply waved away my apology and pulled me into her

rooms, the heavy oak doors thudding closed behind us.

Her chambers were empty, her handmaidens sent away as far as I could tell. Why wouldn't she have wanted them here? Glancing around tentatively, I touched my sister's shoulder. "Isa, what's bothering you?"

Isabele sighed and abruptly turned away from me. She stalked to her window, then to her vanity, then to her window again. Pacing. Stalling.

A bolt of lightning lit the room, and finally, she faced me again. Her eyes were conflicted, fierce but worried, as the thunder sent a deep rumble through her chambers.

"I know this may be brash, Rose, and I have been trying to talk myself out of this . . . this crazy line of thought. But I cannot, and I don't understand it, and it's only getting worse."

I was instantly on edge. "What's wrong, Isa?"

"It's about Prince Gryffin." She met my stare, eyes fervent.

I narrowed my eyes, automatically defensive. "Yes?"

Isabele looked away hesitantly and began pacing again. Window, vanity, window.

Finally, just when following her path with my eyes had become hypnotizing, she inhaled deeply and started again. "This is going to sound absurd, but—there is this . . . *haze* around him."

My eyebrows pinched together as confusion seeped through me. "A haze? What do you mean?"

Isabele looked down to the floor, her forehead furrowed. "When I look at him, I see a fog. A—a cloudiness, hugging around his entire frame."

"Your vision has changed? Isabele!" As a sudden rush of concern warped any possible understanding, I took two long steps to reach my sister. "Why haven't you said anything earlier!" I looked for any sign of abnormality in my sister's eyes. Only clear, brown irises and dark pupils stared back, focused on me. If anything, the whites of her eyes were a bit bloodshot. "Have you been to a healer yet?"

Isabele pushed me away roughly—for Isabele, at least—and groaned in frustration. "No, Rose. It isn't like that. It only surrounds *him*." She turned toward her window. "That's what is so odd. I've never seen anything like this before."

I blinked sharply, finally grasping at tendrils of Isabele's words. "Are you sure? You don't see this around anyone or anything else?"

Isabele shook her head. "Everything else is completely and thankfully normal."

Her words made no sense. I reached for my sister's hand. "Isa, I still think that you should see a healer."

But Isabele didn't seem to hear me. She turned back to me with a distraught ferocity in her wide eyes. "And it's only grown denser the longer that he's been here. I can hardly *see* him!" She grabbed my arm, and I gasped in surprise. Still, Isabele ignored me. "Be careful with him, Rose. I don't understand what I'm seeing, but whatever this is, this strange *aura* around him . . . It scares me." Her words trailed off as she stared hollowly into the thick mist blanketing the courtyard.

No longer able to unearth words, I pulled my sister into my arms and hugged her tightly to me. I felt Isabele's shoulders starting to shake. "My sweet Isabele," I crooned, running my hand down the length of my sister's hair. I even hummed the same lullaby that Zeke had used to comfort me not so long ago.

I felt horribly for my sister. A sudden haze in one's vision is strange and terrifying in itself; a haze focused around a single person? Even more so. I could only imagine that this was some type of coping at work. The past few days' events had been traumatizing, without a doubt. Were they taking an effect on Isabele in such a way? Perhaps even making her project paranoia?

However, whether or not this was paranoia did not matter. Isabele was scared, and that took precedence.

"We will figure this out," I soothed. "I promise."

We stood this way for a long moment, sister clinging to sister, until I finally felt Isabele's frame quiet and calm.

"You know what will distract you, Isa?" I asked with a gentle smirk. "Zeke, Celeste, and Gryffin came up with an interesting theory."

Isabele's voice was shaky when she answered. "A theory about what?"

"Why Sterling cared for Mama so much." I wagged my eyebrows.

Isabele looked up from my shoulders with a confused expression.

"Well," I paused dramatically, "Sterling may actually be Mama's *father.*"

Isabele gasped. "No."

"Mhmm," I said, smiling. "Sterling may be our grandfather."

My distraction seemed to be working. Isabele's eyes grew in disbelief, only a bit of residual fear clinging to their edges. "Grandmother would have *never . . .*"

"Would we really know?" I shrugged. "We've never met her."

"Well, that's true." A small smile began to spread across Isabele's face. "I wouldn't mind having Sterling as a grandfather."

"It's a nice thought, isn't it?"

"I suppose we won't ever be able to know for certain, will we?" she mused. "Anyone who could tell us is gone."

I sighed. "Well, yes. But the idea will make Clara happy."

"Ecstatically so." Isabele laughed, sounding much more like herself.

Relief washed through me as my sister's quiet laughter chimed through the room. Once we are all through this overwhelming confusion, she would be all right.

"I have to go, Isa, but I *promise* I will see you again soon." I held her hands tightly in mine and gave her a quick kiss on her pale cheek.

Isabele nodded softly, her deep brown eyes carrying in them a new, tentative reprieve. *She would be all right,* I repeated internally, and I fervently hoped to will it into existence.

As I pulled Isabele's door shut behind me, a drastic heaviness gripped my mind.

My poor sister, already so emotionally in tune with *everything* . . . Really, it was no surprise that the past few days have affected her so much. While she sat here absorbing everyone's emotions—my stress, Clara's grief, the air of emergency that rippled through the castle, now—she'd been needing to process her own fear through it all. Perhaps her mind had been looking for someone to blame, and it had chosen Gryffin, a stranger to Isabele, to pin as the culprit.

Nothing Isabele had said made any sense, but I knew wholeheartedly that my sister was scared. And that was enough to make me scared for her too.

My mind continued to wander even as I closed the doors to my own rooms with Hazel fretting over me.

I decided that I wanted to practice more with my sword that afternoon, even though Gryffin had suggested a break. I needed a distraction from Sterling's service. I changed from my mourning gown to my trousers, and I tried to push through some of the paperwork on my desk for the rest of the hour, waiting for Gryffin to appear at my door as we'd agreed.

But he never showed.

Even another hour past, he had made no sign of coming by my rooms. I shoved the papers aside in frustration and let out a loud sigh.

Where was he?

I decided that I did not have to sit here and wait; I'd go find Gryffin myself.

Waving goodbye to Hazel, I exited my rooms, and my guards fell into step beside me.

"Where to, Your Majesty?" Thomas inquired.

"The guest wing," I said curtly.

As we walked, I scanned the hallways for any sign of my soon-to-be husband.

Soon-to-be husband. The phrase sent a complex chill through my spine, and I struggled to discern if it had arisen out of excitement or fright.

However, my scanning didn't last very long. As we rounded the corner of the hallway, Lord Brock bolted out of the stairwell. "Queen Rosemary!" His shout echoed down the corridor to me before it was drowned out by another roll of thunder.

"Lord Brock?" I called back, completely puzzled. It was rare to see Lord Brock anything but dignified. "What's wrong?"

My advisor all but skidded to a stop in front of me. "Prince Gryffin has been brought to the prison, Your Majesty. He has been arrested."

CHAPTER FOURTEEN

I STARED AT Lord Brock in silence, my feet frozen in their steps as shock overpowered me.

When I found my voice, I began shouting.

Not at Lord Brock, for I knew this was not his doing.

No, but I was shouting at nearly everything else, through the hallways, inside the stone stairwell, all the way down to the castle's prison.

Damp air struck my face as I opened that final door, and the only light to luminate my path was from torches adorned on the wall. The last time I had been down here, I had sentenced a man to die; so, my mood saw no improvement.

I approached the only cell with soldiers posted outside it—Gryffin's two guards and three posted prison guards. The tight aisle became crowded very quickly, and the closer I got to the cell, I saw Lord Castor there as well, his sneer cuttingly aimed through the iron bars.

Though Gryffin's cell was not far from the entrance to the prison, the dankness was no better, and this only fueled my anger.

"What is he doing down here?" I shouted, to no one in particular.

"I'm all right, Rosemary," Gryffin called from inside the cell.

"Hush!" Lord Castor hissed. "She is the queen, and you will address her as such!"

Of course, this did nothing to calm me. I stopped in front of the bars, and I got my first glimpse of him sitting on the straw-covered floor of the cell, his red leather vest bright in the dim light. At least he looked all right; not a curl out of place on his head, the only dirt on his trousers from leaning against the stone wall in the cell.

"What is he doing down here?" I repeated, more demanding than before.

The prison guards glanced at each other, and finally one of the men answered. "The assassin's bow was found in his room, Your Majesty. Prince Gryffin Danicio has been arrested for conspiring against the Crown."

I was silenced. The assassin's bow?

Then I remembered—

From the woods! He had picked up the bow and attached it to his saddle!

I shook my head vehemently. "This is a misunderstanding. He must be released."

Lord Castor's voice boomed through the prison. "He should have turned in the bow the moment he arrived at the castle, Your Majesty."

Though thoroughly embarrassed now, I straightened my shoulders and stood tall. Regal, or so I aimed to be. "That is on my account. I had asked him to keep the incident in the woods to himself."

"And when the second assassination attempt occurred?" Lord Castor rebutted.

Looking for an answer myself, I now turned to Gryffin, who

admittedly looked a little ashamed.

"If I am to be honest," he said quietly, "in the midst of everything happening, I forgot that I'd even had it."

"Because it is a Tarasynian bow?" Lord Castor asked coldly, crossing his arms in front of him. "Convenient."

That garnered a moment of silence throughout the prison.

A *Tarasynian* bow? My brow knitted together.

"How do we know that the bow is from Tarasyn?" I asked slowly. Skepticism coated my voice.

"It bore the Tarasynian crest, Your Majesty. Engraved just below the grip. Can't miss it. It's now in the armory if you wish to view it yourself."

Well, there was no denying that.

I slowly turned on Gryffin, rotating on my toes to face him. "Did you know this?"

Gryffin's gaze fixed onto the floor of the cell, refusing to look at me.

A wave of betrayal crashed over me, flooding out every other emotion. Even my anger was overcome by the weight of this deception.

"Excuse me, Your Majesty," said Lord Brock quietly, "perhaps this might not be a conversation to have in the midst of a prisoner."

I couldn't find my voice. It was buried too far beneath my hurt and disbelief. But Lord Brock had a point, so, with what strength I could gather, I motioned for my advisors to follow me into the hallway just outside the prison.

When the heavy door closed behind us, I let out an impossibly deep breath. "All right, Lord Castor. What in Haggard's name happened between Sterling's service and now?"

My hotheaded advisor huffed out a story about one of the guards in rotation assigned to Gryffin catching sight of the bow one night, jutting out from underneath Gryffin's mattress. During the service that morning, the guard went into Gryffin's rooms, retrieved the bow, and turned it in.

"And what if it was Gryffin's personal bow?" I inquired.

"The prince admitted that it is not his, Your Majesty."

Come on, Gryffin, you must give me *something.* "I'm sure there must be some explanation." I sounded weak even to myself. "I'd like to speak with him."

Lord Castor grunted in indignation. "Your Majesty, what more do you need? He knew Tarasyn was behind the assassination attempts! Your sister was nearly *killed!*"

"Lord Castor is right, my queen," Lord Brock said solemnly. "Mr. Carfale died at the hands of Tarasyn. Between the cipher and now the bow, we know this undeniably, now."

"The cipher?" I asked, taken aback. "Have our men broken it?"

"No, Your Majesty. A note sent from Colonel Burnstead was left on our desk during Mr. Carfale's service. Two more scouts returned from Tarasyn and reported intercepting a letter that used the same coding as our assassin's message."

I threw my hands up in the air. "Why am I just hearing about this?"

"Because I'd just read the note from the colonel when I heard of Prince Gryffin's arrest," Lord Brock answered with a rueful grimace. "The latter seemed a bit more pressing."

Lord Castor folded his arms over his chest. "Even more reason to imprison the man."

I knew that they were right, that no matter Gryffin's reasoning, Gryffin hiding Tarasyn's transgressions was inexcusable. People had died.

Still, for some potentially moronic reason, I felt that same small tug on my mind to return to Gryffin's cell and hear what inkling of an excuse he might have.

"I'm going to speak to him," I reiterated, no longer a request.

My advisors eyed one another, dumbfounded. In the dark flickering candlelight, I saw Lord Castor's face turning to a deeper shade of red, but he glared at the stone floor and stayed silent.

Lord Brock was the one who eventually answered. "Of course. As you wish, my queen." He and Lord Castor stood back against the wall, leaving the doorway open for me.

I slowly walked back into the prison and turned to the men in the dank space, addressing even my own guards. "Please, I would like to speak with him, alone."

The men looked to one another, and finally one of the prison guards said tentatively, "Your Majesty, it is against our orders to leave this man—"

"As Queen, I order you all to leave."

The guard looked as if he weren't quite ready to relent, with his eyes narrowed and his mouth set into a hard line. Finally, under the heaviness of my glare, he grunted and snapped an order to the other prison guards, and they all trouped through the dark doorway. The men assigned to Gryffin followed.

But my guards hesitated.

Amos looked at me, caution dominating his features. "My queen, are you sure?"

"He is locked behind these iron bars," I said tiredly. "What do you expect him to be able to do?" I hadn't meant for my response to be so brazen, but I was truly at my limit of what I could handle with grace.

Amos gave one curt nod. Then, he shot a warning glare toward Gryffin. "If the queen so much as reports any clue of distress, a jail cell will be the least of your worries."

He turned toward the rest of my guards, and with a jerk of his head, they left me standing in front of Gryffin's cell, alone.

My shoulders fell heavily as soon as the heavy door thudded shut behind them, and I couldn't raise my eyes to meet Gryffin's. I knew his eyes would make me weak. Instead, I leaned against the wall across from his bars, my eyes closed. I heard him take a few shuffling steps toward the bars, but even still, I did not look at him.

"Why didn't you tell me?" My voice, though only a whisper, was hard as marble.

His answering tone was much softer, pleading. "If I would have said that the bow was Tarasynian, you would not have given me even a fleeting chance."

"Gryffin, I can't excuse this as a heart's innocent mistake. No matter how much I would like to." I sighed, feeling the weight of our newfound relationship on its brink. "I only would have admired your honesty, especially about your own kingdom."

He was silent for a long moment, long enough that I opened my eyes and glanced at him through the bars. He was crouched, his elbows on his knees, his head in his palms. "I'm so sorry, Rosemary." His words were ragged, his voice broken and muted against his hands.

I had to actively shut out any sympathy that had managed to creep into my heart. "We have been spending *days* hoping for any solid evidence as to who sent the assassin, and you knew this entire time!" I threw my hands into the air, appalled. My voice had risen now. "You *asked* several times if we had had any idea!"

He looked up from his hands then, his blue eyes gleaming. "And I had hoped each time that you did!" His deep voice ricocheted off the iron bars.

"Gryffin, my sisters or I could have been killed! Sterling *was* killed!" My words trembled against my will. I had averted my eyes again, and tears threatened to spill over now.

Gryffin's voice lowered, soft and pleading once again. "I know that this is unforgivable. I didn't know what to do, Rosemary."

"You knew this entire time that Tarasyn is behind this," I repeated incredulously. That was what troubled me so much. All this waiting, spying, hoping for any sign of plotting from the kingdom. All this time and effort wasted, because Colonel Burnstead had been right all along.

"I have no idea who in the kingdom sent him, Rosemary. My brother would *never* do something such as this. He isn't a killer."

"It's *your kingdom*, Gryffin! This is your brother's responsibility, no matter who sent the assassin. This is an act against the monarchy of a neighboring kingdom! It's an act of war!"

"Please, Rosemary—let me speak to my brother. He may not even be aware! If he knows anything—"

"We found an encoded note on the assassin." I spat the evidence through the iron bars. "One that matches another letter found in Tarasyn. Your brother knows, Gryffin."

I could feel his mixed shock and denial emanating through the cell. A silence stretched between us, and he just shook his head, as if the thought itself was painful. Finally, through the bars, he reached his hand toward me. "Rosemary, even if he does know, you have my allegiance." The sincerity in his voice convinced me to look at him.

Again, his gaze kept me locked in place. His eyes swam with only sorrow and honesty, and, despite his heinous omission, I saw the burn of true regret in the lines of his face. He'd meant each and every one of his words.

I could even understand his point, his reasoning. Had the roles been reversed—if I were visiting a kingdom, a marriage in sight, only to find that my home kingdom may be guilty of a war crime as soon as I arrived—I may have stayed silent too.

As my anger and disbelief slowly subsided, I found that I still trusted him. His brother was the enemy, not him.

But this couldn't go completely unpunished. No, this was much too grave for mere forgiveness.

"You must understand, Gryffin—I can't let you leave the kingdom," I said quietly, my tone still edged, sharp as a sword. "As a ruler, I cannot permit that risk, even if I do understand your actions. My judgement would be deeply questioned, given the evidence we now have."

I reached for his hand, still outstretched toward me. I intertwined my fingers with his and let out a long sigh. "The most I can do is have you moved to your chambers, with armed guards day in and day out. You will not be permitted any privacy," I reminded him, "but it will be more comfortable than a dungeon floor."

"But I am still a prisoner," Gryffin said, his voice carrying its own edge.

"Tarasyn made the first move," I retorted, eyes narrowed.

He let out a short, humorless laugh. "Well, that's something I can't argue." He looked down to the straw-covered floor. "A prisoner in my rooms is a bit more respectable than a prisoner down here."

I stroked the back of his hand with my fingers. "I'm sorry. I will work with our colonel, and once we have a plan, I will see about your release." Then I paused, and I looked up at him through my eyelashes. "We will sort this out, right?"

I knew my question was loaded. This exact situation had been my fear, and it had now come to its fruition. Despite my own careful planning and evading, circumstances had deemed this fate: Gryffin had become a prisoner, viewed as an enemy. Now, everything regarding any possible future between us was at stake.

I believed him. Even Prince Charming could not be perfect; he made a mistake, and he knew it. And though it could have been dire, thankfully, it wasn't. I still believed completely that he was good for me *and* for my kingdom. It would take extreme patience for Lecevonia to see this as well, but I had no doubt that he would eventually be seen as a loyal citizen.

But could he ever see me again in the same light?

I was keeping him prisoner, after all. It was a direct insult to his character, his own royal status, his honor. It was an embarrassment.

But I had no choice.

This entire line of thought passed through my mind as I looked at him, all while Gryffin stayed silent. Surely, he could recognize that.

Finally, Gryffin let out a sigh, a long exhale that encompassed his torrent of emotions, and brought my hand to his lips. He kissed it just as tenderly as before, his eyes never leaving mine.

"You are still a woman worth protecting, Rosemary," he murmured, his lips brushing softly against my hand.

At his words, relief took a daring, delicate hold around the edges of my mind.

I looked down, toward the scum-covered ground. It really was filthy down here. "I will have you moved tonight. How can so much change in such a short time?" I shook my head slowly, disbelieving. "And to think, just hours ago we were going to tell my advisors our news."

"I suppose that particular announcement may have to wait," he smiled wryly.

With a sigh, I released his hand. "I can't marry a prisoner, now can I?" I teased, though only halfheartedly.

After a final smile and a wordless promise, I turned away. When I walked through the dark doorway, exiting the prison, I found all eleven guards and my two advisors standing tense and alert. When they caught sight of me, they lurched to surround me.

I held up my hands reassuringly, palms facing out. "I'm all right."

He stayed behind his bars like a good prisoner, I thought to myself snidely. I turned to the prison guard who had obviously been in charge earlier. "Please, have Prince Gryffin moved up to his rooms."

Protests immediately bombarded my ears.

I held up my hand again, this time to silence them. "Have your normal guard shift for the prison keep eyes on him at all times."

Lord Castor sputtered in outrage. "Your Majesty, the dungeon is much more failsafe—"

"Though he is a prisoner, he is still a prince," I said pointedly. "And second in line for the throne, at that. Tarasyn will retaliate if they hear word of his imprisonment. If we keep him in the dungeon, then we will surely have a war on our hands."

"Don't we already have a war on our hands, Your Majesty?" Lord Castor sneered scathingly.

Though his remark was quite possibly true, I chose to ignore it. "In his rooms. Tonight."

But as I turned away, I softened my tone. "Thank you all for your countless hours of service," I bowed my head in their direction. Then, I continued up the stairwell, my guards in step around me.

As we walked, I brought my fingers to my temples and massaged them softly. I tried to decide my next course of action. I thought of going straight to my advisors' office and calling an immediate meeting to discuss Lecevonia's next step. But, no; I wanted to be sure that General Gambeson and Colonels Burnstead and Holland were there as well, to ensure they knew what actions our military needed to take. Now that we knew for certain that Tarasyn was guilty, we would need to act quickly.

I would call a council meeting with all of them first thing tomorrow morning, then. That was the soonest I could expect the general and colonels to arrive from their homes if I sent word to them immediately.

Now, I wanted to speak to Zeke. And more pressingly, I wanted a distraction. As if Sterling's funeral wasn't enough of an emotional hurdle. Now, my sister was envisioning things, and my potential husband was in prison for hiding crucial details of a war crime. The last thing I wanted to do now was think.

I would put thinking off until tomorrow morning.

As we reached the top of the stairs and stepped into the kitchens, finding Zeke did not take as long as I'd expected. He was leaning against the wall near one of the large hearths, and though I tried to stifle my huge smile, my pulse threatened to grow wings and beat right out of my body.

As we approached, he shoved off the wall and made his way toward us.

"Sir Hugh, I've come to relieve you," he said with a slight bow.

But Hugh looked a bit concerned, his brow furrowing. "Sir Ezekiel, my shift does not end for another three hours."

Zeke laughed, always good-natured. "I know I'm early, but imagine the surprise your family will have to see you come home before dinner."

Dinner . . . I registered for the first time that I was ravenous, not having eaten since that blueberry pastry this morning. The smells of the kitchen were suddenly at the forefront of my mind—the savory scent of roasted beef, the buttery aroma of freshly baked yeast rolls, and the sweet crispness of apple-cinnamon all assaulted my nostrils simultaneously, and I was immediately in a hurry to get to the Great Hall.

"Hugh, that is a wonderful idea!" I chimed in, smiling at him warmly. "Oh, I can already see the happiness on your wife's face. As Queen, I permit you to leave your duty early."

At that, Hugh started to smile. I knew that, though he was as dedicated as the others to his job, he was, first and foremost, a family man. He bowed deeply, uttered several words of thanks, and walked briskly toward the doors leading outside, to the crisp, cool spring evening.

Zeke took his place and smirked at me. "Where to?"

"The Great Hall," I answered immediately. "I believe we *all* need to eat, right?" I asked, looking around apologetically at my guards. Following me around day in and day out, they hadn't been able to sit down for a moment, either.

Thomas chuckled in response. "Well, finally."

"And," I added as we began walking, "I want to practice a bit more."

Zeke glanced down at my trousers. "I gathered that much."

As we ascended the stairway to the main level of the castle, Zeke brushed my shoulder with his hand. He had meant it to look nonchalant, I was sure, but I couldn't stop my blush rising to my cheeks. I sighed. Would this be my new "normal"?

"How are you?" he asked quietly, walking close beside me. "I know, with Gryffin . . ." he trailed off.

Oh, of course he knew. *Word travels*, as Celeste had said.

"I don't know," I answered. "I've decided not to try to sort through this tonight. I can only take in so much in a day."

Zeke chuckled. "Fair enough."

But I suddenly found myself unable to stop talking. "If Gryffin had told us what he knew, we wouldn't have wasted so many resources at the border over the last four days."

"We would have sent our men to the border, anyway."

"But we wouldn't have just been *waiting*."

"You would have called for an attack on Tarasyn?"

"Maybe. I suppose . . ." I shook my head to clear it. "That is what I will discuss tomorrow with my advisors and the general. Not tonight,"

I said firmly.

But still, I couldn't stop the words from tumbling. "And the trouble is that I *see* his reasoning. It cannot fully be excused, of course, but it's forgivable."

Zeke peered down at me, looking unconvinced. "I think your feelings for him are skewing your judgement."

I lowered my voice. "If it were me, wouldn't you think the same?"

He only glared at me before turning his gaze straight ahead, shaking his head, and I could tell that I was right.

"And my poor Isa," I groaned, my voice still hushed.

Zeke looked back at me. "What's wrong with Isabele?"

We had reached the Great Hall now, and we strode through the open doors.

I lowered my voice even lower still, to a whisper that only Zeke would hear. Isabele's trouble was something that I undoubtedly did not want floating around the castle. With the chatter in the Great Hall, no one would hear me. "She is . . . seeing something. A haze, she says."

Zeke's eyes immediately voiced concern, squinting at my words. "What? Has she told anyone? A healer, in the least?"

"I told her so. The strangest thing is that she only sees it around one person. Gryffin." I glanced up at Zeke, trying to gauge his reaction.

"That's . . . odd," Zeke murmured. He pulled out my chair for me, his forehead wrinkled in confusion. He sat across from me before meeting my eyes again. "Is she all right otherwise?"

I nodded. "I think it might be some form of trauma, poor Isa. We have all been through so much recently, and you know how potently Isabele feels everything."

"Possibly," Zeke sighed quietly. "The sooner she sees a healer, the better."

"Agreed." I returned my voice to its normal volume. "Now, after we eat, will you help me practice with my sword for a while? My original teacher is *incapacitated* at the moment."

Zeke smiled. "Of course. Amos can assist again in one-on-one."

Dragging with fatigue, I laid my sword into an open slot on the weapons stand, now perpetually fixed in the corner of the Great Hall. I wiped away the sweat glistening on my forehead with the long sleeve of my tunic and turned back to Zeke, who was wiping his blade with the hem of his shirt.

"You are a less relenting instructor than Gryffin is," I muttered, still trying to catch my breath. "But I thank you for that; this was exactly the distraction I needed." And truly, it was. I was too tired to think now, which had been my goal all night.

Zeke smiled at me and winked. "Your stamina is increasing every day."

I rolled my eyes at his joke, but my cheeks still heated beneath my smile.

Zeke laughed, his golden hair falling into his eyes. "No, I mean that. I only pushed you so hard because you were able to take it."

At that, I smiled and curtsied proudly. "Why, thank you." I could tell that I was improving, as well. Although Amos had once again put me to shame, three times in fact, that last fight was closer than it had ever been. Before he ended his guard shift, he had been almost as out of breath as I was.

Then, I sighed. "I'd like to go visit Clara." Her wordless grief from this morning sent a chill of alarm across my thoughts, through my limbs.

Zeke nodded and sheathed his sword into its scabbard at his waist. Then, with a glance that shared my concern, he held his hand out to me.

I took his outstretched hand, as would have been common between us, but I felt that it meant so much more now. I squeezed his fingers with mine once, then quickly released them. But that didn't stop the wound in my chest from rejoicing at the touch.

My guards—my other rotation, minus Ulric, whom Zeke had replaced this time—and I made our way to Clara's chambers, and I noticed that our little entourage was a bit subdued now. Everyone worried for Clara.

As we approached her rooms, Clara's guards opened them for me, and when I entered, my heart wanted to explode at the sight.

Clara's room was filled to the brim with flowers. Crimson roses and pink peonies, draping yellow forsythia, blue baptisia and purple passionflowers, all cascaded from their overstuffed vases and painted Clara's rooms with endless arrays of color. Even her bedposts were wrapped in honeysuckle vines, the little red bells bright spots against their green leaves. All the floral arrangements from the service had found their way here, brightening the one place that needed them most today.

And there was Clara, *dancing*. Dancing in her night shift amidst the flowers, twirling and giggling, though there was no music. No, only the music of her chiming laugh rang through the room.

I stood, shocked, at the foot of Clara's bed. This was such a dramatic change from the silent, broken little girl of this morning. I hadn't seen Clara this happy for days. Then, as the shock subsided, relief took its place. I felt a smile spread across my face, and my own laugh joined Clara's.

Clara stopped mid-twirl and faced me with a vibrant smile. "Hello,

Rose!" She bounded to my side and took my hand. "Won't you dance with me?"

So, accepting this other distraction, I danced with my little sister, twirling her across the room, lifting her off her feet from time to time and making her giggle. Little Clara's laugh flowed through the room like a babbling river. My own elation only strengthened the aura of the room, and we danced until I felt as if my legs would surely move no longer.

With a happy sigh, I sat on the ground and gathered my little sister into my lap. "My sweet Clara," I murmured into the little girl's curls, "I'm so happy to see you dancing."

Clara lifted her chin, looking up at me, with an expression so certain, so indisputable. "Sterling would want me to dance. Just as we were dancing during my birthday party." Her little gaze traveled around the room. "And I *am* dancing with him, in a way. I'm dancing with his flowers."

And I swore, from then on, that Clara's room would always be filled with Sterling's flowers.

"Why should we wait to attack Tarasyn? They are the culprit—they tried to murder our Queen! They have declared war on us, already!"

Lord Castor's words reverberated off the stone walls of the council room, adding to the edge of everyone's already unnerved mood. The council meeting had taken an antagonistic turn, with Lord Castor and Colonel Holland shouting back and forth at each other.

"As we've said before," Colonel Holland reiterated for what I felt was the eleventh time, "we would *lose* any battle in the mountains of

Tarasyn. We must fight *here*!"

"No, we must storm Viridi and take Snowmont down to rubble!"

But Colonel Holland shook his head roughly. "We don't have the manpower we had six years ago to pull off a stunt like that."

"We don't want to ravage our own countryside with war," Lord Quince bravely interjected in their argument.

"Nor do we want to decimate our troops," countered the colonel.

Their ricocheting dispute was steadily wearing down my nerve. "So, it's either lose Lecevonia's protection if we fight there, or lose Lecevonia's livelihood if we fight here," I summarized tiredly.

"Your Majesty," Lord Castor said, "we *cannot* allow Tarasyn to enter our lands. We are not simply talking theoretically, anymore; we must protect the land of our kingdom!"

"There will be no kingdom to protect if our troops are sentenced to death in the mountains!" Colonel Holland shouted.

General Gambeson cleared his throat, silencing the two men. He maintained eye contact with me as he spoke calmly. "That does not have to be the case, Your Majesty. We of course must accept that, in times of war, there will be losses. However, perhaps we can minimize those losses with a planned attack and quick retreat on our end."

I looked at him through narrowed eyes. "Meaning we attack first?"

The general nodded. "Then fall back, with the hope that they will follow. Exactly what we hypothesize their plan may be, if you remember from our last meeting, should they attack first."

Lord Castor hissed. "They have *already* attacked first." His voice was acidic.

"And we have attacked back by imprisoning their prince," countered Colonel Burnstead.

"Imprisoned." Lord Castor scoffed. "He is tucked safely in his rooms. I hardly call that imprisonment."

"Hush," I said sharply. "He is a prince and still deserves respect."

"He is the prince of an enemy kingdom!" argued Lord Castor.

I felt the edges of my mind darkening, my anger rising. "Prince Gryffin did not commit the assassination."

"He *knew* of his kingdom's actions!"

"Tarasyn's actions were just as much a surprise to him as they were to us," I said, hoping to close the argument.

But Lord Castor banged his fist down on the table, shaking the wood. "Your claim is weak, Your Majesty, and you know it!"

Now seething, I suddenly rose from my seat, my voice rising with me. "Lord Castor, I will have you ejected from this council room should you display this level of disrespect for my decisions again." I looked around the room, making eye contact with each of the men. "Prince Gryffin made a *mistake*. He was shocked, he panicked, and he made the wrong decision. He is aware of his mistake, and I am granting mercy. Just as my parents would have. And if you question my mercy again"—my eyes rested on Lord Castor—"you *will* be removed from your position."

Lord Castor fell into silence. He folded his hands in front of him on the table and turned his glare to the stone floor, and as I looked around the table, no one met my gaze, save for General Gambeson. He held my stare with one of his own, his calm, calculating eyes staring into mine.

In his eyes, I saw understanding. Perhaps he had sentenced too many innocent men to their deaths on the battlefield, or perhaps he remembered my father's notorious compassion. Whatever his reason, whether or not he agreed, he understood.

I lowered myself into my seat once more, and I slowly folded my hands in front of me. Lecevonia was only as strong as its leader, and the silence across the table screamed compliance.

After a few deep breaths, I addressed the general. "So, as you were saying. You suggest that we send a portion of our troops into Tarasynian territory"—I drew an invisible line on the table and walked my fingers over it—"stage an attack on the two thousand Tarasynian troops stationed at the castle, and quickly retreat back onto Lecevonian turf." I walked my fingers back over the invisible line. "If all goes well, Tarasyn will retaliate by advancing into the foothills"—I walked the fingers of my other hand across the line—"where, with any luck, we can hold them near the border." My fingers interlaced and folded once again in front of me.

I looked to the general for affirmation, and he nodded slowly.

"That is what I believe will be the best course of action," he said. "And with more than half of our troops at the border, we have a decent chance of succeeding at the hold. At least at first—it will also depend on how fast the remainder of Tarasyn's army responds, wherever they may be."

"Well, at that point, we can send more men and our cavalry."

"Indeed, Your Majesty."

"How many men would be needed to make this plan work?"

"I'd say around three thousand more men."

I sighed heavily. Even with the rest of the Lecevonian army and cavalry, save for one thousand or so men to guard the castle, Tarasyn's forces still outnumbered mine. However, I was confident in the extensive training of my men, of both infantry and cavalry. Though they may be fewer in number, my army was better conditioned. And, with that confidence, I believed that my army could diminish the Tarasynian army as they approached in their waves, potentially with few casualties on Lecevonia's end.

"All right," I said finally. "When do you propose that we make our move?"

General Gambeson exchanged a look with the two colonels. After a silent decision and an affirming nod, he turned his eyes back to me. "As early as tomorrow would be feasible." His dark, deep-set eyes stared into mine. "It's your call, Your Majesty."

It's your call, Your Majesty.

I closed my eyes and attempted to let the words sink and settle into every corner of my weary mind. This decision, my decision, would lead to a war. A war with Gryffin's kingdom. With the kingdom who had sent an assassin to kill me. And my decision would not leave Lecevonia unscathed. I would lose too. But would my gain be greater?

What would my gain be, after all? Reclaimed pride? Was that truly a large enough prize over which to endanger my kingdom?

But I was wrong; it wouldn't be reclaimed pride—it would be reclaimed *strength.*

Tarasyn had weakened my kingdom, just by revealing that my border—and my city's walls—could be breached. It put a target directly over my head for any ambitious monarch.

And not only my head but my sisters' heads as well.

And my sisters' safety was not something that I could risk.

I slowly opened my eyes, peering into each of the men's faces seated with me around the table. Though this call was my decision, there once again was really only one choice.

My lips parted to speak—

The council room doors flew open, then, grating loudly against the stone floor, the old iron handles squealing against their hinges. The sunlight from the hallway highlighted the silhouette of a man for just a moment, before the man rushed into the center of the room.

His uniform was disheveled, damp and splattered with dark mud, his ashen face and hair smothered with grime. He held his arms out to us, as if to offer something, but his arms were empty.

I didn't recognize the man, but I recognized Zeke's terrorized face directly behind him. His bright brown eyes were thrown open wide, brows raised nearly to his hairline, his mouth gaping in shock.

Colonel Burnstead stood from his seat. "Sir Terrin?" His voice, though booming like thunder, sounded as if he'd been caught in a sudden landslide. "Why are you here? You weren't expected to return until tomorrow."

I gathered then that this was one of the scouts sent to Hiddon. From Zeke's face, though, I knew that something was wrong.

Very wrong.

Sir Terrin gasped, breathing in only enough air to spill his next words. "Tarasyn has overtaken Hiddon."

CHAPTER FIFTEEN

THE MAN'S BREATHLESS words hung heavily in the air for one infinite second.

Then, we all moved abruptly, slamming fists on the wooden table, shooting up from their chairs as the wooden legs shrieked against stone. No one truly knew what to do, but we all felt a need to do *something*, even if that simply meant a shout of disbelief or a pounding upon the tabletop.

"They've *overtaken* Hiddon?" I nearly shouted. An entire kingdom overthrown? What did that even entail? "How is that possible? What did you see?"

Sir Terrin's words ran over themselves as he attempted to rush through an explanation. "Tarasyn's army—the rest, the nine thousand men—we saw them marching, leaving Hiddon's capitol . . . The king and queen are dead." He looked at me with wild, bulging eyes. "That's what I heard the troops saying. King Theon and Queen Alys. King Roderich killed them! Three months ago!"

I felt all color leave my face. A sheen of cold sweat immediately moistened my forehead.

Three *months* ago? That was impossible. I would have heard . . . I'd met with Prince Marcus and Prince Maddox!

Four months ago, I slowly realized.

"How is it possible that we haven't learned of this before today?" I asked forcefully, my gaze cutting through my advisors. "King Theon and Queen Alys have been *murdered* in cold blood! How is this a shock to us!"

Lord Castor snarled in indignation, but I caught Lord Quince shoot him a warning glance. So, instead of opening his mouth, he glared at the ground.

Lord Clark answered, but even he sounded annoyed. "International relations have always needed strengthening, Your Majesty."

I immediately realized that my frustration was focused in the wrong direction. I should only be angry with myself.

But if my advisors hadn't been so invested in finding me a husband—

Colonel Burnstead interjected. "They were marching, you say? Where are they going?" he asked urgently. "What did you hear?"

Terrin's terrified eyes jolted to the colonel. "Here. To our capitol. A sudden attack—just as they had done to Hiddon. They are coming *here*." He emphasized the end of his sentence so heavily that no one dared to question him.

A startling chill ran through the council room as everyone froze. I cut my gaze to Zeke and found him staring at me, terror-stricken eyes absorbing the shock.

"I rode hard, made it here in sixteen hours," Sir Terrin continued. "Their army is traveling on foot. They could be at the castle walls by tomorrow's dawn."

The castle would be under siege by morning.

And more than half of my army was at the wrong border.

I turned to General Gambeson sharply. "We have to send word to our army to return immediately."

"Of course," he responded gruffly, "but they won't be able to get here in time. It's a day's ride to the northern border. The soonest they can possibly arrive is the day after tomorrow."

"Our troops here will have to attempt to hold them off until the rest of our army reaches the capitol," said Colonel Burnstead gravely.

"Four thousand against nine thousand," I whispered, shaking my head. Lecevonia's odds were so much less than ideal.

"Your Majesty," General Gambeson said, "if our men here can hold the capitol wall until the rest of our army arrives, we will be able to hit the Tarasynian forces from both sides. Equos may not fall."

I hadn't noticed Zeke's approach until he laid his hand upon my shoulder. "Our men are well trained, Rose."

I knew that. But Tarasyn's force was over twice the size.

Colonel Holland cleared his throat, demanding my attention. "And our cavalry of two hundred and fifty has grown by fifty new recruits as well. Granted, they have not had their complete training yet."

I shook my head fiercely. I didn't care if they were fresh off the city's streets. "No, that is still good. The more troops, the better we stand." I again faced the general. "We must prepare our men as soon as possible."

He turned to Colonel Burnstead, intensity emanating from him. "Prepare the army and send word throughout the city. We must prepare for a siege."

The colonel gave him one curt nod and strode out of the council room.

Then, the general outstretched his arm to the scout, motioning to a chair at the table. "Sir Terrin, come. Tell us what you know."

The man walked forward and collapsed into the open chair. But I was too anxious to return to my seat. Instead, I started pacing near the head of the table as Sir Terrin's trembling voice struggled through his encounter.

"We didn't even make it to the capitol—we were maybe an hour past the boundary when we spotted the first of the Tarasynian soldiers. In a loose formation. We heard them talking." Then he scoffed humorlessly. "It was Tristan's *brilliant* idea to split up"—he managed a bit of sarcasm—"take two different angles, capture what information we could. When I heard what had happened in Hiddon, to King Theon and Queen Alys . . ." He paused, his eyes widened in some unseen horror.

General Gambeson spoke calmly. "Sir Terrin, you have to tell us everything." He waved his hand forward, gesturing for Sir Terrin to continue.

The scout nodded quickly, taking a deep breath. "King Roderich and his army attacked with full force, sneaking in the dead of night. They overthrew Vena and took the castle, killed everyone inside except the king and queen. Even the princes. They—they locked everyone in their houses, burned down the *entire* city . . . The soldiers were complaining of how the—the smell lingered for weeks."

Lord Quince's quiet gasp reached everyone's ears, but no one else uttered a sound at the news of this heinous scene. I felt my own eyes widened in shock. But I didn't know what to say. What could be said?

"King Roderich held the king and queen hostage for about a week in the castle," Sir Terrin continued, "before killing them himself. There have been Tarasynian soldiers posted at the border ever since, to stop any escape of stragglers from the countryside. They were only just called back to the capitol to join the army's formation a week ago." He ran a shaking hand through his ragged hair and heaved a sigh. "They've been functioning on the element of surprise. And we are their next target. *You* are their next target, Your Majesty." He set his stare on me.

And he wasn't the only one. I felt the weight of my advisors' gazes, of Zeke's.

King Roderich was going to kill me next, since his assassin didn't do the job.

The gravity of it all threatened to fracture any perceived strength I thought I had, and that same vulnerability I'd felt in the woods so many days ago began to creep back into my head.

General Gambeson only glanced quickly in my direction before focusing on Sir Terrin again. "Did you hear anything of their strategy?"

"'Hit strong at first light,' was all I could catch," the scout said with a defeated shake of his head. "I didn't meet again with Tristan." He dropped his head into his hands. "I left him . . ." Terrin's shoulders began to shake, and his stifled sobs could still be heard escaping him.

To give him his privacy, I faced my advisors. "Is it possible to evacuate the city? Is there enough time?"

"And send them where?" Lord Clark asked tiredly.

"The city of Equos is the strongest hold in the kingdom," Lord Brock said, eyeing the other men around the table. "Behind its walls is the safest place for everyone."

"All right, increase the guards at the city's wall, then," I commanded. "Start informing the citizens and gather them all as closely to the castle as possible. Open the kitchens for them, the prison, the corridors. Have as many people inside Hillstone's walls as you can fit."

As the men bent their heads together, I turned to Zeke.

He'd stood by me with his hand on my shoulder, and he slid his hand down my arm to take hold of my hand. With a tight squeeze of his fingers around mine, he tried to reassure me. His voice was fierce as he spoke. "Rose, we *will* keep you safe. I swear it to you."

His words were like a comforting caress in this moment of turmoil, but I refused to savor them. "Zeke, I need you to take my sisters and escort them to Port Della, away from harm."

He immediately glared at me, dropping my hand roughly. "Did you hear even a single word of Lord Brock's guidance?"

Oh, for Haggard's sake. My impatience emanating from me, I shook my head fervidly. "I can't have them inside the castle or the city, anywhere close to King Roderich and his army. They must leave. And Hazel must go with them," I added. If I could protect my sweet lady-in-waiting, I would do whatever I can.

"No," Zeke shook his head once quickly. "Rose, I'm not going to leave you here." He crossed his arms over his chest, signaling finality.

But I stood my ground. Speaking with authority, as I never did with Zeke, I gave him a direct order. "As Queen, I command you to take them to Port Della."

Even still, he ignored me. "Get someone else to take them, Rose. I'm staying with you." His eyes gleamed with determination, stubbornness, and, most of all, concern.

But my determination was greater. "Zeke, you are the *only* person I trust to take them there safely." And that was probably one of the truest things I've ever said. "Please."

"Then you come too," he said angrily. "There is no reason to stay here to be slaughtered."

"And leave Equos to burn? I am their queen. I can't flee, Zeke—you know that." I took his hand, and he looked down toward the floor in a scowl.

"Zeke," I continued, my voice earnest, "I trust you more than anyone else here." I lifted his hand to my chest, and, finally, he returned his eyes to mine. I saw that his were glassy, moist, and my heart panged to see his tears. "Please, Zeke. I must protect my sisters."

He brought my hand to his lips, and I felt his lips quiver in a silent, restrained sob. But when he spoke, his voice was clear. "All right, Rose. I'll do as you say."

I sighed in relief. "Thank you, Zeke." I would forever be grateful for this man. "And . . . take Midas too. Perhaps he can draw the wagon."

"You're just trying to protect *everyone*, now, aren't you?" he mocked with narrowed eyes, but there was no real anger in his voice. Only defeat.

I smiled sadly. "Only those I can."

I turned then to Lord Brock. "Please, arrange with Sir Ezekiel to have my sisters taken to the coast, to Port Della."

"My queen—" Lord Brock began, caution in his tone.

I held up my hand to stop his words. "They will be much safer there. King Roderich will have no idea. Even if our citizens cannot go, at least a small caravan won't cause any alarm."

As I spoke, I started for the open doors. The men in the room protested, but I waved them off.

"Where are you going, Your Majesty?" Lord Quince called after me frantically.

"To our last resort."

Leaving their raised voices behind me, I rushed through the large doors and into the corridor, my confused guards following in my wake.

Our last resort. My advisors, especially Lord Castor, would have never agreed to this. Even my parents might not have agreed to this. What if this backfired?

Or if he said he wouldn't do it?

I sprinted past the Great Hall, my haste alarming several castle workers along the way, down to the guest wing.

I halted in front of Gryffin's chambers and pounded on the door. His two assigned guards looked at me in alarm, and while my own guards swiftly explained to them the impending danger, one of the prison soldiers inside the room opened the door.

"Your Majesty," he said in gruff surprise. "What—"

"Excuse me." I pushed past him brusquely and rushed into the middle of the room.

Gryffin was sitting near his bookshelf, peering at a book laying open in his hands. As he heard my approach, his head shot up, a smile spread across his face. However, after only a second of absorbing my expression, his lips quickly turned downward into a hard, grim line.

"Rosemary?" he asked slowly as he placed his book down beside him and stood to his feet. "What's wrong?"

I hurried to him, aware that my panic was evident on my face. I didn't care. There was no time to feign any calm or control.

He laid his hands on my shoulders. "Please, tell me what's happening."

My expression hardened, my mouth set in a tight, tense line, and each word was almost painful to utter. "Tarasyn is invading Lecevonia. Tomorrow morning."

It took him a moment to comprehend my words. Then, his back straightened stiffly, and his hands fell from my shoulders as his eyes dropped to the floor. "What? No, that's not possible." He shook his head in denial and jerked his gaze back to me. "Who told you this? They—they must be mistaken, surely."

"No, Gryffin," I refuted, my hands outstretched and begging for his understanding. "My scouts returned from Hiddon with the news. They *saw* the soldiers themselves, heard them talking. Your brother has taken Hiddon, and now he is heading Tarasyn's army here." I cautiously gauged his expression as I revealed my next harsh truth. "Gryffin, Roderich *killed* King Theon and Queen Alys."

At that, the hardset denial on his face slowly began melting into shock. His eyes widened and focused on nothing but the empty space above my head. Slowly, he backed into the bench behind him, his knees giving way.

"I . . ." he started, his voice hardly a murmur. "I can't believe . . ." His hands lay limply in his lap.

Finally, his blue eyes found my face again. "I didn't know that my brother was capable of doing something like this."

"He killed Hiddon's king and queen, and I am who he is after now." Speaking this reality aloud did not staunch the fear that accompanied it.

Gryffin's face hardened, lines of determination etched into his brow as he stood. "I won't let him get that far." But even as he said this, so passionate in his promise, a deep hurt flooded behind his eyes.

I pulled him with me back to the bench and sat on the hard wood. "It may yet come to that. Gryffin, I have to ask you to do something. I think it may be our only chance to stop a war." I emphasized every single word. "Do you still believe that Lecevonia is a kingdom worth protecting?"

"Yes. Yes, of course I do." He dropped his hands into his lap, palms facing the ceiling. Offering anything he had. He watched me, waiting.

So, with a deep breath, I made my request. "I need you to ride out to your brother and plead with him to stop this attack. Ask him to come speak with me instead. There must be an armistice we can reach . . ." I trailed off, once again taken aback by how quickly this antagonism escalated. It made no sense. No sane ruler would take this drastic of a measure, completely unwarranted. "You are the *one* person that may be able to speak reason to him."

Immediately from behind us, all three prison guards inside the room objected.

"Your Majesty, he is a prisoner!"

"And he may be the only way that we all live!" I shouted unyieldingly, wheeling around to face the guards. "And soon, he will be your king-consort." The guards fell silent at this, and I found a small, incredulous smile. "As Queen, I release him. If"—I turned back to Gryffin, my voice lowering—"you swear your loyalty."

He grabbed my hands, his ocean eyes burning resolutely through his confusion. "You have it, Rosemary."

But I shook my head softly. "In Lecevonia's official ceremony. It is the only way my advisors and the general will trust you."

I thought again of how much I was asking of him. To turn on Tarasyn, his home, his brother.

But after only a short pause, he looked up at me again. He stood up from the bench, still holding both of my hands in his. "Of course, Rosemary. My brother has given up on reason—he must be stopped."

My heart thudded loudly as I registered his words. Despite my anxiety obstinately spinning havoc through my mind, I felt an inexplicable blanket of calm, of trust. I held our hands to my chest and closed my eyes. Had I ever been so grateful for someone's loyalty in my entire life?

Much to the prison guards' objections, I pulled him out of his rooms after me. As we rushed toward the council room, where I was sure my advisors would still be discussing every possible outcome of tomorrow morning with the general, I readied myself for the onslaught of backlash I would receive for my decision.

Lord Castor would surely be the most opposed, but I hoped that after this morning he would quietly nod along with me. If Lord Brock or Lord Clark were against it, however, I would have to be more tactful. I treasured their opinions the most. General Gambeson, well, I couldn't foresee what his stance would be.

We rushed down the stone corridor, well-lit now with stubborn sunlight struggling to burn its way through the clouds. When we heaved the council room's doors, I saw that Colonel Burnstead had returned, and we found ourselves amidst an argument between Lord Castor and the general.

Well, it was an argument on Lord Castor's side, at least. General Gambeson's gruff, calm voice easily overpowered Lord Castor's shouts.

"That is the fastest we will be able to get word to them."

"That is not fast enough! We need them here tomorrow morning, *at all costs!*"

"This will have to be fast enough. Even riding our healthiest horses, it will take at least until nightfall to reach the border. We can hold the castle with—" General Gambeson stopped mid-sentence upon seeing me at the door, towing Gryffin beside me.

In fact, the entire gathering had frozen.

"My queen," Lord Brock said in quiet surprise, "what are you doing?"

I took a small breath and paused, taking a moment to ensure that my voice would be firm and confident. Unquestionable. "Prince Gryffin may be our sole chance at stopping an attack. I am sending him to the Tarasynian army to speak to his brother." I straightened my shoulders, preparing for the repercussions.

"Absolutely out of the question," Lord Clark stated immediately.

Other forms of "no" quickly followed from my other advisors. As if I'd just suggested that I deliver myself to King Roderich in a golden carriage. Would these men forever be so quick to ignore me? How did they so often forget that I didn't need their approval to do as I pleased?

Prince Gryffin put his hand on my shoulder. He had a small, reassuring smile on his face, and his eyes were steadfast. Then he looked away from me and faced the men around the table.

"Gentlemen," he began, bowing his head. His strong, steady voice rang clearly through the room. "On behalf of Tarasyn, I deeply and wholeheartedly apologize." He held the eyes of each of the men in turn. "Truly. I'm ashamed of my brother's behavior, and I did not know that he was emotionally capable of this type of heinous assault." He looked down, his disbelief plain on his face before he turned his gaze back to them. "I believe that I may be able to speak with my brother. Find where his mind has gone. Surely, if I can talk to him, even if only to make him pause, he would come to some sort of agreement."

Gryffin's voice sat in the air, lingering over the group of men at the table. No one tore his eyes away from him. I could feel each of them judging, calculating, and, from the narrowed glares of my advisors, it didn't seem that Gryffin would gain their trust. Only General Gambeson's face remained unreadable.

I felt my hope fading, and the realization that I'd be making a revolutionary decision without the support of my advisors began to settle into my mind. They would undoubtedly feel insulted, and some might even resign. Those that would stay would question my judgement on any matter for a long time, perhaps for the rest of my reign.

However, as I stood there, accepting the long, ever-fraying tear I was about to rip between myself and my advisors, I began to sense a palpable shift in the council room. A kind of settling. I watched first Lord Quince's brow loosen, then Lord Clark's fists unclench. Lord Castor's arms remained tightly crossed in front of his chest, but his eyes relented to a thoughtful gaze.

Finally, Lord Brock sighed. "You've been aware of King Roderich's building of his army, correct?" he questioned Gryffin, uncertainty weakening his tone.

"Of course—I am his second in command."

"Why haven't you warned us?" Lord Castor quickly accused.

"Because he is still loyal to his brother," Lord Quince assumed quietly.

Gryffin quickly shook his head in denial. "No, no—please let me explain. Our army was weak after our civil war, and of course decimated following Atroxis. We have been building our army back to its former strength. I thought nothing more of it. Is not Lecevonia also striving to rebuild their forces?"

"If you are his second in command, surely your brother told you of his plans in Hiddon," General Gambeson said.

With an odd expression, Gryffin shook his head once more. "My brother told me he was going north, to Borea, and that he was dispersing our army throughout Tarasynian villages for drills. We have many new recruits who needed training, so foolishly, I believed him."

As his eyebrows turned down, I finally placed the look on Gryffin's face as pain. "I've been lied to, as well."

His face changed again, then, to determination. He straightened his shoulders. "I have decided to ceremonially declare my loyalty to Lecevonia." He reached one hand to me, and I lightly grasped his hand in mine. "I dedicate myself to Queen Rosemary and her kingdom."

An air of shock seemed to jolt through my advisors, and another quiet gasp escaped Lord Quince's lips. Lord Brock's eyes fluttered from Gryffin to me, then back again. He muttered something that I didn't quite catch.

I decided to step in, then. "Prince Gryffin can be trusted. He is coming to you of his own accord, ready to declare his loyalty! I trust him, and I believe that he may be able to stop this attack. He may be able to stop this *war*!" My hand tightened around his.

I looked to the general, knowing that my advisors would most likely swing in whatever direction he decided. But his expression still had not yet changed. "Is that not a risk worth taking?" I pressed.

General Gambeson's hand rested on his chin, elbow on the table, and his eyes stayed fixed on me. But I couldn't decide if he was truly looking at me or *through* me. Colonel Burnstead sat to his right, silent and unmoving. Avoiding influence.

Then, to my surprise, the general simply shrugged his shoulders. "Let him go," he said. "We have nothing to lose at this hour. There is nothing he can tell them that King Roderich doesn't already know."

"What? A-absurd!" Lord Castor stuttered. "He knows the layout of the castle, of the grounds—"

"If the Tarasynian army is close enough that the castle's layout would be useful, then we have bigger problems on our hands." General Gambeson waved his hand toward me. "Queen Rosemary is right—this could be our only chance at a truce."

The smallest swell of pride made me lift my shoulders. "Then it's settled," I said firmly. "Prince Gryffin must leave as soon as possible."

"Who will be going with him?" Lord Clark inquired.

I steeled myself once more. "He is going alone."

"Alone?" Lord Castor sputtered. "But—that is ridiculous—"

"Is it?" I countered. "Given what we know of King Roderich, is it so wrong to think that he may kill any unfamiliar riders upon arrival? I will not unnecessarily endanger my men. Not when we already have so few." I looked around the table, daring anyone to question me.

Thankfully, no one stepped up to the challenge. "Lord Castor, would you arrange a brief commendation ceremony? As quickly as we can."

I thought that if I asked him, his distrust would be satisfied. However, despite the need for urgency, Lord Castor bowed all too slowly and deliberately. "Of *course*, my queen."

I rolled my eyes, unable to resist responding just as pettily as he had. "*Thank* you, Lord Castor."

"Gather in the chapel in half an hour." Then, after shooting a final glare toward Gryffin, he marched out of the room.

As everyone else in the council room stood, Colonel Burnstead came forward and reached into his vest. "Can you read this?" He pushed the assassin's weathered scroll toward Gryffin's chest.

Gryffin unwound the scroll and studied the scrawling letters for only a second. "Of course I can." He glanced up at the colonel. "It's a Tarasynian encryption." He sat at the mahogany table and held his hand out for a quill and ink well.

As he scribbled a new message onto the scroll, I couldn't help but feel smug. I'd been right to involve Gryffin; had we done so from the beginning, we might have been more prepared for Roderich.

The colonel and I looked over his shoulder as he worked through the message, until finally, he held it out in front of him with a grimace. "It's barbaric. 'An arrow through the child princess, an arrow through the queen. Wait three days; the rebels will shelter thee. We will march from the west in the night, no fire alight. When the blue dawn blazes, we hit strong at first light.'"

"Darkly poetic, isn't it?" I laughed without humor.

"That is my brother," Gryffin said grimly. "He's one for grandeur."

"The rebels," I turned to Colonel Burnstead. "Does he mean the Rebels of the Red Sun? Why would they help Tarasyn?"

Colonel Burnstead shook his head. "I don't know. But right now, there is work to be done." He snatched the scroll from the table, bowed his head briefly, and jogged through the doors of the council room.

I laid my hand on Gryffin's shoulder. "Thank you."

"My Rosemary." He turned his head and softly kissed my hand.

In that moment, no other words needed to be said between us.

Lord Castor had worked quickly. Positioned at the top of the short steps in the front of the chapel was a large wooden chair, acting as a throne, and the tabernacle itself had been adorned with forsythia from the courtyard. The nerys lily in the window cast stark colors onto the floor and walls.

Hazel had come with the King's Cloak—a black horse hide, lined in cotton, only worn for formal ceremonies. It always emanated an inherent sensation of ancient power. My first time wearing it was my own coronation not too long ago. And it would be draped over my husband and I on our wedding day.

Also in Hazel's hands was my jeweled golden crown.

"Come, come—quickly!" Lord Castor gestured wildly with his hands, summoning me to the throne.

Draping the thick cloak over my shoulders, he commanded me to sit on the throne. Hazel gently laid the heavy crown atop my head, and after a quick kiss on the cheek, she backed away to take her seat in the first row of chairs.

My advisors were seated in the first row, and my guards lined the walls. The general and colonel weren't present, so I assumed that they had gone to ready our men.

Lord Castor positioned Gryffin before me, standing at the base of the chapel steps.

With everyone in place, Lord Castor opened Lecevonia's large ceremonial tome, the same that had been used for my coronation.

And an air of gravity immediately overtook the small room.

Before noon today, the citizens of the capitol would know of the target on their backs. They would be flocking to the castle, seeking refuge that I fervently hoped I'd be able to provide.

Then, it'd be another waiting game. All eyes would be toward the west.

Our best hope at any possible peace with Tarasyn was the man standing before me.

"Prince Gryffin Danicio of Tarasyn, kneel before your queen."

Gryffin lowered to his knees on the lowest step before the throne, and he held his hands in front of him, clasped together. A sign of weaponlessness, of fidelity.

Lord Castor read a long, albeit still abridged, passage from the heavy book, but I didn't hear the words. I instead fixed my attention on Gryffin, and I was again filled with an unending gratitude. This ceremony was the first step of one day marrying this man.

But first, we needed to live through tomorrow morning.

Then Gryffin spoke his part, his eyes never leaving mine. "I, Prince Gryffin Danicio of Tarasyn, swear my loyalty to the kingdom of Lecevonia, and to the Crowned, Her Majesty Queen Rosemary Avelia, Reigning Sovereign."

My job was simple, though I'd never done it before. I encapsulated Gryffin's hands with my own, and my strong "I accept your loyalty" rang through the Hall.

Lord Castor belted, "Lord Gryffin Danicio of Lecevonia, you may rise."

With my hands still wrapped around his, we shared a small smile.

It almost seemed as if the situation called for an applause. But instead, as a sliver of the great tension that had settled upon us since Sir Terrin's shocking outburst rescinded, the few in attendance let out a small collective sigh.

As my advisors stood, our call to action imminent, I laid a hand on Gryffin's cheek. "You must ride out to meet your brother immediately," I said fervently. "I will meet you down in the stable."

Gryffin rested his hand on my waist and daringly brought his lips to mine in a gentle kiss. However brief it may have been, my mind quieted, and I let myself melt into the trust and security he infinitely offered.

"I will see you soon," he said, pulling away.

Then, he turned and hurried out of the chapel, his boots clacking on the stone.

CHAPTER SIXTEEN

A̧S I WATCHED Gryffin leave the chapel, I noticed for the first time a lean silhouette propped against the door frame, and my heart began to thud.

The figure pushed himself from the wall and walked up the short aisle to me. Had my mind not already been so occupied, it might have reminded me of the future I'd envisioned, of Zeke walking up this same aisle in a white vest and waiting for me at the end of it.

I met him halfway until we stood inches away from each other, almost toe to toe. I had to tilt my head back to look at him.

"Well, that was short," he commented nonchalantly. "'Lord Gryffin.' Now, *that* I might be able to compete with," he smirked.

I rolled my eyes. "You know this doesn't strip away his Tarasynian status." But I couldn't stop that same small sliver of hope from passing quickly, like a gust of wind, through my tired mind.

"I know, Rose. Just striving to find the good in this morning." Then, Zeke heaved a heavy sigh. "Your sisters are almost ready."

I felt my chest tighten painfully. "Thank you so much, Zeke. You really are the only one whom I trust with their safety. And, as much as it aches to think of you leaving . . . I'm glad that you won't be here."

"I'm not, Rose." He shook his head once, hard. "I should be here as part of your guard, never letting my eyes off you."

His words knocked the air from my lungs, leaving me breathless as I tried to laugh. "I'll be all right. They may not even make it to the castle. Gryffin may stop them." I hoped to speak it into reality.

"I take it the wedding is back on, then?" Zeke tried to keep his tone light with a smile, but he couldn't hide the hint of disappointment there. I probably only recognized it because I felt it too.

"If all goes well tomorrow," I said quietly. That brought on another thought, and after a moment of hesitation, I took a deep breath. "Would you please hold off leaving until after Gryffin leaves? He doesn't know that you and my sisters are going, or where, and, well, it might be best that way. I still trust him," I said after receiving a pointed stare from Zeke, "but I don't want to take any chances. Not with my sisters."

"Fair enough," Zeke answered with narrowed eyes.

My anxiety was almost at its peak. "I'd better go see Gryffin off."

"We won't be far behind."

We brushed hands, our fingers grasping longingly for the other's, and I had to fight back a sob that had suddenly risen from my throat.

I quickly turned to Hazel, hoping that my anguish was not noticeable.

But, of course, she saw right through my strong façade. She strode forward and grasped my hand.

"My queen," she said, her own sadness shining through her old amber eyes.

I patted her hand softly. "I'll meet you down at the stables to see you off with my sisters.”

“I . . .” she hesitated. Then, she straightened her drooping shoulders and, though her lower lip pouted a bit, stood tall. “I expect that I’ll have a roomful of dresses to tend to when I return, yes?”

“And trousers,” I said, giving her my best mischievous smile. And, with no care of witnesses, I wrapped my arms around the older woman. I held her tightly, praying that this woman, this woman that had become my mother-figure, would never have to leave my side again.

I finally released her. “Go on, get packed quickly. I’ll see you soon!”

Then, I turned on my heel and hurried out of the chapel. I rushed down the stairs, my guards trailing closely, with the path to the stable now at the forefront of my mind.

As I stepped outside into the courtyard, I caught my first glimpse at the shred of sunlight peeping through the thinning layer of clouds today, and I chuckled at the irony. Today was hardly a day for sunlight.

I could tell that being outdoors, no longer in the secure haven of the castle walls, made my guards on edge; they hovered closer to me as I jogged down the stone path and through the old, overgrown iron gates that led to the stables. The dampness of the air engulfed us, the humidity making the spring chill feel even colder. With not enough sun to dry the cobblestones, water from yesterday’s storms pooled in the cracks between the laid rocks, and as the path transitioned from stone to dirt, mud splashed up onto my dress as I hurried to the stable doors.

Once inside, the stable was a tornado of movement. Cavalry horses were being led through the aisles, already half-dressed in metal armor, saddles upon their backs. The hammering of the farriers could only be faintly heard amidst the clopping of hooves, squeals of stubborn horses, and shouting between castle workers and cavalrymen. The dim firelit air was clouded with stirred dust. For the first time since my coronation, no one seemed to notice my entrance.

Briefly through a gap between two horses, I caught a glimpse of Gryffin's white mare, Lucy, in a far stall, with Gryffin stooped near her front legs. I slipped my way through the tumult of the stable to them.

"Gryffin!"

At the sound of my voice through the noise, Gryffin straightened and scanned the stable until his eyes landed on me. Though he wore a focused, intense expression, he still smiled as I approached.

I stopped just outside the stall. "Do you have everything you need?"

Celeste appeared then, from around Lucy's rump.

"I think we've got him taken care of, Rose," she said quickly, refastening one of the saddlebags secured at Lucy's side. "He will probably reach Tarasyn's army in eight hours, at the rate they're said to be traveling." Her worried gaze flickered over to me.

That was not much time at all.

In eight hours, the capitol's fate may be sealed.

And we wouldn't know that fate until either Gryffin returned with his brother's terms, or the Tarasynian army marched over the nearest hill as their answer.

Gryffin patted Lucy's neck. "I believe that's all." Finally, he turned to me, his ocean eyes heavy.

I closed the distance between us and wrapped my arms tightly around him, my head pressed against his shoulder. I clung to him, and his arms snaked around me just as fervently. Though I held my tears, my dry sobs soaked into his vest, and I felt Gryffin's hand cradling the back of my head. He held me to him so tightly, crushing his face into my hair, his lips pressed firmly on the top of my head.

When we released each other, I placed my hands on his cheeks, lifted my face to his, and kissed him with no hesitancy. My body bowed against his as he leaned into me, his hands gripping my waist, and I tried to memorize the feel of his curly hair tangled in my fingers. That same familiar melting was there, but this kiss, with its odd feeling of finality, held more. A stronger emotion that immediately swept my breath out of my lungs. A growing emotion.

A growing love.

Gryffin must have felt it too because when we parted, he was gasping. He pressed his forehead to mine and laughed breathlessly. "They're better each time, aren't they?"

I couldn't help but laugh, despite the turmoil raging through my mind.

"I have to leave, Rosemary. But I *will* be back," he said, placing a finger under my chin and lifting my head. His sincere eyes raked across my face, absorbing, and settled on my eyes.

"I'll be waiting, then."

As he exhaled a sharp, humorless chuckle, he put one foot in his stirrup and mounted his horse. With a parting glance, he walked his horse to the stable's open door, then kicked her straight away into a gallop.

In a matter of seconds, he had disappeared down the westward path.

Then, I heard Celeste's voice in my ear. "Zeke and your sisters are preparing to leave, Rose. The wagon is being packed in the south end," she whispered.

Would the goodbyes ever stop?

"Thank you, Celeste," I responded quietly.

Once again squeezing our way through the chaos of the stable, my guards and I finally emerged from the bustle into clearer air, not as filled with dust. The southern aisle was much quieter, as most horses down here belonged to capitol citizens, and at the end of the aisle, the royal family's wagon sat in front of the gaping wide stable doors. The dark and sturdy wooden carriage had been fitted with a leather covering, and two robust, dark brown horses were harnessed in front of it. The horses stood calmly, almost sleepily, unperturbed by the rush of people packing chests and supplies onto the wagon. I looked around, searching for Midas, until I spotted him tethered to the rear of the wagon, ears back and black tail swinging not so calmly.

"Rose!"

I wheeled around and saw Clara, her hands clutching the ends of a woolen scarf that had been tucked around her neck. Walking more slowly after her were Isabele and Lisette, both dressed in coats, prepared for the chill of the ride and the cold sea breeze that often gusted through Port Della's streets.

I stooped down and took Clara into my arms, hugging her close. I buried my face into her curls and closed my eyes, clinging to my baby sister as tightly as she was clinging to me. She was so small. She didn't deserve this fear that had belayed itself onto my family.

I felt a soft hand on my shoulder, and I looked up to see Isabele's eyes, glassy with tears, peering down at me. I stood, Clara's arms sliding down to my waist, and hugged Isabele and Lisette around their shoulders.

"Thank you so much," I whispered to them, "for making sure she is safe."

"Of course, Rose," Isabele responded quietly, her voice thick. "She's our sister, as well, you know."

I chuckled. "I know." A flood of guilt washed over me again. "I'm so sorry that I won't be there with you."

"Then come with us, Rose," Isabele insisted, her voice growing louder. "Why not? You need to be protected too!"

"I *will* be protected, Isa," I said, trying to assure her. For her benefit, I gestured to my guards who faithfully stood around me. "These men won't let anyone get close to me."

"She can't simply *leave*, Isabele," Lisette said, so matter-of-factly. "She's the queen. This is her kingdom, her capitol. She *has* to stand her ground."

I squeezed Lisette's hand tightly, thankful for her understanding. She would have made an excellent queen; her mind functioned the right way.

I couldn't deny that I so badly wanted to hop into that cart with them and be taken to our port city, far out of reach from King Roderich and his army. To see the sea's deep waters again, feel the sea spray in the air, walk on the rocky beaches hugging the coastline. But I knew that if I went with them, King Roderich would not stop at Equos. I was the one he wanted dead.

I involuntarily shuddered as I thought of King Roderich. I'd never dealt with such unadulterated evil before. He'd killed the king and queen of Hiddon, and I unquestionably knew that he would not hesitate to kill me too.

No. I couldn't leave. If I left, I'd only feel a crushing guilt for leaving my capitol in the hands of those who couldn't leave. Those who swore to face death without question.

That same duty tethered me to the castle now.

"You three will be all right now," I said firmly. Though the reminder was more so for me than them.

I caught sight of Zeke, then, squatting inside the carriage and securing chests and wooden supply boxes with ropes. As we approached, he straightened and wiped a dirty hand across his forehead. He didn't look nearly as prepared for the chill of the journey as my sisters were, with only his thin tunic tucked into his trousers, but I supposed that he knew what he was doing.

I expected him to greet us with my favorite grin, but his face remained grim and displeased. He only smiled as he took little Clara from my arms and then helped Isabele and Lisette into the wagon with an extended hand; but when he turned to me, his hard frown had returned.

"Just waiting for Hazel. Besides that, everything is ready. As you commanded, Rose," he spat harshly.

His vicious tone sent a shudder down my spine. "Zeke, please, not now." Of all the goodbyes, I didn't want this farewell to be smeared with grudges and loathing.

"I should be here with you," he said curtly, jumping off the back of the wagon. He refused to look at me, overly focused on brushing a smudge of dust off his shoulder.

I sighed, feeling my patience waning. I decided to change subjects to something that involved less of an impasse. "Why is Midas tied back here?"

Zeke looked past me, toward my horse. Midas' black tail still swished in agitation, ears laid against his head. Finally, Zeke's eyes rested on my face, and he smirked. That little half-smile. "We weren't going to make him pull the cart, Rose. He's *your* horse, and he's just as stubborn. Besides, those two bays are stronger." He reached around me and patted Midas's rump, making the big black horse grunt and stomp his foot. "But we'll still take him along with us, before he's roped into military duty."

"Thank you," I said softly. Before he could retract his arm, I grabbed his hand and interlaced my fingers through his. "Truly. For all of this."

Zeke's gaze fixed on our hands for a lingering second, and when he finally met my eyes, I saw his glistening with moisture once again. Probably angry tears more than anything.

Then, before I could say anything else, he yanked me to him and encircled his arms around me. I slammed into his chest, quite hard really, and my breath whooshed out of me. But, as I took in my next jagged breath, my throat was suddenly thick with my own tears. I wrapped my arms around his waist and held him to me, and I desperately tried to push out the stubborn reminder that this might be the last time I hug him like this.

The last time I saw him at all, if King Roderich got to me first.

He released me and took my face in his hands. "You'll try your absolute greatest to stay alive, right?" he asked fervently, intensity burning in his features. "I can count on you to keep yourself safe?"

"Why do you even have to ask?" I fired back, glaring at him in indignation through tears that threatened to fall. Did he really think that I *wished* to die?

"Just promise me, Rose."

I hardly had any energy to spare, so I sighed relentingly. "Of course I will, Zeke."

He looked at me, eyes scanning my face for a moment, until he finally seemed satisfied with my answer. His forehead relaxed, and a ridiculous grin began to spread across his face as he shrugged. "I'm just asking that you don't gallivant into danger as you normally would."

I rolled my eyes and punched him in the stomach. I was in no mood for teasing.

But he only chuckled, not phased in the slightest, and trapped my hand in his. He kissed it lightly and held it to his chest. There was an urgency in his grip, and I knew that this goodbye was as painful for him as it was for me.

When he finally released my hand, the wound in my chest ached instantly.

An exasperated huff sounded from behind me, and when I turned, I saw Hazel sidestepping down the aisle, dragging a small chest behind her. Zeke left my side to help, and I held my arms out to the woman once more.

"I'm only spending the next few days with *this* one," she muttered in my ear, nodding her head toward Zeke, "because you ask me to."

Zeke chuckled and held out his hand to Hazel, ready to help her step into the wagon. "Oh, now Hazel. I'm at least bearable for a few days, yes?"

Once my lady-in-waiting was settled into the wagon with my sisters, Zeke hopped down to the straw-covered ground.

"We should arrive in Port Della tomorrow morning," he said as he walked to his horse—a large dapple-gray gelding that has been his companion since he joined the scouts three years ago. Hugo, I believe his name was.

"Now it's your turn," I said. "Promise me you'll stay safe while you're away."

"No need to worry about me, Rose. I'm always safe," he retorted, securing his horse's saddle.

I crossed my arms over my chest. "Oh, I beg to differ."

"I thought queens didn't beg," he said with a smirk.

I groaned in frustration and threw my hands up in the air. There was never any way to win with this man.

"All right, just go now!" I said urgently. Time was running too quickly out of our grasp. For all I knew, King Roderich could have been right over the horizon.

I saw all three of my sisters pop their heads from around the canopy surrounding the carriage, and I recognized the scared grief on their faces. I'm sure my own face mirrored theirs.

I patted Midas beside me and laid my forehead against his warm neck. "Soon, my friend," I whispered.

Zeke, from atop his horse, held his hand down to me, and I took it one last time. "Please be careful," I reiterated helplessly, all other words evading me.

Then, I heard the carriage driver click his tongue and the swish of the reins, and the carriage jolted into motion as the bays grunted and lurched forward. Midas whinnied in protest initially, but after realizing he had no choice but to follow, he lowered his head and obliged, walking forward with no objection. The soldiers accompanying the princesses all clicked their horses forward, and the clacking of hooves against the stone floor echoed through the nearby stalls.

Zeke squeezed my hand in farewell. He mouthed a silent *I love you*, and that was when my first tears finally escaped. He wheeled his horse around, Hugo snorting as he did so, and trotted after the wagon.

I stood there, watching the five most meaningful people in my life disappear down the eastward dirt-covered road. Good. They shouldn't be here, not when the castle walls were the only fortitude between us and the enemy imposing death on my people. Still, my tears wouldn't stop flowing steadily over my cheeks.

Upon exiting the stables, instead of turning left toward the castle, Amos took a right, down a dirt-covered path leading to the castle craftsmen.

"Amos?" I asked. My confusion melded with a bit of impatience; surely my advisors were looking for me.

"Well," he began, "you made a request a few days ago that albeit seemed strange at the time. But, now, it seems to be a request fitting of a queen, Your Majesty."

I had to fight the urge to roll my eyes. My emotions were too wild for riddles right now, and a biting reply was about to fly from my lips. However, as we passed through the increasingly thick mass of people, soldiers and castle workers alike rushing through the workshops, my irritation simply morphed into confusion. Then, when we stopped in front of the blacksmith, I finally understood.

"My request for a sword!" Excitement suddenly began coursing through me. I turned to Amos with a beaming smile, and he chuckled.

Stifling steam and blistering fire welcomed us as we walked into the blacksmith's workshop. The humid air would have been a given on any normal day, but now it swam with the chaos of a smithy preparing for battle; apprentices—the blacksmith's seven sons and one daughter—hustled around the shop, fanning flames and cooling worked metal in large vats of water. Newly forged swords, axes and chainmail lay piled against the wall, ready to be delivered to our soldiers. My heart surged with pride at the sight; my people had not given into despair, and they were readying to fight for our kingdom.

The blacksmith, Jacobin, had just handed off a new lance to one of his boys and tirelessly took up another misshapen rod of heated iron as we approached his anvil. When the burly man looked up at us, the sparks stopped bursting into the air.

"Yer Majesty!" he exclaimed, with a big belly laugh.

Hearing his greeting, the apprentices in the smithy all stuttered to a stop mid-task. And the whispers began to rise.

"Her Majesty?" "What is she doing here?" "Why didn't she leave

the city?"

I took advantage of the sudden uncomfortable silence. "Thank you all for your diligent work. Each and every one of you is doing the kingdom a tremendous service." My own voice surprised me. It sounded unwavering, confident, powerful. More so than I felt, yet still, I continued on. "We *will* see through to tomorrow!"

My little speech sent the boys into a rowdy cheer, whooping and raising their fists into the air. Jacobin's daughter was hard at work straightening out an ax handle, but I saw the corners of her mouth rise. I couldn't help but smile at their enthusiasm, and when I glanced at Jacobin, his proud grin said the same.

"Alrigh', now, ge' back to work!" he bellowed, slowly silencing his children. "Those axes aren' gonna sharpen themselves!"

With the apprentices once again buzzing around the smithy, Jacobin bowed his head to me and wiped his blackened hands on a nearby towel, leaving streaks of soot. Still smiling his large grin, he clapped Amos on the back. "Amos! It's good to see ya, mate!"

Amos chuckled. "Likewise, brother."

Then Jacobin turned to me and took my hands, enveloping them in his large bear paws. "Now, what canni do for ya, my queen?"

I tried to stand a little taller. "I'd like a sword made for me. A strong longsword that'll fit my frame."

The initial shock in his eyes didn't surprise me; he'd probably never been asked to do such a thing for a queen before now. But his shock quickly diminished into a smirk.

"Ah, I've heard that yer learnin'," he said smugly. "Takin' lessons from this one here, eh?" He nodded his head toward Amos. Then he leaned in closely and murmured, "I've always been the bet'er swordsman, ya know."

But Amos overheard and smacked the back of his brother's head.

"How about you just stick to making them?" he teased.

Jacobin turned back to me. "I can do that for ya, but it won' be ready for a few days, now. Unless, o' course, you'd like me to do it firs' thing?"

"No, no," I said quickly. "There are much more pressing needs right now." I was not about to stop him from equipping my army.

He pursed his lips tightly, his mustache brushing his big beard, before waving us to follow. "There migh' be somethin' I can still give to ya," he said. "Come this way."

He led us to a quieter back room, which must have been his office. Or, some form of it—it was a little hard to tell when everything was coated in a thin layer of black coal dust. He lifted a stack of papers that appeared to have hand drawn designs on them from atop a chest and flipped up the unlocked latch.

From the chest, he pulled out a large burlap sack. "This was my eldest son's firs' set of brigandine armor." He reached into the sack and began pulling out individual pieces of heavy leather, riveted with iron studs along the seams. Torso, forelegs, forearms, along with a long-sleeved chainmail shirt. An entire set.

It looked incredible.

"No time for fittin' ya to plate armor, I'm afraid," Jacobin was saying, sounding a bit chagrined. "Bu' I think it'll fit ya well."

"It's perfect, Jacobin!" My amazement was almost certainly clear in my huge grin. "Thank you. Really."

That brought Jacobin's characteristic smile back to his face, and a loud chortle made his beard quiver. "It'll be a bi' sturdier than yer pretty dresses and trousers, a' least." Then, he heaved a very deep sigh. "So, yer stayin' here a' Hillstone, then."

I nodded, suddenly solemn. "I cannot leave my people."

He studied me for a moment, his deep-set eyes boring into mine.

"Tha's very noble of ya," he finally said. "Very admirable. Yer mother and father mus' be smilin' down atcha, no doubt. May their souls res' in peace."

"Thank you," I said, smiling softly. "But truly, it's my duty. Besides," I teased, in an attempt to lighten the mood again, "Hillstone *is* the strongest keep in the kingdom, after all."

Jacobin chuckled. "Tha' it is, I 'spose."

I took his big, scarred hand in mine. "I know it may not seem possible to leave the forge, but if you can, *please* take yourself and your family inside the castle. The doors are open for any capitol citizen seeking refuge."

He smiled warmly. "I thank ya, my queen. I will send my wife and youngest daugh'er, I assure ya. Now!" he boomed, "I got'a return to my anvil! Always a pleasure, Yer Majesty." He bowed his head and ambled out of his office, yelling to his apprentices as he went. "Randall! Tha' sword bet'er be hot and ready!"

As we left Jacobin's workshop, burlap sack slung over Roger's shoulder, I felt the strongest upsurge of fortitude move through me, lifting my spirits higher than they'd been yet today.

Back at the castle, I wrapped myself in work, any work I could find, which undoubtedly helped to distract me from my fear. My advisors hadn't heard any news from the general, so I was down in the kitchens, kneading bread for the bakers and cutting potatoes for the cooks. With the influx of citizens hurriedly making their way into the castle, we had more people to feed than ever. Then I was in the Great Hall, arranging bedding on the floor for the citizens who couldn't be squeezed into our guest quarters—which were already being shared by multiple families. Even Gryffin's quarters were overtaken as we tried to fit as many people as possible.

By the afternoon, between the guest wing, Great Hall, kitchens, and even spilling into the corridors and lining the walls, we had been able to find a space for any capitol citizen that sought sanctuary. From the windows in the halls that overlooked the city, Equos's streets looked silent and lifeless.

For a while, I stared out of the west-facing windows, toward the foothills. I strained my eyes against the setting sun, focusing on the road over the distant hilltop where I expected to see any sign of our impending fate. Would Gryffin appear with good news? Though I knew it was too early for him to possibly make the return trip, I didn't try to squelch my hope.

However, after a fruitless stretch of time, I once again needed to find something to do. So, I returned to the kitchens.

The moment my guards and I walked in, I felt sweat immediately accumulate and trickle down my back. The kitchens were a blistering furnace, with fires ablaze roasting countless cuts of boar and lamb and cooking mounds of vegetables, the stone ovens alight and baking full loaves of bread, no time available to be cut into rolls. Not only did we have the citizens to feed, but also an assembled army of four thousand three hundred men.

I saw some unfamiliar faces—citizens of the capitol who were cooks or bakers by trade, aiding the castle workers in the newly increased workload.

But among familiar faces, I found Lucinda, hard at work kneading bread dough.

"May I help?" I asked quietly, sidling up to her.

After a short curtsy, the little girl nodded tiredly and motioned to a nearby wooden slab piled high with loaves of dark bread. "Those need to be sliced and handed out to people in the corridors."

I nodded, took up a knife, and began my work. This bread was not the normal white bread, pandemain, the kitchens normally served. It was much grainier, maybe rye or barley, and much denser. We must've run out of our nicely sifted flour.

"It's called maslin," Lucinda said from beside me. "It's what we castle workers bake for ourselves."

My head turned sharply in her direction, surprised. "You don't eat the pandemain?" I asked in surprise.

"Only when there's extra. The days when the fluffy white bread is leftover are the best days!" The thought seemed to give her a sudden energy, and she smiled brightly, though her eyes still drooped with fatigue.

Perhaps we could start including sifted flour with their wages. Especially after today, and if we made it through tomorrow, they deserved it.

I took my slab of sliced bread and made my way back up the stairs. The windows showed the darkness of night now. The clouds had fully dissipated, showing a clear night sky with the moon glowing in a crescent. With time rushing past us, I felt my anxiety returning, so I turned my attention to the people lining the halls, who had immediately turned their heads at the sight of their queen delivering fresh bread.

I put the warmest smile that I could muster on my face and handed several slices to a small family on my left—a mother, father, and two young boys. The oldest couldn't have been older than Clara.

"Thank you, Your Majesty," the mother murmured, her head bowed.

I continued down the hall, handing slices of maslin to outstretched hands and bowed heads. All of these people, put in danger due to King Roderich's monstrous pursuits.

Once I'd finished my task assigned to me by Lucinda, and still having too much time to pass, I decided that now was a good time to change into my armor.

In my rooms, I stared at the stretches of leather before me. I was just as enamored by them as I had been in the smithy. Dark, thick leather that would ward off shallow sword swipes, held steadfastly together by deep iron rivets that deftly swirled into a discreet pattern across the torso. Finished off with iron plates at the elbows and shoulders, all laid over a durable chainmail shirt.

My remaining chambermaids helped me into my armor, but my heart ached for Hazel. I felt her absence in my bones, as if a portion of my strength had vanished and left me tired.

But I could not afford to be tired now.

The armor fit almost perfectly, aside from taking away the entirety of my figure. Which wouldn't have bothered me, but the extra leather billowed heavily around my midsection. So I cinched a leather belt around my waist. I secured my cobalt and carmine cloak around me, and since I wasn't entirely sure of what type of shoes to wear, I opted for my trusty leather riding boots.

As I stood before my mirror, taking in my appearance, I again felt that surge of fortitude. Of strength, for I *looked* strong. Of hope, for my green eyes shined back at me almost daringly. However temporary, I felt in control.

Then, back to the westward window I went. It had to be almost morning by now, right? But as I gazed out into the dark western sky, there was no way to know if dawn was one hour away or three.

Then, I saw a light.

A pinpoint of torchlight, traveling over the hill crest, down the dirt-covered road toward the castle.

Gryffin!

Then, two lights. I stared, perplexed. Who would be with him?

A third light came into view then, this time heading from the castle. Riding swiftly to meet Gryffin and his guest.

I stared out of the window for a long while, following the torches that seemed to take an eternity to meet. Finally, the three lights came together and paused, most likely the riders discussing something. Then, all three lights were on the move again, traveling together back down the road toward the castle.

I turned from the window and rushed down the hall, my advisors' office as my destination. I heard quick footsteps around the corner then, and Lord Brock appeared, his face a portrait of intensity. "My queen!" He rushed forward, coming to a halt in front of me. "Prince Gryffin has returned—"

I nodded quickly. "I just saw them. Do we know who is with him?"

Lord Brock shook his head. "Not yet. We've sent a scout to meet them."

By the time Lord Brock and I entered the council room, General Gambeson was already there, studying a stack of parchment intently. The colonels must have been outside the capitol's wall with our army. With the general were my other three advisors, each of their nervous ticks surfacing—Lord Clark's tapping on the table, Lord Quince's leg bouncing, Lord Castor's tuneless whistling.

I paced back and forth across the large room, again too anxious to sit.

And we waited.

And waited.

Finally, I heard footsteps approaching down the hallway. No voices, though.

Then, the scout that had returned from Hiddon, Sir Terrin, stood in the open doorway. My advisors all stood from their seats, and General Gambeson looked up from his papers.

"Your Majesty," Sir Terrin greeted me quickly, "Prince Gryffin Danicio has returned." Then, his voice dropped. "And with him is His Majesty, King Roderich of Tarasyn."

We all stood frozen as stone.

So, Gryffin had succeeded in making his brother just pause and listen. And he had convinced him to speak to me. That should have given me some sense of relief, but, mentally and physically, I remained tense.

King Roderich had come *himself* to discuss terms?

Running off no sleep, my mind could only absorb so much at a time. But I had to keep myself focused.

I was about to face my true assassin.

I turned to my advisors. "Where to meet with him?"

"Typically, you'd receive him in the Great Hall," Lord Clark said, "but the Hall is rather occupied at the moment . . ."

"The chapel?" Lord Quince suggested. "It's quiet, private."

"No," Lord Clark answered quickly, shaking his head. "The chapel is too isolated. With only one entrance, it wouldn't be safe."

"Here, then," interjected the general gruffly. "Right in the council room. It is a war meeting, after all."

His words intrigued me. This was the room in which I'd met my suitors. Had those been more so business matters than I'd initially gathered?

"Move the capitol citizens from the corridor to the Hall," I commanded. "I won't have any citizen close to that man." And I didn't want King Roderich to see the extent of the panic he'd instilled in us. "Once the citizens are safe, have King Roderich escorted here."

Sir Terrin bowed and quietly left the council room.

"My queen," said Lord Brock slowly, sweat beading on his forehead. "Are . . . are you ready to meet with him?"

No. I had absolutely no desire to meet with this ruthless, dangerous man. This man who had killed innocent, *helpless* people for the sake of power that wasn't his to take, and who planned to do the same here.

However, hadn't he *already* done the same here? Hadn't he sent his men to kill me in cold blood, in the solitude of the forest, where I may not have been found for *days*? Hadn't he tried to kill Clara—and instead killed Sterling, a truly innocent man, in the castle's very courtyard? Hadn't that already stripped my kingdom—stripped *me*—of power?

I may have been afraid of the man, but my anger geared against him was stronger. I would not permit him to mangle and destroy Lecevonia as he had Hiddon.

"Yes," I finally answered. "I am ready to meet with him."

Outside the council room, the corridor had become very quiet. I heard only the early morning wind, the only movement in the halls, whistling through the high windows, flickering the candlelight. The spring sun was still an hour, maybe a little less, from shining its first rays over the far hilltops.

The outside world was still sleeping, waiting for the gray of the morning, but my castle was very much awake, and it seemed to almost vibrate in its tension.

Then, I heard boots clicking against the stone hallway. More than one set of feet.

As they grew louder, my advisors all straightened in their seats. One of them—I did not turn to see who—cleared his throat quietly. General Gambeson looked up from his papers, his gaze now trained on the door.

And I remained standing, my feet planted onto the strong stone floor beneath me, my shoulders squared.

I was ready.

"We won't leave your side, Your Majesty," Amos said, his voice low in my ear.

Sir Terrin reappeared at the door then, his face taut in clear discomfort as he bowed to me. "Your Majesty, King Roderich Danicio and Prince Gryffin, of Tarasyn."

Gryffin strode in first, taking long, quick strides, and his blue eyes scanned the room until he found me.

Had I not been so tense, I'd have felt overwhelming relief in seeing him standing there, his eyes on mine. I couldn't deny that part of me had feared that his brother would have killed him on the spot. Even as I saw his torchlight approaching over the hill, I hadn't truly absorbed that Gryffin had returned. But now, with him physically only a few paces away from me, I allowed myself to feel an inkling of reprieve. I felt stronger, more secure in my resolve. It was as if his mere presence was holding me together now.

He didn't offer a smile, and I doubted that I could have returned one. His face only remained grave, concerned. He didn't approach me; instead, he stopped midway between me and the open council room door, and he turned his head back toward the hall. Then, a third man appeared in the doorway.

"Hello, Rosemary."

CHAPTER SEVENTEEN

THE FIRST THING that caught my eye was the massive black crow perched on King Roderich's shoulder. It stayed silent and unmoving, but I would have been almost certain that it too had its head turned in my direction, staring at me through one eye.

The initial resemblance between Gryffin and his brother was unnerving—King Roderich had the same dark brown curls, the same broad shoulders, the same angled facial features. They were even starkly close to the same height.

But as I studied King Roderich more closely, the dissimilarities stood out more so than the resemblance. For one, King Roderich's face was torn through with scars, miniscule white slashes that suddenly gave his face a strange textured appearance.

What had happened to him?

And his eyes. No semblance of Gryffin's kind, ocean blue eyes were to be seen upon this man's face. Instead, Roderich's eyes were almost . . . red. A deep, darkened crimson that could almost be called brown. Like garnets. And they burned with a sickening confidence.

His face was hardened into a smile, his eyes crinkled at their scarred corners.

Gryffin spoke first, turning toward his brother. "You *will* address her as Queen while in her kingdom," he said curtly.

King Roderich chuckled quietly and shrugged his shoulders, his crow silently stretching out its long, dark wings at the disturbance. "All right, little brother. As you insist." His voice was as deep and clear as Gryffin's. Then he turned his lazy gaze back to me. I felt him scrutinizing my every feature, and I tried to stand taller. "So, you're the vibrant, young Queen Rosemary Avelia."

I lifted my chin and refused to break eye contact. As I looked at King Roderich more closely, I saw small red flecks in his eyes, and they gave off an illusion of flames. Dancing, flickering flames.

His crow suddenly flapped its massive wings, the whoosh of air breaking the silence in the council room, and my eyes inadvertently flickered to the large bird. Did crows actually grow this *large*?

"Ah!" King Roderich exclaimed, following my gaze. "How rude I must seem, walking into this room with a giant bird on my shoulder, without introducing him. As if he isn't conspicuous. This is Corvus, a survivor of the Corvid Incident that plagued the Peninsula last year." He shrugged again. "My apologies."

My apologies? What did that mean?

I didn't understand why he was being so polite. Hadn't he ridden here with the intention of decimating my kingdom?

His mannerisms were so similar to Gryffin's—how he spoke, the way he held himself, the air of personable confidence he upheld. But his *intentions* were the exact opposite: as Gryffin stood between us, tense, wanting no fight, Roderich seemed to relish in the threat he imposed.

His deep voice broke my evaluation.

"So, please, what terms would you like to discuss?"

He was asking *me?*

His question nailed me to the floor, sewed my mouth shut. I hadn't expected to be given the opportunity to speak first. Why hadn't I discussed this possibility with my advisors? What on Haggard's green earth did I request?

"You're quiet for the one who wanted to speak with me," Roderich mused with a laugh.

I felt my eyes narrow, my indignation rising through my embarrassment. Fine. I figured the best course of action was honesty.

"What can I give you to spare any destruction to my kingdom?"

King Roderich chuckled. "No terms in mind, then."

His belittlement lit a blaze of anger in me. "Horses. As many as your men can ride."

"No, thank you. I'd rather just take them."

"The lives of your men, then. My soldiers are well trained and *will* leave their mark upon your army. If we end this now, no lives need to be lost."

"I don't shy away from death." He folded his hands behind his back, smirking at me.

My fury only grew. What more did I have to offer?

Gryffin caught my gaze with his own, a wary but very pointed stare, and I suddenly understood.

"I offer your brother my hand in marriage," I declared. "If you leave my kingdom unscathed."

King Roderich paused just long enough for me to think he was considering my offer. He looked to Gryffin with a strange glint in his eye. Sinister. "She *is* quite beautiful, brother." Then, he faced me again, all notion of politeness gone. "But not very smart. Why would that stop me from taking the kingdom as my own and claiming it for Tarasyn?"

Through my periphery, I saw Lord Brock's head turn just slightly in my direction before looking straight ahead again. Encouraged by no uproar from my advisors, I asked, "Is not a strong connection between the two kingdoms worth more than a broken, pillaged landscape?"

King Roderich stood quietly, studying me for a moment. "Do you know *why* I want to claim Lecevonia as my own?" he finally inquired.

But he didn't wait for a response before continuing. "Because, since the formation of the Five Kingdoms, Lecevonia has always been the powerhouse of the Peninsula. Equos's Talent to *create* horses? Amazing!" His laugh sounded incredulous. "If only Tarasyn's Viridi had been given that kind of power! Plants?" He spat upon the floor. "A waste. Viridi was much more cutthroat, and she deserved more. Had *she* been able to build armies overnight, Tarasyn would be the leading power today!" He glanced slowly around the room, eyeing my advisors, the general. "I find it hard to believe that there no Talented here in the kingdom."

Talented? My mind was turning, trying to make sense of his words. Didn't his father *hunt* for Talented in Tarasyn? Didn't Gryffin say that he and his brother despised their father's obsession?

Unless the mad king's obsession had more of an effect on King Roderich than Gryffin had known.

"And what's more," King Roderich continued, "Lecevonia has the most land, not to mention the largest river system! So much fertile land. Viridi would have flourished here. And it has the longest coastline. Tarasyn has no viable coastline, as *wretchedly* mountainous as we are. Trade by vessel?" He scoffed. "Impossible." He took a slow step forward, and my guards shifted with him, shielding me more effectively. "Equos took more than his fair share. With Lecevonia's land under my rule, Tarasyn would be the leading power of the Peninsula." He shook his head slowly. "Why would I want to give up that opportunity for anything less?"

"Then why have you come to speak with me?" I demanded. "Your mind has clearly settled on bloodshed long ago."

"Curiosity, I suppose. I wanted to see who my men have failed to kill." His smile stretched further over his teeth, turning into a wicked sneer. "This won't be your kingdom for very much longer, anyhow."

"How dare you threaten me as you stand in my keep?" I suddenly shot back, my indignation at its peak. "With *my* men surrounding you?"

"*My* men surround *you*, Queen," he shouted, holding his arms out wide. "They surround the capitol walls, and they far outnumber your forces."

"You overstep, brother," Gryffin warned.

Roderich's lips curled as he laughed. "Oh, Gryffin, I overstepped a while ago."

Just then, up in the high window, something flew through the bars. I saw a flash of metal as it glinted in the ambient light and heard the clang as it caught around the bars. A grapnel?

A disjointed noise from the hall outside the council room then reached our ears. Shouts, metal clanging, pounding footsteps.

Gryffin understood what was happening before I did. His head turned sharply in my direction, and his wide eyes were filled with unmistakable panic.

"Go!" he shouted forcefully. Suddenly, he swung around just as Roderich's sword clipped his left shoulder. Gryffin quickly unsheathed his own weapon.

And then my guards closed in around me.

We exited the council room through a concealed narrow door that opened to the maid's corridor, which was an entire labyrinth laid behind the castle walls that was used exclusively by the castle workers. I hadn't been in it since I was a child.

My guards jostled me along urgently, practically running, and I had no idea where we were going.

The strength of my kingdom—and the strength I'd foolishly thought I had—began to dissipate before me as the glint of that grapnel flashed in my eyes over and over again.

I was still reeling from the reality that was struggling to take hold, and I must not have been the only one, for Thomas, as if trying to accept it himself, said breathlessly, "King Roderich's men have already entered the castle."

"He tricked all of us," Amos said, cursing under his breath. "He had us all preoccupied, talking of terms, all while his men had already breached the capitol walls. He must think us very stupid right now."

I surely felt very stupid. My steps faltered, almost tripping Hugh and Robert behind me.

"My advisors!" I gasped, and I tried to turn back. "We must—"

But Hugh stopped me by the shoulders. "No, Your Majesty! They will have to take care of themselves!"

Still, I persisted, halting where I stood. "Some of you *must* go back! I don't need six men to protect me when Gryffin and General Gambeson are the only two in that room with weapons!"

"My queen—"

"I command you and Robert to return to the council room to protect whoever you can!" I looked around at the four other men cramped into this tiny corridor. "Geoffrey, you better go too."

I was met with several protests.

"Your Majesty," Amos said adamantly, "*you* are the most important person in this castle that needs protection. *You* are the sole person who cannot be lost."

"And I have people that I cannot lose," I responded, almost pleading now. But I knew that I didn't need to plead. I straightened my shoulders and hardened my voice. "Hugh, Robert, and Geoffrey—go."

In the need for urgency, they no longer argued. The three men turned around, and my remaining guards and I continued down the corridor hurriedly.

My thoughts went to all the people in the Great Hall. Had I made them sitting ducks, vulnerable to the Tarasynian soldiers, all gathered in one place for their convenience?

No, I stopped myself. Some of my own soldiers were in that room too. I had to believe that my people were protected. Just as I'd done what I could to protect my sisters, Hazel, and Zeke. I fervently hoped that they had made it far from here by now.

There was a flicker then, down the corridor, accompanied by a strange sound. My guards and I stopped abruptly and stood in the dark, motionless.

The light began to grow into view from around the corner. My guards stood solidly in front of me, Roger blocking my view. I couldn't decipher what we had heard. A scuffing maybe? Soft shoes against the floor?

I peeked through a sliver of space between his arm and Amos's, and the light kept growing brighter until it finally rounded the corner.

A small, tattered group of castle workers, two men and two women. With the tallest man holding the torch, they hurried their way down the hall. As they approached, I recognized them from the kitchens. The tall man was one of the bakers.

If they were fleeing the kitchens . . .

When their torchlight finally fell onto us, they froze. One of the women whimpered.

"It's all right," I called to them softly, stepping out from behind Roger. "It is only my guards and I."

The women's shoulders relaxed, but the men began hurrying forward again after a quick bow and a mumbled, "Your Majesty."

"Lucinda?" I asked as they passed.

One of the women shook her head quickly, her eyes glowing sadly in the torchlight. "We didn't see her, Your Majesty." Her eyes drifted then to her group, who had shuffled past us. She turned back to me with a hurried curtsy. "I—I'm sorry, my queen. Excuse me." Then, she hurried off to rejoin her group.

I began to walk forward, the path to the kitchens already formulating in my mind, but Amos laid his hand firmly on my shoulder.

"No, Your Majesty."

His tone was so absolute that I didn't argue.

"Where are we going, then?" I asked as we began moving forward, more cautiously this time.

Amos hesitated for a short second before answering. "To the armory."

"The armory?" I repeated, surprised. Wouldn't that have been the first place that King Roderich would have sent his soldiers?

"We have to get you a sword, Your Majesty."

We continued down the dark corridor, rounding corners carefully, stepping as quietly as we could. With no light of our own, we could have kept our presence here quite hidden, save for the clanking of my guards' armor.

Finally, we came to stop in front of a door that I knew would open into the hallway, spilling us out nearly just outside the armory.

With a warning glance, Amos slowly opened the door and looked through, scanning the hallway, before opening the door just wide enough for the rest of us to slip through and into the castle corridor.

After traveling in the dim maid's corridor, the familiar hallway seemed much brighter than normal. I noticed that the sun had begun to rise, its rays of bright white light just starting to spill through the windows.

We slinked along the wall, but there was no one in sight. Tarasyn must have not found this corridor, yet. The door to the armory was ajar, and Roger stood guard while Amos, Thomas and I stepped inside.

The weapons were in complete disarray. Or rather, what was left of them. In preparation for battle, our soldiers had picked the battleaxes clean, and only a few simple bows with half-full quivers remained. The swords left behind were small, strewn across the ground in discard. As the soldiers who had ransacked the armory were most likely taller and larger than me, these small swords probably held no interest to them.

Which was perfect for me.

After sifting through just a couple, I found a sword that fit me as no other had. I quickly found its scabbard and tied it around my waist. While Amos and Thomas picked through the remaining weapons, a small handle peeking from behind an axe stand caught my eye.

It was a dagger, so trivial and insignificant that it would have been forgotten by the rest of the world had this axe stand not been jostled so roughly out of place. The handle was wrapped in scarlet leather, and a small emerald was fixed into its pommel. Tied around its scabbard was a leather cord, so I quickly lifted the hem of my cloak and secured the dagger to my calf.

Suddenly, the shouts of men boomed through the hallway.

I whipped my head around to look through the open door of the armory, and I saw first one man at the end of the hall, dressed in armor of a dark unfamiliar metal. Like Gryffin's sword. Then, he was joined by three others, one by one rounding the corner. They each had their weapons raised above their heads, and they were running.

Running toward us.

Amos grabbed me by the arm and yanked me through the armory door, back into the hallway and toward the maid's door. I quickly turned my head back down the corridor, looking for Thomas and Roger.

Thomas was hesitating, leaning toward us but looking back at Roger. And Roger was standing his ground between us and the oncoming soldiers, feet firmly planted, sword in his hand and battleax strapped to his back.

"Go!" he shouted to Thomas, his voice unfathomably deep. "I'll hold the hall. Protect Her Majesty!"

With a final nod to Roger, Thomas turned on his heel and sprinted after us.

I saw Roger pick up a stray battleax and hurl it with ease down the hallway, and it collided with the closest Tarasynian guard. We ran through the open maid's door and back into the dark and musty corridor as the man crumbled to the ground in a spatter of blood. I saw the Tarasynian pause for only second, then charge forward once more as Thomas slammed the door shut behind us, all light disappearing with Roger.

The ring of heavy metal weapons clanging against each other followed us as we ran down the musty hall, until it slowly and painstakingly faded into the dark.

We didn't speak as we hurried through the increasingly dark space, but I felt a sad gravity emanating from Amos and Thomas. I didn't think that I could have uttered a word had I even known what to say.

As we continued through the hallway and down small spiral staircases, Amos would pause before each door and listen. But behind each door was the sound of battle. Men shouting, metallic shrieks, screeches against stone. As we passed one door, I thought I heard the incessant squawk of a crow. We did not linger near that one.

Finally, Amos halted in front of another door. The final door, it seemed. Natural light burned its way through the cracks of the well-worn wood, brightly illuminating our dank space. Both Thomas and Amos looked grave, their faces hardened into grimaces. Tear streaks had passed through the dust on Thomas's face. I hadn't realized how grimy they'd gotten.

I was sure that I didn't look much better.

"The maid's corridor ends here," Amos said grimly.

I felt a draft of wind blow through the cracks of the door. "So, this door opens to the courtyard?" I asked cautiously.

He nodded and heaved a heavy sigh. "Who knows what circumstance we'll find ourselves in behind this door. What we do know, however," he said sternly, "is that Tarasyn has the upper hand in seizing the castle. Until our men can capture it once again, it is not safe for you."

Thomas spat on the ground. "King Roderich is most likely scouring every room as we speak."

Despair had begun to creep its way into my overwhelmed mind. Within Hillstone, my own castle walls, my keep, my *home*, there was no longer sanctuary for anyone claiming Lecevonian loyalty. Not with King Roderich jaunting through the stone hallways.

"Where out there will we be safe?" I asked, jerking my head toward the door.

Amos had no reply as he slowly cracked open the door. Sunlight began flooding the maid's hall with such brilliant rays that my eyes took a moment to adjust.

There would be no hiding in shadows this morning.

But as Amos opened the door wider, we found that there was no need to hide.

Battle raged across the courtyard, each soldier so engrossed that no one had the freedom to look in our direction. In all the movement, I could hardly tell who were my soldiers and who were King Roderich's.

I saw that we had exited beneath the council room, and the ropes attached to the grappling hooks that had flown through the windows swung lazily against the stone wall, forgotten for now.

In front of us, in the blazing early morning sun, the scenes of combat overloaded my senses. Swords clashed against swords, and axes clanked against shields; men shouted in anger and determination, or they cried out in pain. I tried not to focus on the men lying like dolls strewn on the ground, their battles forever complete.

Sterling's poor rose bushes were uprooted, and several of his forsythia trees were ablaze. Smoke billowed and swirled into the air, filling my nostrils with the sweet aroma of burning tree bark. But mixed with that smoke was a starker odor.

Burning parchment.

I chanced a glance upward, toward the castle library, and first saw the smoke pouring through the huge window. The wooden shutters had been thrown open, leaving the library gaping open to the crisp spring morning air. And, through the smoke, the red glow of flames danced in the recesses of the room.

Thousands of books and centuries of resources.

My library.

I felt a hand on my shoulder, and when I turned, I met Amos's dark, urgent gaze.

"We must move, Your Majesty."

Almost in a daze, I turned away from my home, my despair only growing as the ashes floated through the bright sky to rest on the grass.

With no place to hide in the courtyard, we quickly slinked along the outer pathway, Thomas and Amos shielding me from the battle. Most of the fighting seemed to be concentrated closer to the castle, for we saw fewer and fewer people as we made our escape, until, when we came to the edge of the castle grounds, we were alone. This was where the main road of the capitol began its winding journey downhill through the city.

But we didn't stay on the main road for very long. We took the first side street we could find.

It had been so long since I'd actually left the castle and traveled through Equos. My work took place inside the castle walls, after all. The shops were quaint, squeezed closely together, and the cobblestone road would normally be bustling with horses and carts. Citizens would be hurrying through the street on their errand runs, or they'd be meandering and visiting with one another. The shop doors and windows would be thrown open, ready to accept their regular patrons.

However, now the streets were ghostly quiet. Silent and still.

We passed by a bakery, where it looked as if a baker and his family had left in such a hurry that they hadn't locked up shop. The coals in the oven were left still smoldering. And, though the doors and windows on most other shops were tightly closed, I could tell by the smell of forgotten meat that a butchery was close by.

We did not encounter anyone in the streets for a while. At one point, the familiar clomping of hooves against cobblestone had us hovering against the wall of a shop, whose swinging sign read "Heriman's Woodworking and Carving," but it was only an old milk goat, a cord tied loosely around its neck, ambling through the street. It must have escaped its farmyard further down the hill.

I didn't know what Amos's plan was. We continued down small side streets, taking connecting backroads, until the street we had been slinking along led to nowhere but the main road. So, after Amos peeked his head around the side of the corner shop and signaled that it was clear, we rushed onto the wide cobblestone road.

Then, the sound of running footfalls reached us from around the nearest twisting curve in the road.

I was about to curl into the shadow cast by the awning above the nearest shop, but Amos grabbed me by the arm and began pulling me across the wide road, to a shop whose door had been left open. As soon as Thomas's foot slid into the shop behind us, I peeked up through a crack in the shuttered window to see three soldiers run into view from around the curve, Tarasynian by the looks of their armor.

One of them was laughing as they passed, and another had his sword unsheathed and was thrusting it into the air. But the third slapped both on their shoulders, a quick clink of metal as his hand hit their armor.

"Hush!" he said, though not so quietly himself. "We're fortunate to have made it past the wall alive! You dare to get us caught now?"

The man who had been laughing cleared his throat abruptly.

"Or did you so quickly forget Marius's fate at the hands of that Lecevonian brute?" the first man continued, genuinely upset now.

"I still don't know how their cavalry jumped on us so quickly," the soldier with the sword said incredulously. Then, their voices faded as they ran out of my view.

I slid back down the wall and rested my head against the damp, wooden windowsill. My heart pounded in my chest, refusing to settle even after the threat had left.

"It sounds as if our men have rallied at the capitol wall," Thomas murmured. "That's a bit of good news, at least."

"That's excellent news!" I exclaimed, with a grin that felt on the edge of insanity.

Amos sighed heavily. "Let's hope they can keep it up, until the rest of our men return. Surely, they must have begun their return march by now." Amos then turned to me. "Your Majesty, escaping the city is not possible right now. I had hoped that we could find a few horses at the capitol's trading post and leave the city, head into the forest. But we may have to wait a few hours now, see how the situation at the wall goes."

Ah. So that had been his plan.

"Amos," I whispered, my grin falling, "I will not leave Equos. I cannot leave my people."

"My queen, King Roderich will have you *killed* if he finds you."

"And what of my people trapped inside the castle with him?" I argued, my eyes widened in persistence. I refused to think of them as slaughtered, not yet.

"What of your people if their queen is dead?" Thomas countered, backing his friend. "Think not only of the capitol, Queen Rosemary, but of the entire kingdom."

I tore my eyes away from them, glaring at the floor. I could not surrender the capitol, the heart of the kingdom that easily. If I left, King Roderich would have his way with more than one city until he'd found me.

But I couldn't deliver myself to him, either.

Amos and Thomas, who still valiantly stood by my side, were right. Lecevonia was much more than Equos. It was Port Della, and Flecte, and the settlements of the countryside. It was Zeke, and my sisters, who were thankfully far away from this havoc. It was the young family whom I had been able to allocate funds toward for the re-building of their home. And I was at the head of it all.

"If horses were what you were after, why didn't we go to the Stable?" I asked, warily giving Amos's plan a chance.

"I feared that Tarasyn would have already raided the Stable, Your Majesty."

From outside, we heard more feet approaching, so we fell silent. As I glanced through the crack in the shutters again, I saw two more Tarasynian soldiers run by, though no words were said this time.

Tarasyn seemed to be trickling past the wall, little by little.

"And I believe that the Stable is where King Roderich would expect us to go," Amos continued, once the men had run out of our view.

I sighed. Maybe the houses in the outskirts of the capitol were our best chance, then.

A hushed voice suddenly spoke from just outside the door, strumming the taut threads that were holding together our tense atmosphere inside the little shop.

"Perhaps I may be able to help."

CHAPTER EIGHTEEN

AMOS AND THOMAS immediately shot to their feet, swords drawn. My hand darted to my calf, fingers curled around the hilt of my dagger.

Then Gryffin appeared in the open doorway. His sword too was positioned in front of him at the ready, and there was a moment of heavy pressure in the air. But, after extending a cautious hand toward my guards, he sheathed his weapon. His blue eyes burned intensely as he gazed through the doorway at us.

Amos and Thomas slowly lowered their swords, and I rushed to my feet. I grabbed Gryffin by the hands and pulled him into the shop with us, and I wrapped my arms tightly around him.

"Thank Haggard you're here," I murmured into his vest. I fought back the tears that had suddenly formed behind my closed eyelids. Then, instead of his vest as I had first thought, I registered another fabric pressed against my cheek. A stretch of linen tied around his left shoulder. And a red stain blooming from his shoulder.

He followed my eyes and looked down at his shoulder. "It's nothing, Rosemary," he reassured me with a small smile. "Roderich barely left a scratch."

Which seemed true enough; aside from his shoulder, Gryffin looked surprisingly unscathed.

"How did you find us?" Amos demanded, sliding his sword into its scabbard.

"When you disappeared through the wall," Gryffin began, "Roderich threw himself into an insane *rage*. I'd never seen him so angry." He shook his head slowly. "Once his soldiers climbed down from the window, he stormed out of the council room and didn't give me another thought."

"Equos's citizens?" I asked tentatively.

Gryffin's eyes dropped to the ground. "Untouched, as far as I know. Your soldiers posted outside the Great Hall were well matched for my brother's intruders. But I didn't linger; I ran to the Stable, as I'd assumed that was where you would have gone." He looked up then and grinned ruefully. "I didn't find you, of course, but I found Celeste."

I exhaled in relief. "Celeste is all right."

Gryffin nodded. "Tarasyn hadn't made it to the Stable yet. So, I had her hide a couple horses in the woods, down the path on which we met, before my brother's soldiers could claim them. My hope was to find you and bring you out of the city."

It seemed that *everyone* had decided that I should flee the capitol.

"Since I no longer knew where to look for you, I began making my way to the main gates into the city." Gryffin squeezed my hand. "I thought that you may have already escaped the capitol. I was walking the main road, and I saw the three of you cross the street and duck into this shop."

"And the Tarasynian soldiers that ran past you?" asked Thomas. "Did they see you?"

"I'm their prince," Gryffin replied with a smirk. "They caused me no issues."

"We'll scour the shop, see if we can find anything useful to take with us on the journey," Amos said gruffly.

As he and Thomas turned away, Gryffin lifted my hand and pressed it against his cheek. He closed his eyes and sighed heavily, leaning into my palm.

"I truly didn't think that I'd find you," he said softly. "After you left the council room, I thought I'd have to scour the entire Peninsula before I'd see you again." His husky chuckle exuded a boundless relief.

"Just the entire capitol city," I replied, mustering up a smile of my own. With Gryffin's presence came a new feeling of strength, of hope.

"We *will* get you out of here, Rosemary." He kissed my palm and opened his eyes to look at me. "I swear that I will keep you safe. Though"—his eyes fell first on my sword, then traveled down my leg near where my dagger was hidden—"now that you're armed, I may not be needed," he amended with a grin.

I looked away hesitantly. "I truly shouldn't stay in the capitol, then." I had meant it as a question, but it instead sounded like a grudgingly accepted fate.

Gryffin lowered our hands, but he still held mine tightly in both of his. "I know you, Rosemary. You will do what is best for your kingdom."

I spoke no more on the subject, for it would have been nothing but wasted energy.

The shop we had escaped into turned out to be a potter's workshop. Under the wooden potter's wheel was a large sheet of leather that Thomas thought could be useful, maybe as a rough blanket or sleeping mat for cold nights in the woods. Inside the cold stone kiln was an iron rod that ended in a small hook, so Amos pocketed that little treasure. There were a few nice bowls and pitchers that could have been useful for collecting water, but seeing as we had no packs with us, we made the decision to leave those behind.

When we had exhausted our examination of the shop, we each took a few swigs from the jug of water which the potter had stowed away for cooling the kiln, and we slunk back into the sunlight.

Gryffin led, for he would be greeted more amiably by Tarasynian soldiers than we would be, and Amos and Thomas remained beside me, closely monitoring the streets around us.

I kept my hand on the hilt of my sword, just in case.

The road remained quiet, but after about half an hour of maneuvering our way through the city, the sound of clinking armor reached our ears. The noise was coming from the direction of the city wall, and this time, it sounded like more than a couple of men.

Much more than a couple of men.

We each looked to one another for a wild moment, and without words, we all decided not to chance so many soldiers, in the case that they may be Tarasynian. Gryffin may have been able to sway a few of his brother's men, but a battalion would have been another story. So, we rushed down a side street and pressed ourselves against the corner wall, with Gryffin just barely peeking around the edge.

As the sound of disorganized soldiers grew louder, I felt beads of nervous sweat gather on my forehead. My heartbeat struggled to match the panicked, hurried footsteps.

Then, Gryffin's face lightened with an exultant smile and waved us forward. I saw Amos and Thomas share a doubtful glance as they sidled closer to Gryffin. But Gryffin shook his head quickly and murmured, "Lecevonian."

Relief made my head spin with pride.

My men!

Thomas stepped out first, and the scuffling and clanging faltered. A murmuring ran through the soldiers before an older man's incredulous voice broke through the air. "Thomas?" There was a shuffling of armor as I imagined a man pushing through the group, shoving his way to the front. "Thomas!" he shouted again, this time in elation.

"Stanton!" Thomas replied joyfully.

I took a step forward, ready to greet my soldiers, but Gryffin brushed my hand.

"I'll wait here," he said quietly, a bit chagrined. "They may not take well to a Tarasynian prince."

But I shook my head and grabbed his hand in mine with a confident smile. "They will soon know their king-consort."

I stepped out from the corner, Amos and Gryffin following closely behind me.

I wished many times over that I could bottle the pride I felt upon seeing my soldiers before me. This was the largest group of soldiers I'd yet to see—during actual battle, anyhow. Of course, scores of soldiers lined the halls and pathways during my coronation, and I'd greeted a large portion of the Royal Army standing at attention in the courtyard that same day. But there was something about seeing them this way, in battle and ready to fight for the Crown, that made me feel wired. This group consisted of about twenty men, battle worn but eyes bright and fierce.

It didn't seem that any of them expected to see me here in the city, for as I came into their view, gasps of "Her Majesty" traveled from lip to lip, and the entire group of soldiers stumbled hastily to one knee.

Only the man who I assumed to be Stanton, who also seemed to be the eldest of the group, maintained his composure as he bowed his knee.

"Thank you all," I addressed them. "Your service to Lecevonia and to the Crown is nothing short of admirable. Please, rise!"

As they rose to their feet, Stanton strode over closer to me. "Your Majesty—" And that was when he first caught sight of Gryffin, who had remained standing very quietly behind me. He immediately reached for his sword and began to pull it from its sheath, but I quickly stepped forward and held my hands in front of me.

"No, no—he can be trusted," I said. "Return your sword to its scabbard."

He paused, eyes narrowed in confusion, but he slowly released his weapon. He cast a wary glance toward Gryffin, but, seeming to understand that there was no time for arguments, he returned his gaze to me. "Sir Stanton Mowbray, your obedient servant, my queen."

"Stanton and I are from the same village," Thomas said with a smile. "From Aridia, down south. He joined the Army just four years after I did."

I lowered my head in gratitude, but I had more pressing things on my mind than introductions. "What is happening at the wall?" I asked urgently.

"We're gaining the upper hand, Your Majesty."

My heart could have leaped straight from my ribcage with joy at the news, and I felt a huge smile stretching across my face.

"The Tarasynians took us by surprise early this morning, before the light of dawn, and they approached with no torches or lanterns." Stanton cursed under his breath. "We didn't see nor hear them—they approached in small waves. A handful got over the wall with their grapnels and ladders.

"But after five long hours of battle, Tarasyn's numbers have now evened with ours. Our cavalry was an unexpected force for them." Stanton smiled proudly. "Their arrival was the beginning of the turning point. They rode in swiftly and took care of the rear lines of Tarasynian soldiers without trouble."

"Thoughtless, Roderich," I heard Gryffin mumble from behind me.

"What of our casualties?" I pressed, hanging on to Stanton's every word.

Stanton smirk waned a little, but his voice didn't falter in its positive tone. "At the wall, we've only had minimal losses."

"Any estimate?" Amos insisted.

"Around two hundred or so, I'd say," Stanton answered. "Then we saw the smoke coming from the castle, so I was leading my battalion to aid our men at the keep. It's truly a relief to see that you're safe, my queen." He bowed his head reverently.

"I wouldn't be, if not for these men," I said, extending my arm toward Amos, Thomas, and Gryffin. After all, had Gryffin not drawn his sword against his brother, we may not have escaped the council room in the first place. "And many others," I added solemnly, remembering Roger.

And my mind was not the only one that Roger crossed; Thomas leaned forward in intensity at Stanton's words. "The castle? Perhaps you'll be able to find Roger . . . or the fiends that brought about his death." His voice had lowered to an octave of anger, fierce vengeance evident on his face.

"Easy, Thomas," Amos warned, laying a hand on Thomas's shoulder.

"I should have stayed with him in that corridor," Thomas spat, his face scrunched in his sudden fury.

"It was Roger's choice," Amos said sternly.

Thomas looked ready to either snap back at Amos's words, or relinquish his head into his hands in grief.

But I'd never find out which emotion of his wrangled its way to the top, for our small moment of repose in the streets was derailed by the blaring caw of a crow.

I looked up to the sky, searching for the blasted beast, when something quickly shot past my right ear. I turned my head sharply, and I found my eyes glued to an arrow that had embedded itself into the thigh of one of my soldiers, just below his chainmail.

He crumpled to the ground with a cry of pain as blood blossomed from the arrowhead, staining his dark green trousers.

Then, the clopping of hooves upon the cobblestone road echoed from the direction of the castle, and soldiers on foot appeared from around the curve in the road, dressed in their dark Tarasynian armor. At the head of the group, on a dapple-gray horse and bow in hand, was King Roderich himself.

The street around me was suddenly a mass of action. One of the other soldiers in Sir Stanton's battalion dragged his injured comrade off the road, and the rest of the men charged forward, led by Sir Stanton's loud battle cry. As they rushed past us, Amos, Thomas, and Gryffin all put themselves between me and the oncoming violence and unsheathed their weapons, holding them at the ready. I slowly slid mine from its scabbard as well, and adrenaline kept my hand steady.

King Roderich barged ruthlessly through the charging group of Lecevonian soldiers, and his eyes, burning in hatred, were locked on me.

Behind him, battle thundered in the street. The battalions had collided with each other, and every man was engaged in his own fight. Shouts of agony blistered through the air, surpassed only by the roars of hate and aggression. Several men from both kingdoms already lay motionless on the stone road. I saw Sir Stanton with his sword drawn, fighting off three Tarasynians, and it was clear that, though Lecevonia had the skill, Tarasyn still had the strength of numbers. The battle pushed ever slightly back toward us.

King Roderich dismounted his horse and stormed our way, sword already unsheathed. His wild, fiery eyes were impossible to ignore.

"Brother," Gryffin called to him, in a tone of warning, "please, stop this insanity! You will have nothing left to rule, no people to govern!"

"While *she* lives, Tarasyn has nothing!" Roderich shouted back. He still advanced forward.

Gryffin then rushed toward Roderich, and Roderich slashed toward Gryffin's injured shoulder. He blocked Roderich's blow with a left ochs, and their weapons shrieked together.

"Why do you protect her?" Roderich yelled. He thrust his sword toward Gryffin's side, but Gryffin parried with a downward cut of his blade.

But this gave Roderich an opportunity; he raised his sword above his head and crashed it down toward Gryffin with such force I was reminded of a great bear charging down on its prey. An incomprehensible shout of panic escaped my lips as Gryffin had to quickly raise his blade in front of him to protect himself. I tried to bolt forward to help him, but Amos slammed his arm out in front of me.

"What does she mean to you?" Roderich asked, his voice gruff with exertion. "You can have *all of this* without her!"

But Gryffin couldn't answer; his teeth were gritted together as he struggled to hold his sword under the weight of his brother's.

The clash between the battalions had almost reached us now, and a trail of dead and injured men splayed out on the cobblestones had been left in its wake. The shouts and determined grunts of fighters, the groans of defeated men, and of earsplitting screeches of metal on metal relentlessly filled my head. Even Roderich's crow joined in the fight; it would swoop down, scratch the faces of some unfortunate men, and shoot into the sky with a screech.

Three Tarasynian soldiers suddenly broke free of the fight and charged us.

Amos and Thomas, still shielding me, stepped forward and met the assaulters head-on, swords clashing. Amos shoved one of the soldiers away from him and took a daring jab at another, right to the neck, but his blade bounced off the man's chainmail. Thomas had the third attacker in a sword-lock, weapons twisted against each other at the hilt.

The man that Amos had shoved away, with no one able to stop him now, ran toward me with an unintelligible shout, sword raised over his shoulder.

I lifted my sword, and, just as in my lesson, my mind was sharpened as the imposing threat drew closer. But the world did not seem to slow; this man still moved forward swiftly, radiating intensity. I was about to move my sword into an offensive position, but Zeke's words returned to me: *protecting yourself should be your first priority.*

I instead adopted a left ochs just as the man's sword came crashing down toward my shoulder. His blade crashed against mine, and the tip of his weapon grazed my shoulder. Thankfully, my armor held, and his sword did no damage. I slid my blade from underneath his and tried to thrust it toward his ear, but he dodged my attack and swung his weapon around his body in an arc, and I saw the sword curving through the air quickly toward me.

I ducked out of the sword's path—or so I thought I did. Just before I hit the ground and lurched away from him, I felt the edge of the blade slice into my forehead. As I rolled hastily to my feet and sank into a low squat, warm crimson quickly dripped into my left eye.

I tried to ignore the deep sting of the cut as I quickly wiped my sleeve across my forehead to clear my eye.

The fight between the two battalions was full-on around us now. Amos and Thomas had each taken on two more opponents, and a man lay unmoving at Thomas's feet. But that was all I dared to register as my own opponent stood with his sword at the ready in front of him.

I heard Zeke's voice again. *Point your blade downward.*

With every emotion swirling through my head, I almost laughed; even in his absence, Zeke was trying to tell me what to do.

But I listened to him as I pushed up from my squat and let the tip of my sword hang downward toward the ground. *Don't relax.* I tried to feign fatigue, which really wasn't too much of a challenge. But I kept my arms taut, ready.

A wicked smile spread across my opponent's face, and he began striding forward, his weapon coming toward me in right ochs.

Then, just before I was within reach of his sword, I shot the tip of my blade upward, and I thrusted my sword forward with every fiber of strength contained within me.

My sword plunged its way through the man's leather, and I felt the grating of the chainmail against my blade as the tip of my weapon broke the metal ringlets and pierced through his skin. The man's angry face went slack with shock as my blade impaled his chest, and his hand spasmodically sent his sword clattering to the ground.

"This is called fool's guard," I said, my words matching the echo of Zeke's in my memory, as the man fell clumsily to his knees. I yanked my sword free from the man, and he slumped to the ground and went limp.

My sword gleamed with bright red blood, dripping down the blade toward the hilt. Before my panic could set in, I tried wiping the blade clean with the hem of my cloak.

But I wasn't quick enough.

I'd killed a man.

A different type of adrenaline swelled through me, this time leaving a sheen of cold sweat surfacing on my arms, my neck.

I tried to force myself to think clearly. Right now, with battle surging around me, was not the time to relent to panic. I looked around me—but never at my feet, at the man that now lay there—and saw that Amos and Thomas were still standing near me, fending off attackers.

And Gryffin and Roderich were still fighting.

"Do you truly *wish* to marry her, then?" I heard Roderich laugh. "If you side with me, brother"—he slid his sword off Gryffin's with a piercing screech and held it in front of him at the ready—"you can have your precious queen." He stretched his mouth into a sneer and nodded his head, eyes wide. "I'll let her live, and you can marry her in her chains!"

I suddenly felt, possibly for the first time in my life, a gush of pure, unadulterated *hate*. No fear fueled this emotion, no cognition accompanied it.

My sisters and my oldest friend—though he was now so much more than that; it *hurt* to think of him—had to flee the capitol in secret. My grandfather had died at the hands of this man's actions; my potential husband was fighting for his life. My home was destroyed by this man, and my kingdom and my power were weakened.

I *hated* this man.

And I lunged.

My sword sliced down toward Roderich's legs as an angry scream belted from my throat. I'd surprised both of them. Roderich was quick to move, but not quick enough, for my blade cut into the back of his leg before bouncing off the top of his armored shin plates.

It wasn't a deadly blow, but it brought him down to one knee on the ground.

He could be defeated.

"Get Rosemary out of here!" Gryffin suddenly shouted to my guards.

What? No!

"I'm not leaving!" I yelled. "The fight is *here*!"

"Rosemary!" Gryffin rushed to stand in front of me. He placed both hands on the sides of my face, gently yet earnestly, his blue eyes boring into mine intensely. "Tarasyn still outnumbers Lecevonia here! There are more soldiers coming!" He pointed up the road, where a herd of figures could just be seen around the curve. "If Roderich dies here, and they don't accept me as their king, you won't be safe! *Nowhere* in the capitol is safe right now!"

Behind us, Roderich grunted as he tried to regain his footing. Though he was injured and panting heavily, his garnet eyes burned through me with fury.

"You *have* to get to those horses!" Gryffin shouted, and he turned away from me to face his brother once again.

Thomas grabbed my arm and pulled me down the street, Amos following close behind.

"Don't let them out of your sight!" I heard Roderich command, and heavy footfalls pounded behind us. I turned and saw two Tarasynians running behind us, both with swords drawn, one with an ax strapped to his back.

"Go!" Amos shouted to Thomas. "I can take them!" Then he turned away from us and faced the two oncoming soldiers.

Behind him, I saw Gryffin force a downward slash toward his brother's collarbone. Then, my line of vision was cut off as Thomas pulled me into a side street, and the crow's hoarse and indignant call reverberated off the rooftops.

We ran, working through the streets like a maze, taking sharp left and right turns, until we reached the edge of the city to the west of the castle. No homes were situated down this slope, only a few small huts that served as stand-alone workshops that eventually became fewer as the landscape melded into the forest.

Once we were in the safe cover of the trees, Thomas slowed to a jog and, as the forest quickly thickened, eventually stopped. He rested his hands on his knees, panting.

I leaned an arm against a nearby tree trunk, gasping for oxygen and my side cramping. The exertion had also made my head wound bleed once again; I felt hot blood trickling down from my temple, trailing down into the collar of my cloak.

"Thomas," I managed to say through gasps.

"We don't have much farther, Your Majesty, I assure you," he responded hoarsely. But when he straightened up and glanced at me, his eyes went wide. He jogged to me and placed his hands on my shoulders. "Sit, my queen."

I slid down the trunk of the tree and sat in the scratchy leaf litter at its base. I didn't feel great, and from Thomas's reaction, I probably didn't look so great, either. As my adrenaline drained away, it left my body weakened and fatigued. I felt pallid and tired, but my eyes refused to close. They stayed wide and darted from tree to bush to Thomas and back again. I couldn't control them. But as I struggled to take deep inhales, I was eventually able to close my eyelids.

Thomas cleaned the blood from my face and neck with moss from the ground and held it to my head. "This will staunch the blood," he said quietly. "It isn't as bad as it seems."

I surely hoped so. The dirt from the moss did not help to alleviate the stinging pain. I sighed quietly. "Thank you, Thomas."

"Of course, my queen," he said softly. "I've had a few wounds of the same nature in my lifetime."

As we sat catching our breath, I slowly began to feel a bit stronger. My head eventually stopped bleeding, and I was finally able to relax my eyes behind my closed eyelids. I was parched, as I'm sure Thomas was too. We had no water to drink, but I knew we'd have to pass the stream to get to the trail on which Gryffin and I had first met.

Once I felt well enough, I stood, and we were off again.

We were not following a laid path, so we went a little more slowly through the brush. I was once again thankful for my leather armor. The brambles would have torn any dress to shreds and my legs along with it. We also weren't very quiet. The sprouting spring leaves rustled as we pushed through them, and the discarded twigs and leaves from the past winter crunched beneath my feet. More than once, I twisted around quickly to look behind me, thinking I heard more footfalls on the loud forest floor, only to find our newly forged path empty.

The sun was directly overhead in the sky, filtering through the leaves of the highest trees. Sweat trickled down my back underneath the heavy leather, and the dense forest allowed no breeze through to offer relief. But the farther we traveled, the closer we were to safety.

Once we reached the horses, where would we go?

Potentially Port Della, I hoped, though we had no supplies for the trip. We'd of course have to make stops along the way. But the thought of having my sisters near me again encouraged me to take my next few steps. To have little Clara in my arms, her tinkling laugh filling the air; to have Isabele's sweet eyes looking over her shoulder at us as she shared a smile with me, and Lisette nearby with her arms crossed in disapproval. I pictured them so clearly that it was almost as though I could feel Clara's hand in mine already.

And Zeke.

The wound in my chest left by our impossible future throbbed once more as I thought of him. The warmth of his hands, his arrogant smile, and his chocolate brown eyes all dared me to remember the warmth of our single kiss, the heat he left trailing along my back with his fingers, my hand twisted into his hair. But it wasn't only the physicality of the kiss . . . I recalled the safety I felt, the *homeness*. These memories were like forbidden delicacies to my battered mind, and it relished in this newfound contentment.

After Sterling's funeral, I'd hoped that I'd be able to look past these feelings, to marry Gryffin and find happiness there knowing I'd done what I needed to for Lecevonia. But now I was unsure.

Finally, the whisper of free-flowing water perked my ears.

"Thomas, we're close!" I rushed ahead of him, my aching throat now leading the way, and the whisper grew to a murmur, then to an energetic buzz as we broke through the brush to the stream.

The stream was flowing more strongly than it had been the last week—probably runoff from the storm that passed through. But it was still crossable, and definitely drinkable.

As my lips touched the surface of the stream, the chilly water almost instantly satiated the ache in my throat. I could tell that Thomas too was relieved. He sighed heavily and smiled as he splashed water on his face.

I took the same opportunity and washed the dried blood from the side of my face, carefully working around my head wound. The gash would still trickle a bit from time to time, but I had hopes that it was mending on its own. I tried not to think about the dirt, sweat, and grime that had caked inside it.

With water and a cleaner face, I felt a bit more human again, and more strength returned to my tired limbs. I decided to take the time to clean the blood from my sword, about which I had tried so fervently to forget. I grabbed some moss from the forest floor and ran it over the blade, as I'd seen Gryffin do when we'd first met out here, scrubbing away the dried brown flakes of blood.

I had to do it, I told myself, repeating it over and over in my head. I would have been killed had I not done it.

Still, I'd taken a man's life. I'd stopped his heartbeat. *Myself.* Not through a command or a sentence, but through a life-ending blow inflicted by the weapon in my hand.

Just as my mind began to spiral into a downward bleakness by the transgression I'd done, Thomas spoke from behind me. "That's actually really good for your blade, you know."

Thankful for the distraction, I glanced up at him. "Oh yeah?" I asked, managing a tiny smile. "I just figured it'd be rough enough to get through the grit."

He grinned. "Indeed. Blood can be corrosive if left on for too long. But peat mosses also contain a bit of oil, perfect for maintaining a quality blade."

I looked back down at my sword, and I supposed I could see a bit more of a shine to it.

Thomas sighed, and it sounded like he slumped down to the ground near his tree. I was reminded of a time not so long ago that he and I had been in the woods together, taking a rest near this same stream. Only then, I'd actually had control over my kingdom, though it hadn't felt like it at the time.

"How often should I oil it, then?" I asked. I wanted to keep him talking, to keep him acting as my distraction. I wiped my clean blade against the hem of my cloak to dry it of any remaining stream water, steering clear of the bloodstains from my hastened attempt at cleaning the blade earlier.

But for some reason, he didn't answer. I was about to sheath my sword and turn to Thomas when, in my blade's bright reflection, a dark figure loomed behind me.

Roderich.

I gasped and lurched to my feet, sword in hand, and I spun around to face him. How did he find us out here? How did Gryffin let him *live*?

But when my eyes finally focused on the man, I realized that, though the frame and hair were the same, this man's eyes weren't burning garnets.

It was Gryffin who stood before me.

CHAPTER NINETEEN

I INSTANTLY RELAXED in his presence, though what my eyes perceived made no sense.

What I saw was Gryffin, sword drawn in one hand, blue eyes piercing through the grime on his face, and a small, relieved smile stretching across his lips. That little smile sent me into a place of refuge.

"Rosemary," I heard him say. But his voice oddly sounded far away and muffled, as if he were speaking through sheep's wool.

I saw bright, wet blood on his hands, and held tightly in his other palm was a small dagger, also gleaming with crimson.

And I saw Thomas, slouched against the tall oak tree. From his neck still ran fresh blood, slick on the front of his armor.

"Rosemary," Gryffin said again, more urgently.

But I couldn't look at him; my eyes were glued to Thomas. Through my periphery, I saw Gryffin take two long, slow steps to reach me.

"My Rosemary, it's all right," he said imploringly.

I *felt* his words. I felt them course through every fiber of me, cloaking my mind in a lovely, warm, woolen blanket of security. Yes, everything was all right. But why did I feel that way if my trusted guard lay bleeding out just three paces from me?

"I *saved* you, Rosemary," Gryffin's far-off voice insisted. "He was about to attack you, while your back was turned, and I found you just in time. Please, trust me, Rosemary."

Trust.

But Thomas. Would Thomas do such a thing?

My mind wanted to curl in on itself, for two separate sides were warring with one another. Most of my senses were physically compelled toward Gryffin. Gryffin was a good man. He wanted to protect me—that's all he'd ever wanted to do.

But something in Thomas's lifeless face tethered me to one particular sense. My sense of vulnerability.

I felt danger. I felt weakness. Just as I had in the face of death at the archer's arrow.

Gryffin had laid down his dagger and gently placed a bloody hand on my cheek. His eyes delved deeply into mine, and his voice became a little clearer through the haze. "My Rosemary, please, you *must* trust me."

But . . . I didn't.

With that decision, everything surrounding me snapped into crisp focus.

My mind felt as if, for far too long, it had been stretched into a thin, threadbare sheet, so near to tearing, and had only just been released back into place. And the first thing I felt was fear.

It had been there from the first day that I met him, but I hadn't been able to recognize it, concealed and cowering in the corner of my mind, until now.

The eyes staring into mine, as I was seeing them clearer than I ever had, were no longer the deep ocean eyes I'd grown to admire. They were still blue, but his deepening silver flecks had turned red.

Identical to Roderich's.

But these blazing red flecks burned with so much more intensity than his brother's had. They flickered so strongly that they reminded me of that old adage. *The greedy will bleed while the righteous will heed.*

I slapped his hand away from my face and held onto the hilt of my sword tightly in front of me. I didn't understand what he'd done to me, or how he'd done it, but I knew that I was seeing the true Gryffin for the very first time. I'd never met this man before.

His small smile hardened into a tight line. He sighed, an exasperated tone infiltrating his words. "Ah, Rosemary, why did you have to make this so much harder?"

"What did you do?" I demanded shakily.

"*I* didn't do anything," Gryffin clarified. "It's what you did."

I shook my head weakly. "Enough games. What is going on?"

"Lower your weapon, and we'll talk."

"I prefer to keep it raised, thank you."

"Rosemary," he implored again. "I don't want to hurt you, I swear it."

"Just as you didn't want to hurt Thomas?" I asked, my voice cracking. My eyes cut down to my fallen guard again, dead against the tree trunk, and I felt my throat close at the sight of his blank, oblivious stare.

Gryffin kept his voice low and calm, but his eyes narrowed in dismay. "All right, have it your way." He didn't sheath his sword, but he relaxed his stance a bit and leaned on one foot. For a moment, the only sound in the forest around us was the rushing stream.

"My brother wanted to take Lecevonia by force, just as he had with Hiddon," he started, turning his gaze to the trees above us. "But I'd talked him out of it for the time being. It would have been an utter *waste* of resources. He'd absolutely decimated Hiddon." He shook his head in disappointment, closing his eyes. "My brother lived to conquer, by any means necessary. Cities and villages destroyed. Forests leveled. It truly was barbaric." Gryffin opened his eyes and looked at me sadly. "Killing the royal family, I understood. But the citizens? That was an entire workforce! Always a shame, loss of innocent life."

"You knew of his plans, then." My voice was little more than a breath.

Gryffin gave a small, morose smile. "As I said, I am his second-in-command."

My mind returned to our breakfast, though the memory was now shrouded with a haze, when he'd asked if our map of the Magian Peninsula was updated often. *Stupid, Rose*, I chided myself. He'd *known*. "You knew he'd planned to kill me." The weight of his betrayal threatened to bring me to my knees on the forest floor.

"No, no—not quite. Like I said, I thought I'd talked him out of it." His eyes were so earnest. "I told him there was another, less destructive way. So, I embarked on my own effort to secure Lecevonia—with a marriage."

It'd *all* been a lie. I had no strength to stop my tears of hurt from escaping, but I conjured up what willpower I could to wipe them away before they slid silently down my cheek.

"Oh, my Rosemary, please don't cry." Gryffin stepped forward, arms open wide to me, but I cringed away from him. He froze, looking at me with overflowing concern, before dropping his arms.

"I wanted to prove to Roderich that this needless violence was wasteful," he repeated. "But I didn't want to take any chances at losing, either. So, we agreed to an arrangement that might have given me the upper hand right from the beginning."

My eyes widened. "The archer in the woods."

With a small nod, Gryffin smiled. "Valiant, yes? I excluded that bit from the assassin's cipher. But that was where my brother lost his patience, it seemed." His lips turned down into a scowl. "I didn't know he'd had his own agenda to kill you. I swear, I didn't know." He lifted his shocking, fiery eyes to mine, full of sincerity and remorse.

I was a mouse, trembling under the stare of a viper.

"Please, Rosemary," he begged. "I can be trusted. I am on your side, Lecevonia's side!"

His eyes bored through me, and I felt nothing but vulnerability.

After what was too long of a second, he ripped his eyes away from me and groaned. "Agh, it's useless now," he spat, suddenly agitated.

A sliver of impatience helped me find my voice. "What is?"

"My Talent," he said slowly, as if he were explaining this to a child.

My heart jolted at his words.

Gryffin was *Talented.*

But how was that possible? No one has been Talented in centuries.

As confusion riddled my brain, I replayed scene after scene in my mind, looking for any clue. Our first meeting, our picnic, our kiss, our sword lessons. I was able to remember them all, but they were . . . hazy. And that in itself was evidence.

"What did you do?" I asked again, my voice laced with distrust.

"Rosemary, again, it's not what I did, but what you did!" he exclaimed, eyes wide in frustration. "The second you shut off your will to me, my Talent became powerless. Had you just continued to keep an open mind, had you continued to see the *good* in me, we could have had *everything* through your trust!"

Trust. There it was again. That feeling that had come so easily and simply before, yet seemed so foreign now.

New scenes began to hound my memory: our breakfast, when I'd wrongly decided that he was innocent in all of this; in the prison, when, even in the face of each damning piece of evidence and his sorry excuses, I'd been convinced that his heart had meant well; our last council meeting, when the air had changed, and my advisors had slowly slackened; even just a moment ago, in the potter's shop, when Amos and Thomas had laid down their weapons . . .

My words left my mouth very slowly as I struggled to fit each piece together. "Your Talent is to make people *trust* you?"

Gryffin beamed. "See, Roderich was wrong. You are smart."

"Your eyes—"

"Frightening, aren't they? I've found that hiding those pesky red flecks makes them much more appealing, more trustworthy." A childish grin darkened his features.

With a blazing guilt, I realized that with my mistakes, the largest of all putting my trust in this man, I'd failed my kingdom. I'd failed Sterling, and I'd failed Thomas, two of the most loyal men I'd ever met. Truly, I was nothing more than a mouse, with a flimsy crown on its head. Unfit to rule over even a breadcrumb.

But there was a familiar voice willing me out of my mouse's burrow.

Lecevonia is only as strong as its leader.

So I found the strength to glare into his red-flecked eyes. "You deceitful *snake*," I hissed.

Gryffin scowled. "Oh, no, Rosemary. Deceitful, maybe. But a snake? No, that was Roderich. Had he given me just a *week* before changing his mind, all of this loss could have been avoided."

"You had me entirely blinded!" My hand tightened on the hilt of my sword. "Every time I looked into your eyes, I thought I was seeing sincerity. But I was only seeing deception." I set my mouth into a hard sneer.

He smirked. "You were easy to influence. Though I almost lost you twice. My Talent has always been more effective with eye contact and . . . *merciful* minds. Mercy greatly weakens the resolve, you see."

His scathing remark fueled an anger that had begun to rise from within my little mouse's burrow. "Unfortunately for you, I'm no longer feeling very merciful. You deceived my entire court!"

"Almost," he muttered, amending my statement. "Not everyone was as easy to influence as you were. Zeke, Lord Castor . . . I eventually got them to relent, however. But your sister Isabele! Well, just from looking at her I thought she'd be easy, as feeble as she is! But I hadn't seen her Talent in quite a while." His tone was almost admiring.

Isabele?

"And to be wasted on someone so oblivious! If I had someone with a Talent such as hers in my court, I'd undoubtedly be exploiting their Sight."

His words were foreign to me, but before I could even think to inquire, he took a daring step toward me.

I whipped the tip of my sword upward. "Don't come any closer," I warned. If I took another step back, I'd be calf-deep in the stream. The rushing water bellowed loudly in my ear now.

He looked shocked by my reaction, and he held one hand up peaceably. "My apologies, I didn't mean to frighten you." He eyed me carefully, as if he were waiting for me to run. "It's only that the flies are starting to find our friend here." He nodded his head toward Thomas's body.

Thomas. Another man dead because of . . . because of *Tarasyn.* "Why did you kill him?" I tried to sound threatening, but my anguished voice betrayed me.

"I would have spared him had I known how attached you were to your guards." He gave a surprised snort. "I didn't think his demise would make you doubt me in the slightest. But I needed you alone."

"Why?"

Gryffin pursed his lips, then, disappointed. "Well, to be honest, I'd planned to parade back to Hillstone with you, victorious against my brother and sole savior of the queen. There are only two horses, after all."

I narrowed my eyes. "You are just as evil as your brother is."

"'Was,'" he corrected me. "*Excellent* fighting, by the way! Your attack made killing him much easier. And how you skewered that one poor man?" He laughed almost proudly. "I taught you well."

I gasped aloud. "You *did* kill Roderich?"

He shrugged, so disgustingly nonchalant. "I would have killed him at some point, had it not been today. He'd have been the only thing standing between me and the power just *waiting* to be claimed throughout the Peninsula. My brother set his bar much too low; he'd had the right idea with invasions and conquering, but he'd barely scratched the surface of the Peninsula's potential."

His words sent a shot of confusion through me. "The Peninsula's potential?"

Gryffin looked at me incredulously. "You don't think I am the only Talented, do you? How can you be so blind, with the Rebels of the Red Sun using Equos as their home base?" He shook his head and smiled. "No. Magic runs deep into the mere *rock* of this land. The strength of the magi still courses through the blood of each kingdom!"

The Rebels of the Red Sun again. How deeply involved were they in all of this? What did they even stand for? "Impossible," I managed to utter. His words were so overwhelming.

He looked at me with sympathetic eyes. "There is so much you don't yet know, my Rosemary. I am going to reawaken the Talented—it's already started in Tarasyn, thanks to my father. But, unlike my father, we will no longer hide in the fear that he had thrust upon us." A determined intensity formed in his red-flecked eyes. "Yes, I am Tarasyn's King now. And to grant me full access to the Lecevonian people, you are going to marry me."

I spat at him. "The thought of marrying you makes me *sick*."

"Rosemary, don't you see?" He extended an arm, gesturing around him. "We can still have *everything*! You will be my queen, and you can still rule your people, by my side! We already have Hiddon, and there won't have to be any more destruction—no more loss! There has been so much loss today already, hasn't there? Look at what happened here." He turned in a circle with his arms extended and shook his head in disappointment, closing his eyes in convincing anguish. "So many men, so much time lost. And the castle library! Oh, so many ancient maps and pieces of literature, burned to nothing!" He opened his eyes and looked at me sadly. "I'm truly sorry for that loss."

He was right; there had been so much loss today. And here in the forest, I'd been made more vulnerable than ever. If Lecevonia was only as strong as its leader, my kingdom stood with its arm open wide for the next attacker.

"We don't have to lose, anymore," Gryffin implored. His lips had softened into a gentle smile. He made a move toward me and reached out his hand, maybe to caress my face. But, keeping my sword at the ready, I didn't let him get close to me.

He lowered his hand and glowered at me through squinted eyes. "Then Lecevonia will suffer."

His threat snapped something inside me, then, through my weakness. From the inner walls of my vulnerable little mouse's burrow blossomed a new type of strength. A determination to regain my kingdom, to live to see the day Lecevonia stood victorious once more.

I hissed through gritted teeth. "Don't you *dare* threaten my kingdom."

A rose with the strongest thorns had emerged from my mouse's den. The sudden pulse of energy flowing through my hands at my sword hilt felt as alive as the fast-flowing stream behind me. Lecevonia would *not* be lost today.

Gryffin must have sensed the shift in my resolve. His eyes widened, and he took a small step back. Still, he laughed incredulously. "Who between us is in the better position to threaten? My men still hold the castle."

"The rest of my army is marching here as we speak," I shouted vehemently. "And we will outnumber you! Your men will fall!"

"Not before I have every one of your citizens holed up inside the castle slaughtered!"

My people.

Gryffin quietly studied my face, looking for some sign of a fracture in my composure.

Everything I'd done, every decision I've made. I *lived* for my people, and Gryffin had always known that.

"I could kill you now." I glowered at him with thick menace in my voice, sword held steadily in front of me.

Gryffin chuckled. "Could you?" He still held the hilt of his sword loosely in his hand, but I'd seen his skill, and I had to admit he had a point. That loose grip could quickly change into a powerful death threat.

"You don't even belong on the throne," he added, "with that gardener's blood in your veins."

I cut my gaze through him harshly. "Sterling's blood changes nothing.”

“I think some wouldn’t agree with you. So, now you must choose. Marry me, and peace will ensue between our kingdoms with our union. Your grip on the Crown will be more secure than ever. Or, if you refuse me, you and your capitol citizens die within the hour, and Lecevonia will be ravaged by the worst war it has ever experienced.”

I stayed silent, fuming.

Neither of the choices this monster had given me was acceptable. If I married him, my life would belong to him. He wouldn’t truly let me reign with him. I’d be lucky if he didn’t keep me in chains, just as Roderich had threatened.

But my people and my kingdom would live. Under a different name and a different rule, but they’d be breathing, moving.

Unless I explored a third option. If I could get to those horses—

I spun around and sprinted into the stream.

The cold water infiltrated my leather boots, weighing them down, but I splashed through the stream and didn’t hesitate as the water crept up my knees, then to my thighs, until I dashed up onto the opposite bank. I heard Gryffin wading in after me, but I refused to look over my shoulder.

If I could just get to those horses . . .

I tore through the forest, jumping over gnarled roots and bursting through thick bushes. I should have thought to sheath my sword before making an escape; the blade knocked against trees and pulled vines along with us, and it made my arms very off balance. But I didn’t chance stopping and sliding it into its scabbard now. I was solely focused on getting away from the beast behind me.

I crashed my way through low-growing branches and leaves, and my foot landed in a rabbit hole. A burst of pain shot upward from my ankle, but I regained my footing and shot forward once more until I was suddenly exposed to the spring wind, no longer surrounded by brush.

The trail.

I darted to the left, away from the castle, ignoring the pins of pain pricking their way up my leg. Gryffin and I had met just a bit further down—the horses must have been close!

Then, I heard Gryffin's grunt of exertion behind me as he too burst through the brush to the trail. I lowered my head and ran as quickly as I could across the overgrown dirt path, but his footfalls fell closer and closer.

As my very last resort, I slid to a stop and turned on my good heel to face him, my sword jutting out in front of me.

Gryffin's eyes widened as he was suddenly confronted by a sharp blade, but he skidded to the right last minute. He yelled in gruff pain as my sword sliced into his right arm, but it was only a shallow cut. He cursed loudly and unsheathed his sword.

"Rosemary," he said, a smile playing at his lips. "I'm going to win."

But I didn't care. I attacked.

I wasn't thinking about maneuvers or guards; I was only slashing my weapon left and right, hoping to land somewhere, anywhere. He blocked each of my onslaughts, but he didn't try any counterattack.

"I'm not going to hurt you, Rosemary." He grunted, dodging my downward cut to his shoulder. In a final move, he locked his sword around mine near the hilt and yanked my weapon from my hands. It bounced and slid across the ground, billowing up small clouds of dirt behind it.

But I reached my hand down to my calf and unsheathed my dagger. My hand shook as I pointed it in front of me, arm extended.

Gryffin lowered his sword to his side. "Oh, now Rosemary, there's no need for this. Do you even know how to use a dagger?"

"Of course—I slash you open with it!" I feigned an attack, my whole body moving to the right, and Gryffin followed. But my arm stayed steadily to the left, and I plunged it into the left side of his chest.

But before I could even feel a moment of victory, I realized that my blade missed my target. It landed instead near his shoulder, hitting bone before it could do any real damage. He still uttered a pained cry, but his fiery eyes showed more frustration than anything. He pulled the dagger from his shoulder.

I tried to run, but the pain in my leg had reached my hip, and he was already too close. His steps quickly caught up to me, and he grabbed my arm.

I was slung into his chest, banging my forehead against his collarbone, hard. I felt my head wound sting and split open once again. Then, a hard blow rammed into the side of my head, and I saw no more.

The gentle swaying beneath my body greeted me as I awoke.

But when I registered my throbbing head, that swaying morphed into turbulent waves rolling in my stomach. I groaned quietly and kept my eyes closed; I was afraid opening them would only make the waves angrier.

The fresh crispness of forest air. Faint, musky sweat. Prickly horsehair. These were the things I slowly began to comprehend as I fought through my heavy grogginess.

What else?

The unrelenting pain of my head . . . centered just above my temple . . . Agh! Yes, that was exactly where it was radiating from.

The worn leather of a saddle. Warm sunlight. Cracked dry blood on my forehead surrounding my stinging cut.

I tried to move my hands to wipe away the sweat trickling into my head wound, but I found that impossible. Coarse ropes bound them together at the wrists.

That jolted me out of my stupor. My eyes flashed open, which did induce a rush of nausea as I knew it would, and they fell upon the gray horse's big head bobbing in front of me. I recognized her. Lucy.

I tried to throw my body to the right, but a strong arm caught me.

"Rosemary, you shouldn't fling yourself off a moving horse."

I narrowed my eyes as Gryffin chuckled in my ear. I whipped my head around to look at him, but an involuntary groan escaped me as my head swam.

"I'm sorry that I had to do that to you," he said, sounding genuinely penitent. "You weren't being cooperative."

Gryffin had me sitting in front of him on his horse, his arms extended on either side of me holding the reins. I heard the clopping of a second horse's hooves. He must have tied the other horse to his saddlebags. My hands were tied to the horn of the saddle, so he was probably sitting on a blanket or such behind me.

"This is *treason*," I snapped. "You swore an *oath* to Lecevonia."

Gryffin paused for a moment, mulling over my accusation. Then, he sighed heavily, and I felt him shrug his shoulders. "Lecevonia will soon belong to Tarasyn, so it's no matter."

"Why haven't you killed me yet, then?" I asked through narrowed eyes.

There was amusement in his voice, "I saw another opportunity for peace. How are you feeling?"

Oh, he was *concerned* now. "Livid and in pain," I answered shortly.

He let out one quick laugh. "Ah, how I adore your temper. We'll have you cleaned up in Viridi, and I'm sure you'll feel a bit more forgiving afterwards."

Viridi? So, he'd abducted me. Marvelous.

Though I was fuming, I forced myself to speak to him. I needed to get my bearings. "How long have I been unconscious?"

"Oh, not very long. One hour, maybe two," he answered calmly. "Long enough for me to find my general and have him pull back our army."

"Pull back? Why?" My muddled brain couldn't see a reason. If he'd had the castle, why not keep his claim?

"As I said, I don't like wasting resources. Besides, I have what I want," he murmured into my ear, lowering his voice an octave.

I glowered straight ahead, still too queasy to turn my scathing eyes to him. "You disgust me."

"Well, I'm still hoping that, once you see the benefits of our marriage for Lecevonia, you'll change your mind. I'll give you another chance to choose me *and* your kingdom. I will be a perfect gentleman to you all your life, I swear it."

I couldn't bring myself to answer him, for I refused to believe a single word he'd ever utter to me again.

Instead, I began trying to conceive some way to return to my capitol.

As already proven, making a quick escape was out of the question. I couldn't jump out of this saddle, and even if I were able to weasel my way off Gryffin's horse, I could hardly keep my eyes open without my stomach rolling. Not to mention my injured ankle.

I considered for a moment the second horse. He'd eventually have to let me ride on my own, so poor Lucy wouldn't have to bear two people for long. Depending on how fast the other horse rode, perhaps I could outrun him. But would he release my hands? Would he even untie the horse from his saddlebags?

Probably not.

Though I didn't see an opportunity for escape now, I swore that I'd take advantage of the first chance I could grasp.

Then another thought began to consume me: would anyone from Lecevonia know where to find me? Or even know to *look* for me?

Gryffin may have already convinced them of a lie, have them all fooled into thinking I'd agreed to marry him and was going to Tarasyn willingly. Surely, they knew that Roderich was now dead. Perhaps they thought the danger had died with him.

If no one knew to look for me, I could be imprisoned in Tarasyn indefinitely.

I closed my eyes as panic slowly unfurled its livened tendrils through my mind, and I had to stop myself from spiraling down that road any further. I beat back the infectious dark thoughts and tried to think rationally once more.

Neither Zeke nor my sisters would ever let me simply disappear. They'd know that I wouldn't abandon my kingdom, never to return. And Isabele would most certainly know that Gryffin was behind it. She hadn't fallen under his spell—or whatever it was—as the rest of us had. They'd send someone to Tarasyn eventually.

And Amos!

Joyful relief immediately radiated through my chest.

Amos had been there! He'd known that we were going for the horses!

But would he know where to look?

Caught up as I had been in my own thoughts, I'd noticed a bit late that the green forest surrounding us had begun to thin. Before long, the large oak branches that had canopied our path broke away, and warm sunlight enveloped us as the trees exposed a brilliant blue sky.

Surprised by the sudden openness, and having forgotten my

pounding head, I twisted my gaze back and forth around us in an attempt to absorb everything I could manage.

Over Gryffin's shoulder, I saw now that our path had brought us to a high hillcrest—we must have been deep into the Beryl Foothills now. And, as far into the horizon as I could see, the glorious expanse of Lecevonia stretched behind us.

I'd never seen my kingdom from that viewpoint before, and for a moment I was mesmerized by the large waves of grass swaying in the spring breeze. A shimmering light would dance and ripple through the long blades along the hillsides and disappear over the gentle slopes, only to begin again at the base a moment later.

I could certainly appreciate that old Lecevonian lullaby with a new understanding now.

As I tore my eyes away from the verdant grassy sea, I frantically focused my attention toward the south.

My heartbeat quickened as I found what I had been searching for: there in the distance, situated along the slope of a low hill, was Equos. Its walls still stood strongly around the city, and there was no sign of ongoing battle as far I could tell.

So, shockingly, Gryffin had told the truth: he'd pulled back his forces.

Hillstone remained proudly in the city's center atop the hill, and the billowing pillar of smoke had now diminished to a thin wisp rising feebly through the air. Though I knew my library was burned beyond repair, I was relieved to see that at least the rest of the castle had endured.

And, though it was just a small speck of color at this distance, my cobalt and carmine banner waved vibrantly to me from atop the chapel turret.

My grand capitol may have appeared dwarfed in this green expanse, but even this stretch of land could not compare to my rising jubilation upon seeing my home victorious.

That waving flag told me that Equos had persevered, my citizens had survived, and my men had reclaimed Hillstone.

Lecevonia had continued to fight for me. I must continue to fight for my kingdom.

Then, Gryffin's hushed voice in my ear sent me plummeting into anger once more. "*This* is ours. Beautiful, isn't it?"

I turned away in disgust and glared ahead of us once again. The Silver Mountains towered closer than I'd ever seen them before, glistening with snow-laden peaks.

Amos would know where to look for me. He'd find Celeste and ask her where she'd hidden the horses. Or he'd see our haphazard path through the woods.

Then, he'd see Thomas's body—he'd *know* that something had gone wrong. Yes, Amos would find me.

So, I needed to stay alive until then.

Even if that meant living in shackles. Gryffin couldn't kill me; he needed me to marry him for his most efficient ending. If he wanted me dead, nothing would have stopped him from killing me in the woods, right next to Thomas.

I could play his game, for now.

Making my first move, I leaned my body back against Gryffin's chest, though his touch repulsed me now, and closed my eyes. I felt his lips very gently press against the top of my head.

I tried to think back to the small moments when his gentle kiss had comforted me, excited me.

But the haze that accompanied them was impenetrable, and only made my head ache that much more.

To disguise my shudder, I let out a small, tired sigh and hoped to

Haggard that it was convincing.

Stay alive.

EPILOGUE

ZEKE WAS RIGHT. I felt the change in the atmosphere the moment we stepped into Tarasyn.

It was not the towering mountain peaks, nor the frozen snow-covered ground that made the world around me feel like a perpetual winter, that told me we'd crossed the border.

It was the energetic charge in the air—a begging, persistent buzz filling my ears. It was the breathy sway of the tall, needle-leaved trees surrounding us. The way they almost seemed to object when Gryffin would pull off their branches to make a bed for us over the stretch of leather Thomas had taken from the potter's shop. How the water in the small stream at which we rested whispered loudly in a hushed current of babbles.

It was almost overwhelming to my senses. Which didn't combine well with the elevation change my body was still trying to comprehend.

We'd been traveling for almost a week, following a valley line for the past few days. Gryffin had stopped in a small town called Pruin to gather up some supplies for our journey through the wilderness, and he'd hidden me in the dense forest while he went through the crooked wooden shops. I'd thought to run, then, but I'd quickly decided I'd die of the elements if I tried.

When Gryffin told me that we'd be approaching the capitol soon, I imagined the horrors I'd see of a civil war-ridden city: sad and disheveled structures, bloodstained stones, echoes of persecutions in the streets.

But as the trees thinned, the heavy layer of gray clouds hanging above us suddenly and inexplicably did as well, and the sun shined radiantly over Viridi.

Everything was suddenly so *bright.*

The clean cobblestone road stretched through rows of colored shopfronts. Their walls and roofs were striped in green and gold, coated with opulent blues and purples, wrapped in whorled red and silver. Evergreen trees like blue spruce and holly had been planted along the streets, accenting the city's vibrant palette of hues.

But Gryffin didn't take me through the city. I needed to be "cleaned up first," he'd said. So, we stayed partially concealed in the trees, bringing no attention to ourselves. He took us on a small frozen dirt path around the city; on my left was the back of a few small homes, and on my right was an ever-thickening evergreen forest. As the minutes passed, Lucy began pawing at the ground as if she sensed that she was almost home.

Finally, the tall trees opened, exposing the castle looming ahead.

I had a hard time deciding if the imposing structure was beautiful or unsettling. I could tell where an expansion had taken place—the huge laid stones looked lighter, cleaner. Some had even been painted. The original section had been modest; two stories compacted into the corner of the castle grounds. But the new areas were extravagant. As Gryffin helped me dismount my small bay horse, for my hands were still tied, I tried to make sense of the lavishly colored stone patterns. Was that a *sixth* floor?

The castle's shining spires towered over the city, and the color red dominated the parapets. In a brief glance before Gryffin ushered me through a hidden door, I was certain that I saw an enormous crow circling one of the gaudy turrets.

Gryffin's castle.

My prison.

OF LEGENDS AND ROSES

1

A MAGIAN PENINSULA NOVEL

ACKNOWLEDGEMENTS

Wow. What a journey this has been—and it's only the beginning!

I am so thankful to you, the reader, for picking *Of Legends and Roses* out of your undoubtedly lengthy to-read list and starting your journey with Rosemary.

Nick, my amazing husband, my love, thank you for making this dream possible. Without your love, support, and encouragement, this book would have stayed tucked away as an old Word Doc file from 2011 on my computer. You have talked me through bouts of self-doubt, imposter syndrome, and panic attacks, and look what's happened now! We have a book, babe!

Rebecca, thank you for always having my back! When I need something read or need a second opinion, your answer is always, "Sure, send it on over!" You have seen the very earliest forms of this book in all its rough glory, multiple drafts in fact, and you still supported me! Your words and encouragement have gotten me through some pretty tough moments!

Thank you, Kristine, Lauryn, Sam, Hilary, and David for being the best beta readers I could have ever asked for! Each of your comments, opinions, and suggestions led *Of Legends and Roses* to where it stands before you today. Thank you for giving Rosemary's story some love, even if it still needed some work! Every single "I'm so proud of you" from you guys struck my heart and mind with a renewed sense of "I can do this."

A huge thanks to Gina, my amazing editor, for seeing the diamond in the rough even after I thought I'd polished it all nice and pretty. Your dragon's eye for literary greatness has lifted *Of Legends and Roses* to its full potential!

Thank you, Lena, for an absolutely gorgeous book design cover, bringing Rosemary's world to life in such an eye-catching manner. As a debut author, I had no idea what to expect, and Lena was so patient with me and answered all my newbie questions!

Thank you to my English teachers and librarians I've had throughout high school and college for nurturing my passion for literature and creative writing. Your own passion inspired me, even when I tried to hide it.

Thank you, Mother Dear and Daddy, for supporting my endeavors and raising me to always believe I am smart enough and strong enough to achieve my goals in life. I love you both so much!

I thank God every minute of every day for giving me this ability to share a story and for blessing me with the opportunity to set out for my dream of becoming an author. Only with His love, mercy, and strength am I able to feel capable of achieving anything to which I set my mind!

READ ON FOR THE FIRST CHAPTER OF

OF DECEIT AND SNOW

BOOK TWO OF
THE CROWNED CHRONICLES

(Contents following this page are not finalized. Subject to change after editorial revisions.)

2

CHAPTER ONE

THE BOOK SLIPPED through my fingers and slapped shut with an echo upon the stone floor.

Jolted back to the present, I groaned heavily and plucked the little book off the floor, only to plop it onto the cushion beside me. I hadn't been absorbing the tiny, printed words, anyway.

My mind had instead taken me far from these Tarasynian walls, to the snowy forests upon a horse—probably Midas, but I hadn't paid that much attention. We'd been riding, part of a hunting party, but my prey hadn't been an elk or a wildcat or a fox. No—it'd been something invisible yet so tangible, something that meant *home.*

But I'd been under a deadly pursuit, too, by a beast I hadn't known had been hot on my heels. And as I'd caught my first hopeful glimpse of the low-lying Beryl Foothills through the dense evergreen trees, an armored hand had caught my shoulder, spinning me off my horse to face my beast's deep blue, red-flecked eyes—

I shuddered. Letting my mind wander had not been in my best

interest.

As I massaged my temples softly, my fingers grazed the raised scar across my forehead—another reminder of why I needed to get out of here. I understood that the Tarasynian soldier was only following orders, but what would the other soldiers think of the woman who'd killed their comrade? Even if that woman were to become their queen?

What had I even been reading? A glance down at the book's binding reminded me—oh yes, *The Fawn and the Fanciful Frog*. Again. It was a happy little story, at least, though I've read it three times now. I've read every book on the tiny shelf in this room at least once since I'd been held here.

My brain always felt hazy these days, always muddled, any semblance of concentration scarce. I attributed it to being knocked unconscious, but part of me also believed it was some type of aftereffect from Gryffin's Talent. And truly, I'd be lying if I said that I was not afraid that Gryffin might *still* be tricking me, influencing my mind.... After all, what did I know about Talents? Gryffin hadn't necessarily been the most enlightening person this past month.

One entire month.

One month of no word, no suspicion of foul play, and no sign of a search party.

One month of knowing absolutely nothing. [As far as I could tell, Lecevonia believed Gryffin's lies, that I had come willingly with him to be wed in Tarasyn.] With no correspondence from Lecevonia, and with Gryffin as my only informant, I had no knowledge of what was going on outside these castle walls.

Or inside, for that matter, for now it has been one month of playing prisoner here in Tarasyn.

It was not as if I couldn't bear it, however. Gryffin hadn't kept me in chains or locked in the castle's dank dungeons, as I'd thought he would.

Contrarily, my arrangements were actually quite *comfortable.*

On that first night, Gryffin had led me instead to the castle's guest chambers. The castle corridors had been so dark, just as my scouts had reported, so I was not quite sure where the guest chambers lay in regard to the castle's layout. However, each time my door had been opened since that first night, I'd glimpsed the flickering of every possible candle lit in this hallway.

The guest chambers of Snowmont may have been in severe need of updating, seeing as they haven't actually welcomed guests in seventy-odd years, but the plush chair with furred cushions upon which I sat upon in this moment was admittedly more comfortable than any of the furniture I'd had in my own rooms.

The downfall was that these were *not* my own rooms, these rooms that felt smaller with each day.

This was not home, nor will it ever be.

I've picked up weaving again, something I hadn't done since I'd been a small girl, with the help of the handmaidens I'd been given. In fact, I have almost finished weaving an entire square meter of blue sky. Exhilarating.

I've memorized the tapestry of the elk hunt that hung upon the wall opposite the bed. Probably the source of my daydream. Even my trouble with concentration couldn't compete with the only other thing in my rooms to look at aside from books. Fourteen hunting dogs, all very large with long, wiry coats. Six men on horseback, three bay horses, two chestnuts, and one white. Four bows, two spears. Seven trees, twenty-three bushes.

If Gryffin didn't kill me first, my boredom would surely do the job.

What was taking the most effort to acclimate myself to was the *cold.*

Yes, my capitol city saw snow almost every winter, but the rising temperatures of spring always melted away the powder and slush. Here, the frigid crispness of the air was perpetual. I was thankful every day for the thick furs and the burning fireplace that kept me warm, but that also meant that I opted to keep my window shuttered most of the time to trap in the heat and block the most unwelcome chill. Which usually led to another round of utter tedium.

This morning, however, I kept my window open, for I refused to go another day with only that tapestry to look at. I stayed cocooned in my unbelievably soft brown fur blanket, sitting upon my cushions, and let the breeze escaping from the frozen world outside nip at my cheeks, my nose.

The soft knock upon my door, quickly followed by the turn of a key, did not surprise me, but my heart still painfully fell to my feet as the door's bolt released with a resounding click. The door swung open creakily on the old hinges, and my captor strode into the room. His searing gaze immediately found me bundled near the window, and a wide smile spread across his face.

"Good morning, Rosemary."

I actively fought the urge to convulse as his soothing voice tormented my ears. "Hello, Gryffin."

He came to see me at least twice daily since I'd been brought to these chambers. His visits usually lasted anywhere from just thirty minutes to two hours or so. Where he was during the rest of the day, I did not know. And] he was, unfortunately, the only face I saw besides my chambermaids.

And the Tarasynian guards posted outside my door, of course.

He walked farther into the room and, as always, greeted me with a gentle kiss on my hand before sitting on the corner of my bed. I tried to disguise the hostility rolling from me with a quick bat of my eyelashes, but from his frustrated expression, I could tell he was seeing right through my act.

The red flecks in his eyes still unsettled me, so I turned my gaze out the window to the sunny courtyard.

The reason as to why the snow clouds skirted the capitol city still evaded me, but in a way, I was grateful for it. I was always able to be amazed by the colorful vibrance of the city. Even just here in the courtyard, trees of blues, reds, and oranges stood out starkly against the evergreens of the forest. Sterling would be astounded.

Gryffin's irritated voice brought me back to my room. "Rosemary, this dismissiveness is getting old rather quickly."

That tends to happen when one is held against her will. The acidic thought almost passed through my lips, but I stopped it and only shrugged in response. I tried to speak only when necessary to him, for I feared he'd use whatever I said against me. I did not trust him with my words or my thoughts.

However, I also knew that in order to stay alive, I needed to give him *something* to believe. So I reached my hand out to him and let him take hold of it.

He heaved a deep sigh as he pressed my hand to his cheek. "Have you eaten, yet?"

I shook my head, but it'd been silly for him to ask. He always ate breakfast with me when he visited in the morning. As if to prove my point, a castle worker from the kitchens came waltzing through my door with two plates of steaming food, followed by another with a bowl heaping with fresh fruits. With a flourish, they placed the food onto a little table at the foot of the hunting tapestry and left just as gracefully as they'd come in.

What Tarasyn lacked in warmth, they made up for with their food. The meat tasted different here, though I couldn't quite figure out why that was yet. I believe it was altogether a bit fattier, which made it all the more deliciously juicy and flavorful. And the fresh produce! They must have had acres upon acres of greenhouses.

Gryffin continued his own end of the conversation—how he'd slept last night, how his sword practices have been going, how Roderich's memorial service had gone yesterday. I'd refused to attend, though it would have given me an excuse to leave this room. I couldn't bring myself to be around people who were mourning a man that had been a monster, who'd threatened my kingdom and almost killed me.

Gryffin had told his people the truth, for the most part. He'd told them that Roderich had been power hungry, that he'd gone about conquering surrounding kingdoms in a brutal, wasteful way. He'd told them honestly that *he* had killed Roderich, for Roderich had been standing over me—the love of his life, his *queen*—, with his sword poised to kill.

That last part of a bit of an embellishment.

And, of course, with Gryffin's Talent, there was no doubt in his subjects' minds that killing their former king was the right thing to do. There was no ill will whatsoever toward the man that had killed his own brother. They all accepted their beloved prince, their new king.

I nodded along through Gryffin's rambling while nibbling at my crisp pear, cutting myself a little slab of roasted ham, tearing apart a piece of bread. Their bread was not quite as fluffy as Lecevonia's, but the plump raisins that they added was a nice touch.

He'd just finished telling me of the latest on his brother Yaris, who was technically the older of the twins, when he suddenly said, "I'm going to officially announce our engagement to the citizens."

I froze mid-nod, and my eyes widened involuntarily. No. Not yet.... I slowly placed my raisin-studded bread back down onto my plate and sat a bit straighter in my chair. "Gryffin, I'd–I'd like more time—"

But to my surprise, Gryffin laughed. "So, she *can* still speak!"

A sigh that was a confusing mix between relief and frustration escaped me. "Gryffin," I began again, steeling myself now to tell a lie, "Marrying you would of course benefit Lecevonia. I just need more time to heal from your . . . deception." I practically spat the last word, but I tried to keep my voice soft. "I don't want our marriage to start on any mistrust."

As if that were possible.

If Gryffin knew I never planned to marry him, he'd kill me. I was sure of that. He'd killed his brother for standing in his way, and he'd undoubtedly do the same to me. But not until he was *certain* that our marriage was a lost cause.

No, I would never marry him. But I needed to give Amos more time. And Zeke, and Isabele—surely, they were back from Port Della by now. So, I needed to continue to stay alive.

Gryffin looked at me with such convincing remorse that I almost believed that he felt sorry for what he'd done. Almost. "Rosemary, I do hope that we can eventually move past what happened. You'll see that it was all for us, and for the Talented."

"It was all for *you*." My words were sharp like shattered glass, cutting through my façade.

I instantly regretted it, for a shadow of anger darkened my captor's features. He glared at me, then down at the table, the knife he'd been using clenched tightly in his white-knuckled fist.

Angering him was not what I should be doing. Showing him how disgusted I was by his actions, even less so. But I'd meant what I'd said, and he knew it. We sat in a lengthened silence, the tension across the table as taut as a bowstring.

Finally, Gryffin took a deep, shaking breath. "You're wrong." He turned his gaze up to me, and thankfully it was no longer a glare.

"Everything—the use of my Talent, my *imprisonment* in Lecevonia, Roderich's death, my bringing you here— I carried out and endured all of it with only us as king and queen in my mind."

And Thomas's death? I wanted to ask him, but I refrained. I knew that was only for him. To make his goal of getting me alone easier. Besides, he'd already told me during one of his past visits like this that he'd regretted it now. A waste of life, he'd said. That he should have just used his Talent on both of us. Especially since it made *me* see through his Talent.

He'd also admitted that his imprisonment had not been part of his plan. Yes, he'd known from the moment I rode through those woods that his and Roderich's staged plan would work flawlessly. And afterwards, when things had no longer gone according to his plan, he'd known without a doubt that his brother had been behind the second assassination attempt.

But he hadn't expected to be *caught* knowing such things.

So, he'd come up with the ridiculous lie of chasing after my heart. He had truly played me like a perfectly tuned harp, thrumming across my heartstrings with each deceptive stroke.

He told me that he'd almost lost me in the prison, that he'd felt my will slipping away from his control. I'd almost been free from his power, had my sheer stubbornness to trust him been a little weaker.

"Would you have ever told me?" I asked suddenly.

But he hadn't been in my head. My question confused him, and he only looked at me with puzzled eyes.

"About your Talent."

"Ah . . ." he mused aloud. "I hadn't truly decided. Possibly, in a less direct way. In some way to make you see that it is a useful tool rather than a deceptive one."

"So you would have still lied to me," I said flatly.

He clicked his tongue in dissatisfaction. "We are only going to go in circles this morning, aren't we?"

I parted my lips, ready to let some equally snide remark fly, when a heavy knock on my door reverberated throughout the room. When neither of us acknowledged the interruption, a deep voice called from the hallway. "Your Majesty."

We both turned our heads to the doorframe sharply, though I did so out of reflex. I knew I wasn't the one being called for, and Gryffin was "His Majesty" here now, no matter the means of how he'd obtained the title.

"What is it, Campton?" Gryffin answered gruffly.

"You're needed in your office, Lord King."

There was a brief second of tense silence, as if Gryffin were deciding whether or not he was willing to shirk his duties a bit longer for the sake of winning our argument. Finally, he nodded his head once. "I'll be there in a moment. Tell Fendrel to make himself comfortable."

The man named Campton bowed and padded away down the hallway, and with a heavy sigh, Gryffin put down his fork and knife. My chambermaids immediately began clearing the plates from the table, but I kept my hands hovering over mine, signaling that I wasn't quite finished. They nodded quickly and backed away as Gryffin stood from the table. "I suppose I should let you get some rest, then. Are you still comfortable?" he asked, and there was true concern evident in his voice. "Is there anything that I can do to make you happier here?"

Happier? No. But more comfortable . . . "Well, if I'm to be completely honest, I've run out of things to *do*, Gryffin. Of course, I enjoy weaving," I added, nodding to my chambermaids in thanks, "but I've read every wretched book here, and I've stared out into the courtyard so much that I see it with perfection in my dreams."

"Would you like more books, then?" Gryffin asked. "I'll have some sent up. Or maybe you'd like to learn an instrument? I can have a flute made—"

Why was he so bent on keeping me merely occupied?

"I want to *leave* this room, Gryffin!" Then, to soften my brusque interruption, I lowered my voice to a coy timbre. "I want to see the rest of the castle. You've always talked so highly of the work you and your brother have been doing to make improvements." I moved toward him tentatively and extended my hand, grasping his in mine gently. "I'd like to see what you've done."

He looked down at our hands, and his expression softened. This was the first time *I'd* taken *his* hand since I've been here. When he looked back up to me, there was a new twinkle in his eyes that almost disguised the red flecks. "Of course, Rosemary. You aren't a prisoner."

The constantly locked door told me otherwise.

"Just tell me when and where, and I'll gladly show you around." He lifted my hand to his lips and kissed it tenderly before letting go. His smile lit his features, all traces of anger and frustration gone. "I'll see you tonight."

Then, my captor strode from my chambers, the bolt of the door's lock sliding into place behind him.

The sun had already set behind the low snow clouds, dinner had come and gone, and torches in the courtyard below my window had been set aglow by the time Gryffin returned that evening. This time, I looked forward to the click of the bolt and the creak of the old hinges. When he appeared through my door, I was already standing to greet him with an exuberant smile on my face.

He looked shocked for a moment to see me so enthusiastic, and I had to admit that my mood felt a bit out of place. But he'd told me that I could leave my rooms, and I was ready to hold him to his word.

As he came forward and took my hands in his, a smile of his own stretched from cheek to cheek. "Ah, my Rosemary," he said, "now you're looking more like yourself."

I continued to smile, but truly, how would he know? The only *me* he'd known had been trapped under his treachery. I kept my tone light, however, to hide my thoughts. "Well, I've been thinking of your offer this morning, and I've decided."

"Oh?"

I nodded fervently. "I'd like to go now, and I'd like to go anywhere," I said matter-of-factly, answering his *when* and *where* stipulations. *Anywhere* did not give him a reason to say no, and I was determined to see anywhere else but here as soon as I possibly could.

He raised his eyebrows at my response, but his unwavering smile told me all that I needed to know; he'd agree, as long as my mood stayed as happy as it was now. After a second of thought, he asked, "How about I take you to the conservatory?"

Snowmont had a conservatory? How . . . classy.

"It's something that I've been wanting to show you," he continued, "and I think you'll be amazed." His laughter shook his dark curls, which I would have found charming once upon a time.

He offered his arm to me, and, moving quickly to hide my mental hesitation, I looped my arm through his as if it were still as natural as ever.

The release I felt as we stepped through my door was

insurmountable. Even just this narrow corridor felt freeing! And I had been right—every candelabra had been lit, brightly illuminating our way. Signalizing that the king was home.

For a fraction of a second, I considered my appearance. This was the first time anyone in Tarasyn would see me, aside from my guards and chambermaids, and I was not quite dressed to be seen by the public. At least, not to be seen as a queen. And the simple knot of hair upon my head would have made Hazel cry. Nevertheless, I was happy with the mauves and navies that had been conjured up for me here, so I decided to give my looks not another thought. Less attention was perfectly fine with me.

I inferred quickly that the guest chambers must have been in the original part of the castle, for the dark stone hallways were rather tight with low ceilings. New candelabras had been added amidst the older to give more light, but the smell was mustier than in my rooms.

"I'm sorry that this is the first you see of Snowmont," Gryffin said with a bit of chagrin. "We hadn't focused on renovating the older section. Only adding on the newer."

"'We' as in you and Roderich?" I asked, doing little to hide the murderous accusation in my voice. Then I silently chided myself; I'd lose my new freedom before I'd even get to enjoy it if I couldn't keep my tone in check.

Thankfully, Gryffin was not phased. "And my other siblings, of course," he with a smile. "They have a say-so, too."

There was no door separating the old section of Snowmont from the new section, and from the moment we stepped through the gaping doorway at the end of the corridor, it was as if I'd been dumped into a new world.

As the hallway suddenly opened into a massive room, the first thing that caught my eye was the exorbitant amount of *color*. The large stones that built the walls had been painted just as they had been on the outside, in great swaths of reds with flashes of golds and innumerable hues of blues, greens, and yellows. It reminded me vaguely of the stained glass nerys lily in my chapel, but these collections of color didn't seem to have any rhyme or reason to them.

The ceiling soared above our heads, with rafters crossing over one another in complicated arrangements. From the rafters hung banners of what must be the Tarasynian crest: a crimson sun peeking around a white mountain, embellished with green and gold grape vines around the border. I thought I'd heard the croaky call of a crow, so I quickly averted my eyes from the rafters and instead studied the tapestries that covered every wall.

They certainly liked their needlework here in Tarasyn. I wondered vaguely if insulation from the cold had anything to do with it as I studied the different scenes depicted on the tapestries: another hunting party, though this time they seemed to be hunting rabbits with a pack of small dogs and large red-tailed hawks; a quaint garden, with two women in extravagant clothing conversing with one another; the same women in the same garden, but with a little girl running around them with a little white dog now; a regal throne room with a grand king accepting the fealty of one of his subjects. Smaller tapestries also hung above the mantle of the colossal fireplace, but I could not see what scenes those had been woven into.

The warmth emanating from the blazing fire caressed me even from this distance, which was impressive more than anything. Though, with a fireplace large enough for even Roger to step into with ease, I supposed it shouldn't have surprised me.

Gryffin must have seen the reluctant awe on my face, for he chuckled quietly and announced, "Snowmont's new Great Hall."

As I shrugged off the fur blanket I'd kept wrapped around my shoulders, I ran a hand over the nearest burgundy velvet couch, one of many that were spread throughout the room, all with plush rugs laid underneath them.

This was surely not what I'd expected the castle of two killers to look like.

"Come," Gryffin said, nodding his head toward the left end of the room. As he led me across the Great Hall, I found that my earlier concern for my appearance had not been needed; there was not a single soul in this grand room. Each couch and chair were empty. There were no dining tables in the room, only small side tables near the ends of the couches, so there were no stragglers from supper conversing around the edges of the room.

I thought it odd—surely it was not *that* late in the evening?

We came upon a set of large, wooden double doors. With a growing smile on his face, Gryffin held one of the doors open for me, and I found myself standing in a glass globe.

Truly, the conservatory felt as if I were standing in a gigantic soap bubble that had settled onto the ground outside, the landscape around us slightly disfigured. The icicles on the trees along the edge of the castle grounds danced and twinkled in the moonlit breeze, yet it was still *warm* inside our bubble.

An innumerable collection of plants surrounded us, lining the cobblestone walkway that curved through the conservatory. Plants of all different varieties, most of which I hadn't seen before. The low-growing plants with large, plump leaves and trees bending overhead with shady fronds looked like they belonged in the tropical climate of Loche. There were others that were more familiar, like roses and violets, and I thought I caught the slight pink of a peony peeking from around a linden tree, bringing Sterling's kind, sun-wrinkled face to mind.

When I looked at Gryffin, he had the smuggest look I'd ever seen on his face.

"Well?" he pressed.

It was ostentatious. It was arrogant. It was domineering.

But it was beautiful.

Anyone with any appreciation for nature would have to admire the sheer amount of *life* in the room. What's more, this globe felt more alive than any dining hall and courtyard I'd experienced. These plants had the same energetic buzz as the evergreen trees out there in Tarasyn's forests had. But here, in this controlled environment, it was a little less unsettling.

"I've never seen anything like it," I finally admitted.

As a satisfied smile spread across Gryffin's features, an unfamiliar and starkly feminine voice suddenly spoke from behind him. "You'll get used to it. I assure you."

"Always a ray of positivity, this one," he said dryly, rolling his eyes. He sidestepped, exposing the young woman who had stealthily crept up to us. "My sister, Kathryn." He waved his hand lazily between the two of us in introduction. "Kathryn, this is Rosemary."

Even without the introduction, I'd have been able to tell there was some relation. With her cascading dark curls that seemed black in the dim light, and tall statuesque frame, she was the female incarnate of Gryffin. And her deep blue eyes did not have the frightening flecks of red, only the grey of the ocean's depths, holding a sharp, smiling intelligence.

Could she really be only seventeen? I recalled my sweet Isabele, her innocently wide brown eyes and shy demeanor, the timid droop of her shoulders. Surely, if Kathryn was seventeen, growing up with brothers had accelerated her maturity. I didn't even think that *I* held myself as confidently as she did.

"What other woman would you be walking with so late in the evening, brother?" Kathryn replied smartly, which instantly made me want to grin. Then, she turned a great white smile toward me. "I've been dogging my brother about letting me meet you *before* the end of civilization. And even still, this was an accident!" She shot a glare in Gryffin's direction. "Has he even given you a proper tour of Snowmont, yet?"

Before I could answer, Gryffin cleared his throat. "This was actually the first time Rosemary requested to leave her rooms."

Requested to leave my rooms? Ah, yes, the locked door was *clearly* an inclination that I could have done so! But I held my tongue against any acidic remark. I'd still play this game.

"I've been taking my time adjusting," I lied, plastering on my best rueful smile. "I apologize if I've been a bit . . . anti-social."

Kathryn was studying me closely. I couldn't place the emotion that was churning in her fierce eyes. Something like doubt, or mistrust, but surely that wasn't right. We've hardly spoken a word to each other.

Gryffin chuckled, flawlessly playing along. "It's a big change, undoubtedly. No need to apologize. My sister has just been impatiently eager to meet you," he eyed Kathryn pointedly.

At Gryffin's accusation, she looked away and crossed her arms over her chest. "Well, how would you expect to feel if the only *woman* aside from yourself has moved into your home, and you have yet to meet her?" She turned her eyes to me again, a grin pulling at one corner of her lips. "You're absolutely gorgeous. I can't believe Gryffin isn't showing you off to the entire court."

Her blatant compliment would have normally taken me by surprise, but it felt so sisterly that I smiled. I liked her.

"Well, you've met her now," Gryffin interjected, "and it's getting late. You should sleep soon, Kathryn."

By the indignant set of her eyebrows, his sister looked as if she were about to argue. But the longer she thought, her face settled into a resigned mask. "Fine," she grumbled. "But don't keep her from me as long next time. I mean, really, what has he been up to, keeping you locked away for so long?" She met my eyes again, and there was another emotion that was more easily readable. Empathy.

Locked away. Interesting choice of words on her part.

Before I could think of any way to acknowledge her remark, she gently touched her hand to Gryffin, outstretched finger to finger, palm to palm. An old greeting and farewell among loved ones on the Peninsula. So old, in fact, that I hadn't seen it used in Lecevonia for years.

"Good night." Kathryn dipped her head to both of us, and slowly walked out of the conservatory, closing the thick door behind her.

Without her presence, the conservatory felt a little darker.

"I must meet with her again," I said immediately, turning to Gryffin.

"She'd like that, too," he answered with a small smile. "Tomorrow, I'll tell her to meet you in the Great Hall."

For the first time in over a month, I felt an inkling of gratitude toward this man.

IF YOU ENJOYED THIS BOOK, PLEASE CONSIDER LEAVING A REVIEW ON GOODREADS AND/OR THE WEBSITE OF PURCHASE.

REVIEWS ARE INVALUABLE TO AUTHORS. REVIEWS INCREASE EXPOSURE OF LITERARY WORKS YOU LOVE AND ENABLE AND ENCOURAGE THE AUTHOR TO CONTINUE CREATING STORIES. AUTHORS APPRECIATE EACH AND EVERY REVIEW THEY RECEIVE ON THEIR WORK.

THANK YOU FOR YOUR CONSIDERATION IN LEAVING A REVIEW.

MORE WORKS BY ASHLEY W. SLAUGHTER

THE CROWNED CHRONICLES

Of Legends and Roses, Book One

Of Deceit and Snow, Book Two

Of Reign and Embers, Book Three
Forthcoming

Short Story Anthologies

Eumonia's Monody and Five Other Stories
Exclusive to Amazon and Kindle Unlimited
Read it for free on KU!

JOIN Ashley's MAILING LIST FOR
EXCLUSIVE CONTENT, COVER
REVEALS, AND UPDATES!

(Don't worry, she won't spam you. She's still
figuring out the whole *mailing list* thing.)

Visit Ashley's website to join:
https://www.ashleywslaughter.com

VISIT ASHLEY'S SOCIAL MEDIA PAGES FOR THE MOST UP-TO-DATE PUBLISHING NEWS!

Instagram: @ashleywslaughter
Facebook: Ashley W. Slaughter, @AWSwriting
Twitter: @AWSwriting
TikTok: @ashleywslaughter

Follow Ashley on Goodreads!
https://www.goodreads.com/awswriting

ABOUT THE AUTHOR

Ashley W. Slaughter was born in south Louisiana and grew up amidst the sugarcane fields lining the banks of the Mississippi River. She received her bachelor's degree in Biology from the University of Louisiana-Monroe in 2018 and worked as a veterinary assistant and wildlife biologist before pursuing her career as an author. Writing has always been a passion of hers, as shown through her near-to-bursting manila folder of short stories she'd written throughout grade school, and a collection of life events has allowed her to rediscover this passion. She enjoys spending time with her husband and pets, hiking, kayaking, beach-going, and, of course, reading.

"When one finds a good book, they hold onto its characters and plot as tightly as possible in hopes of instilling the memory of that reading experience forever. Happy reading!"
- Ashley W. Slaughter
author, coffee drinker, pet mom, nature lover, beach bum